THE DEBT OF TAMAR

The
DEBT
of
TAMAR

NICOLE DWECK

THOMAS DUNNE BOOKS
ST. MARTIN'S PRESS
NEW YORK

THOMAS DUNNE BOOKS.
An imprint of St. Martin's Press.

THE DEBT OF TAMAR. Copyright © 2015 by Nicole Dweck. All rights reserved. Printed in the United States of America. For information, address St. Martin's Press, 175 Fifth Avenue, New York, N.Y. 10010.

www.thomasdunnebooks.com
www.stmartins.com

The Library of Congress Cataloging-in-Publication Data

Dweck, Nicole.
    The debt of Tamar : a novel / Nicole Dweck.
      pages cm
    ISBN 978-1-250-06568-1 (hardcover)
    ISBN 978-1-4668-7269-1 (e-book)
    1. Sleyman I, Sultan of the Turks, 1494 or 1495–1566—Fiction.   2. Inquisition—Fiction.   3. Holocaust survivors—Fiction.   4. Jewish families—Fiction.   5. Muslim families—Fiction.   6. Portugal—Fiction.
    7. New York (N.Y.)—Fiction.   I. Title.
    PS3604.W43D43 2015
    813'.6—dc23

2015017948

Our books may be purchased in bulk for promotional, educational, or business use.
Please contact your local bookseller or the Macmillan Corporate and Premium Sales Department at (800) 221-7945, extension 5442, or by e-mail at MacmillanSpecialMarkets@macmillan.com.

First Edition: September 2015

10   9   8   7   6   5   4   3   2   1

For my parents
For Andy

PART I

I

1544

PORTUGAL

José observed his aunt Dona Antonia, an aging aristocrat who'd taken him in as her own. Sitting across from him at the center of a long bronze table, Dona Antonia Mendez held her chin slightly raised over the stiff fabric of her modest ruff. A smattering of fine lines stemmed outward from the corners of her bright eyes, and her oval face, still pleasant in her age, was framed by a dangling cluster of sapphire and pearl drop earrings. She had raised him alongside her daughter Reyna since infancy. In his twenty years of life, she was the only mother he'd ever known.

As she looked out at Lisbon from the covered terrace of the royal compound, Dona Antonia's expression was drawn, her eyes narrowed and lips stitched into a neat line.

"Your daughter would make a fine wife to my cousin, Alfonso of Aragon," the queen said from her high-back chair at the head of the table. "I thought we would discuss the matter."

Patting her brow with the edge of her handkerchief, Dona Antonia appeared nervous. "I am honored." She glanced toward José, her blue eyes flashing alarmingly in his direction.

"Yes. The match was thought up by the emperor. It's an honor that he should have involved himself in such a trivial matter." The queen turned her attention to the dwarf spaniels prancing at her heels, tossing bits of cheese in their direction.

"Reyna is very young for marriage," Dona Antonia replied. "I know my nephew agrees." She swept a gray tendril from cheek to temple, then eyed him directly from across the table.

José nodded, although he knew very well that his opinion was meaningless. He was brought along on this day for a show of male guardianship. His brilliant, widowed aunt would make her own decisions. He was simply there to lend a touch of masculine determination that her husband would have provided had he been alive.

Glancing over his shoulder, José let his gaze wander beyond the tasseled red and gold canopy edges toward the manicured grounds beyond. He spotted Reyna standing by a tall hedge, her fingers grazing the trim bushes in the garden. She had just turned seventeen, old enough to marry by anyone's standards.

"I'm afraid she is too young." Dona Antonia fumbled with the diamond cross around her neck. "Just a skinny little thing, hardly a woman." Her voice faded with each breath.

"Speak up!" The queen raised a hand to one of the braided muffs fastened over her ears.

A servant appeared with a basket of bread, and José chuckled to himself, envisioning an updated version of the queen's coif featuring two of the olive rolls atop his plate.

"It's just that you may want to consider someone older . . ." Antonia continued.

"She will be older." The queen was clearly losing her patience. "Next year she'll be turning eighteen, then nineteen. I'd wager the year after that, twenty. I've yet to meet anyone who grew younger by the year."

Dona Antonia said nothing.

A moment passed with only the sound of the queen's quiet, steady breaths as she toyed with a strand of carnelian beads. Having heard rumors of their embarrassingly tenuous financial situation—apparently expensive wars and expeditions had not been as lucrative as the emperor had hoped—José was not at all surprised that the royal family saw it within their interests to align themselves with the widow and her fortune. The daughter of Spanish merchants who, having fallen on hard times, had emigrated from Spain to Portugal toward the turn of the century, Dona Antonia had married a prominent Lisbonian whose family boasted social ties with all the great houses of Europe, as well as a lucrative trade empire that was the envy of all who knew them.

Dona Antonia's daughter, Reyna, was now the heiress to that great fortune. By marrying her off to a cousin under their command, the royal family could easily come to control her vast inheritance and alleviate much of their burden. What surprised José was his aunt's reluctance to accept such a mutually advantageous union. Any other mother would be thrilled.

The appearance of a dark-skinned beauty in a straw hat put an end to his musings. The girl kept her eyes to the ground, fanning the queen for a few moments before slipping away behind the boughs of an exotic potted plant from the new world. The plump red fruits dangling from its branches were known as *tomatoes,* or so he'd been told. Drumming her fingernails on the table's surface, the queen continued: "The emperor has made up his mind. He hasn't been known to accept no for an answer." She pursed her lips and her gaze bored into Dona Antonia. "With that in mind, do take some time to consider it. I'm sure you'll come to the right decision on your own and there will be no more unpleasantness."

"Yes, Your Highness."

"You'll go ahead and sort out any financial considerations, such as your late husband's fortune, your daughter's inheritance, and what other trifling matters might need to be sorted. Within the next two months, we expect to officially receive word of your acceptance of the match. That should give you ample time to get your affairs in order."

"Then it's settled," José said and lifted his goblet just as the cupbearer approached to replenish it. He nodded, as though nodding one for all, then took a sip of the spicy red wine. "I should go find Reyna." He stood and found himself crouching beneath the low roof of the canopy. He kissed the queen's outstretched hand, then looked up and held his boyish stare a little too long, so her wrinkled countenance turned noticeably red. The same devilish grin he had offered up to the queen was met with his aunt's scowl before he headed off along a red gravel path to the royal gardens.

"Reyna!" he called out from the maze of shrubbery that concealed him. "Cousin, where are you?" As he strolled in the shadows cast by tall, flowering hedges, he was suddenly jolted by two hands fastened tight upon his shoulders. He turned about quickly and wrestled his assailant to the ground.

"I frightened you!" Reyna's eyes sparkled with mischief. She struggled to get up as he pinned her shoulders down.

"Frightened me?" His heart was pounding in his chest. "That would be like a lamb frightening a lion."

Her long hair fell away from her tilted face, spreading over the green moss. She laughed fiendishly.

"Your mother's right!" he continued as he tossed back a few wisps of his long, dark hair. "You're not ready to marry. I pity the fool they've chosen for you!"

"What are you talking about?" she said, her body suddenly still.

"The prince can barely mount his horse! I've no idea how he'll be able to tame the likes of you."

"Cousin, tell me!" She struggled once more to free herself from his hold.

"Get up." He grabbed her by the wrist and lifted her from the ground. "Before they see you and change their minds completely."

She turned serious. "What's happened?"

He smiled mischievously, then dropped his voice. "Just moments ago, the queen proposed a match."

"And?"

"Naturally, your mother is being difficult."

With hands clasped toward the sky she mumbled under her breath: "Heavenly Father, give me the strength to overcome the seven-headed beast whose womb you chose to send me out—"

"Reyna!" He glared down at her.

"I'm not really surprised." She shrugged casually. "She doesn't want me to marry. Not now, not ever. She'd prefer I grow old alone and die bitter. That's the route she's heading for."

"No." José took his cousin by the arms and quieted her with his eyes. "That won't happen to you."

"Will you be arranging my marriage, then? You're worse than she is."

"Cousin, stop."

"Well, you did turn her against my last two suitors, did you not?"

"Antonio Agostinho Lopez da Susa? He was practically a midget with wings for ears! He could have taken flight at any given moment. I should think you would have thanked me for intervening."

"I quite liked him."

"If he were standing just so and the winds picked up to just the right speed . . ."

"He was a perfect gentleman."

"Perfectly dim-witted."

"I thought he was handsome."

"Uglier than a monkey's rear!"

"Lower your voice."

"Personally, I don't see why any of us must marry at all. I think we're doing just fine how things stand."

"The bachelor, the widow, and the spinster. What a fine household we three make!"

"Stop these theatrics, Reyna. If you want to marry, you'll marry. I'll make sure of it."

"And how will you make sure of it? You'll be spending the winter entertaining Prince William in the Netherlands, or have you forgotten?"

"Don't remind me. The boy is duller than dirt. I don't know how I got through it last year."

"Apparently you got through it quite splendidly!"

"Is that what they say?"

"Enjoyed yourself like a dancing dwarf, so they say."

"*They* say a lot, don't they?"

"Your reputation precedes you, dear cousin."

"Oh, enough about me!" He clapped his hands together. "I'll speak to your mother. I know I can talk some sense into her."

"You're so ugly when you lie." She turned and walked off through the tall hedges.

He watched as she strutted away, then called after her, "And you're lovely when you're angry!"

José stood in the garden and for the first time seriously questioned why his aunt had not yet accepted one of a number of proposals. There was no shortage of fine young men pursuing Reyna. They came to the villa often to request her hand in marriage. Some came from Lisbon, others from the fringes of the countryside. There were Spanish dukes and city aristocrats. German counts and French noblemen would boast of vast palaces and fortunes abroad. They persisted until Dona Antonia's tone turned nasty and she'd send them away with a tongue-lashing. A dozen men with wounded egos would recount to their peers that the widow Dona Antonia Mendez had simply gone mad.

* * *

The roads were steep and the carriage threatened to give way as it maneuvered down the winding trail home. José sat on the bench opposite the ladies, gazing east through the carriage window at a picturesque scene of tall leafy palms and city dwellings. "The emperor has proposed a match." Dona Antonia did not bother turning to her daughter as she spoke.

José and Reyna's eyes met momentarily before Reyna turned to address her mother from the edge of her seat. "What was your response?"

"I said nothing." The widow patted the moisture from her neck. It was a warm, windless day in May and the scent of musk filled the dark carriage. "But I am disinclined to accept the proposal." Reyna fell back into the plush burgundy bench cushion, shooting José a pleading look with her big brown eyes.

He coughed against his fist, then addressed his aunt sternly. "*Tia*, you should be very pleased. A royal prince will make a fine husband for Reyna."

Dona Antonia rolled her eyes.

"*Tia!* She *wants* to marry, and in case you've forgotten, you've not much choice in the matter. You're to give your approval in just two months' time."

"Is that so?"

"It seems to be the case."

"It was merely a request."

"It was merely a direct order handed down to you by your queen."

"Suddenly so serious?"

"Only idiots and jesters wouldn't take this seriously."

"I think I'd prefer the jester. Sounds like more fun."

"I'm sure it won't make a difference, dear aunt. Fools of all sorts have been known to end up with their heads rolling. And what a large head yours happens to be."

"Stop it. Both of you," Reyna interrupted. "I can't put up with one more minute of this."

They journeyed on quietly, the only sounds the trotting of hooves and the occasional whinny of the stallions as they made their way home beneath the midday sun. As they neared the neighborhood square, a low rumbling sounded. The noise grew louder until the carriage, having just turned a corner, became surrounded on three sides by a rowdy irate mob.

One side of the carriage was butted up against a brick wall, so José leaned out of the free window, wondering what all the commotion was about. The charioteer had dismounted from his perch and was elbowing his way through the crowd toward the carriage door. "Senhora!" He removed his hat and tilted his head. "We must wait for the crowd to disperse. It's impossible to move on."

"José, what do you see?" Reyna sat forward. "A revolt perhaps?" She beamed delightedly. Since she was just a girl, Reyna had always been partial to a bit of mischief.

"Most likely nothing quite that dramatic." José cleared his throat but instinctively felt for the dagger beneath the folds of his cloak. "What a vivid imagination you have, Cousin."

"Move away from the window." Dona Antonia's voice was stern from the far end of the carriage.

"Perhaps the commoners are protesting the queen's new coif," José said pointedly. "If ever there was a thing in need of protest . . ." His carefree demeanor cracked upon hearing a scream among the rabble-rousers.

The carriage rocked as a foul-smelling throng of men shoved up against it, pushing it tighter to the wall.

"Away from here!" Dona Antonia grasped the tip of her lion-headed cane and, crouching toward the open window, began poking at the jumbled sea of heads bobbing up against it. "Roaches!" she muttered as she went to work with her stick, forcing the cluster of bodies away from the carriage and back against the crowd.

Reyna twisted her neck to catch a glimpse of the commotion. "José!" Reyna cried out as her anxious eyes came upon him.

José wriggled uncomfortably and tugged at the drawstrings of his collar as a layer of sweat formed beneath his shirt. "What is it, Cousin?" He brought his cheek beside hers and for a moment was unaware of just what he was looking at. "Satan's wretched city." Dante's words escaped his lips.

In the square beyond, chained dogs snarled at passersby. Wenches flapped about like screeching ravens, and stray cats sought refuge along the low rooftops. Mothers silenced their children with openhanded slaps and the threat of white-knuckled fists. Pyres burned at the center of the square, and the smell of ash began to infiltrate the carriage.

"Auto-da-fé," Reyna whispered. The tremor in her voice suggested this was not the sort of mischief she had anticipated.

José's neck stiffened, and he was suddenly incapable of pivoting any direction at all. Barely able to utter a response, he huffed, "Death by burning." The grotesque scene took shape before his eyes and had now been named for what it was: The Sixth Circle of Hell.

Hordes had gathered to witness a public execution by fire.

"Swine! Heretics!" a filthy man raged. When he happened to turn and face José directly through the window frame, his eyes blazed ferociously. Startled, José shrank back. "Kill the Jews!" The vein in his sweaty neck bulged as he spat out the words. "Kill the pigs!"

At the center of the square an execution of the city's unrepentant Jews was taking place. Tied to wooden beams, six condemned heretics wriggled while the flames of the Inquisition danced about their flesh. Inquisition guards stood smugly to one side with fresh-faced district officials.

Horrified, José blinked back tears. Another hot flash assaulted his body as his eyes froze upon one of the condemned. Black tresses fell about her face and dusted the length of her waist and hips. As they set her legs on fire, her body twisted like a caged beast. A jolt of agony ripped through him.

"Don't look at them!" Dona Antonia commanded. She grabbed José's collar and tore him from his paralysis. He sat stunned as she examined his pupils one at a time, pulling back his lids for closer inspection. "The damage is done," she whispered.

He pulled away and shook his head in disbelief. Was he supposed to believe that these helpless souls were the same beings his priest had once called roaches and vermin—pests that needed to be rooted out and exterminated from society? He'd not known a Jew in all his life, but in this moment, the wailing victims appeared more human than the monstrous hordes that stood cheering around them. Never before had José stopped to consider the secret Jews he'd only ever heard of. Then again, he'd never come face-to-face with such evil and suffering. "We are witnesses," José said after a long moment. "We cannot look away."

Reyna was rocking nervously now, her head buried in her arms and her hunched shoulders shaking.

He forced himself to turn back toward the lurid scene. The victims, all in tatttered, bloodstained clothes, were thrashing about in flames that rose from glowing bundles of dry wheat secured with hemp chords around their ankles. There was an elderly woman with powder-white hair, along with two red-haired men with beards who might have been brothers, or perhaps father and son. There was a raven-haired girl and two others whose faces he could not see because the flames had already risen above their heads. Old and young, men and women—it seemed none were spared.

Just as the heat in the carriage had become unbearable, a wild fury overtook him. "Stop!" José lunged at the door. "Stop at once!" he shouted again before Dona Antonia leaped forward and grabbed the drenched fabric of his shirt with her bejeweled fingers.

"Sit down!" Dona Antonia pushed him back against the bench. Her glare frightened him to stillness. A moment of silence passed in the carriage before she spoke. "Do not raise your voice again. You will get us all killed!"

His knees began to tremble as he sat in his place. "We have to do something." He covered his face.

"Tell them who you are," Reyna pleaded. "They'll listen to you, Mother. Make them stop!"

José took his aunt by the wrist and opened the carriage door. "There are condemned souls not yet burning. You can save them. You can end this!"

"There's nothing we can do!" She pulled her arm free of his grip, only to have him reach out and grab her even more forcefully.

"You have to speak up. Tell them you have just come from the queen. Tell them who you are! You must stop this!" He kicked open the door with the heel of his boot, then pulled her forcibly to the street below.

"Wait!" Reyna seized the edge of her mother's skirt.

With his free hand, José pushed Reyna back inside, then flung the door shut. "Guard Reyna!" he shouted back to the charioteer. A bulging pillar of a man, he heeded his master's directive and planted himself in front of the carriage door, his arms crossed.

Above the barbaric cheers, the determined voice of the inquisitor general announced the names and sins of the condemned. The stench of seared flesh crept through every pore of his being. José squinted to shield his eyes from the char and dust and dirt as he pulled his aunt through the crowds toward the platform at the center of the square. "Do something!" he yelled back to her as she struggled to break away from his grip.

Halfway between the carriage and the grand inquisitor's podium,

Dona Antonia folded to the ground and collapsed into sobs. A dirty shoe kicked her in the gut as the stampeding crowd unwittingly began to trample her. José shoved them aside and clutched his aunt in his arms.

As he stood there, the stench of charred bone nearly suffocated him. Out of the corner of his eye, he could see flames dancing. He turned his gaze upward as though trying to escape into an empty patch of sky. Could this be the same sky he had gazed upon earlier that morning? All he saw was smoke. With his head tilted toward the heavens, he closed his eyes and for a brief moment managed to blot out the hideous world around him.

Without warning, they were swept away by the violent mob like twigs in a river's current. José held onto his aunt so tightly, he nearly smothered her against his chest. "Don't let go," he told himself over and over again as they were pushed and prodded along. He nearly dropped her at least once but managed to lift her back up quickly. Eventually, they were spat out at the far corner of the square.

She was choking for air when they finally emerged. He laid her down on the cobblestone pavement, a safe distance from the edge of the crowd. Dona Antonia sat up, her lace dress muddied and her hair matted with sweat and dirt. She pulled him close and nearly poured the words into his ears. "We are them!" She was sobbing so heavily, he was not sure he heard her correctly.

"What are you saying, *Tia?*" He shook her when she did not answer. "I don't understand."

"Your parents did not die of the fever," she gasped.

"What?" He was more baffled than ever before.

"We are them!" she cried out angrily.

"No." He nearly choked. "No!"

Perhaps she was just being cruel with her words? What exactly did she mean? In his peripheral vision, he could see the podium where the victims were still burning, perhaps even still alive. He shook his head as though the forceful motion might be enough to sweep away a reality that was slowly settling in on him. "It can't be!"

Her words came as gently as the tears that were now streaming down his cheeks. "They were Jews." She squeezed his hand as the world he knew came crashing down. "*I* am a Jew," she added quietly.

"But you are a respected Catholic noblewoman!"

She took his hand in her own, closed her eyes, then shook her head limply. "Better the devil you know than the devil you don't," she whispered.

In that moment, he realized the dire situation they faced. His parents had been secret Jews. His aunt was one too. If she was discovered, they could all be executed. He reached out and let his fingers clasp the diamond cross that lay flat against her chest. His thoughts turned to the parents he never knew. He shut his eyes and felt his hands tighten around the warm metal. The smell of fire filled his nostrils. The fog of smoke clouded his memories. He heard a snap. Upon opening his eyes, he discovered that he had ripped the necklace from his aunt's neck. A bright red scratch showed against the side of Dona Antonia's neck where the chain had come apart.

"You are the senhor of the house now," she said.

He nodded once, then squeezed the cross in his palm until his flesh turned raw.

2

That night Antonia and José sat silently in the candlelit parlor of their home. A thousand thoughts and sights and sounds were careening through José. His mind was spinning beyond control, and though he searched for words, he found only the memory of screams.

José heard the wooden floor creak and turned to find Reyna standing in the doorway. Her damp hair fell loose, glistening against her cotton nightdress. Barefoot, she stepped forward and moved across the parlor, then took a seat beside José on a rigid monk's bench.

A warm breeze wafted through the open shutters, and José turned his gaze to the dark sea beyond. Outside, the moonlit waves crashed against the rocks and splashed up toward the billowing canopies, spraying the elevated marble pavilion with salt and sea and sand.

He was stunned out of his reverie by the feel of fingertips stealing over his own. He looked up, though as he did, Reyna slid her hand away discreetly, tucking her fingers back into the sleeve of her dress.

As though having been summoned by the warmth of her touch, his lips parted and he heard himself begin to speak. "All my life, I believed a fever had taken my parents." His hands clenched into fists and he tried to calm his voice. "I can't pretend today didn't happen. I know what I saw."

Dona Antonia closed her eyes. The room was quiet except for the faint tick of the grand clock. An exquisite rarity, it measured the passage of time, replacing the sand-filled hourglass that had once stood in its stead. José had been mesmerized by the priceless contraption when it first appeared in the house some months ago. Now he thought only of what he might use to smash the thing to pieces and put an end to the relentless tick.

It was several minutes past midnight, and though the servants had long ago been dismissed and were sleeping soundly in their quarters, there was still the sense that the walls had ears.

The hands on the clock inched forward with determination. Moments passed like lifetimes—violently, steadily, silently.

And then, quite suddenly, Dona Antonia spoke, her voice hushed, the words rippling throughout the room in baritone waves. "You were just an infant. Of course you don't remember. They wanted to make an example—" She stopped speaking mid-thought and her mind seemed to retreat into some dark, faraway memory. "Like so many others, my own parents fled Spain in 1492, the year of the Edict of Expulsion. It wasn't poverty they were escaping, as I'd always led you to believe."

José blinked, his dry eyes stinging as he tried to steady his nerves.

"On the contrary," she continued quietly, "they were among the Spanish elite, belonging to one of six hundred prominent Jewish families invited by the Portuguese king to settle in this country away from the threat of Spanish oppression. Each was forced to pay a fee of one hundred cruzados in exchange for permanent residency and the freedom to live as Jews."

"But you weren't free for long?" José rasped. "What happened?"

"A marriage happened," Dona Antonia replied. "A marriage between a Spanish infanta and a Portuguese king. With that marriage came a political alliance that would bring the horrors of Spanish tyranny to the doorstep of every Jew in Portugal. By the time I was born just seven years after they'd settled here, my parents had already been forcibly converted. Though they publicly adhered to Catholicism, like many other New Christian families, they secretly remained true to the old faith, and that's how I was raised. Unlike the rest of us, José, your parents insisted on openly flouting their Hebrew ways. Your father, my brother-in-law, was so very stubborn. Your mother was too." Antonia shook her head. "At times it seemed they were taunting the authorities, brazenly placing Sabbath candles in the windows or failing to appear at Sunday mass. Perhaps they wanted to change things, to stand up and fight. It was only a matter of time before the authorities caught up with them."

José was beginning to feel light-headed. The more she revealed, the more it seemed he needed to know. "Go on," he whispered.

Taking a deep breath, Dona Antonia continued. "It was Festa do Corpo de Deus, the day of the Corpus Christi feast. I was five months' pregnant. La senhor and I thought it wise we all go to church to witness the grand procession of the Holy Sacrament. I knew how important it was for us to be seen at religious festivals, and unlike your mother, I was cautious to a fault. Of course, José, it didn't surprise me that your parents refused to take part, but I asked, no—*insisted*—that you come with us. I simply couldn't forget the stories I'd heard, of how the babies of unrepentant Jews had been taken from their parents, shipped off to distant islands to be raised as Catholics in the homes of strangers. I wouldn't take that chance, not with the nephew I loved as my own son." Her voice trailed off.

"Eventually your parents relented, and we took you to witness the Eucharist as it was being paraded through the streets amid wreaths of flowers, song, and prayer." His aunt lowered her lids and a few tears slowly slipped from her eyes. "I brought back a garland of roses, thinking your mother might hang it over your crib. As I look back on it now, it was stupid of me to think that she would ever hang those processional flowers in her home." She pulled her linen cap from her head and crumpled it in her hands, her padded shoulders sinking as she did. "We were different, your mother and I. Where I saw flowers, she saw betrayal."

Why couldn't they have just pretended, like Antonia had? José lamented as he tried to piece together his broken past. He fixed his eyes on the bowl of floating rose petals atop the table by his side. Their brilliant red petals looked bright and alive, and yet upon closer inspection, he could make out their wilted edges beneath the glow of a nearby candelabra.

"The authorities came for them." His aunt's words pierced his thoughts. "They left behind a red star, garishly painted on the door to their home." Antonia remained silent for a long moment. When it became clear she'd said all she'd intended to, a panic crept through José.

"That can't be all?" He heard his voice breaking. There was so much more he needed to know.

Antonia's fingertips made their way to her temples. "I never saw or heard from them again."

Unable to speak, José tried to imagine his parents as his aunt had so often described them before. Only now, for the first time, he could conjure up no images, could no more envision their faces than he could the worn portraits upon the oldest coins in his collection.

"We had the two of you to think of," Dona Antonia said steadily. "And after all that had come to pass, I thought it best to shield you both from the truth. By the end of that year, Reyna was born, la senhor had died unexpectedly, and I was left to raise an infant and a toddler on my own. I did what I had to. I continued to profess to be a devoted worshiper of Christ. I donated huge sums of money to the church and to the queen and soon fell under her protection. She took it upon herself to guide me through my widowhood as a devoted Catholic noblewoman, and in return the donations never stopped. All the while, I managed to stay true to my faith. I lit the house with dozens of candles every night, all in an attempt to mask the two sacred ones reserved for Friday sundown. I observed the fast of Yom Kippur, our Day of Judgment, even when it meant pretending to be ill, coughing my communion wafer back into my handkerchief as my mother had taught me. I avoided leavened bread during Passover, and declined many festival meal invitations for fear of being served pork, which is forbidden to Jews. I made sure you attended weekly mass, were educated in all the relevant disciplines, and displayed all the trappings of respectable Catholic children, though within these walls, I never spoke the teachings of the church."

She paused, her eyes wandering to the silk tapestry hanging over the mantel, a masterful woven illustration of the Savior's last supper. As he watched her examine it, it occurred to José that the illustrious work of art was no more than another prop in his aunt's elaborate deception. "The outside world has a name for us," she said despondently. "They call us Marranos, pigs. But that's not what we are," she continued, shaking her head. "We are the Anusim." She raised her head defiantly. "We are the *forced ones*."

José could not quite believe what he was hearing. Before him sat the woman who'd loved him and raised him in her home. She seemed almost a stranger to him now. He cradled his head against his palms, propping his elbows on his knees as he leaned forward, when a sharp object poked into his side. Reaching into his robe pockets, he searched for the source of his discomfort, withdrawing the diamond cross he'd unwittingly torn from his aunt's neck earlier that day.

Looking upon it, José realized that the woman he'd thought he'd known had never existed at all. Rather, perhaps for the first time, he was seeing who she truly was.

As he held the cross before him, Dona Antonia laughed sadly. "Every secret Jew has one." She drew her fingers over the bright red scratch against her neck—a scratch marking the moment when her lie had come undone. "In my heart, I have never forgotten who I am." She turned to her daughter. "Reyna, you must understand that my reluctance surrounding your marriage has never been a matter of age."

Reyna's eyes searched the room as though examining the parlor for the first time. "It was a matter of faith . . ." Her voice trailed off as she finished her mother's thought.

"I had always planned to pick spouses for the both of you from among other families in our secret society," Dona Antonia continued. "As the years passed, I told myself that I'd reveal the truth to you both on your respective wedding days, for surely then you'd no longer be children."

Reyna spoke softly. "So why is it that I am still unwed?"

"I had hoped you would be by now." Dona Antonia sat forward and frowned. "But over the past few years, many well-known Catholic noblemen have asked for your hand, and have made a public spectacle of it at that. I couldn't very well announce your engagement to an unknown from within our own secret ranks. It would be highly suspicious after all the seemingly impressive suitors I've refused on your behalf."

Blinking slowly, as though unsure of what to make of all she'd heard, Reyna stood up, her chest and shoulders rising as she took short, anxious breaths. "It's been a long day. Please excuse me." The hem of her white gown hovered just above the floor as she glided away.

"My parents died for something," José said once her silhouette had disappeared into the dark corridor. "They chose their faith over me. They chose this faith over their own lives. And for what? I want to learn."

Dona Antonia frowned, then shook her head. "It's too dangerous."

"Better to die standing than to die kneeling."

"Careful, *niño*. Your tongue runs faster than your wit."

"I need to know why they left me." His voice cracked and Dona Antonia remained still for a moment.

"The risks are too great."

"Then why do you still choose to practice?"

"I never had a choice."

"This is the life *you* chose!"

"You fool, you don't choose your faith. Your faith chooses you."

"I want to learn."

"No!" She rose to her feet. "It's not the right time."

"I'm not here to ask your permission." He stood and was suddenly towering over her. "Only your blessing."

Dona Antonia scoffed. "I am your guardian and I will decide what's best for you."

"No," José leaned forward. "I am the senhor of the house." His voice was calm and cool. "I will decide." For once the widow was stunned to silence. José pulled her into his embrace.

"I am the senhor of this house," he repeated softly.

She pulled away and looked into his eyes as though peering into the future. "I can't stop you, can I?"

He shook his head. "I'll do what I must, with or without your help."

"You're a fool," she whispered.

"Someone must have the books I'll be needing. I shall ask around discreetly."

With her mouth slightly open, she took a step back and examined him. "A sure way to get yourself killed."

"Perhaps *you* know who can be trusted?" he said with a hopeful, wide-eyed enthusiasm. "Will you have it arranged?"

She huffed, then brought her hands together as though in prayer. "When your parents died, I swore to the heavens that I'd protect you no matter what." She turned down the corners of her lips and continued hastily. "Goodness knows, I had no idea that would mean protecting you mainly from yourself." She stared hard at him for a long moment. "But it seems you've forced my hand. I'll have it arranged."

Several days had passed since Antonia's revelation had sent a shock wave through the household. José took his breakfast on the seafront terrace while reading the latest book he had acquired, a translated edition of

Kitab al-Manazir, The Book of Optics. It was blasphemous. It was won-
drous. Could it be possible that light traveled at a particular speed?
Alhazen, the tenth-century Arabic philosopher, thought so. If it was
true, the implications would be staggering. As he sat contemplating the
possibilities, an elderly man with a hunchback and a trim gray beard
approached with a stack of books in his arms.

"I'm your new Latin tutor."

"What happened to Don Miguel?"

The man shrugged. "I do not know Don Miguel." He clutched his
books as a moment of silence passed between them. The old man began
to back away. "I see you were not expecting me."

"No," José said before bidding him farewell in Latin.

The old man's blue eyes darted about in confusion, a peculiarity not
lost on José. He shifted from one foot to the other and then turned away
hurriedly.

"Wait," José called out. He was puzzled that the man did not speak a
word of Latin in return, but even more so by his anxious demeanor.
"Did my aunt send for you?"

The elderly man hesitated.

José gestured for him to sit. "Join me."

He placed his books on the ground and sat down on the stone bench
opposite José. He glanced around, then introduced himself quietly. "I'm
Don Carlos."

"Please, eat something," José said casually while trying to set the man's
nerves at ease.

Don Carlos picked up a roll and took a bite, then leaned in and whispered, "I'm not here to teach you Latin."

José downed the remainder of his tea and returned his cup to its saucer. Their eyes met and exchanged a knowing look. "I suspected as
much." José sat forward. "I was hoping you could teach me something
far more valuable."

The man nodded slowly and slid a leather book across the table toward
José. "Do not open this until later tonight when you are sure all the
household is sleeping."

Over the next few weeks, Don Carlos and José met each night after sundown. Don Carlos would bring books whose covers indicated the study

of Virgil, the collected works of Julius Caesar, and the archives of the first-century historian Tacitus, but beneath the false book covers lay a secret world of ancient Hebrew texts, beginning with Portuguese translations of the Talmud, the basis from which all Jewish law was gleaned.

José plowed through several tractates in a matter of weeks, approaching his studies methodically for hours each night. Searching, always searching, José was on a mission.

During that time, dark rings formed beneath his eyes and his once robust frame began to thin out. José was losing weight and losing sleep. Don Carlos began to grow concerned about his new pupil.

"Why are you doing this?" he asked one night as they studied together.

José laid down a recently completed volume of Mishnah. "Another," he instructed Don Carlos without bothering to answer his question. When Don Carlos failed to make a move, José reached toward the far end of the table and took the book himself.

"My boy, why are you doing this?" he tried for the second time as José hunched forward on his bench and cradled the book.

José did not bother looking up when he answered, "I can't stop." His voice was raspy as his eyes settled on the text of the opening page.

"José!" Don Carlos brought his fist down hard, causing the table to shake.

Startled, José finally looked up. He could feel his eyes burning, glazed and bloodshot. "I can't stop," he repeated himself. "I need to understand why my parents left me."

Soon he was delving into metaphysics and once again astronomy, through the spiritual teachings of the Zohar. Never before had his mind been able to operate on so many different planes simultaneously. It was as if Kabbalah—the ancient tradition of Jewish mysticism—was a language stored in his memory before birth and the process of learning it merely an exercise in recollection.

One Friday evening after supper, when the breeze had come through the window and extinguished the candle in his chamber, José spent a few minutes squinting at his book before giving up trying to study in the dark. Exhausted and spent, he made his way downstairs in search of Reyna.

He found her in the parlor, doing needlepoint in a chair by the window beneath the dim glow of the moon.

"What is it?" She placed her embroidery on the table beside her.

"Will you walk with me?"

She smiled and stood up from her seat.

They made their way to the beach, where they strolled for several minutes with the sand between their toes, swinging their shoes at their sides. Eventually they came upon a small cove sheltered from the wind. There José unhooked his cloak and spread it out before them. They made themselves comfortable and lay out beneath the stars.

"What if one of the servants discovers your books and reports you?" Reyna's voice was serious, even angry. "You don't need to do this."

"Of course I need to do this." He'd been naive to think she'd understand. They'd never before hid anything from one another, but now he questioned himself for having entrusted her with his secret just five days earlier. Since Sunday—the first day of the week belonging to God (or so he'd once been taught)—she'd done nothing but fuss and agonize over the trouble he might face.

"It's not too late to go back to the way it was."

"Go back?"

"Yes. Burn your books. Forget all this."

"Can you do that? Can you forget what you saw? Can you really pretend that nothing's changed?"

She turned away, fixing her gaze on the dark ocean instead.

"People are being massacred. My people, *your* people. I need to know what they're dying for." He shook his head. "I think I'm starting to understand."

"What is it?"

José thought it over. "It's something I won't let anyone take away from me. I can't explain it."

"Try."

He shook his head again. "I can't teach it to you any more than I can teach you the feel of this sand." His voice trailed off. "You have to touch it to ever know it."

She sat up and caressed the sand in her fingers. "I don't care about any of it. I just don't want to lose my best friend." They sat quietly for a few moments.

"See that?" José pointed toward a cluster of stars that took the form of an archer and his bow. "Do you see?" he repeated, still pointing.

Her eyes scanned the night sky.

"I'm not sure they are actually there," he explained.

"But they're so bright?"

"They only appear that way. Those stars burned out long ago. It took some time for the light to reach us."

When she didn't reply, he tried to explain further. "What you see is their legacy. It's what's left behind." He leaned forward, propping himself up on his elbows as he focused on the sky. "It never fades. It never dies." For a time, the sound of crashing waves filled the silent lull between them.

She twisted her body toward him and rested her cheek on her hand. "Promise I won't lose you?" Even in the darkness, her eyes glistened brightly.

"Never."

In the morning a messenger arrived, a scroll of parchment bulging from the inner folds of his cloak. It had been a month to the day since Dona Antonia had been called to the palace to discuss the matter of Reyna's marriage. "The king and queen request that you relay your blessing upon the betrothal of your daughter, Dona Reyna Mendez, to Prince Alfonso of Aragon, cousin to the emperor." He handed her a gilded mirror encrusted with rubies, diamonds, and pearls. "A gift from Her Majesty as a token of her affection. I take it I may relay your blessing to the king and queen?"

Dona Antonia swallowed the knot rising in her throat and tried to steady the tremble in her voice as she spoke. "With great sadness, I am forced to decline this proposition, with all due respect to the king and queen. We cannot let our blood mix with that of the holiest of Christendom. That would be a sin in itself. We are common people, of no importance. We could not bring honor to the royal family any more than a candle could bring light to the sun. Our place in this world is at the feet of Her Highness, as loving and loyal servants, but we dare not try to rise above our station. For such ambition is not favorable in the eyes of the Lord." She did not wait for a response but turned from the messenger, gathered her skirt in her hands, and hurried up the front steps.

She made her way into the grand foyer and rang the bell for the servants. An elderly maid appeared in an instant. "Find Reyna and José and tell them I'd like an audience with them in my study immediately."

The sound of creaking wood pulled her gaze up toward the second-story landing of the mahogany stairwell. His hands gripping the balcony railing, José looked down on her, his expression tense and knowing. For a long moment, he did not move.

"Will you be requiring a formal invitation, then?" she called up before again gathering the hem of her skirt and hastening toward her study.

She sat in the grand throne chair, then stood, then sat again, then paced for a short time until Reyna and José appeared before her.

"Sit down," she instructed and ushered them into the two armchairs opposite the desk. Reyna seemed concerned, but it was José who sat rigidly, his hands pressed flat against his knees.

Dona Antonia continued pacing, though the tone with which she spoke was decidedly unruffled. "You'll both pack a small bag. Only essentials. Whatever you may need for a short journey."

"Where are we going?" Reyna's eyes widened as she grasped onto the oak armrest.

"There's no time to explain. Now pack your things." She turned to José. "Are you hearing me?"

He nodded, just barely. It occurred to her that perhaps he was only beginning to understand what it meant to be a secret Jew.

"They're coming for everything," Dona Antonia said before withdrawing a key from the folds of her dress. "If it can't be through marriage, it will be through confiscation." After slipping the key into the hollow notch in her desk, she lifted the hinged flap, retrieved her ledger, and raised it up for them to see. "I've been transferring our assets overseas for some time. It's all right here. I thought it might come to this." She lowered the desk flap, then slapped the ledger down atop her desk. "Make haste and ready yourselves to depart."

"Depart?" Reyna wondered aloud. "It's all so very sudden."

"I thought we had more time," Dona Antonia mused to herself. "The queen said two months. It's only been four weeks." She looked up, then sank down into her chair. "Never mind that now. We'll be leaving a fortnight earlier than I'd originally planned."

"You've been *planning* for this?" Reyna fretted.

"Of course I have. You didn't think we'd all just wander off the peninsula with no plan in place?"

"Do we really have to *leave*?" It was as though the reality of their plight was only just settling in on Reyna.

Dona Antonia looked upon her daughter with pity. "My dear, what did you think was going to happen once I refused the queen?"

"I don't know," Reyna mumbled. "I suppose I hadn't thought it through." She turned to José, who looked on anxiously.

"We haven't any time to discuss this further," Dona Antonia continued. "I suspect the authorities will be returning in the next few days. In any event, we'll all three be long gone come nightfall." After a moment, she rang the servants' bell and instructed her maidservant Isabel to gather the household. It took only a few moments before the entire domestic staff was before her.

Dona Antonia began by doling out a small fortune in gold ducats to each one of them. "Some of you may have realized something is amiss in this household. Leave Lisbon for a while if you can. Return to your families in the countryside. You are no longer safe here. I trust you will keep anything you may have heard to yourselves. I want to thank you for your loyalty."

Just as fate had determined and Dona Antonia had anticipated, the house was raided the very next evening. Dona Antonia, José, and Reyna lodged at the edge of town under false names while the authorities stormed up the marble stairs leading to the grand villa. They broke down the door to discover absolute stillness, the house in perfect order, not a soul in sight. They scoured all four wings of the mansion.

Outside, a young soldier was holding a glowing torch when he heard his heel clang against a slab of metal hidden beneath the earth. He crouched low to the ground and swept away some loose strands of grass and dirt with his free hand. Beneath that small mound of fresh, cool earth, he discovered a hidden door with an iron lock. He shouted out to his superiors, "Over this way!"

They smashed the lock and descended the stone stairs to the damp subterranean lair. Beneath the flickering light of their outstretched torches, they uncovered countless Torah scrolls, prayer books piled high, a spectacular menorah of solid gold, prayer shawls. And within an innocuous wooden crate, a broken mirror encrusted with rubies, diamonds, and pearls.

3

With the help of the Jewish underground, Dona Antonia had arranged her family's escape. They were smuggled out of Portugal en route to Spain, where they rendezvoused with a band of gitanos bribed to escort them east to Italy and away from Iberia.

The origins of these Gypsy peoples were as cryptic as the chants, spells, and black magic potions they dispensed on European passersby. Some claimed them to be the accursed descendants of Cain, while others maintained that they were among the lost tribes of Israel. And yet they themselves boasted of their noble Egyptian origins.

And though Europeans had long debated the ancestry of these exotic drifters, the question of their origins was of no consequence to Dona Antonia Mendez and her family.

It was where they were headed that mattered to them now.

For weeks they journeyed along the Tagus river basin. At the cost of two exquisitely woven lace mantillas, a copper kettle, and a gold and ivory hair pin plucked right out of Reyna's hair, they'd come to possess a pair of she-goats that would provide a steady supply of cheese and milk along the way, as well as an affectionate, floppy-eared mule whose hee-haw bray never failed to elicit a small smile. And though they carried coinage on their persons, Dona Antonia decided it best to keep it hidden from view altogether, lest they become the victims of caravan pickpockets with sharp eyes and fast fingers.

José traveled by foot with the goats tethered to his wrists, while Reyna rode atop the mule and Dona Antonia in the small wagon secured behind it. They got by on milk and cheese, nuts, eggs, and dried fruit bits. The caravan would camp out along the edges of small towns and big cities, where the Gypsy people would go to peddle their potions and charms and knickknacks. All the while Dona Antonia, José, and Reyna stayed behind, hiding in their tent.

It would be foolish to venture into town while they were still in hostile territory.

They kept mostly to themselves as the caravan journeyed through fields and abandoned vineyards, trekking east across the hilly Spanish terrain beneath the midsummer sun and far beyond the river source into southwestern French territory. More than a month had passed, and though she would not approve of mixed bathing back in Lisbon, Dona Antonia—fatigued and spent—turned a blind eye when Reyna and José escaped together to spend a few quiet moments in the streams and ponds they passed.

They'd dunk themselves entirely clothed, Reyna in full vestiture with her skirt bouncing up all around her. But over the weeks, after several dips, she set aside propriety, stripping down to her innermost layers before jumping in and cooling off with nothing but a thin cotton dress draped over her figure. They were a hundred miles from home, somewhere beyond the mountains and north of the sea, when it occurred to José that his cousin was no longer the girl he'd once teased and played alongside in his youth. He watched her in a pond, wading gracefully and smiling primly as drifting white petals got caught up in her hair. At some point, beneath her layered frocks and the veil of her lace mantilla, Reyna had transformed into a striking young woman. The sight of her now, with her full breasts bobbing along the water's edge, was more than he could bear. José forced himself to turn away as she emerged from the pond to shed her wet layers and don her dry clothing. When she was once again decent, she tilted her long neck to the side and wrung her hair so that droplets of water fell to the grassy earth below.

"Is something bothering you?" she asked while pulling her hair back into a damp bun.

"Not at all," he lied, and forced a smile.

She examined him quizzically, then fastened her cloak.

Forcing his attention toward the horizon, he took note of the hour. The sun was low and the temperature was cooling. "We should get back," he declared before slinging his sack diagonally across his shoulder and hip. He was more than glad to avoid another awkward moment.

They made their way through the thick brush, emerging into a lavender field, where just beyond, the caravan had set up camp for the evening. They pressed onward for a few moments through the lean, sloping stalks as the labyrinth of tents and wagons in the clearing ahead drew nearer. When they arrived, Reyna was quick to enter her mother's tent, but José lingered behind.

With the sun setting behind, he withdrew a pocket-sized siddur from his satchel. Though he could not quite make out the Hebrew words etched upon its yellow pages, he clutched the book in his hand—a simple act of prayer in itself. There beside the tent, in his own words, he prayed for the safety and well-being of his family. He prayed that God deliver them beyond the reach of those who'd see them be destroyed, just as had been done nearly three thousand years before, when He'd brought their people forth from Egypt, not as slaves, but as free men.

The next morning, after the poles and tent fabrics had been packed away in their wagons, the caravan resumed its onward trek, but exactly where the Mendez family was heading, Dona Antonia would not reveal. José did not press the matter. If she refused to tell him, he knew it was for their own good.

Two full moons had come and gone by the time they reached an abandoned field at the edge of Veneto, a northeastern Italian territory under the control of the Republic of Venice. The peddlers and sorcerers emerged from their tents with crafts they had fashioned, trinkets and talismans they planned on selling to gadjos living in the town beyond the field.

It was late morning when Drina, the clan leader's wife (and mother to his nine children), appeared at the flap of their tent. José was in his usual spot at the rear of the tent, cracking nuts with a rock, while Reyna sat on a straw mat weaving a basket from branches she'd collected

"*Lachós chíbeses.*" Drina announced her arrival with the customary greeting of her people.

Startled, Dona Antonia rose quickly from her straw mattress and made her way to the flap of the tent. It was an odd occurrence, the tribal leader's wife here at their tent, the only time she'd ever called upon them.

"Good day, *Madre* Drina." Dona Antonia addressed the leader's wife in the manner of the clan.

"For you." Drina refrained from entering the tent, but held up a small scroll between her gold-ringed fingers. "Messenger bring this," she explained in a mix of Spanish and broken Portuguese. "Say he wait many weeks for your arrival."

Dona Antonia took the scroll and nodded. "*Najis tuke.*" She thanked Drina with one of the few Gypsy phrases they'd picked up along the way.

The clan leader's wife headed away, the clang of her bangles fading in the distance.

Reyna set aside her basket and stared anxiously at her mother.

"You need not fret if this is what I think it is," Dona Antonia explained while unrolling the scroll and scanning the message hidden within. Then she glanced up and announced enthusiastically, "They've been anticipating our arrival."

"Who has?" Reyna stood from her straw mat and made her way over to examine the scroll for herself.

"Our agent here in Veneto. He will take us somewhere safe." She breathed a sigh of relief, then put her arms around Reyna and rocked gaily for a moment. "We're almost there!" She turned about and took José's hands in her own.

"Will you *now* tell us where we are going?" Reyna pleaded.

"You'll know soon enough." She pulled José and Reyna back into her embrace and squeezed them both excitedly. "I'll need your help." She backed away and set her stare upon José. "In three days' time, you'll venture out to this place here," she said while handing him the scroll and pointing out a set of coordinates mapped out upon the parchment.

"Let me go with him," Reyna said, her sense of adventure getting the best of her.

"No," Dona Antonia replied. "A woman like me, let alone a girl like you, would be fairly conspicuous in the place he's to go." She turned her attention back toward José. "You'll have to do this on your own."

"Whatever you need, *Tia.*" He tried to sound calm, though his heart was racing.

"Here is the rendezvous point. You'll make your way there in three days' time, ninety minutes after sunset. See here, it's not far from the harbor," she explained while turning the map. "When you arrive at your destination, you'll wait until the Spaniard who sent this letter comes for you."

"How will I know it's him?"

"The man will reveal himself to you in the sacred manner by which the priests of our people have always blessed the nation. With his hands."

"Hands?" José asked, bewildered.

"When he places his hand on the table before you, he'll do so like this." She lifted his hand in her own, then separated his middle finger from his ring finger such that they formed the shape of a *V.* "Do you understand?"

"I think so." José nodded.

"Good." She sighed, then released his wrist. "This will all be over soon, I promise you that. In just a few days' time, we'll start a new life." She smiled brightly and lifted a dirty pile of clothing in her arms.

"Now I'm going out to wash our linens so that we don't look like beggars when we do arrive at our new home. I'll not be more than a few moments. Everything is falling into place now." With her linens in her arms, she rushed out of the tent.

Not a half hour had passed before Reyna looked up from her weaving. "Do you hear that?" she asked, her expression tense.

José froze for a moment. The hair on the back of his neck stood on end as he slowly made his way to the tent's entrance. The sounds of screaming women and children soon filled the field and entered through the flap of their tent as José looked out.

"What's happening?"

"The authorities! They're raiding the camp!" José turned to Reyna. "Quickly, give me your finger."

He took hold of her hand and withdrew his dagger. "They must know we're here."

"What are you doing!"

He said nothing and made a small slit along her fingertip with the blade. She winced in pain. José then did the same to his own finger. "Look up," he instructed a bewildered Reyna. Her eyes were glazed over. She was filthy and exhausted. He spread the blood from his fingertips across her cheeks, nose, and forehead.

"José?" Her voice was raspy as she spoke.

"I'm darkening your skin. You should appear to be a Gypsy when they find you." He continued to blot the blood across her face until she was noticeably darker.

He did the same to his own face while the commotion outside their tent grew louder. Mothers and babies were crying as the authorities stormed the tents one at a time.

Suddenly a hulk of a man wielding an enormous bludgeon in one hand and a sword in the other burst into their tent. The red-haired man took one look at their dark complexions, grimaced, and stormed out as violently as he had burst in.

Reyna let out a deep gasp and could not catch her breath. José tried to calm her. "You're all right." He strained to sound convincing.

When the raid had ended, José and Reyna emerged from their tent to a cloudless blue sky. There was an uneasy stillness throughout the caravan. The snake charmers and peddlers hid in their tents while Reyna and José wound their way through the narrow caravan lanes in search of Dona Antonia.

"*Tia!*" José's anxious cry spread throughout the makeshift village.

"Mother!" Reyna's foreign call sounded throughout the camp.

Reyna tightened her grip around his arm. "They've taken her," she said in a faint, breathy voice.

"We don't know that." José's tone was bitter, though in his gut he knew that Reyna was right. "Let's just keep looking."

They scoured an abandoned well and a dilapidated roofless struc-ture that might have once been a barn. Calling out for Antonia, they stormed through the camp, checking in each and every tent, dodging the malevolent hisses and curses of the dwellers within. They were con-sidered gadjos, outsiders, whose presence was seen to have brought about the disastrous raid. It was clear that they were no longer welcome within the ranks of the traveling caravan.

As dozens of angry Gypsies emerged from behind the openings of their tents and gathered around them, José took hold of his cousin and instructed her firmly, "Follow me." He led her away through the maze of tents and out to the edges of the encampment. It was there, by a nar-row stream, that they spotted a deserted washboard. Only a few steps farther, they came upon Antonia's lace collar, muddied with the fresh bootprints of those who had come to take her away.

Though grief-stricken, they were forced to carry on. Taking shelter in dodgy inns along the decrepit alleys of the Venetian mainland, José and Reyna changed their hideout each day, moving from one rat-infested lodging to another. The inns they patronized housed the city's cripples and drunks, but they would not take any chances on more upscale accommodations. The Republic of Venice was on alert for two wealthy runaway Jews.

As Antonia had instructed, José arrived at his rendezvous point at the specified time and place. He'd followed the map, stealthily making his way past the enormous clock tower and down the dark streets of the Venetian city of Mestre. Beside the marshy shore of a shimmering canal, he arrived at his destination—a whorehouse and tavern where no self-respecting clergy or officer would dare risk being spotted.

Taking a seat in a back corner of the inn, he averted his eyes from a handful of drunken patrons. In his periphery, he noticed a tall man in a hooded cape rise from the opposite end of the room. He ambled past a bosomy redhead straddled over a big man's lap and around two younger lads playfully wrestling in the center of the room. The tall man drew nearer without so much as a flinch.

Not a moment passed before the stranger was upon him, hovering closely over José. Without a word, he laid out his hand on the oak table in the very same manner Dona Antonia had informed José he would.

José nodded once, and the man lowered himself onto the bench just opposite.

The Spaniard's face was sunken back beneath the shadows of his hooded cape. He looked over his shoulder before pulling the hood back with his long, pale fingers. He had chiseled features and a sharp-pointed chin. His long ebony hair fell forward, masking much of his face from view. He was one of hundreds of secret Jews in the resistance network.

"We've been trailing your movements," the man said in a low, even tone.

"I don't understand." José looked up incredulously. "How did you even . . ."

"Your aunt has been funding the underground movement for some time."

"My aunt? But—"

"Her involvement has been of great importance to our mission. Naturally, we've kept an eye on her and her family."

"I never suspected . . ." His voice trailed off.

"She hid it well from both you and your cousin."

José furrowed his brow and said nothing.

"You mustn't be upset. The less you knew, the safer you were. The safer we all were."

"What happens now?"

The man took a breath before carrying on. "More likely than not, she is being interrogated at this moment." His thin lips seemed to disappear behind his frown.

"What sort of *interrogation*?"

"Who can say for certain? The important thing is, we believe she can withstand the pressure."

"Pressure?"

"José, our people are loyal. The last time one of our men was caught, he chewed off his own tongue, so afraid he was he might name names."

"My God," José gasped.

"You have to understand, your aunt's whole life has been dedicated to the cause."

José blinked back tears. "Why did she stay? Why not carry on with the mission from a distance, somewhere safe! Somewhere where they couldn't reach her?"

"She stayed for them."

"Them?"

"The others. The ones without means. She used her money to fund the movement, to bribe officials and district authorities to release prisoners and turn a blind eye at the border. We often tried to get her to leave, but to no avail. She was convinced her efforts wouldn't be as effective if she weren't situated on the peninsula overseeing things. She arranged for their hideouts, their escape routes, food, shelter—everything and anything to ensure that they were delivered to safety. All those poor souls, crouching in the shadows. From the shadows, she brought them out into the light."

"Were there many?" José asked.

"I stopped counting long ago."

"All this time . . ." José sighed, then shook his head.

"I believe she would have stayed in Portugal if she could, but she was forced out. A marriage between the prince and Reyna would have given the royal family control over your family's finances. It would have been impossible for the mission to continue."

"What do we do now?" José asked. Life as a fugitive was taking its toll. He had not slept more than a few hours the past three nights. Tormented by visions of his aunt being tortured in ways he tried not to imagine, he felt completely helpless for the first time in his life.

The Spaniard withdrew a weathered map from his satchel, unfolded it, and placed it before José. He tapped his finger on a narrow strip of land nestled between the Black Sea and the Aegean.

"That's where you're to go—Istanbul. The capital city of the Ottoman Empire."

"Istanbul? But why?"

"Because there you will be free. Free to practice your faith and free to arrange your aunt's rescue. We have an agent there waiting. He and your aunt had been working together to smuggle those in hiding out of Iberia. I'm told he has strong ties to the sultan."

"You're *told*? Do you mean to say you've never met this man? What if it's a trap?"

"You'll have to trust me."

José sighed. "I haven't much of a choice, do I?"

"You have no choice."

"My aunt is imprisoned here. I can't just leave." He shook his head in disbelief. "No, I won't. We won't . . . not until we're all together again."

"There's nothing left for you here. Get out now."

"But my aunt!" José brought his fist to the table.

"The sultan is your only hope." The Spaniard's eyes darted around the room as he leaned in closer. "Think of the girl. You are her guardian now. They'll have the two of you strung up in quarters if you're caught," he said, grabbing the edge of the table. "Listen carefully. Disguise yourselves. Take a gondola at sunrise down the channel and across the lagoon to the island port of Malamocco. It is the busiest of just three inlet ports where ships sail in and out of the lagoon. There you will board a merchant ship that will take you to your final destination. It is my hope that you both will slip through this busy hub unnoticed. Stay quiet and keep your ears open."

"Now, wait just a minute—"

"Our agent will come to collect you in Istanbul once you arrive."

"I need some time."

"Every uniformed man for miles is out right now looking to hunt you down for a fat bounty. Don't you understand? The Portuguese are offering a handsome reward for the arrest and return of all three of you. *That's* why the authorities are holding your aunt, and *that's* why they'll be here in the morning asking after a young Portuguese traveler. With your smooth skin and foreign tongue, how long do you think it will take them to track you down?"

José swallowed hard.

"Do as I say." The Spaniard tapped Istanbul on the map, then folded it back into a neat square and returned it to his sack. "Leave." He pulled the dark hood back over his head and gathered his belongings. "You're running out of time."

At the Malamocco harbor, just as José had expected, they were approached by district authorities demanding to know their travel purposes.

"My wife and I are missionaries," José explained to a rotund young man with dopey eyes and thick brows. He handed the officer the forged identity papers.

"Have you heard of the Mendez children?"

"I have not."

"*Jews.* They're on the run. You two fit the description quite nicely."

"I assure you we are not Jews." He laughed, perhaps a little too loudly. José tried to steady his pounding heart as the officer looked over their documents. The man squinted as though something wasn't quite right.

A shrill whistle sounded, and José seized the opportunity.

"Officer, we really should make that ferry. I'm afraid it's going to leave in just a few moments."

The whistle sounded once more. The young guard twitched nervously, then pulled the hood down from over José's head. He ran his fingers through José's long dark curls. Assured that José did not possess horns or the stubs that indicated their removal, he ushered them onto the boat.

"Hurry, you both!"

With that, José pulled the dark hood of his cloak back over his head and hurried up the wooden planks with Reyna by his side. They boarded *Le Grand Marie*, an enormous ship much like the ones Ferdinand and Isabella sent to explore the new world. Thick ropes and netting soared overhead. Four enormous sails ballooned out from tall masts rising from the deck like spears piercing the heavens. Boys as young as eight or nine hustled by with leaking buckets and tall mops. Muscular deckhands and bronzed sailors tugged and tied their ropes in accordance with the will of the winds, cranking their wheels and hollering orders.

José and Reyna were ushered to their shared quarters, a musty cabin in the lower deck fashioned with endless rows of barracks. They could not risk staying in the cabins of the upper deck, where they might be recognized by diplomats and young noblemen lodging in luxurious private cabins and socializing in first-class dining quarters. The House of Mendez had been entertaining dignitaries and aristocrats for as long as José could remember, and the chance of rubbing shoulders with someone they knew was not altogether impossible.

As they waited their turn to descend the hatchway ladder into the lowest point of the ship's hull, José spotted several dandy-looking young men greeting one another. No doubt these fellows were enjoying the newest fashion among the Continent's most privileged classes—a grand voyage around Europe with an entourage of servants available to cater to their every whim. Along the way, they were supposed to learn about art and culture before returning to their remote family estates and resuming the idle, leisure-filled lives they'd left behind. And while these wealthy young men would surely disembark before reaching the southernmost tip of Italy's boot, José and Reyna would be journeying onward, beyond the Aegean and toward the Mediterranean, never to return to the home of their youth.

The conditions in the lower cabin were nearly intolerable. They slept with linen cloths pressed over their mouths to avoid the fevers that at week's end had spread to countless passengers. Reyna and José spent most of the journey holed up among the commoners, the sickly, and sealed cargo boxes, worrying about Dona Antonia's fate as well as their own.

By the time the fevers had claimed two lives below deck, the threat of disease outweighed the threat of recognition. After carefully considering the risks, José determined that most of the touring young men had disembarked at the last port of call. Traveling Europeans generally did not venture beyond Italy's southeasternmost tip. They were far beyond that point by now, somewhere in the far reaches of the Ionian Sea.

With that in mind, Reyna and José made their way up to the open air of the upper deck. There, priests and diplomats relished the salty sprays brought aboard by easterly gusts. Reyna closed her eyes and let the hard winds assault her cheeks and ravage her hair. Her pale face was covered with smudges of dirt and grease, and her once full hair was flattened under too much oil and filth. And though he'd always be able to recognize the glimmer in her eye, he was sure that no one else in this world would ever guess that the scrawny girl before him now had once been among the most sought-after heiresses in all the land.

Though he chuckled at the thought, he knew by the startled look upon her face that he himself was in no better shape. Their once fine linens had turned to rags and their skinny, dirty faces were hardly recognizable to each other, let alone anyone else.

They strolled the deck, stretching their legs and taking in the view, before making their way to the rear of ship. There they came across a portly young man with a cloud of smoke escaping his lips. He smoked rolled bundles of dried tobacco, a fashionable new affectation among Europe's upper class that had been brought back from the New World by Portuguese sailors and explorers of the day.

"If it's good enough for our dear lady Catherine de' Medici, it's good enough for me!" he proclaimed while leaning up against the railing and blowing smoke into the wind.

"Mind if I have a try?" José asked the man.

He examined José pitifully, then plucked a cigar from a wooden box and handed it to José. "The good Lord knows I've not been a charitable man, but one look at your sorry state and I can't help myself."

José smiled cheerily, then brought the cigar to his lips while Reyna eyed him as if to say, *Be careful what you let on.*

They leaned over the edge of the deck, flicking ash into the sea below. "That your wife there?" The man gestured toward Reyna as he sucked in smoke to his cheeks.

José nodded. Then he turned to Reyna and, in the most honest moment of their three-week charade as husband and wife, enveloped her in a kiss so passionate, violent, and persistent, she tore herself away and stumbled as she did.

"Newlyweds!" The man laughed wholeheartedly. "Good luck to you both!" He tossed his cigar overboard, leaving Reyna and José alone on the rear deck.

That night, their minds raced with thoughts they'd never dared to entertain before. They lay in the barracks beside each other, bodies parted by the invisible spark between them. At some point during those long sleepless hours, she reached out and pulled his arm over her body so that they lay like spoons.

4

At the dock in Istanbul, a handsome old man with a trim gray beard approached José and Reyna. Smiling, he exposed a row of perfectly aligned teeth as bright and spotless as the long white tunic and turban he wore. "You must be the Mendez children?" he asked in near-perfect Spanish. It was one of several languages Reyna and José had learned, thanks to the rigorous education Dona Antonia had provided.

Having taken such pains to hide his identity for the past few weeks, José stood speechless.

"It's all right, you are in Ottoman territory now," the man said. "No one will harm you here."

"We can't thank you enough, Señor . . ."

"Hamon," the man said. "Dr. Moses Hamon, personal physician to the sultan. I am also Jewish." The man explained further. "Here you are free to follow whatever faith you choose. You're a citizen of the Ottoman Empire now." Glimpsing over at Reyna, he took in the sight of her matted hair and drab frock. A web of dust veiled her face, but did little to conceal her beauty.

"You are lovelier than your mother promised."

José and Reyna exchanged a bewildered glance.

"I am also from Iberia," he continued as he led them toward a sedan chair manned by two muscular Africans. "Granada, to be exact. My family fled the year of the edict. I was just two years old when we came to Istanbul, but here I was raised, here I was educated, and here I have thrived. I've been working for the sultan for many decades now."

"I'm sorry, Doctor, but how did you manage to find us?" Reyna said as they all three continued onward.

"I've been exchanging letters with your mother for many years. She'd been planning an escape for quite some time. Over the years, she's funneled her assets here little by little. She'd always planned to come to Istanbul."

"Dr. Hamon," José cut in. "Have you had any word of our aunt? Of her condition?"

"I have good news," the doctor said. "The sultan is insisting she be released. Preparations are in motion as we speak. I expect the Venetians will give her up in the next day or so. They'll not risk a military response from the sultan." They stopped before the sedan chair and he turned around to face them. "My goodness, the girl looks as though she is going to faint. Come! You've had a long journey." He took Reyna's hand and helped her mount the step leading up to the sedan chair. "You'll be taken to my villa, where you'll stay until we can arrange for more permanent accommodations for you both. A full staff awaits you there and is prepared to attend to all your needs."

"We cannot thank you enough," said José.

"Just get some rest," the doctor replied. "In the morning, you'll be presented to the sultan. Now I'll excuse myself. I have some business to attend to back at the palace."

Reyna reached for the doctor's hand and bowed her head to kiss the large emerald on his finger.

"Please, don't thank me." He reached for her dirty cheek. "It's only natural. Why shouldn't I help if I can?"

"Not everyone would."

"I am a close personal friend of the sultan. He would do almost anything to help any member of my family."

"Family?" Reyna questioned.

"Well, it's only a matter of time."

Stunned, Reyna and José said nothing.

"Why, hasn't Dona Antonia told you?"

"She has not," José replied frostily.

"I'm sure she intended to tell you both. Reyna is promised to my eldest son. It's been agreed upon for nearly two months now. Yes, it's all very exciting." Hamon clapped his hands together. "But you'll not meet my boy just yet. He's to spend several more months training at the hospital, where he'll finish his studies and return home with a degree in medicine. A thousand apologies." His smile was bright. "I can see you are exhausted from your journey. I won't keep you a moment longer. Welcome to Istanbul!"

Neither José nor Reyna uttered a word as the sedan made its way beneath the cypress trees along the hilly streets of Istanbul. At every turn, glistening domes and spiked minarets thrust skyward from mosques throughout the city. They passed tall wooden houses with latticed windows and breezy second-story porches overlooking narrow alleys and vaulted walkways.

Their hands rested next to each other, so close that the fine hairs of her skin grazed his palm. He looked away, acutely aware of the infinitesimal space between them. As the sedan came to an abrupt stop, she seized his hand in her own. He turned to her and their eyes met. He knew nothing of the customs in this land, but her eyes, as did his heart, begged the question. If she was truly betrothed to another, might this be the last moment they'd be permitted alone together? She brought his fingers to her lips and kissed his rough, dark skin.

He struggled for breath as the world seemed to close in on them.

The door flew open, and in an instant he was back at the far end of the bench, his heart thumping and his insides reeling.

A young servant nodded politely. "Welcome to the House of Hamon. I hope the trip wasn't too arduous. I know these roads can be bumpy." He offered a hand to help Reyna disembark.

They'd arrived at a small stucco villa nestled up against the edge of the Bosphorus. Pink, red, and blue wild flowers blossomed from shrubs all about the secluded property. Without a word, they retired to separate quarters, where they were stripped of their tattered rags and bathed in lavender-scented water. At sundown, they dined in separate quarters, on sea bream and artichokes served on silver trays by their handsome attendants. That night they both tossed and turned in the plush pillows and silken fabrics lining their beds. For the past week they had slept side by side upon thin mattresses in cramped barracks smelling of must and perspiration. In the past few days, he'd grown accustomed to her soft body tucked against his torso, she to the warmth of his breath on the nape of her neck. Now in bedchambers at opposite ends of the villa, Reyna and José lay awake, each wondering how it was that their first taste of freedom should be so bittersweet.

Though their enemies had taken Antonia, it was their friends who would soon tear them apart.

In the morning, José was ferried across a narrow waterway, then carried a short distance by sedan chair to the gates of Topkapi. The palace was situated on a peninsula overlooking the place where the Sea of Marmara met the Golden Horn. Unlike the grand, singular structures of European palaces in Portugal and Spain, the sultan's residence was more of a fortified city, a labyrinth of covered pavilions, disparate quarters, and conjoined apartments.

Stepping down from the sedan chair just outside the palace walls, José found himself standing before the Gate of Salutation. It was an intimidating structure, a vast, crenelated passageway flanked on either side by two enormous watchtowers. Guided by two palace guards, José passed through the gate as though he were walking into a lion's den. Beyond the dark shadows of the gated tunnel, he found himself standing in the midst of a plush green paradise, where strutting peacocks poked their heads up from the grass and gazelles grazed the low shrubs blossoming with blue and pink hydrangea. He passed through another set of gates before being led to a chamber where the sultan was waiting to receive him.

José smoothed down the burgundy caftan that Dr. Hamon had given him earlier that day. He'd accepted the gift reluctantly, knowing very well that he'd taken charity from a man who'd return to claim that which José held most dear. He knew it was only a matter of months before Reyna would join the House of Hamon. Reason would dictate that he should have begrudged the doctor, and yet on the whole he couldn't help but admire the man. Had Dr. Hamon not displayed tremendous concern for their well-being since the moment they'd arrived?

He was more confused than ever.

José shook his head wearily, then forced the matter from his mind. He'd come to this place for one reason, and one reason only. Returning to the task at hand, he made his way through the azure-tiled sanctuary thinking only of his aunt. At the far end of the room, beneath a gilt canopy, Sultan Suleiman the Magnificent sat on his jewel-studded throne. José was led across four enormous oriental carpets before he finally found himself kneeling at the base.

Sultan Suleiman the Magnificent, the tenth sultan descended from

Osman, had been named for the wise ruler of Judea, King Solomon. It was said that in greatness he had surpassed his namesake. He wore an enormous cloak secured with a gleaming diamond and a huge white turban fashioned with a green feather atop his head. He was not a handsome man, with his prominent nose and sunken dark eyes, yet there was a kindness about him, a certain grace in his composed demeanor.

"Rise," the sultan instructed José, who promptly came to his feet. "My physician has informed me that you are concerned over the well-being of your aunt. You needn't be. I have secured her release, and I assure you, you will be reunited shortly. Here, and in all the territories throughout my empire, your people are welcome to live freely as Jews."

José raised his gaze toward the sultan and understood that he was indeed in the presence of greatness. From the Persian Gulf to the North African coast of Algiers, from the farthest reaches of Hungary to the Mamluk state of Egypt, the sultan did not pass laws that he did not believe were just. It was said that he ruled his lands and conquered territories with the resolve that he would better the lives of their inhabitants. He was the first sultan to sleep and live with just one woman. A Polish slave by the name of Roxelana, she was his one true love and only wife. Suleiman governed by day and wrote poetry by night. He was a great patron of the arts. A man who sought to be inspired, he inspired all within his domain.

Still, he was not the first sultan to welcome in persecuted Jews; rather, he followed in the magnanimous footsteps of his predecessors. His grandfather, Sultan Bayezid II, had sent his fleets to collect thousands of stranded Jews who sought to flee Spain and Portugal in response to the Edict of Expulsion. Trapped between sea and land, they faced death whichever way they turned. If they took to the seas, they could be killed by pirates waiting offshore. If they stayed on the peninsula as unrepentant Jews, they risked being burned at the stake. Sultan Bayezid's ships transported the refugees, who came and settled throughout the empire, free to practice their faith in peace. And even before that, his great-grandfather, Mehmed the Conqueror, had famously proclaimed, "Listen, sons of the Hebrews who live in my country . . . May all those who desire come to Constantinople. May the rest of your people find here a shelter."

Now Sultan Suleiman the Magnificent seemed to be intent on continuing their work. Since the start of his reign more than two decades prior, he had been welcoming Jews into his empire with open arms.

They came by the thousands, penniless and empty-handed. They entered Istanbul as a convoy of promise, rich with the education and experience that Ferdinand and Isabella could never confiscate. With them, the Hebrew nation brought the printing press, along with their knowledge of science, medicine, astronomy, and weaponry. They came with their professional trades as well as expertise in European banking and finance. "How can anyone call Ferdinand wise when he is impoverishing his kingdom and enriching mine?" Sultan Bayezid II had once said.

Beyond the wisdom and skills they would bring, among themselves there was one thing they treasured above all else. It was not to be carried in pouches or stored in the mind. When it came to the religion of their forefathers, that of Abraham, Isaac, and Jacob, such a treasure could only make its way over land and sea stored safely in the heart and in the soul.

These were the sacred traditions of a nation that had survived thousands of years of intimidation, persecution, and tyranny—the same traditions that had been handed down from the time of Moses, nearly three thousand years prior, from mother to daughter, father to son.

In Iberia, their faith had been hidden away, for decades residing only in the depths of their hearts. Now it had been unveiled. Out of the darkness and into the light, from the churches of Iberia to the yeshivas and synagogues of the Ottoman lands. The Hebrew calendar would be dusted off and embraced anew. The glow of Shabbat candles would once again fill the Jewish home. All the days of the Tabernacle Festival would be commemorated in bamboo-covered dwellings known as sukkoth. From the passover seder to the blessing of the new moon, men and women, old and young, would embrace and perform the rituals of their forefathers. And for the Jewish people, Rosh Hashanah would once again fulfill the promise of a sweet new year.

For the Jewish nation, it meant the survival of a people, but for José, it meant something more. He resolved to bring the faith his parents had held to deeper into his heart. José was convinced it was what they would have wanted had they been alive. He'd not disappoint them now, not when they were surely looking down on him from Olam Ha-Ba, the world to come. He imagined their spirits, night and day, peering through a veil of stars or a sky laced with clouds, watching, always watching, the son they'd left behind.

5

Three weeks had passed before the vessel transporting Dona Antonia Mendez sailed through the Dardanelles and arrived at the port in Istanbul. The ship bobbed gently upon the ebbing tide and against the easterly winds as it was moored to the harbor. José scanned the area. Throngs of Inquisition refugees had come out to witness the arrival of the legendary Dona Antonia Mendez. It was known all throughout the Jewish community that this was the woman who had rescued so many of their persecuted brethren, who had in many instances saved them. For this reason, she had earned the nickname La Madre de los Anusim. Over time, she had come to be known simply as La Madre.

Near the docked vessel, José and Reyna stood side by side, both painfully aware of the tension that had developed between them. During the days they'd spent in Dr. Hamon's residence, they'd hardly spoken to each other at all.

Now their silence seemed to simmer, like water just before it begins to boil. Her eyes met his briefly and a stab of pain—or was it pleasure?—sliced through his core. She turned away, freezing him in that state of agony.

A low murmur rose from the crowd, and José looked toward the cabin door. His aunt appeared, moving slowly with the aid of two young Janissaries.

Reyna gasped at the sight of her mother, then gathered her dress in her hands and ran toward Antonia.

José followed quickly. As he approached, he saw a broken woman with ashen skin and sunken eyes. She was nothing more than a sack of bones.

Dona Antonia's skin hung over her withered frame, but it was the dark void in her once-bright eyes that frightened José most of all.

The fingers that clasped the head of her walking stick were gnarled and bruised. "José." The raspiness in her voice grated his ears. She held out her shaking, withered arms. "My boy. My *son.*" The word stirred something within him. He dove gently into her embrace, careful not to crush whatever was not yet broken. For a long while, he could not let go.

"I was afraid I'd never see you again," Reyna confessed to her mother that evening.

They sat in Dr. Hamon's exquisitely decorated parlor, a vast space outfitted with sumptuous curtains and broad oriental carpets. An enormous candelabra hung overhead, casting a ring of light against the vaulted ceiling.

"Even the longest day has its end," Dona Antonia marveled aloud. With trembling lips, she offered up a weak smile before bringing her hand to her chest and filling the room with the sound of a dry, heaving cough.

José looked at her with concern, though Dona Antonia waved her hand dismissively. "It's nothing," she assured.

A servant appeared with a tray of grapes, figs, and cheese. Her presence seemed to cast a wedge between them.

Reyna held her breath. The servant girl retreated and the intimacy of the reunion was restored. She brought her kerchief to her eyes and addressed her mother. "I'm ashamed I haven't matched you in courage."

Dona Antonia extended a bony hand. "You and I are cut from the same cloth." She wove her fingers through her daughter's. "As long as you remember that, it shall always be true." She held the edge of her chair as another barrage of coughs issued from her chest.

With tears in her eyes and a tremor in her voice, Reyna lowered her chin and shook her head. "What did they *do* to you, Mother?"

She began in a tone not much louder than a whisper. "By my wrists." She held out palms branded with purple rope burns. "They took me up by my wrists, hoisted me above a pit of fire. It wasn't long before my shoulders were dislocated and I *did* confess my sin. 'Hear O Israel, the Lord is our God, the Lord is one.' This had been a prayer I'd silently recited every night of my life. For the first and only time in my life, I screamed these words aloud."

Antonia's words rang in José's ears.

"After my confession, they threw me into an underground cell. A space so small that even the rats fought each other for a corner to claim as their own. In that hell, the sun never rose and the moon never shone. I lost all sense of time. Sleep came in fits and starts. I can't tell you how long had passed, but soon I came to exist in a space between nightmare and reality, where I could no longer tell my interrogators from the demons in my head. Putrid scraps not fit for a dog were the only sustenance provided me.

"I slept in a bed of filth, barely able to tolerate my own stench. I prayed for God to take my soul and then, from the depths of the darkness, a light materialized in the distance. It moved toward me and I was certain my time had come. I recited the kaddish, the mourner's prayer. A prayer never intended to be said by the dying, but rather by those who would be left behind once the loved one has passed. But I was alone, and there was no one else there to pray for the elevation of my soul. The light neared, and with it, the voices of brutes. Huffs and snorts and cackles. With my cheek pressed against the wet floor, I saw four columns moving down the long dark hall leading to my cell.

"Men were exchanging angry words. The glow of a lantern illuminated a red, knotted face.

"'You'll do what you're told,' I heard the more authoritative voice command. 'The sultan has made his demands perfectly clear. The hag is not worth the threat of attack. The Grand Turk can have her if he pleases.' Upon hearing those words, I let out a torrent of air, breaths of the living I hadn't known were still in me. I was consumed by all the trappings of the physical world—searing pain and hot tears against my human flesh. I cried out for joy, but my human voice failed me. I heeded not the burning sensation in my throat. My time had come, and I understood that I was to be released from the world of the undead, old hag that I was. My heart filled with joy at the knowledge that I would live another day. The jingling of keys sounded and the door came crashing open. I knew that I'd been saved."

"You're safe now, *Tia*." José reached for her hand.

"My greatest fear all throughout was not of fire or death or illness. My greatest fear was for you, my children. Were you hungry? Were you safe? Were you suffering? I cannot tell you what immeasurable joy it gives me to see your faces. I was prepared to die for my faith, but to live, I was prepared to live for *you*."

His aunt's words rattled throughout José's mind. And though they brought him some comfort, they also brought him pain.

He'd been an infant, incapable of having wronged his parents in any way. And yet he wondered if he'd displeased them somehow. Had his cry been too grating? His face perhaps too wrinkled and ugly? For what could have led them to choose death over life? What could have led them to abandon their only child?

Questions like these lingered in his mind. Of doubts, he had many, but of answers, José had none.

As the indigo sky gave way to the thick black of night, the silences between words and sentences grew until there was nothing more to say. Reyna and José mounted the stairs with Antonia—hunched and limping—supported between them. As she shuffled to her quarters, the sound of her labored breathing disturbed them. They watched as she disappeared behind her door, leaving Reyna and José a moment alone.

"Do you think she'll be all right?" José whispered.

"I do." Reyna replied. "She's stronger than you and me."

"Reyna—"

"Good night then, Cousin." Her words took on a forced formality that broke his heart.

He reached for her hand but only grazed the tips of her fingers as she turned from him and rushed away.

Ever since the moment they'd shared together in the sedan, Reyna had been taking great pains to avoid him. He recalled that on the silk divan earlier in the evening, she'd positioned herself as far from him as possible. He'd tried to engage her in conversation, but she would respond with only one or two words. Dutiful daughter that she was, her behavior could easily be interpreted as concern for her mother. But even when they'd pass each other in the corridors, she'd avert her eyes and angle her shoulder inward so that she might not brush up against him. The servants spoke of her as a shining example of modesty, but José knew the truth. There was no turning back. He felt it. He knew she felt it too.

Somberly he made his way to his chamber at the opposite end of the hall. He was welcomed by the warm glow of the fireplace and the fresh scent of gardenias floating in a crystal bowl. His bedsheets had been turned down and some sticky, flaky sweets were placed on the tray by his bed.

He sat at the edge of his mattress and watched shadows from the fire dance against the floor and walls. He covered his eyes with his right hand and recited the Shema, the prayer that Jews the world over had been reciting for millennia, the very same words his aunt had shouted aloud while strung up above a pit of fire.

"Hear O Israel, the Lord is our God, the Lord is one."

Were they the words his mother and father had uttered in their last moments of life? José wanted to believe so. He needed to have that, if nothing else—these holy words, shared between them.

He remained still, his eyes closed and his mind racing. Everything was changing so quickly. Once he had been a boy he now barely recognized. A boy with the world at his feet and not a care to keep him up at night. He watched the boy saunter through the corridors of time, his stride ir-reverent and unknowing. The boy turned and disappeared beneath the hood of his black cloak, and just like that, he was gone.

José changed into his sleep suit and climbed onto the low featherbed. Though he longed for sleep, his mind would permit him no rest. Grati-tude to the sultan and to his God whirled in tandem, while visions of Reyna flickered before his eyes. Soon his thoughts turned back to the mother and father he'd never known. Their already hazy faces blurred further and then faded before him. As his anxiety mounted, he began worrying about the woman who'd loved him as though he'd been her own. After all that she'd been through, could Dona Antonia be expected to make a full recovery now?

Tossing and turning, José conceded defeat and flung his covers to the ground. He slipped into his robe and slippers, then hurried from his chamber down the wide spiral staircase to the grand foyer below. A full suit of armor guarded the far end of the hall. It stood well over six feet tall, the shell of a man who'd once been a giant. As José made his way past, he envisioned the soldier eying him from behind the slits in the helmut.

Drawn to the sound of muffled voices beyond the foyer, José made his way down a narrow passageway to a door lit up all along its edges. As he pressed gently, the panel creaked and the voices came to a halt. His body turned to ice and he remained suspended in that position, his shoulder against the door.

"José, is that you?" Hamon's voice sounded from within.

His muscles relaxed and he pushed on the door ever so slightly. "Excuse me, Doctor. I couldn't sleep." He addressed his host through the crack in the door.

"Nothing like a bit of night walking to set your mind at ease. Do come in."

He entered the serene glow of Hamon's private study. A dim orange light blanketed the room, illuminating the narrow two-story chamber he'd never had the occasion to enter before. Three unremarkable chairs surrounded a table one might expect to find in a monastery. A bamboo ladder rested against a wall of books that reached all the way to the ceiling.

"This is Rabbi Hayyim Ibn Yacoub." Hamon gestured to an old man with a flowing white beard sitting next to him. "Our community's chief rabbi and the greatest scholar of his generation."

José brought his lips to Ibn Yacoub's pale, fleshy hand and kissed it.

"I have heard of you," the rabbi intoned. "Hamon tells me you can recite the book of Bereshit by memory. Is it true?"

"I'm afraid not." A pang of inadequacy swelled from his gut to his throat.

"He's being modest." Hamon directed his words to the rabbi. "I've heard it myself. Just yesterday, I spied him in the salon reciting verse while gazing into the garden. There wasn't a book of Tanakh in sight."

"I have much to learn," José interjected.

"What are you doing wandering around the house at this late hour?" the rabbi queried.

"I hope you'll forgive my intrusion. I have much on my mind."

"Why don't you join us then?" Ibn Yacoub's smiling eyes welcomed him.

"I'd like nothing more," he replied, lowering himself into an empty chair by the rabbi's side.

"We were just contemplating this passage of mystical scripture. When a man accomplishes the divine will below, he causes a parallel rectification above."

As the rabbi read the verse aloud, black letters swelled out from the page under the eye of Ibn Yacoub's magnifying lens. The old man looked up.

"What does it mean to you?" Hamon asked.

"I don't know." José felt his cheeks flush. "If I had to guess, I might say that it suggests that the actions of mankind move the universe toward some kind of ultimate destiny."

"Very good," the rabbi said with a satisfied smile. Leaning forward, he continued. "My boy, it is my sincerest belief that man's actions rebound between the universe and the earth. When a kindness is bestowed on earth, the universe takes notice. It craves balance. It demands a kindness be paid in return." He stroked his long white beard. "Through man's actions, such a debt is eventually paid."

Enthralled by the rabbi's words, José leaned in.

But the rabbi said no more. Instead, he rose from his seat, his joints creaking as he stood. "If you'll excuse me now, *rabotai*," he said, addressing José and Hamon. He let the book fall shut before announcing his intention to retreat for the evening. He brought the holy book to his lips, then returned it to an empty place on the shelf before disappearing beyond the door.

The wooden chair scraped the floor as José rose to his feet. *When a kindness is bestowed on earth, the universe takes notice.* Ringing in his mind, the rabbi's words conjured the sultan's magnanimous act—the deed that had rescued not only his family but all the generations yet to be born of his blood and faith.

Taking Hamon's hand, José asked, "Doctor, how does one repay a debt such as the one we've spoken of tonight?"

The doctor's kind eyes softened. "You're just a boy, aren't you," he said as though taking note of it for the very first time. "The celestial forces pursuing this balance flow like ocean currents," he began to explain. "Mankind floats upon these invisible currents, though he still has the power to choose another way, for even a simple-minded trout may sometimes swim against the tide."

"But, Doctor, how does one know which way to swim?"

"You need not chase the opportunity, José. The universe will ensure that the ultimate destination is the same: The debt will be repaid, even if four hundred winters must first come to pass, even if you never even know it. The universe will take notice."

6

Several weeks had passed before the family vacated Hamon's residence and resettled in the Galata neighborhood of Istanbul, in a stone country home surrounded by lush gardens and vineyards. The neighborhood boasted vast sun-drenched piazzas and orderly parallel streets. Diplomats and Ottoman officials frequented coffee shops in the area to play backgammon, smoke nargilehs, and discuss the politics of the day. It was in this neighborhood that foreigners and diplomats came to live, so it possessed all the qualities of a well-manicured European village, rather than the jumble of byzantine dwellings that characterized the heart of the city.

Together, the family agreed the time had come to revert to the surname of their ancestors, Nissim. It was a name meaning *miracle*.

While they had been fortunate enough to escape one danger, another was still with them. Though she'd dismissed her ailment as nothing more than a pesky cough, Dr. Hamon ultimately determined that Dona Antonia's inflamed lungs, fever, and abdominal pain were symptoms of the deadly illness known throughout the region as peripneumonia. He cautioned her to rest and take oil of hyssop.

With Dona Antonia confined to her bed, Reyna received religious instruction under the tutelage of the chief rabbi's wife. In a small room just off the kitchen of their new home, Reyna first began learning the ways of her people, the dietary laws of kashruth, the forty-nine prohibitions pertaining to the Sabbath. And while Reyna dutifully carried on with her studies, it could not be said that she carried the same flame that Dona Antonia and José held in their hearts. She yearned for the life they'd left behind—for the home of her youth, the sound of her native tongue ringing in the streets. Though she was ashamed to admit it, there were times she wished the truth had never come out. There were even times she wished to belong to another people.

Not a week had passed since they'd settled into their new home when Dona Antonia informed Reyna that in preparation for the day she'd soon be wed, it was time for her to commence with the study of Jewish family law. Having been sheltered all of her life, Reyna had been stunned to discover just what that meant. The laws of family purity were a strict set of rules governing the relations she would soon share with a complete stranger. The next morning, pretending to fall ill, Reyna asked to be excused from her lessons, then stayed in bed all day. The thought that she might share such intimacy with a man other than José was more than she could bear. She longed to go back in time and place, to the simple life she'd once known beside a boy she now realized she'd loved all along.

And while Reyna spent the mornings locked away in study, José passed the hours in the synagogue alongside a quorum of men whose incantations rose to the heavens through open windows and cracks in the roof tiles.

He prayed, believing that through prayer and study, a piece of his parents might always live on. He prayed as though through prayer alone, he might somehow bring about his aunt's recovery.

After the shaharith, the morning prayer service, he'd meet with Hamon and Ibn Yacoub in the doctor's private study. As Hamon had said, his son had several months left of training at the medical university in Manisa, and José filled the void his boy had left. In the same way, José couldn't help but seek out the doctor's approval. Though he was regarded as a man at the ripe age of twenty years, it seemed José Nissim was still very much a boy, craving the love of a father he'd never known.

It was there in the doctor's cloistered sanctuary that Hamon, Ibn Yacoub, and José sat for hours on end, hunched over the ashen pages of ancient tractates of the Talmud. Those were mind-twisting hours spent picking apart, then piecing back together an intricate web of Judaic scripture. Problems contemplated became problems solved. Revelations came like flashes and ideas evolved to maturity at lightning speed.

Only when the doctor was called away on palace duties did José allow his mind some rest. He would visit the local coffee shop, where he'd

drink tea and flex his mind in a game known in Europe as backgammon, but which went by the name of Tavla here in the Ottoman lands.
There in the coffee shop he'd play opposite the Bosnian, a formidable
opponent who was said to have once beaten the renowned mathematician
Matrakçı Nasuh when he was just a boy and the latter an old man. Jews
did not often frequent the coffeehouses, but José relished the opportunity
to mingle with different peoples from all walks of life. Besides, the game
was the perfect training ground for the mind. Through its study, one
might hope to master the most intricate and powerful nexus of all—
man's control over his own destiny. Though the currents of the universe
would always push man toward his fate, *even a simple-minded trout can
sometimes swim against the tide.*

With the dice in midair, José was already contemplating the benefits
and drawbacks of an infinite number of moves. How they would fall
was a matter of fate and chance. And yet his next moves would be determined through sheer will and human intellect. He would direct the
movement of his chips.

He would steer the course of his destiny.

With the sharpening of his mind came the sharpening of his sensitiv-
ities.

The die had been cast and the distance between him and Reyna had
never been so great. The further she pushed him away, the closer he
yearned to be. In the dead of night, he found himself imagining the
curve of her thigh beneath her full skirt and petticoat, but then his lust
would turn to sorrow, and what he yearned for most of all were a few
honest words between them. He missed his confidante. His cousin. His
best friend.

It was a breezy morning in early autumn, a month since the family had
relocated to the Galata villa, when José spotted Reyna picking fruits
from a young date palm in the garden.

He approached her slowly, taking care not to startle her. When their
eyes met, he greeted her cheerily, only to be met with her tepid smile.
"Can I help you?" he offered meekly.

"Of course," she responded too politely.

José began gathering dates from the low branches and placing them in
the box on the ground.

"A gift for Rebekka," she explained as she plucked the ripened fruit from the sprawling tree. A vision of Hamon's niece flashed before his eyes. A plain girl with swollen calves and a pale, freckled face, she had been kind to Reyna, welcoming her into a group of girls that met in the afternoons to invent stories and concoct theatrical plays for their own amusement. "I was thinking of calling upon her for a visit before shabbat," she continued.

"I'll escort you." He felt his insides churning. As the man of the house, he'd been charged with escorting Reyna anywhere beyond the walls of their home in Galata, as it would be unheard of for a lady of her station to venture out into the streets alone. And yet Reyna had not come to him once, calling upon her maids and servants to chaperone her outings in his stead.

"All right." She sighed.

They continued picking dates until she seemed satisfied with the amount they'd gathered. He admired her as she squatted to tie a hemp cord around the parcel she'd assembled. She lingered there a moment too long, causing him to hope beyond hope that perhaps she too enjoyed this briefest of improprieties. She stood abruptly, as though coming to her senses.

"Shall we go?" She fastened her veil to her headdress, then lifted the parcel and began walking, first at a leisurely pace but soon more quickly, sensing he was trailing too closely behind. He stepped up his pace until they arrived at a two-story wooden house with large windows and a big balcony. She rapped gently at the door.

"Speak to me," he called out to her from the base of the steps.

Reyna spun around. Her weary eyes blinked back tears beneath the thin fabric of her veil. "Please, just let me be, José!"

"Tell me you don't love me. Say the words and I'll not bother you again."

"Please, don't make this harder for me." She turned from him and again began rapping hastily on the door.

"I'll speak to your mother."

"And drive the nail into her coffin?" She glanced back with pleading eyes. "The shame of it would kill her." The door swung open and Reyna hurried through it without another word.

José made his way home, saddened and confused. He stopped to

smoke some nargileh in the coffeehouse, even though he had long de-
tested the smell of tobacco in his clothes. From the coffeehouse, he went
around to the synagogue, where he spent the afternoon studying sacred
texts alone at a table in the rear of the sanctuary. Though he normally
debated scripture alongside Hamon and Ibn Yacoub, on this day he
could not bear to face the good doctor, knowing full well what he would
soon be asking his aunt to do.

By the time he returned home, the sun was low in the sky and the
afternoon had drawn to a close. José removed his turban and handed it
to a servant at the door, then made his way up the stairs to Dona Antonia's dimly lit chamber.

He found her shivering, her pale, fleshy face peeking out from beneath
a vast fur coverlet. It was a disturbing sight. Though the leaves were
speckled with orange and yellow, autumn was barely upon them.

"José," she called to him. "Come in."

He made his way over and kneeled by the side of her bed. "I'm sorry
to disturb you, *Tia*. I know you should be resting."

"I have all eternity to rest." She smiled weakly. "Tell me, my son, what
is it that is bothering you?"

He lowered his eyes and wrapped his fingers through hers. "Is it so
plain to see that something is bothering me?"

She squeezed his hand in her own. "A mother always knows."

He gritted his teeth and committed himself to speaking his mind. "I
want to be with Reyna." In his ears, the proclamation sounded more
timid than he'd planned.

Dona Antonia frowned. "It's just the affection of children for each
other."

"That's just it, *Tia*. We're no longer children. I want to marry her. I
know she feels the same."

His aunt shook her head limply.

"You haven't even heard me out," he said calmly.

"You're practically brother and sister."

"You know very well we are not brother and sister."

"She's been promised to another."

"Promises can be broken."

"I wouldn't be here if I hadn't given my word!"

"And I won't be here if you don't take it back."

Dona Antonia closed her eyes and pursed her trembling, purple lips.

"I beg of you," he went on. "Ask Dr. Hamon to call off the wedding."

She'd not gotten out another word before she began heaving and coughing blood into her handkerchief.

"Forgive me." José rose from her bedside, filled a glass with water, and brought it to her lips. "I didn't mean to upset you," he said before stepping away from her bed.

He made his way to the window that overlooked the garden below and the vineyards beyond. Reyna, having returned earlier, was now swaying gently in a hammock strung up between the linden trees.

Reyna had been right. Dona Antonia was far too weak to handle the matter herself. He'd be better off dealing with the doctor directly. Hamon had once claimed that José was like a second son to him. If he had spoken words of truth, then he would do José this kindness. He gathered his courage and determined to speak with the doctor himself.

"The Sabbath is coming." His aunt's soft voice interrupted his thoughts. "They'll be expecting you at the synagogue."

"I don't need to go. Perhaps it's best I stay here with you."

"Nonsense," she muttered. "Off with you now."

He moved to her side and kissed the top of her head, leaving her chambers to ready himself for the evening. He washed his face and hands, changed into a fresh tunic, then placed his Sabbath turban squarely on his head.

Looking in the mirror, he barely recognized himself. No longer did he possess the boyish charm of his youth. His eyes were glazed over from too much worry. A trim beard covered the lower half of his face. His expression was stern and his heart was heavy. He had finally made it to this great land, where he could practice his faith freely. The chains shackling his spirit were finally broken, only to be replaced by the chains now shackling his heart.

Making his way through the narrow winding streets of Istanbul, José passed Ashkenazic Jews and Romaniote Jews, Italian, Spanish, and Portuguese Jews as well. He was greeted at least half a dozen times by the faithful on their way to synagogue. They tipped their brightly colored turbans, bent forward in their wide-sleeved cloaks, and uttered "Shabbat shalom" as they passed. Then they would go their separate ways, the German to the German synagogue, the Italian to the Italian synagogue, and José to the Spanish-Portuguese synagogue that his aunt, along with Dr. Hamon, had helped to establish.

As he traversed the dark alleyway leading to the synagogue, the glow of Sabbath candles filled the windows of homes along the way. He could hear the melodic song of the cantor through closed wooden doors as he approached the modest sanctuary. Upon entering, he greeted acquaintances and neighbors with a quiet nod or a smile before heading for an empty seat on one of the long wooden benches. The room was packed with men, young and old, some hailing from the old country, others born on Ottoman soil, but all Inquisition refugees united by a fate that had led them to this place. There was camaraderie among these men.

The rabbi addressed the congregants in both Spanish and Portuguese and led the evening prayer beneath an enormous oil-lit chandelier.

The congregants partook in the spirited liturgy with enthusiasm. Anyone passing by could easily have mistaken the service for one in a Catholic church. Having been forced to attend mass for the better part of their lives, the congregants adopted much of the chorus-like tempo of the churches they'd left behind.

At the end of the service, José spotted Dr. Hamon in conversation with a few of the community's elders. He was standing tall with his hands locked behind him, nodding in his measured, gentle way. As the elders bid the doctor farewell, José approached.

"José. So good to see you." Hamon's smile was warm and welcoming. "Is everything all right?"

"I'm all right, but there is a matter I'd like to discuss with you."

"José! You haven't yet had the occasion to meet my son?" The doctor turned to a tall boy approaching the two of them. "He's only just returned from the training hospital."

The young man bowed slightly. "My father has told me much about you. I am glad you and your family have made it safely to Istanbul."

"Yes." José tried to keep his voice steady. "Well, thank you." Jealousy sunk its ugly fangs deep into him.

"Tell me," the doctor cut in. "What's troubling you, José? Was there something you wanted to discuss?"

The younger Hamon stood before him in an exquisite black-and-gold-embroidered caftan. He was a head taller than José, with powerful shoulders and sparkling hazel eyes set off by his Arabian complexion. This, then, was the man Reyna was betrothed to.

"I've a matter I'd like to discuss with you in private." His voice was low.

"Of course, José."

"Can you come by tomorrow?"

"I'll be by after sundown."

The next evening, José greeted Dr. Hamon in the grand foyer. The doctor returned the greeting with a few kind words and a modest bow.

Smoothing down his vest, José suggested the doctor check in on Antonia before they commence with their business.

When the doctor finally appeared in the parlor twenty minutes later, José ushered him over to the chair across from the divan. "Thank you for coming," he said as they took their places opposite each other. "You must be wondering why I've asked you here."

"I'm not wondering, José." Hamon stroked his thin white beard.

"You're not?"

"I know why I'm here. You are going to ply me with cheese and dates and cakes, maybe offer me a handsome sum of money, then ask that I release Reyna from the betrothal."

Stunned, José said nothing.

"Does that sound right?"

At that moment, a servant appeared with a tray of cheese and a bowl of olives.

Dr. Hamon took one look at the tray and laughed hard.

"How did you know? How could you possibly . . ."

He waved his hands and smiled. "Let me save you the time. I don't want your cheese and I don't want your money." He leaned back.

José felt a screw tighten in his chest. If the doctor would not release Reyna, he'd take his chances and marry her anyway. But at what cost? To break a promise made to the sultan's most trusted physician would have dire consequences for the entire family. "Is there something you *would* like, then?" José asked.

"Maybe some wine?"

"Wine?"

"Sure. We are men. We are brothers. Let us drink wine together. It is, after all, the only worldly pleasure in all the empire that we as Jews are permitted, while our Muslim neighbors are banned from even the smallest drop."

"All right. But what about—"

"Do not worry, José. I release her, of course." He waved his bony hand as he spoke. "I saw it in your eyes when you arrived. You are very much in love."

"Thank you, Doctor!" José leaped up from his place.

"Marry her. You have my blessing."

He took the doctor's hand and kissed the ring on his finger. "What of your son?" He looked up suddenly. "Will he contest it?"

"He will be upset, of that I am certain, but we are not brutish men. His ego may be wounded, but nothing that won't heal in time. After all, he's been back only a week and hasn't yet met the girl. Besides, you've seen him, a boy like that, he can marry any girl he chooses."

"How can I ever thank you?"

"The price, I'm afraid, you might find a bit steep."

José froze in place and let the doctor's hand fall from his grasp. "Well? What is it you want then?" His body was rigid.

"I told you."

José clenched his fists and tried to quell the mounting frustration within him. Whatever the price, he would find a way to pay it.

"The vineyards on this land are legendary. Does a case sound fair?"

José's body went limp as something bright and warm began to rise within him. He kissed the doctor on both cheeks, then clapped his hands together. "Good doctor, you'll have wine from our vineyards for the rest of your days!"

That same month, José and Reyna married.

The modest ceremony was officiated by the chief rabbi and took place at the foot of Dona Antonia's canopied bed. Though she was dying and in pain, Dona Antonia Nissim proclaimed this day above all others to be the very happiest of her life.

And when José stamped on the ceremonial glass signaling their very first moment as husband and wife, Dona Antonia shed tears of joy. It seemed she could no longer recall why she had ever opposed their union in the first place.

When the ceremony had ended, Dona Antonia presented José with an exquisite ritual washing cup of hammered silver and gold. "The senhor of the house must have his own cup," she whispered. José brought her hand up to his lips and did not try to stop the tears that came streaming down his cheeks.

"How I have loved you, *hijo*." Though her voice was fading, her sparkling eyes were still very much alive.

And while it was tradition for a bride and groom to celebrate their marriage by feasting with friends, José and Reyna dined alone that evening.

With her children by her side, Dona Antonia Nissim clung to life for six days more. After that, her soul left through the open window, extinguishing the candle by the ledge as it made its way up to the heavens.

As she took her last breath, José tore his chemise from collar to sternum, exposing a pale, concave chest beneath. He beat his fist against his chest as he recited the mourner's kaddish for the woman who'd taken him in, raising him as her own flesh and blood.

News of La Madre's death spread quickly throughout the Jewish community and for the next week, Reyna and José were comforted by the throngs of visitors that came to offer their condolences.

Even Don Albert Toledano, the illustrious Portuguese portraitist whose services had once been called upon by kings and queens and popes alike, came to their home to extend his sympathies. After being presented by his man in the grand foyer of the home, the painter tipped his feathered hat and folded low from the waist. "Don José, I come to offer my condolences, as well as something more." At his side, the man held a tall, framed canvas. "You see, many years before his death, I was commissioned by Dona Antonia's husband to produce a portrait in her image. I accepted the offer, was paid a handsome sum up front, and soon after that began working. But I am ashamed to admit, I never had the opportunity to finish until now. Like so many others, my family fell under the suspicion of the authorities. When I expressed my concerns to your aunt, she arranged for our immediate escape. Well, Don José, I may not have been able to finish what I'd started then, but I am a man of my word." He leaned the canvas against the wall. "It's done now."

"Senhor?" José stepped forward, not quite certain what the painter meant.

"So that she shall always be remembered."

José looked on, but said nothing.

"May God comfort you among the mourners of Zion." The painter again tipped his hat and left.

After the door closed behind him, José turned the canvas around to reveal a resplendent portrait of a young Antonia, set within a thick gilded frame intricately carved with a leaf-like motif and scrolling corners. Toledano had painted her wearing a brocaded gown of black, silver, and gold velvet, fitted tight against her chest and upper torso but flowing freely from her waist to the ground below. Her hair was pulled back and secured with a netted cap of opal beads, and upon her neck was a handsome strand of black sea pearls adorned with a shimmering tassel at her breast. Illuminated by the rich glow of the gilt frame, the most striking aspect of the portrait was Antonia's deep-set indigo eyes—eyes that seemed to bore straight into José's soul now, as they always had.

"So that she shall always be remembered." José echoed Toledano's words before making his way into the parlor and setting the painting atop the grand fireplace mantel.

7

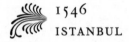
"Moiiiiiise!" José charged down the stairs with the force of a stampeding herd. At the base of the stairwell, he leaned against the banister and called again for his servant in a strained voice.

Moise appeared from beyond a dimly lit archway, hastening through the hall with the edges of his dark cape flapping against his pleated trousers. Atop his head, a small, Spanish-style cap tilted to one side.

"Call for the doctor at once," José urged. "The midwives believe the baby is breech. They say they can do no more. We need help, right away!"

"Of course, Don José."

"Come with me." José hurried into his study while his servant trailed behind. He fumbled through his drawers and withdrew a blank scroll of parchment.

Wasting no time with formalities, he began scribbling the message hastily:

> *Dona Reyna in grave danger.*
> *Has been in labor for more than twenty-four hours, and mid-*
> *wives say there has been little progress.*
> *Your assistance urgently needed. Please come at once.*
> *Yours,*
> *Don José Nissim*

He sprinkled a dash of cuttle powder over the parchment and waited for the ink to dry, then rolled the parchment and secured it with his seal.

As he did, Reyna let out a piercing cry, rattling the walls and windows throughout the grand villa.

"Hurry, Moise!" José commanded.

"Yes, effendi." He bowed and left the room.

José hurried back upstairs and for the next few hours recited psalms by her side. Reyna lay moaning on the bed, her pregnant belly bulging out from beneath her cotton dress. Her maid was there patting a damp cloth over her forehead and eyes, while the midwives fretted over what else they might do to coax the baby from her womb. All the while, Reyna cried and shook and gritted her teeth.

Two years had passed since they'd been wed, and with the years, two souls conceived and lost too soon. José prayed that this third child would survive. He prayed for some time until he was startled by the sound of Moise's voice.

"Senhor!" his servant called loudly from behind the crack in the chamber door. "The doctor is here!"

"Thanks be to God," José mumbled under his breath, then rushed down to the foyer below. As he neared the man at the banister, he discovered that it was Dr. Hamon's son. "*You?*" José examined the young doctor from head to heel. With his medical kit hanging by his side, he stood unmoved, his shoulders squared and his chin elevated.

"Yes. My father sent me," he answered in his deep, clear voice.

"But where is he? Didn't he read my message? This is an urgent matter!"

"His services were called upon at the palace, so I've come in his stead. I understand you're concerned, Don José, but rest assured, I've been practicing medicine for years, working and learning alongside my father. I've even treated the sultan himself on several occasions."

"That's all well and good, but your treating the sultan means little to me now!" José wrung his hands. "Tell me you have some experience delivering a breech baby?" He held his breath while the younger Hamon stared on lamely. "Tell me you have experience delivering *any* baby!"

"I've not," the young doctor admitted. "It's a rare thing for a man to deliver a child. You know that yourself. I've only the case studies in my textbooks to go by."

Though he felt sick to his stomach, José pressed his lips together and strived to appear calm. He saw no other choice but to place his trust in the man before him. "We're wasting precious time," José said, his voice almost a hiss. "Follow me."

In the room upstairs, they discovered Reyna sitting up in bed, her face twisted in anguish and her breathing labored. The room was dark and warm.

"Who is this man?" she managed to ask between gasps.

"This is Dr. Hamon's son. He's here to deliver the baby." He clasped her hand and brought them to his lips, then forced himself to say, "You have the very best doctor in the city." He lowered his eyes so she'd not see the fear in them. "He has even treated the sultan himself."

"Dr. Hamon's son?" Reyna's voice grew faint. "He's *here*?"

"Yes," the young doctor cut in. He took a few steps forward. "I've delivered many babies," he lied. "Not very long from now, you will hold one in your arms."

Reyna's eyes teared up as the doctor nodded gently, possessing the kind eyes and calm temperament of his father. "It might be a while before the baby comes. Try to steady your breathing." He turned to the midwife at the edge of the bed. "Has she had anything to relieve the pain?"

She shook her head. "Just a touch of rosewater syrup with cinnamon spice."

"Go fetch a jug of wine, quickly."

José kissed Reyna on the forehead, then knelt at her side.

"I now must ask that you leave us." The young doctor addressed José.

Startled, José looked back at the doctor and rose to his feet. "Are you really asking me to *leave*?" It was the last thing he felt he should be doing. He dug his palms against his eyelids and shook his head as he walked toward the doctor. "Shouldn't I stay by her side?"

"Certainly not." The doctor lowered his voice so Reyna would not hear. "This labor has been long and complicated. I can have no distractions—for the sake of your wife and child."

José felt a ring of heat around his neck.

"I must insist that you go now."

José drew a breath and wiped the sweat from his brow. "For the sake of my wife, I shall do your bidding."

As the night wore on, José recited psalms beneath the glow of an oil lamp in his study, his body swaying to the singsong chant. A dozen of his most loyal servants remained by his side, praying in unison from scattered chairs throughout the room, until he forced them away and back to their beds. "You must rest now! Return to your chambers," he instructed mere hours before dawn. Exhausted and spent, they heeded their master's directive and left him to his own devices. He prayed for the safety of the woman he loved and for the delivery of a healthy baby boy. He invoked the name of God and collapsed to his knees, which is where he awoke several hours later.

His neck was stiff and his back, a canvas of knots. He groaned as he peeled himself up from the coarse carpet.

The sun outside was bright and the room was covered in red and orange light cast through the stained-glass window. He straightened up and found the young doctor sitting in a chair by the door. "What news have you?" José's voice was hoarse.

The doctor leaned forward. "The baby was born several hours ago. Your wife is asleep."

"Why didn't you wake me?" He squinted to shield his eyes from the light.

"I won't mince words with you, José. When the baby finally did arrive, your wife had already lost a lot of blood."

In an instant, José was fully awake. "Doctor, tell me she's all right?"

Hamon hung his head, then loosened the collar of his shirt. "She will be."

José covered his face and rubbed his aching eyes. "Is she in much pain?"

"Not now. The opium solution I prepared seems to have been quite effective. I've left a vial by the bed. In a few months' time, she should be fine. We'll have to just keep an eye on her."

"And the baby?"

"I was a bit concerned, especially since your wife was in labor for so long, but the baby came out healthy. A bit small, but healthy."

"A healthy boy," José said to himself.

"A girl," the doctor corrected. "A beautiful, healthy girl."

"So it is. One great lady has left this house . . ." José lowered his head and thought of his *tia*. "Perhaps another destined for greatness has entered in her stead." He forced a sad smile. "Perhaps with the next birth, we will have our boy. Thank you, Doctor." José took a few quick steps toward the door, patting the doctor's shoulder as he passed.

"There is something you should know." The younger Hamon cleared his throat in the manner of his father. "The labor was very hard on your wife."

José stopped in the doorframe and shifted in place. "Yes, you mentioned that. But as you said, she'll recover." José twisted back and locked eyes with the doctor's.

"Yes, of course. I'll be here, and she will make a full recovery. It's just that—" The doctor paused.

"Tell me, please!"

"Don José, I'm afraid this will be her only child."

José stood motionless. "You said she would make a full recovery?"

"She will live a long and healthy life. She is a mother, you are a father. José, you have a *child* now, but it pains me to tell you, there can never be another."

"How can you be certain?" He'd always dreamed of having a house full of children, six or seven or even more. But he'd especially wanted a son. Wasn't that what every father wanted? To see the son born in his image grow to be a man? To one day fill his shoes?

"I'm sorry, senhor."

José was about to reply when the shrill cry of his daughter came from beyond the walls of the study.

"Listen to that," the doctor urged.

José nodded and headed up to the second-story landing, his infant daughter screaming in the room to the right, his wife resting quietly in the room to the left. The doctor trailed behind him as he shuffled into Reyna's chamber.

She looked angelic, her long dark hair framing her pale face as she slept peacefully. He made his way to her bedside, wanting to kiss her gently, only to pause at the sight of the bloodstained sheets.

José cradled his head in his hands as he strained to think clearly.

The doctor spoke in from behind. "She needs to rest."

"What of the baby?"

"The wet nurse is in with her now."

José lowered himself into a rocking chair by the bed. "When she is done feeding her, have the wet nurse bring the child in," he instructed the nurse lingering at the edge of the bed. "I should like to look upon the face of my daughter, the first and last child we shall ever know."

He kept his eyes on his wife as he rocked in his chair.

"Effendi?"

"You can go now."

The baby's cries continued to echo throughout the stone house. He closed his red, stinging eyes and rested his head against the back of the chair.

Once the doctor had left the room, José closed the door gently and made his way back to the bed. He drew the coverlet up over Reyna's shoulders, then stepped out of his slippers and assumed a place on the mattress by her side. He nestled in close so that they lay like spoons. With eyes closed, he wound loose tendrils of her hair around his fingers and with care draped his foot across her exposed ankle. In that moment, he desired nothing more than to touch and be touched, to hold his wife close, flesh on flesh, breath on breath. He closed his eyes, and the room began to sway, the sound of the sea all around. When he opened his eyes once more, he was startled to find himself someplace other than in the stinking hull of a merchant ship.

Several hours passed before José rose from the bed. He made his way to the basin in the room, taking great pains not to wake Reyna. He reached for a ritual washing cup, and as he did, was overcome with emotion. For this was the cup Dona Antonia had given him on the occasion of his wedding, just days before she died.

Pouring equal measures of water over one hand and then the other, he closed his eyes and recited the blessing over the washing of hands. He dressed himself for the day, then headed out through town to the synagogue, where he joined the minyan—a quorum of at least ten men—readying themselves for the morning prayers.

Dr. Hamon and his son were there among the crowd, offering their well-wishes along with friends and neighbors who'd heard the news. Facing toward Jerusalem, the men were a sea of rocking bodies cloaked in blue and white prayer shawls as they silently prayed alongside one another. In his prayers, José gave thanks for the birth of a healthy baby girl and resolved to trust in the ways of the Lord.

During the reading of the Torah, a special blessing was said for the health of the new mother and the welfare of the child. They had named her Tamar, as Reyna had insisted.

"Tamir if it's a boy. Tamar if it's a girl!" Both names were derived from the Hebrew word meaning *date*. For Reyna had been nibbling on that sweet fruit when the signs of labor first appeared. In those early hours, she'd joked with José that perhaps the child had savored a bit of that sun-dried sweetness and—thinking it a taste of the outside world—began kicking and wriggling to be free and born. If it was a boy, with a name like that, he'd be destined to grow tall and lean and strong like a date palm. If it was a girl, she'd surely know nothing but sweetness and bounty in her lifetime.

José prayed that Tamar would indeed know nothing but sweetness in the coming years. He envisioned her growing to become a wife, a mother, and a queen among her people.

Like her grandmother before her, she too would be entrusted with the sacred task of preserving the faith for the generations to come. For José saw it as no coincidence that Dona Antonia Nissim and her granddaughter were both born under the same star.

The girl Tamar would follow in the footsteps of La Madre de los Anusim, the late great Dona Antonia Nissim.

Encouraged by the enthusiasm of well-wishers, he drank an entire cask of sweet red wine after the kiddush. The fruity libation set his head spinning as he headed out of the building into the narrow alley below. "Good-bye then," he called out to his friends as he made his way back home, feeling gay from the fog of wine and his own good fortune.

He was rounding the corner leading into the square beyond the synagogue when two young men wearing cone-shaped hats moved swiftly toward him. These were hats unlike any an ordinary Ottoman civilian might wear. He immediately recognized these men to be the sultan's Janissaries by their signature mustaches. Each wielded a falanga, the infamous whip unleashed on civilians who were found to be publicly drunk or inciting ruckus. Could they have noticed José stumble? Was it possible that they were able to detect his drunkenness? José straightened his posture and tried to compose himself.

"Are you Don José Nissim?" One of the Janissaries spoke up.

"I am." José swallowed hard. "What's this about?"

"You'll have to come with us. We've been instructed to escort you to the palace."

"Topkapi?" His palms began to sweat. He was sure he could hear his heart beat in his chest. "What was the reason given?"

"Please come with us, effendi." The two men escorted José around the corner and into the sun-drenched piazza where their chariot was stationed.

"Please, I have a newborn daughter at home. My wife will be worried."

"We will send word to your wife that you will be home later today."

"Later? How late? Gentlemen, if you could just tell me what this is about."

"You will find out soon enough." They took hold of his arms and led him toward the chariot.

It was the second time in his life that he'd been summoned to Topkapi; only this time he could not fathom the reason.

8

On his first visit to the palace some two years earlier, José had entered through the majestic grand gates. This time he was escorted through a nondescript side entrance that blended seamlessly in the slate-gray walls surrounding Topkapi. He was led through a windowless maze of narrow halls that zigzagged until finally opening into a small sun-drenched courtyard walled with terraced gardens.

He stepped out into the space. "Will you now tell me what I am doing here?" He spun around, only to find that his escorts had vanished. He was alone. José took a few cautious steps forward and examined his surroundings. Then he climbed a few steps leading up to a marble terrace with a breathtaking view of the sea. On a stone bench beneath the shade of a vast chestnut tree, he sat looking out at the Golden Horn for what seemed to be eternity.

"So you are Don José the Jew!" a voice sounded after some time.

José winced. He forced himself to his feet.

Before him stood a strapping young man with yellow hair and honey-brown eyes. Perched on the leather sleeve of his bulging forearm was a beady-eyed falcon with a gray-spotted coat.

"Yes, I am Don José Nissim."

The two men stood eye to eye. José cleared his throat, but the man said nothing. He stood there for a moment, seeming to assess everything about José, from his fingernails to his physique, from his shoes to the way he wrapped his turban.

"Have you been drinking?" the man sniffed.

"Effendi, it was just a small amount earlier today, to celebrate the birth of my daughter."

"The birth of a child!" the man exclaimed. "Yes, certainly an occasion worthy of celebration."

"Can you tell me what this is about?" José spoke up against his better instincts.

"This is an unofficial visit," the man replied. "I am Selim. I believe you met with my father, the sultan, several years ago?"

Dumbfounded, José fell to his knees. "Your Imperial Highness, please excuse my ignorance."

Selim laughed and tossed back a whip of yellow hair. "Come on. Get up." He thrust his arm into the air, sending his falcon into flight. Within an instant, the bird was making vast circles overhead.

José came to his feet but said nothing.

"I hope I haven't startled you. It's just that I need someone I can trust, and Dr. Hamon tells me that you are a man who can be trusted."

"I'm afraid I don't understand."

"Come, José. Sit." He took a seat on the bench and gestured for José to do the same. "You've heard of the unfortunate death of my brother Mehmed some years ago?"

"Yes, Your Highness." José recalled the tragic loss of the sultan's son, the firstborn child of his beloved wife, Hürrem. "May I extend my condolences. A great tragedy."

For a long moment, the prince remained silent. "He was very ill." Selim's jovial manner disappeared and his face seemed long and drawn. "My father didn't take it well. We all presumed Mehmed would be our father's heir." He turned to José, his expression determined. "My father the sultan is getting old. He will step down one day. He looks upon me favorably, but I would like to cement his goodwill so that he considers no other son but myself as his heir. There must be no doubt in his mind that I shall be his successor."

"Your Highness?"

"You see, I spend much of my time away from the capital, governing the province of Manisa. I need someone to be my eyes and ears here on the ground at Topkapi. I need to know what political intrigue is brewing here. But it's not just that, José. When I inherit the throne, and I *will* inherit the throne, I will also be taking on the tangled mess of international diplomacy that comes with it. I'm going to need someone who is familiar with European affairs."

An awkward silence passed between them.

"Me?" José questioned.

"Naturally!"

"But I've never worked in politics."

"And I have never been outside the empire!" Selim threw his hands in the air. "I don't know how to deal with these Europeans. We could rule all the world, bring our citizens peace and bounty for ten thousand lifetimes, and they'd still call us barbarians." He leaned toward José. "But you, you have lived among them. You understand them. You're one of them."

"That may have been true, but that time has passed."

"Dr. Hamon tells me that you were a frequent visitor in the European courts before your arrival in Istanbul, that you are acquainted with many of the powerful ruling families throughout Europe. Is that so?"

"I suppose it is. I was just a child, raised alongside Spanish and Portuguese nobility. At times I was sent farther off, to the Low Countries, where I held court with a few lowly princes."

"So you have seen much of Europe?"

"It could be said."

"José! How many languages do you speak?"

"A few. French, Spanish, Portuguese, Latin, Dutch, and of course, now Ottoman."

"An educated man." The prince slapped his knee and stood up from the bench. "Hamon also tells me that there isn't a man in Istanbul who can outwit you."

"He speaks very kindly indeed."

"That you spend your free time in the coffeehouses drinking tea and playing Tavla?"

"When you put it that way, it does sound rather decadent."

"Is it true that you've even beaten the Bosnian?"

"You've heard of the Bosnian?"

"Most certainly! My Janissaries are always searching for talent in the most unusual places. Were you aware that no one has beaten the Bosnian at a game of Tavla in over twenty years?"

José flushed. "It's just a game," he went on modestly.

"It is *not* just a game." For the first time, the prince seemed agitated.

"He who can master the game of Tavla quite often masters the game of life. You see, once the die is cast, man has no control over the outcome. Now, a novice might throw his chips in the air and lament that Allah has dealt him a poor hand, but a master—a master will keep his wits about him and use his intellect to steer his chips to the very best possible outcome. A master understands that Allah does not choose for us. Rather, He sets forth a set of paths for man to consider. And though Allah knows precisely just what man shall choose, a master never forgets that he still possesses the power—"

". . . to steer the course of his own destiny." José finished the thought. "For man has been granted the freedom to choose."

"Precisely." Selim smiled. "We do think alike, you and I. Diplomacy is not unlike Tavla. At times you will be presented with unfavorable odds. How you move your chips, that separates the novice from the master."

"Yes, effendi." José bowed his head.

"You've got the perfect mind to serve as my right hand, and the correct background too. One of the most important qualities of any future sultan is the ability to pick the appropriate people for the tasks that lie ahead. You shall make a good impression at court."

"Yes, Your Highness."

"I know you won't disappoint me." Selim's expression was stern. It seemed he was gambling on an unknown and was hoping to be rewarded handsomely for it.

The falcon swooped down from the sky and landed gently on Selim's outstretched arm. The bird flapped, revealing a majestic blue and silver undercoat.

Selim turned his attention to the bird. "This majestic creature has been trained to carry messages to and from officials in neighboring provinces. Only the most important messages, those worthy of the sky." He examined his bird and then, as though remembering he had more important business to attend to, turned back to José.

"Now, tell me, José. Can I trust you?"

He slid off the bench and bowed his head to the ground. "I am your servant."

"Good. Now get up off your knees. You'll report to the palace tomorrow morning and the morning after that."

José could hardly believe what he was hearing.

"I'll be splitting my time between my palace at Manisa and my living quarters here at Topkapi."

Selim snapped his fingers, eliciting the prompt return of his servant, who wrestled the falcon from his possession and headed away down a flight of steps. Just then a squeal sounded from behind.

The prince stood up and turned toward a voluptuous woman approaching them. In her fleshy arms, she cradled an infant swathed in purple velvet.

"Ah! Here comes the wet nurse with my boy now!"

Following the prince's lead, José rose to his feet and trailed behind as Selim bent over and scooped the child up into his arms. Beaming with pride, he lifted the boy in the air momentarily and exclaimed, "My son."

Son. The word pinched José's heart. His inner voice chimed, *Such as the one you'll never have.*

José mustered all his goodwill. "A handsome boy," he declared.

"He lives here with his mother," the prince explained.

"Topkapi? Do they not accompany you back to the provinces?"

"His mother, Nurbanu, prefers to reside here. Istanbul is the home she's known since the tender age of twelve," the prince said. "Or perhaps it's just that she can no longer bear to witness the ever-growing harem at my Manisa palace," he admitted with a smirk.

"I understand, Your Highness." José bowed his head. It was well known that the prince enjoyed the company of far too many women.

"I do think it best that the child be educated here, in the shadow of his grandfather, the sultan." His expression stiffened and the twinkling in his eyes disappeared. "There should be no confusion as to the line of succession, you understand?"

José nodded, understanding all too well Selim's intentions. The child would be raised in the shadow of the sultan, winning over his grandfather and cementing the line of succession for the next generation.

"One day you will be able to say that you have met three sultans of the empire."

José studied the infant prince. He had a pensive face with large brown eyes, heart-shaped lips, and a delicate crown of sable-colored curls.

"His name is Murad. I'm not ashamed to admit it, the boy gets his good looks from his mother. Look at that sublime chin. And his hair!

These cocoa-colored locks certainly don't come from my side of the family," he said while fingering the baby's dark curls.

José was unsure of the proper protocol for being presented to an imperial heir, let alone an infant at that. Certainly he should not coo or reach out to touch the child. Whatever the proper conduct, he had managed to get this far without insulting Selim.

"See how intelligent he is?" the prince went on. "You can tell just by looking at his eyes. He's observing us right now."

José nodded.

"And you will bow to him one day," the prince continued. "You along with all the empire will bow to him."

The boy gurgled as tiny bubbles began to foam from his lips.

"That day is still far off." Selim smiled and handed the boy back to his wet nurse. "Now that we've settled our business, how about we celebrate with a drink?"

José studied Selim's relaxed demeanor, not sure if he was being tested or if the prince was actually serious about defying one of Islam's more serious prohibitions.

"Even a Muslim prince needs to have some fun once in a while. And telling from the purple stain on your tongue, I can tell you are a man who likes to have a good time too."

"Your Highness, I . . . I . . ." José stuttered.

"Let's keep this our secret." Selim winked as a tray with two silver goblets was presented to them. He took a swig of wine, smacked his lips, and squinted. "I think I like you, José." He took a moment to consider his own statement, then nodded in agreement with himself. His eyes twinkled with delight and his smile was warm and playful. He slapped José on the back before turning and heading away from the garden. "See you tomorrow!" he called out as he disappeared from the courtyard.

José lowered his face to his palms and felt warm tears of gratitude on his hands. Standing alone in the middle of the sultan's garden, surrounded by fluttering tulips and the smell of the sea, José closed his eyes tightly and recited a prayer of thanksgiving to the Lord.

He would return home and take his daughter in his arms, recite those same words of gratitude, and give thanks to the Lord for the miracle of life.

9

 1551

Five years had passed with José employed in the palace. In Selim's absence, he represented the twenty-seven-year-old prince at court, slipping into his new role quite effortlessly, with a cheery confidence and a calm disposition. He was soon charged with representing Ottoman interests abroad, focusing his dealings on European diplomats from the Old World. And though they were initially weary of dealing with a self-proclaimed Jew, it was not long before these diplomats were completely taken in by the strapping Portuguese exile. They could not help but hold him in a kind of curious esteem.

He was a deserter of Christ living an exceptional life in a faraway land under the protection of an Ottoman sultan. At their homes back in Europe, they'd not dare claim him as a friend. But here, in this exotic land hundreds of miles from the place of their birth, Don José Nissim was the man that every European diplomat and merchant sought to befriend.

Among the foreign elite, it was rumored that within his pocket robes, Don José Nissim held the keys to the gates of Topkapi Palace. Even among the palace servants, odd rumors began to spread. There were those who whispered that Prince Selim's wife was a cousin, sister, or even daughter of the House of Nissim. Others would swear to it that Prince Selim himself was no son of Suleiman, but rather somehow of Nissim blood, smuggled into the harem and passed off as an infant prince in the place of a stillborn heir. It seemed Prince Selim's enthusiasm in extolling the virtues of José had the unforeseen effect of evoking truly bizarre tales throughout the capital.

Despite the gossip, Selim's right hand seemed to be doing everything just right.

With his family's extensive European banking connections, José managed to set up a robust trade network, providing financial services and importing and exporting goods between Ottoman lands and the West, including wine from his vineyards to the Christian lands of Europe.

When he entertained foreign dignitaries at his Galata villa, the liquor never ceased to flow. After the wine and lamb and honey cakes, once his visitors had succumbed to a woozy, drunken haze, José would pry from his guests invaluable secrets pertaining to the latest technological advancements in weaponry coming out of Europe. With José at the helm and his vineyards in full bloom, Europe could not hope to keep any secrets from the empire.

But his achievements did not begin or end there. Master diplomat that he was, José further strengthened the Franco-Ottoman alliance, and even succeeded in rounding up the support of Protestant princes to join the efforts against the advances of Charles V's Catholic Empire. As Ottoman influence expanded, both Selim and his representative grew in the sultan's esteem.

Back at the Ottoman court, José Nissim was by far the brightest star.

It was a charmed life by all accounts. Reyna assumed her position as one of the great ladies in society. She oversaw the distribution of charitable funds throughout the community and at her table hosted refugees and noblemen, peasants and princes. People from all walks of life were welcome in the Nissim household—Muslim, Christian, and Jew.

Dr. Hamon and his son would visit José often, and the three would devote several hours to study and prayer. In the evenings, after supper, José would retreat to the parlor and examine the portrait of Dona Antonia Nissim over the mantel. As he peered into those indigo eyes, he would marvel at all that had come to pass in his short life.

And when his five-year-old daughter would nuzzle beneath his arm—the fluffy hairs on her head tickling the smooth skin of his neck—he knew that all the gilded treasures of the world could in no way compare to the time they shared. In those moments when he held his daughter in his arms, when the beauty of the world seemed almost too bright to behold, he was reminded of the kindness that had rescued his family. If it hadn't been for the sultan, perhaps this daughter of his faith and blood would never have come into the world.

It was during these times that José would turn his eyes to the window and search the starry sky.

The universe takes notice. The words of his mentor sounded in his mind. He was now a loyal servant of the sultanate, and yet José could not shake the feeling that the unpaid debt still hovered over his household.

Many nights had come and gone, one followed by another—close to two thousand, five hundred, and fifty of them. But in all that time, José was somehow certain that his debt remained.

As winter approached, the winds swooped down from the mountain steppes, rattling the lattices and the shutters of the Nissim villa. A blanket of snow descended from the gray sky. The fish in the ponds had grown lethargic, barely swimming at all. Winter in the villa was a quiet, somber affair.

One afternoon, as Reyna wrapped herself in Siberian fur and drank eucalyptus tea alone by the fire, her chambermaid, Arabella, approached and handed her a scroll secured with a jewel-studded seal.

Reyna lowered her cup to its saucer and took hold of the scroll. The outer parchment was ornately decorated with a blue and gold floral motif. She unrolled it and scanned the words. "It's an invitation."

"I figured as much. Look at that seal. How many aspers do you think you could get for that?"

"Why don't you find out, Bella," she called to her maid affectionately and handed her the seal. "It's yours."

The girl beamed, wrapped the gift in a linen cloth, and placed it in the folds of her dress. "Thank you, senhora."

Reyna turned back to the invitation. "I've been invited to a ladies' party hosted by the prince's beloved in three days' time. A celebration in honor of the birth of her daughter." Reyna studied the invitation carefully, settling on the words at the very bottom.

"What is it, senhora?"

"I'm to bring Tamar." She let the parchment fall to her lap and looked up at Arabella. "Why would they want me to bring Tamar?" She turned to the window and pulled open the shutters. In the square frame, snowflakes drifted by. Beyond the gray veil of winter, Tamar could be seen with Miriam, the nurse who had continued to care for her long after she'd been weaned. "No, *Nana*, no!" she could hear Tamar call out as Miriam tossed a snowball in her direction.

Dwarfed by her purple wool cloak, Tamar squealed with delight as the snowy sphere came crashing over her. She fell to the ground and rolled about gleefully, throwing her arms and legs out in all directions. A halo of auburn ringlets framed her pretty face and wide-set green eyes. Her cheeks were two bright pink splotches against her caramel-colored skin, but if she was cold, she didn't notice or mind at all. *"Anne!"* The little girl turned her gaze to the window and spotted her mother spying through the window. *"Mamãe!"* She waved enthusiastically with both arms, calling out *mother* in both Turkish and Portuguese.

"Hello, little dove!" Reyna called back down to her.

"I don't recall you ever having been invited into the harem before." Arabella brought the kettle and poured some tea into her mistress's cup.

"You're not mistaken, Bella." Reyna shifted her attention from the window back to her servant. "Only the most trusted of *kiras* are permitted entry, and I've no goods to peddle behind the harem walls."

"It seems your husband has been making quite an impression at court! You'll need to have something made. What about the new fabric I brought back from the bazaar last week?"

"I was hoping to save that one for the seder meal come spring. We'll have scores of guests at our table if José has anything to do with the guest list."

Arabella reached for the fireplace poker and began stoking the flames.

"What about that brocade linen we received last week?" Reyna asked.

"The one gifted to you by the pasha's wife? You felt it yourself. Coarser than a three-day stubble," Arabella said while placing the fireplace poker back against the wall. "I thought we agreed that fabric wasn't fit for a foot muff."

"I recall something to the effect," Reyna mumbled.

"I'll call the dressmaker and have her bring over some new fabrics."

Reyna popped a grape into her mouth and chewed thoughtfully. "Perhaps we should have a dress made up for Tamar as well."

"As you wish, Dona Reyna." Arabella said before clearing away a cluster of grape stems. "I'll call for the seamstress at once."

* * *

Reyna was eager to meet and know the legendary women sequestered behind the guarded harem walls. Throughout Europe, the Imperial Harem was rumored to be a place of sexual decadence the sultan entered to have his every whim pleased, but that depiction was far from reality, as Sultan Suleiman had been loyal to his one true love and wife, Hürrem Sultan. Aside from being part of the imperial family's private living quarters, where a sultan's female relatives and young sons lived, the harem also served as a kind of high-end finishing school. The most beautiful young girls of the empire were brought there to receive the very best education available. They were fortunate enough to receive an imperial education and to live alongside the daughters and relatives of Sultan Suleiman.

Though they were technically slaves, the girls—some so young they still clung to dolls—were rigorously trained in literature, music, poetry, and art. Their schooling was strict and took up much of the day. After nine years of training, they were granted the freedom to leave. Very few exercised this freedom.

The harem produced the most refined, educated, and sought-after women in all the empire. By the time they'd come of age under Suleiman's reign, those who chose not to return to the homes of their youth might be married off to high-ranking officials or Ottoman princes. In many instances, the sultan himself chose their husbands, provided their trousseaux, and gifted them with stately villas in which to begin their new lives.

The girls entered the harem as slaves, were educated alongside exalted princesses, and strove to become the sultan's beloved, all in hopes of birthing a male child who might one day rise to the throne. In that way, every sultan was the son of a former slave. It was the sultan's mother, or valide sultan, who governed harem life and was oftentimes intricately involved in matters of state. It was she who would wield the most influence over her son, the sultan.

Very few outsiders were granted access to this private world, but when they were, they came back with tales of riches and political intrigue. In the parlors of wealthy *kiras* and at the tables of diplomats whose wives were lucky enough to be granted entrance, privileged women spoke of the diamonds they'd seen, stones of titanic proportions; luxuriant silken fabrics; furs; and extravagant coverlets from a place called Kashmir. They would also report sightings of heavenly creatures, beautiful women from every conquered corner of the empire.

Reyna had heard her fair share of harem tales, but to be invited to visit—well, the prospect quite delighted her. Presented with nearly two dozen reams of fabric and the seamstress's finest ready-made clothes, Reyna settled on a turquoise fabric beaded with pearls and a silk veil she would secure to her head with a gilded feather headdress. For Tamar, she selected a velvet caftan of glittering gold, with white fur trim along the collar and cuffs.

The party was grander than any Reyna had ever attended before. On the gold-leaf-tiled pavilion, an orchestra entertained the women with flutes and harps, while a troupe of belly dancers undulated to the music, brass bells attached to their hips, ankles, and wrists. All the while, steaming trays of duck, veal, and mutton were ferried out from the royal kitchen.

While Tamar clutched the fabric of her mother's robe, Reyna looked about the premises. Apart from the sexless eunuchs guarding the premises, there wasn't an adult man in sight. She estimated that there must have been over a hundred and fifty women gathered there along with their young sons and daughters, as well as a legion of servants to cater to the guests. Reyna took in the sight of Persian beauties mixing with ladies of the Caucuses, Venetians, Greeks, Ottomans, and Jews. Conspicuous in their Western-style, full skirts, even the wives of foreign dignitaries took part in the revelry. While dancing to the merry sounds of musicians' tunes, they sipped on their sherbet or salted yogurt drinks.

In the center of the courtyard, beneath a green-and-gold-fringed canopy, Reyna spotted a handsome woman with ivory skin, hair like fire, and brows stitched into two neat arches. Reyna felt her jaw slacken as she looked upon Haseki Hürrem Sultan, the exalted wife of Sultan Suleiman the Magnificent. Bending low to greet the sultana was none other than Esther Handali, the legendary Jewess who had managed to make a fortune selling rare jewels, sable furs, and the occasional odd secret to the women living behind the harem walls.

As the musicians neared the end of a lively concerto, Reyna noticed a tall woman coming her way. Her imposing stature and unrivaled beauty far outshone that of any other lady at the party, signifying to all her celebrated rank. Reyna recognized her immediately. She could be no other than Prince Selim's beloved, Nurbanu Sultan, in whose honor the party was being held. It was said that as the only daughter-in-law residing in Sultan Suleiman's family compound, Nurbanu was granted the unprecedented freedom of entering and exiting the sultan's harem quarters at will. Though she lived under the sultan's protection within the walls of his private family quarters, she belonged only to Prince Selim, the presumed *şehzade*, or crown prince of the empire. During the long months her husband would spend away governing the provinces, she would move out of his princely quarters and into a grand residence situated along the wall that separated the harem from the inner courtyard. The apartment was rumored to possess a hidden door that opened to the outside world—a door to which only she held the key. As such, Prince Selim's beloved was believed to be the only free woman in all of Topkapi, the envy of all who knew her.

On that splendid evening, the privileged lady wore a jade-colored silk gown, dotted with a sparkling array of diamonds sewn on with threads of gold. A feathered headdress and a sheer veil did nothing to hide her beauty, but only added an iridescent sheen to her porcelain complexion.

"You must be Dona Reyna," Nurbanu said as she approached breezily.

"How did you know?"

"You're the only one I don't recognize here." Her voice was bright and cheery. "Fish in a fishbowl." She raised her hands to the air and surveyed the surroundings. "And here you are, a swan in our midst."

Reyna bowed low from the waist. "I am humbled, Princess. May I congratulate you on the birth of your daughter."

"You may." She tipped her head ever so slightly. "I take it this is your daughter." Nurbanu lifted Tamar's chin with the tip of her finger so that she might have a better look at the girl. "What a lovely child," she marveled. "I only hope my own daughter grows into such a beauty."

With the snap of her fingers Nurbanu summoned a servant girl, undoubtedly one of scores of the underlings in the complex harem hierarchy. "Take this girl to the garden to play with the other children," she said to a slender Asian girl with long lashes. Then, glancing back at Reyna, she clapped her hands together and smiled. "I have a message for you. I do think you'll be pleased when you hear it."

"A message?"

"From Prince Selim," she said. "It concerns your daughter."

"Tamar? What about her?"

The princess drew in a deep breath as the corners of her pouty lips curled upward. "It's been decided that she'll be granted an imperial education inside the palace." Nurbanu paused for a long moment as if to let the enormity of the honor sink in. "She'll be schooled in music and poetry, embroidery and literature. I've invited you here tonight to tell you this good news in person. It's a rare honor bestowed on the sultanate's most loyal servants."

Reyna blinked. "I don't quite understand."

"Come now." Nurbanu smiled casually. "I know it's hard to believe. I was surprised myself when I heard."

"But I don't think I could bear to be separated from her just yet."

"I can understand that." Her expression softened. "It's a difficult thing for a mother, but she won't be far, and she'll have to begin her education at some point. It truly is a blessing. What more could you hope for?"

"Yes," Reyna replied dazedly. "Thank you."

"In three days' time, my man Jaffar will arrive at your villa to collect your daughter."

"Princess." She dropped her voice and reached for the hamsa good-luck charm she wore around her neck. The gold hand-of-God pendant felt cool between her fingertips. "What of my husband?"

"Your husband will be pleased. An imperial education is the very best any father could hope for his daughter."

"It's just that he's always had his own ideas about education," Reyna pressed on. "I know he's already secured a place for her in the Hamon school this coming year."

"The decision has been made," the princess said dismissively. "I thought you'd be pleased."

Just then a dazzling display of fireworks filled the sky above the sea.

The two women looked up instinctively as flurries of fire dissipated over the sea like gold dust sprinkled from the heavens.

"Spectacular, isn't it?" Nurbanu kept her eyes up to the sky.

"Yes, Princess." Reyna's voice was barely a whisper.

10

The guests dining in French ambassador d'Armon's courtyard turned their attention to the fireworks show in the sky overhead. "A party taking place in the palace, no doubt," Ambassador d'Armon noted.

"The Prince's beloved has given birth to a daughter," José explained. "My wife and daughter are taking part in the festivities as we speak." He lifted his glass in the air. "To the new princess!"

"Hear, hear!" The other guests cheered.

José turned to the ambassador, hoping to bring him back to the matter at hand. "Yes, yes, Ambassador, splendid indeed, but should we not get back to discussing the future of our long-standing Franco-Ottoman alliance?"

For the past several decades, Ottoman and French forces had been united in their efforts to stymie the advances of the Spanish and Roman Empire of Charles V. Together they had warred relentlessly against the emperor of the Old World. José was eager to ascertain where the French stood on a recently proposed skirmish to wrestle back control of the African coastline from Christian forces along a strip of land known as Tripoli. It was expected that the mostly Muslim population would welcome the return of Muslim rule, and in the process, the Catholic Empire of Charles V would suffer an embarrassing defeat.

José had been zealously advocating for an attack. The more he considered the prospect, the more his anger simmered. When it came to Ferdinand and Isabella's progeny, he could see nothing but red. For Charles V was the grandson of the Spanish regents who had ordered the expulsion and execution of thousands of Jewish souls throughout the kingdoms of Iberia. Had it not been for their vicious policies, thousands of innocent lives might have never been lost. Had it not been for their hatred, his mother and father might still be alive.

"We'll get to our alliance soon enough, José," the ambassador said, interrupting José's thoughts. "But I daresay, we haven't yet concluded with our pastries." He smiled and popped a cube of baklava into his mouth.

And so it was that instead of devising a way to further torment the Spanish Empire, José passed a leisurely evening debating spiritedly with d'Armon's merry entourage. Guillaume Postel, the philosopher, Kabbalist, and religious universalist, was in attendance, as were other scientists, poets, and naturalists. The French explorer André Thévet dazzled the crowd with tales of world travels and promised to deliver a published account of his explorations to all. Debates about religion, science, and human existence continued late into the night until the guests retired to their quarters and collapsed upon the silken lining of their plush featherbeds.

Arriving back at the villa the following day, José made his way up the front steps and through the grand entrance. Once inside, he discovered Reyna sitting at the base of the staircase.

"I've been waiting for you," she said as the doors closed behind him.

Taking note of her anxious demeanor, he quickened his step until he was kneeling beside her. "What is it?"

And so she told him of all that had come to pass the previous night. By the time she'd finished explaining, José could barely move at all, for he was sure that when he did, the world he knew would shatter into a million pieces.

"I'm sorry, José," she whispered. "They will come to collect her the day after tomorrow." Upon hearing those words, he stormed off to his study, leaving Reyna alone at the edge of the stairs. Hovering over his desk, he slammed his fist down upon a map of the empire, then took his quill in hand and snapped it in two.

Selim had been at the palace for the past few weeks, having journeyed the long way home in anticipation of the birth of his child. He would preside at Topkapi for sixty days more, but José wasted no time requesting an audience with the prince.

As the prince was expected to be out all that afternoon hunting with his dogs, José managed to secure an appointment to appear before him

on the following day. The palatial heart of Dar al-Islam was no place for
a Jewish child to be educated. He didn't know if he had the right to refuse, but he had to try.

"If you've called this meeting to thank me, José, there's no need," Selim
began. "Only the children of my most trusted servants receive a palace
education. It's a privilege bestowed on those most deserving."

José bowed low. "We are honored," he said before bringing the hem of
Selim's cloak to his lips. "But how can we ever accept this kindness?" He
promptly returned to his feet and crossed his arms behind his back. "We
are not deserving of such an honor."

Selim waved his finger and smiled. "I won't take no for an answer," he
chided affectionately.

Whether spoken in jest or spoken as truth, once pronounced, the will of
an imperial prince was final. José took a step back and considered his op-
tions. "Perhaps she might return home in the evenings, after her studies?"

"No, no, José. My children were quite taken by your green-eyed girl.
They'd like to keep her as a playmate."

"Keep her?"

"Of course. Nurbanu tells me that she's quite charming. My children
couldn't bear the thought of her leaving after all the fun they had at the
party. You are a lucky man, José. Your daughter will live alongside my
children."

José's voice dropped to a whisper as he hung his head low. "She is our
only child."

Selim was still, his eyes narrowed and his yellow brows steeped in confusion. "I take it that you're not pleased with my generosity?"

"On the contrary." José tried to sound cheerful. "It's just that my wife
can no longer bear children. I'm afraid that she will grow lonely without
Tamar."

Selim nodded in agreement. "I understand."

"You do?"

"Of course. A mother must be with a child."

Upon hearing these words, José breathed a sigh of relief. "I'm so glad
you agree—"

"And if she cannot bear children, things can be arranged," the prince
continued.

"Arranged?" José could not comprehend what the sultan meant.

"Take a girl for yourself, Don José. There are so many to choose from. If you can't decide, I can select one for you. She will be young and healthy and she will give you much joy. When she delivers you a baby, the child will be passed to your wife to be raised as her own."

José was stunned by the very suggestion.

"So it's settled," the prince said. "Tamar will be educated in the palace, and all the empire shall know of the honor I've bestowed upon you. And one day when I am sultan, you'll serve beside me as the second most powerful man in all the land. Had not Yusuf, son of Yakoub, left the home of his birth to rise up and become the right hand of an Egyptian pharaoh? You, José, shall follow in the footsteps of your namesake Joseph, the leader of your people." The prince leaned in and caught José in the force of his gaze. "You shall have power beyond your wildest dreams." Selim's wild eyes flickered as he spoke.

"Yes, Your Highness." José forced himself to say the words.

"You are dismissed now, José." With downcast eyes, José withdrew from the prince's chamber. Despite all the power he'd been promised, he could not help but return home feeling as though he were the most helpless man on earth.

Upon entering the villa, he found his wife sitting at the table in the dining hall, staring blankly at the damask-covered wall ahead.

For a long moment, José was motionless.

Reyna looked up and greeted him with tired, empty eyes.

"This is not what I wanted," José said quietly. "I always thought, I always planned . . ." His voice trailed off. Having collected his thoughts, he leaned over the table as he spoke again. "Dr. Hamon's wife runs a perfectly suitable girls' school. That's where I wanted her to be educated, with her people." Reyna turned away. "They will come for her in the morning."

José backed away and sunk into an empty chair.

"I have had some time to think about it," Reyna pressed on. "An education among noble people. She'll be well taken care of."

José examined his wife and understood that it had taken all her courage to say such a thing. She took a deep breath, then continued. "She'll be by far the most educated and respected among her peers. She could have any man you choose for her. When she finishes, it will be with all the skills and graces necessary to assume her proper place as a leader of our people."

"Is that what you think?"

Reyna rubbed her eyes and shook her head. "I *have* to think it."

"Reyna," he said with all the compassion he could muster, coming to his feet and standing beside her. He cradled her in his arms.

"Was not Moses provided with an imperial education?" she went on tepidly. "Did he not rise to become the greatest leader our people has ever known?" She looked up at him with wide, questioning eyes.

José let his hands fall to his sides before shaking his head and walking away. "This is the second time today someone has tried to convince me of something by invoking the name of our forefathers!"

"A leader of our people!" Reyna called back after him. "Like her grandmother before her, the great Dona Antonia Nissim!"

His body was still upon hearing La Senhora's name. "May her soul rest in peace." He whispered the words. *"Aleha ha-shalom."* He turned back to Reyna. "We both know that we cannot refuse this honor," he said wearily. "Not after everything that has come to pass." He stood at the doorway of the parlor and studied the portrait of Dona Antonia hanging above the mantel. "An imperial education," he said after a long moment. "If it will help her to one day follow in the footsteps of her grandmother, so be it."

The next morning Reyna and José greeted an Ethiopian man at the door. Jaffar was at least six foot six inches tall, with a powerful build and the cocoa complexion of his people. He wore a caftan the color of saffron, secured at the waist by a thick belt of ivory shards.

"Just one moment to say farewell." Reyna turned from the man and crouched low to talk to her daughter.

"You'll go to school at the palace today," Reyna explained to Tamar.

The little girl, having never spent a day apart from her mother, was wide-eyed with worry.

"I'll see you in a few days." She and José hugged their daughter, then sent her away with Jaffar, the eunuch tasked with escorting her into the harem.

That day, like most, passed slowly for Reyna. As a woman of means, she was not allowed to venture out of her home unaccompanied by her husband. She spent the morning in the parlor, working on a tapestry she'd begun with threads her servants had brought back from the bazaar. When her fingers began to ache, she rang the bell for the maid and requested a meal. She dined on eggplant and lentils, and then, for something sweet, crystallized fruits and honey cake. Wondering what time it was, she tilted her head up and took note of the position of the sun through the window. It was far from midday. Nevertheless, she retreated to her room, collapsed onto her bed, and drifted off into a fitful sleep.

She woke up a few hours later. A chill filled the room and the light was dim. Still in a sleepy haze, she rose from her bed and peered through the lattices. The sun, low in the sky, seeped along the horizon like the pierced yolk of a broken egg. She turned her attention to the courtyard below. "Tamar!" she called out.

But Tamar did not appear or call back to her—not at that moment or the next. She called down once more, then scoured the empty courtyard for any sign of Tamar or her governess.

It was then that she recalled the governess had been relieved of her duties earlier that morning, sent away with a basket of figs and a half-dozen lengths of costly velvet and silk.

It was then that she recalled her daughter Tamar had been taken from her home, her life, and her very arms.

Four agonizing weeks had gone by before Reyna was invited back to Topkapi. Though she had wished to visit sooner, entry to the private quarters of the Imperial Palace was by invitation only.

She joined Nurbanu in her private garden, where she drank tea and waited for news of her daughter. Through the bamboo lattices, she could see Tamar sitting atop the jewel-studded saddle of a miniature pony with a young boy. "Let me go to her." Reyna stood from her place.

"What's the rush?" Nurbanu seized her by the wrist. "Relax with me and watch them play a little longer." With her long torso and fair legs sprawled out across the silk divan, Nurbanu was a picture-perfect odalisque. She was Selim's beloved and looked the part.

"Is it safe? Tamar's never ridden before," said Reyna.

"Perfectly safe, and she's ridden often since her arrival."

Returning to the cushions of the divan, Reyna tried to appear comfortable.

The high-pitched squeal of children's voices sounded from beyond the garden. Reyna peered through the lattices and saw that Tamar was being lowered from the saddle by one of the servants. "She looks happy," Reyna said quietly.

"She is, but you can't feel bad about that. It's natural that a little girl would want to be with other children her age. This is a wonderful place for a child to be raised."

"Does she ask for me?" Reyna's voice sounded pitiful in her ears.

"When she arrived, but she's stopped that now."

"Princess, may I speak candidly?"

"Why bother asking? I suspect you shall, one way or the other."

"Might such a thing as this be improper?"

"What's that?" Nurbanu held out her hand as a servant girl went to work filing her nails.

"A little boy and a little girl, not linked by blood, spending so much time together."

"They're so young. It's plain to see, they're enjoying each other's company," Nurbanu replied. "And what's the harm anyhow? Murad will be gone before he's old enough for anything serious."

"Gone?"

"Sent away to the men's imperial quarters. You don't see any grown princes around here. Your daughter is well guarded behind these walls."

The frenzied shuffle of little feet in motion sounded from the corridor. "Here they are," said Nurbanu as the children stumbled in with grass in their hair and dirt along the hems of their cloaks.

"*Anne?*" Tamar questioned when she noticed Reyna's presence. Her eyes smiled as she climbed atop the divan and nestled herself in her mother's lap.

"Tamarciğim." Reyna drew a ring with her finger across the girl's cheek and nose. "You shine for me like a gold ducat."

Tamar studied her mother's face as though searching for something far in the distance. After a moment she slid off Reyna's lap and headed over to Murad. She wrapped her chubby arms around him, and he, in an instant, returned the embrace. With their little faces pressed together, they appeared as two beaming cherubs. "I'll catch you a goldfish as big as a house!" Murad proclaimed.

"You've never seen a house!" Tamar countered. They both laughed, because it was true, then debated whether a palace could be considered a house, because if that were to be the case, Murad had seen many houses in his lifetime. He counted, at the very least, two. They played with marbles on a sprawling carpet by Reyna's feet for a few minutes before heading off together to try their hand at skipping stones in the pond.

Not even a good-bye. Reyna thought she might burst into tears. "May I visit again?"

"As often as you'd like." Nurbanu glanced up from behind the rim of her teacup and smiled.

And so it was that Tamar was raised in the Imperial Harem, reared by an army of women that included the sultan's favorite imperial princesses, servants, and relatives. It was known to all that this was the child of the prince's most trusted adviser and friend.

Almost a decade would pass, and during that time Tamar would return home for monthly visits. She'd proudly display drawings and recite poems and perform charming dance routines to the applause of Reyna and José and all the staff that had come to greet her. Over dinner, she'd tell her parents of all that had happened in the weeks since her last visit. She'd speak of boat trips and ball games, dancing troupes and the princesses and princes she'd grown fond of. But mostly she'd speak of her affection for Murad, the boy prince who'd proven himself to be a loyal playmate since her very first day at the palace.

To José, it seemed as though just yesterday she'd been bouncing on his knee and playing with wooden dolls. But by all accounts, she was growing into a beautiful young lady, prim and chaste. He would present her with a new doll, and she'd smile demurely, as if to say *I'm too old for that, Baba*. He'd be reminded right then and there that the little girl that had once nestled in the nook of his arm would soon be gone. In her stead was a slender beauty with all the grace, wit, and charm befitting a lady of her stature.

The years passed and the time of Tamar's return drew nearer.

It was midnight on the eve of the New Moon Festival, sixteen years to the day of Antonia's death. José sat alone in the parlor with a goblet in hand. Atop the iron-banded oak chest before him, the blood-orange flame of the *meldado* candle burned bright, commemorating the legacy La Madre had left behind.

Within the halo of that glow, Dona Antonia's somber eyes gazed out at him from Toldedano's portrait above the mantel. Her portrait commanded his absolute attention, reeling him in until he was lost in the depths of her eyes. He traveled through the spiral of her blue-speckled irises toward a hazy reflection. As he neared it, the reflection grew clearer, but it was not Antonia who looked back at him.

Emerald eyes, luminous in the dark, beheld him.

Tamar.

In just a few weeks' time, she'd return for good, and he'd sit her down by the fireplace and point out the portrait hanging above the mantel. Beneath the watchful gaze of the great Antonia Nissim, he would impart to his daughter the story of how they had come to live in this great land, all the tragedy that had befallen their people back in the Old World.

He'd choose a husband for her among the ranks of the Jewish elite. Perhaps a wealthy merchant, one of Hamon's nephews, or better yet, the chief rabbi's grandson. A leader, a scholar, a man of unimpeachable repute: He would select someone worthy, and as her grandmother before her, she would take her rightful place in society, as a wife, mother, and guardian of the faith.

I I

Murad rested the oars in their holsters and let their small boat drift aimlessly. The shore was just a faraway cluster of miniatures now. He hung his arm over the side of the boat and slapped the water playfully.

"I don't see you enough," Tamar said matter-of-factly.

"And I don't see you at all." He nodded toward her veil. "This thing, it doesn't seem right." He wiped his wet hand on his silk caftan. "I'll never get used to it."

"What's the difference? You know what I look like."

"It's not the same."

"Murad, it's proper."

"Proper? We used to bathe naked together in the fruit fountain. Don't talk to me about proper," he quipped.

"We were seven," she shot back.

He leaned in close. "You've never been in trouble a day in your life, have you?"

"The day's not ended."

He leaned back against his elbows and smirked. "Don't ever change."

Becoming more serious, he said, "I don't like talking to you through this, but I'm grateful we at least have this time together."

She smiled a smile he could not see. Then she pulled a few pins from her veil and let the fabric fall away, exposing auburn hair that fell loose in long waves.

Specks of sun glinted off the water's surface, freckling her caramel-colored skin with dots of white light.

He stared at her for a time, as if she were a gift he could not quite believe he had received.

The buzzing of a wasp came between them. Murad instinctively reached for her veil, now set off to the side, and used it to swat the insect away. As he did, he accidently flung the muslin fabric overboard.

"Murad!" Tamar stood up and wobbled in her place.

He shrugged apologetically.

"How am I ever going to explain this!" Her emerald eyes narrowed to slivers as her veil sank away beneath the water's surface. She was already on edge as it was. Murad had stolen the key from his mother's robes and sneaked Tamar out of the harem through the secret door in her chamber. Cloaked in his dark robes, they'd passed as two young princes strolling innocently through the courtyards. With her head down, the fact that she was actually a girl had gone unnoticed. Now with her long hair and face fully exposed, it would be impossible to sneak back into the harem. "I'll marinate you!" She reached down and shoved him hard.

"I'm truly sorry! Let me dive in and get it," he offered sheepishly, then stood up and removed his shoes.

"Do you see it?" She stepped forward, causing the boat to sway dangerously, and stretched out her arms for balance.

Murad grabbed hold of her arms, falling forward as he did.

An invisible force exerted a downward pressure, plunging them deep through the sharp surface of the sea and into the dark waters below. They dove to some unknown depth, at which point they spun around and beheld each other through the water that engulfed them. As they floated in place, their eyes were wide and their lungs still. It was a quiet world, a world without veils or rules or rituals. A world without any noise except for the sound of one's heart thumping in one's chest and the rush of one's blood coursing through one's veins.

Tamar looked up toward what could only be the sun, a runny, yellow mark on the water's surface. When she kicked her feet, Murad followed suit, and the force of their kicks shot them skyward.

In an instant, they had surfaced in a ring of ripples and gasps and were taking huge gulps of air into their lungs.

Murad swam to her. "Are you all right?"

"I'm fine." She coughed up some water.

"Look what I managed to find!" He held out her soaking veil and flung it over the edge of the skiff. When she didn't respond, he took a closer look at her. "You're shivering." He pulled her toward the boat. "Let's go." He unhinged a small ladder on the side of the boat and helped Tamar up before boarding himself.

"Take off that robe before you freeze."

She obliged and slipped off her caftan, laying it flat at the back of the boat to dry.

Murad shed a few layers himself, exposing his thick, muscular arms from shoulder to wrist.

They sat there quietly, baking dry under the warm, steady sunshine.

After a time he spoke up. "They're going to send me away."

She glanced up. It was clear the thought had weighed heavily on his mind for some time.

"Soon." He answered the question she hadn't asked. "Feel this." He took her hand and brought it to his face.

She moved her fingers across the length of this jaw. "So rough?"

"I've been using a blade to scrape off the stubble for months." He pulled away. "It's only a matter of time before someone catches onto it. I know Jaffar has his suspicions already."

"Murad." She moved a few inches closer to him.

"Most of us are sent away by the time we're thirteen. I know Mustafa managed to stick around until he was fourteen, but I'm already fifteen. I have no idea how I lasted in the harem this long."

"So they're sending you away?"

"You know they will."

"When will I see you?"

Murad turned from her.

When he didn't answer, she frowned disappointedly, then reached for her sopping veil and flung it back at the sea. As she did, the corner of the fabric caught along a splintered edge of the skiff and Murad moved to retrieve it.

"You'll need this," Murad seemed to chastise as he handed back the drenched fabric.

"So that's it?" She let it drop to the bottom of the boat and form a puddle by her feet. "You're just going to leave because they tell you to?"

"What choice do I have?"

"There has to be something we can do."

"You know very well. No men inside the harem."

"If you have to go"—she lowered her voice—"I'll go with you."

He leaned back and scoffed at the suggestion. "And your father?"

She rubbed her hands together and rocked in her place. "I think he would be pleased."

"Are we talking about the same person? The man they call Don José the Jew? They say you'd be hard-pressed to find a Hebrew more fervent in his faith."

"My father is an enlightened man, an educated man!"

"I heard he risked everything for a religion forbidden to him, even his very life!"

"If what you say is true, then surely he must understand the importance of freedom."

"Your father doesn't care for your freedom, he cares only for his faith. Have you spent so much time away from your father's house that you no longer know him at all?"

She shook her head and reached for the oars. "Don't talk about my father as if you know him." She fumbled with the oars and began rowing in the wrong direction. "I may not know him well, but it's fair to say you don't know him at all." She gave up on the oars and let them fall loose in their holsters. "I want to go back now."

"Tamar—"

"It's getting late."

"Now wait just a minute—"

"I need to get back," she snapped. "If you're not going to help me turn this boat around, I'm happy to swim."

He locked his eyes with hers, then leaned in close until she could feel his breath on her lips. "I'm sorry," he said after some time. "I want us to be together."

She softened and put her arms around his neck. "I'll go where you go."

"And your people?"

She looked up toward the place where the sea met the sky. The image of a scared little girl flashed through her mind. She was held in the arms of an African giant ready to take her away from the only home she'd ever known. Over his shoulder, she could see her parents' figures in the doorway, standing by idly as they faded from view.

Her voice was low and pensive when she finally replied. "You are my people," she said, her eyes still on the sea.

Murad nodded.

There were no more words, nothing left to say as they drifted farther from the shore, the moment sealed by the weight of the silent oath between them.

As the weeks passed, Murad began to notice the eunuchs eying him suspiciously as he and Tamar rode out on their horses or took long walks in the gardens. It had become impossible to hide the shadow of a beard that crept up along the length of his cheeks and above his lip. He had grown tall—a head taller than every other boy in the harem. He knew that at any moment, he could be sent out from his mother's apartment to live with the other adolescent princes in the royal residences of the inner courtyard. On that day he'd be considered a man, and would henceforth be prevented from entering the Imperial Harem.

It happened quite suddenly on an otherwise unremarkable day. He had just left his tutor in the Second Courtyard of the palace and was on his way to the harem when he was stopped at the entrance by Jaffar, one of the African eunuchs tasked with guarding the gates. Invoking his princely status, Murad tried to press on, but was politely informed that he could no longer be granted access to the women's quarters.

He was now barred from entering, just as Tamar was barred from leaving.

He was assigned to his own quarters in the Third Courtyard, where his mother could call upon him for visits. His two-story residence was outfitted with splendidly tiled archways, marble columns, a private garden, and a bathhouse. He was granted his own staff of servants and butlers, as well as beautiful slaves from the Imperial Harem, all courtesy of his grandfather, the sultan. As an imperial prince that had come of age, he was now also entitled to receive a daily stipend of a hundred aspers to do with what he wished. And yet there was nothing he wanted that money could buy. Murad thought only of Tamar.

Attempts to sneak back in through his mother's chamber door would prove to be a fool's errand. Murad knew the door could be unlocked only with the bronze key that his mother had suddenly taken to wearing around her neck after his and Tamar's secret river rendezvous. Might he have somehow aroused her suspicions? Perhaps he had returned the stolen key to the wrong pocket of her robe? Though he might never know the truth, it was of little consequence now.

Murad reminded himself of the only thing that mattered.

Tamar. He had to find a way to see her again.

A full moon had passed since his departure from the harem, but still Murad could think of little else but Tamar. He spent the afternoon as he often did, pacing along the path in the outer palace courtyard, hoping to catch a glimpse of Tamar as the harem doors swung open and shut to receive food trolleys ferried over from the imperial kitchens.

Murad spied Jaffar guarding the door. He watched as the tall eunuch mouthed directives to one of his subordinates before the unknown eunuch took his place and Jaffar headed off in the direction of the kitchens. Murad trailed a safe distance behind as Jaffar rounded a corner and disappeared behind a thick wall of bushes.

"Jaffar!" Murad called out as he quickened his pace. "Jaffar!"

He spun around to face Murad. "Your Highness, what are you doing in these parts?"

"How are you, Jaffar?" Murad's attempts to sound casual fell flat.

The eunuch's expression stiffened. "Is there something I can help you with?"

Murad took a step back and cleared his throat. "I just thought you might have some news from the harem."

"It's been only a month, Your Highness."

"Much can happen in a month's time."

"You know, most boys can't wait to graduate from the harem and live their lives as men in the princely residences, but you, you're different, aren't you, Murad?"

"I'm afraid I don't understand—"

"You want to find a way to sneak back in. To see the girl. You're plotting and scheming this very instant, and you think I can help."

"Can you?" Murad leaped at the suggestion.

"Of course not," said Jaffar. "Are you trying to get me executed?"

Murad's posture withered.

The eunuch shook his head and dug his walking staff into the dirt. "There may be another way for you to see her."

He felt his heart jump up into his throat. "Please, go on."

"The girl is almost fifteen. It's been decided that her time in the harem has come to an end. She'll be returning home shortly, effendi, so there is no point in trying to sneak your way back in."

"When is this happening?" His breath quickened. "When does she leave?"

"In seven days' time, I'm to escort her back to her father's house."

Murad looked around. "Here." He pointed to a low, sprawling willow tree, then pushed away its branches and disappeared beneath it. "Can you see me?" Murad called out from behind the wall of leaves.

"You are well hidden, effendi. No one can see you there."

Murad emerged and was standing by the eunuch once more. "Then this is where I will wait. Bring her to me."

"You know that I can't."

"Do me this favor. I'll remember your kindness one day when I am sultan."

Jaffar seemed to mull it over. "All right. Just this once. After the sun goes down, at the time when it is no longer day, but not yet night."

Murad clasped his hands together loudly. "Thank you, Jaffar! I won't forget this."

The eunuch frowned. "I already wish you would."

Seven days later, in the twilight hour, Murad took his place in the hollow space beneath the tree and waited for Jaffar to escort Tamar his way. While he waited, kitchen staff bustled past with rattling silver trays. Sacks of rice and grains were transported to the imperial kitchen in wagons pulled by donkeys. To pass the time, Murad began to count the heels of servants walking by. When he reached sixty, he pulled back the branches and studied the evening sky. Though the moon shone faintly, he could not make out a single star.

And yet he knew that somewhere hidden in those heavens, his and Tamar's star signs overlapped. He'd just come from Sheikh Suca's dark sanctuary in the Second Courtyard of the royal compound. The old Sufi confirmed what Murad had felt all along. The heavens embraced their union, no matter that she was a foreigner and a Jew. Islam permitted a man to marry any woman who practiced a monotheistic religion. Tamar, daughter of Don José the Jew, was a perfectly suitable match.

The sound of snapping twigs interrupted his daydream. He spotted Tamar through the thicket of jade- and lime-colored leaves. Her turquoise caftan wrapped her in a silk cocoon as she ducked under the canopy of leaves and lowered herself onto the ground by his side.

They sat enveloped by the tree, its sweeping branches shielding them from view. After several moments of silence, the air pulsated with a question in waiting.

He lifted her veil and peered into her emerald eyes. "I have something for you." He passed her a small ring, a ruby cast in yellow gold mined from the rich soils of India. She examined the stone. The inscription on the ring read: *To my queen, my sultan. I'll sing your praises always.*

Murad slid the ring over her finger. "In a year, it is my father's will that we be married."

She looked up at him, awed and tongue-tied, before raising a hand over her mouth and suppressing a smile. Then she shook her head, leaned forward, and set her lips upon his.

As they kissed, a flurry of sensation filled him. He didn't dare pull away, but rather pushed in closer, taking in the salty taste of her lips and the heat of her mouth. They remained that way for a long moment before she tore away and stared at him, breathless.

He could still feel the heat of her kiss burning his lips. He ran his fingers through her hair, squeezed her hand, and let out a breathy laugh.

"*Murad,*" she whispered as the wind came through the leaves.

He pulled her close and held his breath, savoring the sound of his name upon her lips.

"I love you," she said.

Holding her close against his chest, he felt himself free-floating and free-falling all at once.

For the next several moments, they lay on the ground side by side, hand in hand, peering through the branches into the dimming world beyond. Amidst the sound of rustling leaves, they could make out a muezzin's call to prayer, announcing the hour.

"Go." He sat up reluctantly. "Your parents are waiting."

She turned to him with playful eyes and a smile confined to the corners of her lips.

They shared one last kiss before she said good-bye and slipped away.

12

That evening José entered the dining room, elegant as always in new clogs and a spotless white turban. He was beginning to show signs of aging, his trim beard boasting a few specks of gray, his shoulders and torso thickened with wine and cheese and the complacency that often accompanies too much success.

"How I have longed for this day," he said as he approached his daughter. "Today you have returned to live in the house of your father." He put his arms around her and drew her in close. "You must be hungry?" he said as he pulled away.

"A bit," she answered shyly.

"Let's be seated," he said before all three took their places around the table. "Are you well? What news do you bring?"

"You know very well, *Baba*. Little changes in the harem. I'm afraid I don't have exciting news to share."

"Ah, come! You must have some stories for your *baba*. How is Nurbanu? I hear she has lost the favor of the prince to a younger, prettier thing from the East."

"José!" Reyna flashed her husband a disapproving glare.

Though he'd never been known to engage in idle chatter before, José found himself struggling to relate to his daughter. She was a young woman now, no longer a girl. What did one talk to young women about? He simply couldn't recall.

"Angling for a bit of gossip, *Baba*?" Tamar chimed in.

"Gossip?" he replied. "Certainly not!" José threw his hands up and offered his most innocent smile. "You know how I hate the word. Let us call them stories about life."

"How eloquent you are, *Baba*."

"What? In my own home I shouldn't be permitted to speak? Isn't that what you ladies spend your days doing anyhow? Chatting among yourselves?" He wondered if that might truly be how she had passed her days. What did he know of palace women? What did he really know of his daughter? Though their interactions over the years had been pleasant enough, he had little insight into her private world. She was now sitting just an arm's length away, and yet he could not help but feel that they were still somehow separated by the many years they'd been apart. He wondered if perhaps she felt the same way.

Tamar looked up at him and smiled blankly.

"Nurbanu hasn't much to worry about anyhow," José rambled on between bites of mutton. "She's positioned herself well, hasn't she? That son of hers is the smartest of the bunch." He held his fork in the air to punctuate the point. "The boy was already reciting poetry when the rest of the lot were still in diapers. He's got a head on his shoulders, that Murad. Mark my words, he'll make a fine sultan."

Tamar's cheeks flushed conspicuously.

"Enough about that." He turned to his daughter. José couldn't remember the last time he'd felt so nervous, though he was now trying his best to sound at ease. "Are you happy to be home to keep your old *baba* company?"

"I wouldn't have it any other way."

José nodded approvingly, then took a hearty bite of meat. "Now, for some news of myself." He released his fork and took a swig of wine before bringing the glass down hard. "It seems I've been honored by the sultan." He glanced about for a moment and waited for the enormity of the news to sink in before continuing. "I've been granted my own province to govern. A piece of land straddling the Sea of Galilee in the Holy Land. They call it Tiberias," he explained proudly.

"*Mashallah!*" Tamar exclaimed.

Reyna smiled modestly, though her eyes beamed with pride.

"Of course it's practically a wasteland right now, but it won't be for long. I'm sending over whole villages to populate the area. They'll be charged with cultivating the land and growing trade relations."

"Will we have to relocate?" Reyna seemed concerned.

"Heavens no!" José laughed. "You ladies wouldn't survive a fortnight there. You see, it's a lawless place." His tone turned serious. "The city walls have been destroyed. It's quite vulnerable to attack and yet it is our homeland. A Jewish land governed by Jews. What more could we ask for?"

The table grew silent.

As Tamar reached for her spoon, José noticed a shimmering ruby on her finger. His eyes moved from the stone to his daughter's downcast eyes. "I've shared my news." He leaned in closer. "It seems you have some of your own?" His voice took on an oddly inquisitive tone.

Their eyes met as she slid her hand back under the table.

"It's nothing."

"Nothing?"

"Nothing important."

José did not spare his daughter his long, hard gaze. "Go wait for me in the garden. I'd like a moment alone with your mother."

Tamar sat unmoved, her spoon in midair. "Have I offended you, *Baba*?"

He sighed wearily. "You can no more offend me than the light of the moon."

She nodded, then stood up and headed out to the garden.

José turned to Reyna. "Is there something I should know?"

She took a sip of her sherbet, then looked up innocently enough. "I'm not sure I know what you mean."

"You know what I mean."

"The ring?"

"Yes, the ring!"

Slowly she placed down her cup, folded her hands in her lap, and smiled serenely. "It's no crime to accept a gift. Certainly not one as beautiful as that."

José got up from his chair rather abruptly, tossed down his napkin, and headed out to the garden. He discovered Tamar sitting on a stone bench beside a flowing fountain depicting a sculpted rendition of Jonah being spat from an enormous whale. In the courtyard, two squawking geese poked about the shrubbery for caterpillars to feed their hatchlings.

"Tamar," he began. "What is this?" He reached for her hand and peered at the ruby on her finger.

"It's a ring."

"Yes, but where did you get such an exquisite gem?"

"It's just a gift."

"A gift from whom?" He took her arm firmly. "Who gave you this?"

"Murad." She pulled her arm free, held up her hand, and examined the ruby. "We'll be married in a year. *Baba*, tell me you are pleased."

He tilted his neck and studied his daughter as though seeing her for the first time.

"You've always spoken highly of him. You yourself said what a fine sultan he'll make," she pressed on while her father simply stared.

He lifted his daughter's face until her eyes met his.

"*Baba?* Please, say something."

José glanced around at his surroundings as though lost in a place that was vaguely familiar. "What can I say?" He shrugged. "You don't know who you are." He thought of all that he'd planned to tell her: of her grandmother Antonia, of the parents he'd never known, of all the lives lost.

"*Baba*, please," Tamar pleaded.

But José had no words. He reached to the ground and grabbed a fistful of earth with each hand. He closed his palms and felt the smooth grains seep between his clenched fingers. Memories fluttered through his mind. Books hidden beneath a loose floorboard. A starry night on the beaches of Lisbon, a quorem of men shrouded in a sea of blue and white prayer shawls.

"*Baba!*" Tamar's voice echoed against the silence of the night.

With his eyes closed he hardened himself to the memory of love. A chill rippled through him, limb by limb, until finally he was frozen.

He held his fists before her. "This earth here." His voice was barely a whisper. "You have to reach it to ever know it." He loosened his grip and let the cool earth slip away through his fingers.

Tamar cast her eyes to the ground. Her satin slippers, once white and pure, were covered in a thin layer of dust.

José turned abruptly, leaving his daughter alone in the garden with nothing but the clucking of the geese as her only consolation. His wooden clogs slapped against the stone steps as he marched up to his suite. He closed the door and looked around the room. With the force of a wild boar, he charged the console, toppling a vase of wild flowers and several vials of scented oil. Pools of water and oil spread across the floor, filling the room with the scent of honeysuckle and lavender. José scowled. Never before had he taken such offense at something so sweet.

He made his way to the window and peered out at the garden. Tamar was still there where he had left her. She held her hands up to the light of the moon. He watched as she spread her fingers wide, then bent down low and pressed her hands against the soft earth. She dug her hands in deep, trying to feel for something she did not know.

During the three days that followed, José lived and prayed and worked as though existing in a world of mere shadows. He'd rise earlier than usual to make it to synagogue in time for the exalted *vatikin*, or sunrise prayer, then be out all day and night until close to *chatzot halayla,* or midnight. José was content to have missed supper at home those evenings, opting instead to dine at the villas of foreign dignitaries or study late into the night with Hamon. In the brief time she'd been back, he'd barely seen his daughter and was glad of it. He drew no warmth from her smile, no comfort from her embrace.

He mentioned nothing to his wife about what he'd been told. "Burn your books, forget all this," hadn't Reyna once said? He thought back to that night so long ago on the beaches of Lisbon. She hadn't understood then. He'd no reason to think she'd understand his feelings now.

If she knew about the proposed match, Reyna didn't let on. Rather, she seemed more relaxed than ever now that her daughter was back at home. She called on the seamstress to have a dozen new dresses made up for Tamar, spoiling her with the most expensive and luxuriant fabrics that money could buy. From the garden bench where they worked on needlepoint tapestries, the women whooped with laughter as though two old friends.

But while a blissful aura surrounded his daughter and wife, a storm was brewing in José's heart. When Tamar and Reyna lit candles a short time before sundown that Friday evening, it was not the glow of the Sabbath light that filled his senses. Rather, it was the flames of Inquisition fires that raged through his mind. The smell of charred flesh crept through his nose and stuck to the back of his throat, bringing him back to the hellish day in Lisbon nearly seventeen years earlier. The screams and sweat and misery of that horrid day would forever be branded in his memory.

He thought of his mother and father. How was it that they had died for a belief that his own child, his own flesh and blood, could so easily relinquish?

The next night, long after the havdalah candle had been lit, marking the end of the Sabbath and the start of a new week, as her mother had explained, Tamar awoke to find her father standing over her bedside. "*Baba?* What's wrong?" She glanced beyond the lattices into the dark. By the thick curtain of night, she calculated that it was several hours before sunrise.

"Is everything all right?" She sat up in her bed. "Tell me what's happening?"

"Pack a small bag."

"Why?"

"Be quiet. Dress quickly."

"I don't understand," Tamar whispered.

"There's nothing to understand. Trust me now. Get your things." He kissed her forehead. "Meet me at the gates."

Just a few moments later, Tamar stood by her father in a hooded cape with a satchel in tow. He took her things along with a large square parcel wrapped in linen and led her toward a long winding road. They walked the path silently for what seemed to Tamar to be an hour or so. Finally, a dim shadow emerged before her eyes. A large man with a red beard appeared atop an enormous black horse.

"This man will take you the rest of the way," José said to Tamar.

"What are you talking about?" The panic in her voice was mounting.

"Go with Mustafa," he said flatly. "He'll escort you."

"Please, don't send me away. I'll be better. I promise." She threw her arms around his waist. "Don't send me away."

"I love you," José whispered as the man dismounted the black stallion and made his way toward Tamar.

"No!" She cried in his embrace. "Tell me what I've done wrong!"

He turned his cheek so that she wouldn't see the tears trickling down his face. "Be good." He held her for the last time. "Take this with you." He handed her a flat wrapped package. "To always remind you of who you are." He could feel her body trembling against his. "Go now."

"Where is he taking me?"

The red-bearded man took the package and placed it along with her other possessions in the covered wagon.

José spoke in a low whisper. "You're to live in Tiberias."

"No, *Baba*! I won't go."

The man stepped forward and pried Tamar from José as she sobbed loudly. He tossed her slender body over his muscular shoulder and lifted her onto the black horse. As José prepared to look upon his daughter for the very last time, a high-pitched scream whipped through the air—an otherworldly cry, a sound no human could ever make. José lifted his chin to the heavens. Overhead, an enormous spotted bird was making broad circles in the night sky.

A chill ran through him. Falcons were not known to travel at night.

The bird soared without so much as flapping, its silhouette like a smudge of ink against the crescent moon.

As he peered up into the night sky, he heard the words of his mentor. *The universe takes notice.*

"Off with you!" he shouted to the messenger of the sky. "Be gone!" He picked up a rock and threw it in the direction of the majestic bird. José then fell to his knees and watched as the horse carried his daughter into the darkness, and with her, the falcon too disappeared beyond the dark horizon.

Returning to his house, he seated himself in the parlor across from the fireplace and gazed up at the empty space where Antonia's portrait had once hung.

To the spirit of Antonia, he whispered the words: "She shall always remember who she is, with you by her side."

In the morning, when José revealed to Reyna what he had done, they stared at each other for a quiet moment. Her chest began to heave and her eyes swelled red. He went to embrace her, to try to explain, but she drew her arms against her stomach. Her lips parted as though she was about to speak but could not gather enough air in her lungs to make a sound. She struggled for breath as she leaned against the bedroom wall. Several moments passed before she made her way to the basin by the bed and reached for the ritual washing cup Dona Antonia had given José on their wedding day. Reyna clutched it in her arms before smashing it to the ground. As it hit the painted tiles, one of its richly carved handles broke away and sped across the room. Reyna uttered something before losing her breath once more.

José had been unable to make out her words. Imagining was more frightening than knowing ever could be.

Don José the Jew did not arrive at court the next day or the next. On the third day of his absence, he was summoned to the palace. The grand vizier warned José the imperial prince was in a foul mood. His beloved falcon had managed to escape from his cage and had now been missing for days. That he'd not yet returned was a wonder to all.

"Has he been spotted?" José asked.

"Not by a soul," the vizier replied. "I fear he may be lost forever."

José entered the quarters of the sultan's chambers with tattered clothing and his head slung low. He'd rehearsed this speech many times over the course of the three days. It was a perfect plan. Consumption was sweeping across the region at a rapid pace and the whole city was in mourning. There was barely a family who could claim they had not lost a loved one to the mysterious fever. Certainly the prince would not question it. José didn't even need to display a body. To prevent the spread of disease, the sultan had issued a *fatwa* deeming it permissible to cremate the bodies of the dead.

"A thousand apologies," José explained. "Our daughter . . ." he whispered in a tone of hushed grief. "The fever . . . Yes, it was awful . . . Two days ago . . . There was nothing we could do . . . If it is God's will, let it be." José could feel his heart thumping in his chest as he lied through his teeth. His mouth and jaw stiffened. He had not expected the sense of shame that quickly overpowered him. Don José the Jew fell to the ground and wept at the feet of the prince. He might never see his daughter again. José had banished her in his grief and killed her with his lies.

He took leave of his duties at the palace for a month of mourning. José mourned the loss of all that he held dear. He had lost his daughter, he had lost his wife, and when it came to his faith, he had lost his way.

13

"She is gone," Prince Selim said to his son.

Murad looked out of his window. Below, people were moving about their business as usual. The gardeners tended the bushes, as though they still believed it were possible for life to grow. Jaffar, along with the other eunuchs, continued to guard the gates under the mistaken impression that there was anything left on this earth worth protecting. A bird chirped its song in oblivion. White doves brazenly spread their wings and dove recklessly through the wanton sky—a sky so bright and blue and without shame that Murad clenched his fists in rage.

He wanted to scream down to all those passersby, "You scurrying fools! Your appointments, your plans, your dreams! Go ahead and forget them all. Only take up your shovels, for we must bury it all. How disappointing life is!" But he didn't shout these words. He did not speak, only let out a low growl, a deep rumbling from within.

Murad was silent for six days. Day after day, Prince Selim sat at the edge of Murad's bed, talking to him and trying to coax him to eat. The room was kept dim, the shutters drawn tight. In the darkness, Murad sat curled up, his knees tucked up to his chin.

On the seventh day, he finally spoke. "I only loved her a little."

Murad said the words quietly, as though trying to convince himself.

The prince calmly asked his son, "Can fire rage only a bit? Can flood-waters drown *only a little?*"

Murad fought back his tears. "*Baba.*" He caved into his father's embrace. He had always seen Tamar as a force of nature, an enchanting, mysterious force with the power to entice, to pull, to shape. Like gravity, a charm so potent, it had the ability to affect, but never to be affected. The idea that a force as unshakable as death had taken her away, that *he,* the son of the holy Ottoman emperor—the conqueror, the ruler of Dar al-Islam—could do nothing to bring her back thoroughly stunned him. That she was only human was inconceivable. In fact, it was more than he could bear.

"I do not accept," he breathed in a tone so eerily low and dismal, it sent a chill through the room.

"I do not accept," he told the servants when they attempted to serve him his dinner.

"I do not accept," he would hiss, his eyes cold and distant, as he waved away the delicacies brought before him from the farthest corners of the empire.

"I do not accept," he repeated again and again as dozens of beautiful servant girls were brought before him.

"Dismissed." He sent them all away one by one, with the same scorn he used to dismiss his meals.

"I do not accept," he pleaded with Allah as he knelt on his carpet during the sunrise prayers.

"I do not accept," he threatened menacingly in his prayer at sundown.

"I do not accept!" he cried out in his sleep.

In Murad's distress, visions of Tamar weighed heavily on his lids. Her mischievous smile, her emerald eyes, her bronze skin—these haunting images all found their rest in the hollow space of almost-sleep.

Just a few hours before sunrise on the night marking the one-month anniversary of her death, Murad was startled awake. His sheets were drenched in a cold sweat. Crickets chimed in the still of night and a silver mist hung low over the sea. He summoned the Halveti Sheikh Suca, the interpreter of dreams.

"Murad, what is it?" The sheikh's long robe trailed behind him as he hurried to Murad's bedside.

"A strange dream." Murad kicked his legs over the side of the bed as he sat up. "You must tell me what it means."

"You will dream many dreams. Best not to ponder the meaning of each and every one."

"This one's different." Murad leaned forward anxiously. "I know it."

Their eyes locked for a moment before the sheikh nodded. "Go ahead, then. Tell it to me."

"I was weeping in the courtyard, beside a tree most dear to me, thinking only of the loss of my beloved, when from that tree, I heard a rustling of sorts. I turned quickly, trying to ascertain who it was that dared trample upon that sacred earth." Murad stopped to take a deep breath.

"What happened next? Take your time, Murad. It's important you remember the events just as they unfolded."

Murad nodded, then sealed his lids tightly. "I hurried over and pulled back the branches, but to my surprise, no one was there. Not even a songbird or a squirrel in sight."

"Go on," the sheikh said as he stroked his long white beard.

"I backed away slowly, convinced that my mind had been playing tricks on me. But as I moved away, a flash of turquoise appeared and disappeared beyond the leaves and branches. Someone *was* there. I froze in place." Murad stopped, and without even realizing it, was now holding his breath. "It was then that I saw her." His lids fluttered to a wide-eyed gaze as the words rushed forth from his lips. "Her emerald eyes flashed through the leaves as she brushed the boughs aside, revealing her luminous face. She looked down and smiled. As I hurried toward her, she took a few steps back and disappeared beyond the leaves. She vanished." Murad turned his attention back to the sheikh, who was now fingering a strand of lapis lazuli prayer beads in his hand.

"A willow tree, you say?"

"I did not say."

"But it was a willow tree, was it not?"

"How could you know that?"

"I saw it, just as you did."

Murad nodded.

"Was that all?"

"I awoke shortly after."

"Strange, indeed." The sheikh nodded slightly.

"Have you any idea what it could mean?"

"I've more than an idea."

Murad sat forward. "So I was right to summon you. I was feeling so very foolish."

"This is not the dream of a fool, Murad. It is a window into the future."

"Tell me what it means. Tell me now and tell me quickly."

"A tree such as that can mean only one thing."

"Please go on, good sheikh!"

"A tree such as yours can only mean life."

Murad looked on, bewildered. "Life?"

"Yes, dear boy. The girl lives on."

"But the girl in my dream, she is *dead*."

"Murad," Sheikh Suca continued, "the girl is certainly not dead. The debt of her household follows her to a faraway land."

"*Debt?*" Murat's voice was faint.

Holding his beads in his lap, the sheikh pressed his lids down tightly, accessing a world of secrets and spirits beyond. "Your forefathers rescued her household and all its descendants, those living and those yet to be born," he said with his eyes still sealed. "For this, a debt lingers in the heavens. A time will come when she returns to see it paid."

"What do you mean, *paid?*"

"Make no mistake, Murad. The sun will rise on a day when the saved becomes the savior. Then and only then shall this debt be repaid."

Mystified, Murad looked at the sheikh.

"You are your father's son, are you not? The girl inherits the debt of her father, and you, my boy, shall inherit the deed of your household."

Murad stared on blankly, then headed toward the open shutters and peered out over the dark, empty courtyard. "So Tamar lives on?" he asked, his heart thumping.

"She does."

He spun around and challenged the sheikh. "If she's not dead, then where exactly *is* she?"

The old sheikh frowned. "Perhaps it's best you leave Topkapi for a time." He continued without waiting for Murad's response. "Memories can be just as haunting as ghosts and do little to heal the heart. This place," he said while shaking his head, "there are too many memories for you here." He gazed toward the window, then turned back, wide-eyed and seemingly inspired. "Perhaps now would be the right time for you to join your father in Manisa." He brought his hands together so that just his fingertips met, holding that pose for a long moment. "You're to be sent there next year anyhow to study the art of governance. I think an early departure is in order. I shall speak to your mother at once. In the meantime, try to get some rest."

"I don't need to rest!" Murad snapped.

Wincing, the sheikh shuffled to the door and muttered to himself before turning back to Murad. "Yes, some sleep will do you good," he said faintly before heading away.

But Murad could not sleep. Beneath a netted canopy embellished with a thousand shimmering sea pearls, he thrashed about until the sun rose, thinking only of her debt, his deed, and the day they might soon be reunited.

14

Murad waited. He prayed that Sheikh Suca was correct—that Tamar was alive and she would come back to him. He waited. All the while, three moons came to pass and the day of his departure was soon upon him.

Just as the sheikh had prescribed, Murad was sent off to join his father in Manisa, a bustling Anatolian province southwest of the capital. There he would be educated in matters of state and be prepared to take over an empire.

On the voyage, he passed ancient Greek ruins, temples belonging to the Greek god Zeus. From the distant grounds to the west rose ancient stone goddesses of the Hittites. To make an image of God was forbidden according to Islam, but Murad let his eyes drape over every inch of the crumbling monuments and carved imagery.

The caravan passed the mourning head of Niobe, daughter of Tantalus, king of Lydia, and wife to Amphion, king of Thebes. This was a tremendous rock structure bearing the image of a sitting woman. It was said that Niobe was turned to stone as punishment for her sins. There she rested, to the side of the road, a river of tears streaming down her face for an eternity of weeping. She sat there waiting, her heart a slab of stone, waiting for her spirit to free her from the trappings of God's punishment, from the carvings of a mountainside.

Murad too waited. Weeks turned into months. Seasons passed and colors changed. The sky darkened and lightened and the moon waxed and waned. Years went by and still he waited. He grew more desperate in time, certain she was alive and that one day they'd be reunited. Guards and Janissaries were put on alert for an emerald-eyed girl possessing an exquisite ruby ring. This girl, he explained, was indebted to him. His soldiers searched far and wide but nowhere did they find Murad's beloved.

Decades would pass. Tamar's father, Don José Nissim, would retire from palace life, while Murad's own father would die in the arms of Nurbanu Sultan, his one true love. In the winter of 1574, Murad ascended the throne and began ruling the land from his lonely niche. Still heartbroken by the loss of Tamar, he retreated from state politics and allowed the empire to be governed for the most part by his grand vizier and mother.

Upon his ascension, Nurbanu ordered that potential rivals be executed, even those who shared Murad's blood, even those who were his half brothers. He resisted his mother's command for eighteen hours, but after coaxing him into a drunken stupor late one night, Nurbanu managed to get hold of his commanding seal. By morning, the order had been carried out.

Murad became no more than a puppet on a string. Nurbanu was the one who truly occupied the throne. And Nurbanu Sultan reigned with an iron fist.

Of Murad, it was said that he'd gone mad. Lashing out for no apparent reason, he turned ever more embittered and reclusive. In time, he sought comfort in the arms of his concubine Safiye, fathering a child who would one day stand to inherit the throne.

At the hour of his death at the age of forty-nine, he summoned the royal scribe to his chamber. Murad was still waiting. Waiting for a debt that was never repaid. Waiting for the return of a love that had been stolen away. In the chapter on his life in the Osman Secret Chronicles, it is written that Sultan Murad III died *in waiting*.

Interlude

Over four centuries had passed and much had changed in the ever-shifting world. New countries were born and others swept away. In some parts, the old ways held strong, and in others, modernity and technology reigned. Borders were drawn and redrawn and pushed and reclaimed. Nations of slaves worked the fields and wars were waged and men died for freedom. Leaders were born and their lives taken too soon. Millions flocked to Mecca as they'd always done before, while millions more sought refuge in a land said to flow with milk and honey. Science illuminated secrets of the universe, and where mankind had taken a stride forward, so too it would go hurtling back. Despots were cradled in the warmth of a mother's lap, taught to crawl and walk and talk and one day rise to decimate the peace of the earth. And the acts of mankind, both good and evil, continued to ripple through every realm in the universe.

Through it all, the very same sun and moon and stars never wavered, never once failed to rise and fall and shine their light upon the world. And though mankind itself had run amok, the universe never once collapsed in on itself.

Through seismic shifts, wars, famine, and mankind's great experiment with its own free will, the universe never lost sight of even its most infinitesimal need for balance. Two dynastic paths that had once been intimately aligned had come to be separated in the heavens just as they'd been separated on earth. As such, a mark of unbalance hovered over the descendants of those dynasties, never to be settled until they crossed paths once more.

And so it was that among the boundless forces rippling through time and space, the debt of the House of Nissim came careening into the twenty-first century. The world, as always, was seeking balance and goodness, despite the chaos and horrors mankind continued to unleash.

PART II

15

Selim Osman was born waiting. Waiting for love, waiting for enlightenment, waiting for the meaning of the tragedy of his life to make itself known. From one day to the next, thirty-two-year-old Selim Osman, the sole living descendant of the last Ottoman sultan, was waiting.

Selim pulled into a circular driveway around a tall stone obelisk at the center, brought his car to a stop not far from the entrance to the hilltop villa, and waited.

As the engine ran, the headlights of his Bimmer illuminated a few parking attendants in white suit jackets and bow ties hustling to collect the cars ahead of his in line. He reached over to the empty seat beside him and popped open the glove compartment, withdrawing a white plastic pillbox. His headache had worsened throughout the day and was now nearly intolerable. Ignoring the recommended dosage instructions, he knocked back four ibuprofen tablets, downing them with the last drops of a warm bottle of Diet Coke that had been rolling beneath the backseat all throughout the drive. A few moments later, the door was flung open. There to greet him was a skinny boy who didn't look like he could be a day over fourteen. Stepping out of the car, Selim handed over his keys and some loose change. "Keep it close by, will you?"

He followed the winding red-carpeted path before him, enclosed on both sides by lush, towering hedges. There were a few neatly planted torches lighting up the otherwise dark path to the old Western-style villa. The ten-bedroom mansion had been built by an Italian architect and had last been inhabited by an Egyptian dignitary and his family several decades back. Now the place was an upscale nightclub, rented out occasionally by wealthy individuals for weddings or charity functions.

The evening's gala was meant to benefit Istanbul's children in need, and Selim had written out a sizable check to the charity and mailed it in along with his RSVP three weeks earlier. As he entered, he said hello to fat Musa, the security guard who worked the club on weekends. White-gloved waiters stood at either side of the doors, offering up glasses of champagne to Istanbul's elite and a smattering of well-to-do European expats. Inside, there were extravagant orchid arrangements, a sleek Lucite bar stationed at the far end of the room, and a steaming dinner buffet that could have fed the charity's hungry children for months. The smell of spring rolls and sweet sauce filled the air.

A life-size ice sculpture of Kemal Atatürk, the national hero, was situated beside the bar, melting under the warm glow of the orange and rose spotlights.

As he circled the room, Selim spotted all the usual attendees, many of whom were friends he'd grown up with and known since childhood. They were all part of a small community of privileged Turks who had been educated in private French or Swiss lycées, and summered with parents and grandparents on the Turkish Riviera or along the pebbled shores of the Côte d'Azur.

He said his hellos, then made his way over to the bar, where he was immediately captivated by the sight of a stunning brunette sipping on a plum-colored martini. Standing just a few feet away, she seemed to be observing the room, her long slender fingers wrapped delicately below the rim of her glass. In her four-inch heels, she stood a hair below his six-foot frame. She was angularly built with golden-brown skin, chiseled shoulders, and striking collarbones. Her untamed hair cascaded down her back and swept across her narrow waist in full, dark waves. She had a small beauty spot at the tip of her cheekbone beside alluring upturned eyes. In her slinky black dress, she looked familiar, but where he knew her from, he could not say.

The band onstage began strumming Turkish party favorites, and just like that, the woman with the martini glass wandered away, her hips swaying. He grabbed a drink from a tray and was soon trailing a safe distance behind her. He moved when she moved and slowed when she slowed. Standing beside a narrow bar table, he watched as she smiled and tossed back her hair. His eyes rested on her lips as she mouthed little nothings and nodded serenely to those around her.

After a moment she turned and eyed him directly.

Selim felt the blood rush to his face.

Smiling coolly with just the corners of her lips, she lifted her glass ever so slightly in his direction.

In that moment Selim realized exactly who she was. The young lady before him was the twenty-four-year-old soap opera star Ayda Turkman, and raising a drink in the air was her character's signature move.

He returned the gesture, then smiled self-consciously into his cup as he downed the remainder of his whiskey.

Placing the empty glass on the bar table, he relished the moment. Ayda Turkman had noticed him after all.

A few feet away, he spotted the Dogan twins. They sipped wine and laughed coquettishly with the minister's son, gossiping in French while casting sideways glances at Ayda. They spoke more loudly than they normally would have in their native tongue, confident that Ayda, with her presumably limited education, would not understand their petty insults. Speaking French while not in France was an elitist affectation Selim's contemporaries took up upon their return from whatever boarding schools they'd attended.

These Euro-Turks regarded the city's rising glitterati with a mixture of intrigue and scorn. Models were considered glorified strippers, disposable arm candy for upper-crust playboys, and actresses were regarded as temporary playthings for the aristocracy's naughty adolescents. Though they debuted the latest designer trends on billboards across Istanbul and Ankara, they would not be welcomed into the homes of the old-world elites. Despite the country's modernization, Istanbul's upper class was still a closed society, its membership regulated by a strict grandfather clause, bequeathed at birth to those whose ancestral lines could be traced to some legendary war hero or to the prophet Muhammad himself.

If his father had been alive, he would have reminded Selim that it was improper for him to mingle with actresses who wore short-shorts and drank martinis, but his father was gone, and as far as Selim was concerned, Old Istanbul was gone with him.

He made his way to the center of the room, where a large table was covered with place cards. He discovered his own, directing him to table three. Scouring the room once more, he spotted Ayda, sitting alone at table eight. He watched her for a long moment. There was nothing bleak about her solitude. Rather, she looked like a queen on her throne, somewhat distanced from the little clusters of conversation all around. He reached for his pen, changed the three on his place card to an eight, then headed over and seated himself by her side.

A waitress passed with a tray of finger foods. "Some kibbe for you, sir?" He shook his head and turned his attention to Ayda. She waved away the waitress politely as other guests began filling the seats around them.

Selim leaned over to say something but found himself tongue-tied.

She glanced discreetly in his direction. "Are you following me?"

Without answering right away, he leaned back in his chair. "What would make you think a thing like that?" He offered up a charming smile.

She uncrossed her legs and reached for his place card. "The original seat assignment is written in black ink," she said evenly. "Your additions here are in blue." She placed her elbow on the table, resting her pointed chin on her palm, and challenged him with her big brown eyes.

Draping his arm over the back of her seat, he studied her. "Would it bother you if I were?"

She turned away and muted her smile.

In the background, the rambling speech of a committee chairman sounded from the speakers.

Selim kept his eyes on the speaker, who was saying something about children in Istanbul suffering from iron deficiencies. "I'm so tired of these talking heads," he said low enough that no one but they could hear. He sipped on his second glass of whiskey, closing his eyes as the burn trickled down his throat.

"I couldn't agree more," she said and looked at him. "By the end of the night, they'll have raised close to a million dollars." As she adjusted her hair, the ends of her waves grazed his fingers, a move so slight, he was unsure whether she had even perceived it.

"What's wrong with that?"

"Come next year, the bellies of all those children will still be empty, and the pockets of all these guests will still be full." She surveyed the room as she spoke.

"Then why are you here?" Selim pressed.

Her eyes met his, studying him for a long moment. "It's in my contract."

"Excuse me?"

"My producers think it's good press," she continued in a low, breathy voice.

Selim frowned.

"It's not the whole truth," she admitted after a time. "I did *push* for it to be in my contract. I thought it would force the network to be more socially conscious." She leaned in, her expression uncertain. "They're sponsoring the event, which is what I'd hoped for, but the more I learn about how these organizations are run, the less certain I am of what, if any, goodwill come of it." She placed her hands in her lap and sighed. "What about you?"

The shifting spotlights did nothing to turn his attention from her, as the chattering crowd and music retreated to the periphery of his mind. He dared not avert his eyes for fear such a move might cut the flow of electricity between them.

"What would you like to know?"

She smiled primly, then shifted her eyes elsewhere. "Are you here on your own?"

"I am."

"And you don't have anyone waiting at home for you," she said matter-of-factly.

"What makes you so sure about that?" He smiled.

She took a sip of her drink, placed the glass back down, and looked up. "I saw you walking alone."

"That doesn't mean a thing."

"But it does. You're very good at it."

"Good at walking alone?" he scoffed.

"Most people look terribly uncomfortable walking on their own." She paused, then blinked a few times. "But not you."

He studied her quizzically.

"You look like you've been doing it all your life."

He inched forward and studied a sphere of black and amber bands radiating out from pupils dark as granite. "I could say the same about you."

She lifted her chin and held his gaze. "I've had all my life to practice." She frowned.

"If practice makes perfect, I'm a pro."

"I don't normally talk this way," she continued demurely.

"Nor should you."

"No?" She pursed her lips and raised her brows.

He shook his head slowly, then fixed his stare on her mouth. "Someone could get hurt."

"How's that?" she asked playfully.

Leaning back against his chair, he eyed her skeptically. "Mademoiselle, do you really have no idea just how dangerous you are?"

Rolling her eyes, she lifted her napkin from her lap and brought it to rest at the edge of the table. *"Pardon."* She stood, then surveyed the room for a moment, her lean and stunning frame reminding him of the obelisk in the courtyard.

He studied the sculpted cliffs of her bare neck and jutting, almost masculine jaw.

She removed a tall cigarette from a jewel-encrusted purse. With it perched between her fingertips, she leaned forward to catch the flickering candelabra beside him. As she did so, she brought her lips past his, taming the flame with a few short breaths and offering him a tantalizing trace of her eau de parfum. She straightened up, smiled, and polluted the air nonchalantly before reaching for the fur shawl draped over the back of her chair.

"Leaving already?" he asked evenly.

She swept her hair to one side and took hold of her purse. "I think it's just the right time. Besides, you should be thanking me."

"For what?" He looked up.

"For getting you out of harm's way, of course."

She smiled slowly, and when she did, a warm tingle ran down the back of his thighs. She turned, exposing the smooth, fleshy scoop of her backless ensemble, and sauntered away.

He watched the tiny vertebrae in her back as she walked in the direction of the exit, and a moment later found himself following her out of the banquet. In the grand entrance hall, his steps echoed off green stone tiles and high-vaulted, flat-frescoed ceilings. From the banquet hall came laughter and a round of applause, muffled by the thick, wood-paneled doors that had closed behind them.

He followed her until her silhouette slowed and stopped at a centuries-old wrought-iron gate. With her back to him, she shifted ever so slightly so that the outline of her lips and nose were on display.

Selim watched the stem of her cigarette glide toward her mouth. His eyes lingered as a cloud of smoke escaped her lips.

"You're doing it again," she said without so much as flinching.

"What am I doing?" His voice sounded low and raspy in his ears.

He moved toward her so that when she turned to face him, she seemed surprised to discover no more than a few inches of space between them. With upturned eyes and a lowered chin, she said softly, "You're following me."

Without so much as blinking, he took hold of her cigarette and let it fall to the ground, grinding it beneath the tip of his shoe.

"Do you always just take what you want?"

He leaned away slightly. "Sometimes the thing I want comes for me first."

Lifting her face haughtily, she brought her hands up to his cheeks and pressed her lips up against his. She pushed in close, delivering a warm kiss tasting of plum-flavored martini and cigarette smoke. After a moment, he backed away and gently scolded. "Bad habit."

"There are worse things."

"I'm sure," he whispered.

"Don't you want to know my name?"

He ran his hands down the back of her dress, then pulled her into him. "I know your name." He smiled, took hold of her hands by his side, and kissed her once more.

16

They drove to his apartment, small but luxurious and situated in Bebek, one of the more chic areas on the European shore of Istanbul. He parked his car out front, then came around to open the door for her.

"This way." He took her hand and led her into the dimly lit lobby, stopping at the base of the staircase leading to the second level. Running her hands down the length of her fitted black dress, she smoothed out the creases and adjusted the fur shawl draped around her shoulders.

"You look great." He moved in closer.

She pursed her lips, then eyed his parked car through the building's entrance.

"I can drop you home if you'd prefer." He was surprised by the words that escaped his lips.

She turned back to him. "Is that what you want?" She seemed taken aback.

"No, but I just thought—"

"You thought I was a girl who didn't know how to make up her mind?" Ayda crossed her arms. "I'm not one of *those* girls."

Selim felt his throat go dry. Looking at her now, he saw a woman who could hold her own in any situation.

As she stood there smugly, he could not help but admire her. He felt the corners of his lips curl upward right before saying, "No, you certainly aren't one of *those* girls."

Her stance softened as she flattened her lips and tried to hide her smile.

Though he'd never thought much of the women he brought home, something in Ayda's demeanor set her apart. He suspected that she was the kind of woman who could be vulnerable and yet not give up an ounce of strength. Certainly, Ayda Turkman was a woman who knew her worth.

"Mind if we go up?" she asked casually enough. "I could use your powder room."

He nodded without much fanfare. They ascended the flight of stairs, turned at the top, and continued down the dark hall until they came to a halt before his door.

"Looks like the bulb's out." He reached into his pocket and felt for his keys. "Just a minute." They stood quietly with only the sound of keys jingling between them.

He stepped inside, flipped the light switch, and turned to Ayda.

Leaning against the door post, a slim cigarette holder between her fingers, she exuded an air of old-world elegance. The sight of her there—with her clear-eyed gaze and impish pout—made him smile. "Do come in."

She dropped her shawl on a low console as she stepped inside, her stilettos clicking against the hardwood floors as she moved gracefully through his apartment.

She stopped before a long corridor leading to his bedroom. The hall walls were covered with framed portraits of men, some old, others young, but all wearing enormous white turbans and the same stern expression.

"Who are they?" She turned to Selim.

He smiled shyly. "The sultans." An awkward silence passed between them. "All thirty-six of them."

"Your family?"

"That's right."

Her eyes scanned the portraits along the length of the hall, settling on one in particular. "Who's that one?" Ayda pointed at a young sultan with a glint of madness in his eyes.

"Ah, that's Murad the Third." He placed his hands behind his back. "Awful legacy," he thought aloud.

"Why? What happened to him?"

"It doesn't matter what happened to him. It only matters what happened *after* him," he said teasingly.

"What do you mean?" She turned and faced him directly.

"Every sultan descended from Murad is thought to be cursed."

"I've never heard that, and I know my Ottoman history."

Selim laughed. "There is Ottoman history, and then there are the Os-man Secret Chronicles. This isn't the sort of thing that made it into your Turkish history textbook. The chronicles have been well guarded through-out the generations. They document the private life of every sultan through-out history, passed down from one sultan to the next."

"And you have these chronicles?" Ayda asked incredulously.

"I do."

"And you'd give up these secrets so easily?"

"They're family secrets."

"Go on."

"I have no family." He put his hands in his pockets and shrugged lamely. "And so there is no need for secrets." He cast his eyes downward, pretending to take an interest in the scuffed tip of an otherwise polished shoe.

They both stood quietly for a long moment.

"Did you still want to use the powder room?" he said, hoping to turn the conversation.

She shook her head. "So what do the chronicles say about Murad the Third?" she pressed on.

Selim took a deep breath. "His chapter was written on his deathbed by an imperial scribe charged with penning Murad's most intimate thoughts. It seems his beloved died before they could marry. The body of the girl was never found. No grave was ever marked, and so, unable to accept the loss, he kept soldiers on the lookout for an emerald-eyed beauty possessing a ruby ring. He spent the rest of his life waiting for her return. Those around him believed that he had simply gone mad. It is said that Murad's bitterness was so great that after his death, it rose above the palace and hovered like a curse, casting a dark cloud over every future sultan. It is said that each and every one was haunted in his own way, possessing a bit of the madness and despair that eventually destroyed Murad."

"And you?"

"Me?"

"Yes, you."

"What would you like to know?"

"Are you cursed? I need to know what I'm getting myself into." She smiled mischievously. "Do you possess the *madness*?"

He grabbed her by the waist. "I certainly do."

"My eyes are brown. Does that mean we don't stand a chance?"

"We can always fit you for colored lenses."

She shoved him playfully. "Are you *mad*, Selim Osman?"

"The only thing that's driving me mad right now is you." He pulled her close and kissed her hard. And though her eyes were closed and her lips parted, Selim could sense some hesitation on her part.

"What is it?" He pulled away.

"Oh, it's nothing." She shook her head and tried to kiss him once more.

"No." He pushed back. "Tell me what you're thinking."

She sighed, then looked away. "It's just that, you mentioned before that you had no family."

"*And?*" His tone grew defensive.

"I guess I was just wondering what happened to them. I mean, that's quite a bomb to drop without explaining further."

He raised one brow incredulously. "You know very well what happened to them." He let his hands fall from her waist and took a few steps back.

"Selim—"

"I'm sure you read about it in the gossip pages."

She shrugged apologetically. "I was never one to read the gossip section."

He sighed. "I'm sorry. It's just that—"

"You don't need to explain anything. I shouldn't have pried."

He shook his head. "My brother passed away. He was fourteen. We were on a motorcycle. The thing skidded, lost control."

"My God. Fourteen? He couldn't have had his license at that age?"

Selim dropped his head. After a moment, he looked up. "My mother ran off to stay with her aunt in the countryside. I was sixteen. I think it was just all too much for her to bear."

"Selim—"

"It wasn't her fault. Don't think that for a minute," he was quick to add. "She was the kindest woman I've ever known. All goodness. When it all went down, something inside of her just cracked."

"You can't blame yourself."

"Can't I?" Selim countered, then added quietly, "When Ali died, a piece of her died too. She said good-bye to us as though she were stepping out for a few hours. She left us with nothing more than a pantry full of groceries and a note with the combination to the safe containing precious jewels the Osman women have had for generations. We waited several days before driving out to get her. My father was so sure she'd come back if only we gave her the space she needed to grieve. By the time we arrived, she was already gone. My great-aunt couldn't say where to."

"And that was it?"

"My father kept looking," Selim explained. "I think it was something he thought he should do on his own, something he should protect me from."

"What happened to him?"

Selim again shook his head. "He slipped into a depression. Passed a few years ago."

"Was it the *madness*?"

Selim leaned back and scoffed. "*Excuse* me?"

"The curse maybe?" she pressed on.

"I'm a modern man," Selim snapped. "That's all nonsense. It's not *real*."

"I'm sorry. I shouldn't have said that. I guess I just don't know what to say."

He looked at her, sensed nothing but sincerity, and calmed down. "Let me fix you a drink. Cabernet, merlot?"

"Make it a whiskey."

He poured her a drink over at the bar, then made his way back to the leather chair where she had seated herself. He handed her the whiskey but remained towering over her.

She threw back her head and gulped down the strong stuff as though it were a penance for a crime she could not name but was sure she had committed. When she was done, she wiped her lips with the back of her hand and looked up at him. "So you forgive me?"

"For what?" He feigned ignorance.

"My big mouth. It always gets me into trouble."

"I like your mouth," he said cheerfully. "It just says whatever it wants to."

She set her empty glass aside, stood up, and sealed her lips.

"Does that mean we're done talking?"

She nodded, then took hold of his tie and swung her arm playfully.

"That's it!" he teased as though he'd had enough. He lifted her up and carried her away, but before reaching the hallway leading to his room, he put her down so they might walk through together. She took his hand and led him down the long corridor.

As they walked, the gaze of thirty-six sultans bore into Selim from either side of the hall. They were silent, but they still prodded him, pushed him. They were constant reminders of the past when the past was all he ever yearned to be rid of. On this evening especially, he needed to forget. He squeezed her hand as they walked along. On this night, he couldn't bear to be alone.

He took her to his bed that evening, but it was Ayda who made love to him on the eve that marked the anniversary of his only brother's death.

17

Slow down, Brother. Slow down!

Selim was startled awake in the early hours of dawn. Those words
never ceased to haunt him. It was not just his head, but now his jaw was
aching too. He reached for the pillbox beside his bed and tried to pop
open the tight lid with one thumb. The pills went flying in the darkness
and rolled over the hardwood floor throughout the room.

He got out of bed and felt along the floor with his open palm. He
found one pill, brushed it off with his hand, and swallowed it, not
bothering with the water by the bedside. Branches rustled beyond the
window as gray shadows moved about the room like a caravan of night-
wandering Gypsies. The sheer curtains shivered in the breeze, their
tattered edges creeping out beyond the windowpane as the dark river rose
beyond.

Ayda lay on her side, her bare figure twisted upon the sheets. As the
sun pushed toward the horizon, he gazed at her body in the pastel hues
of dawn. Her pale torso undulated as she breathed, mirroring the quiet
ripples of the Bosphorus outside.

The wailing cry of a muezzin sounded from a mosque somewhere on
the Asian side of the sea. A moment later, another sounded closer to
home. Soon at least half a dozen muezzins could be heard calling the
faithful to prayer, their voices echoing from mosque minarets that pierced
the clouds all along Istanbul's skyline.

A blanket of fog hovered over the sea as the scent of morning dew
filled the room. Selim sat in the old rocking chair by the bed, waiting for
the ibuprofen to kick in and his headache to pass.

And still she slept. Her body, as sumptuously sculpted as a violin's frame, reminded him of the instrument *Baba* had given him years back. It was an original Stradivarius, a gift from the king of Spain to his grandfather on the occasion of his sixtieth birthday. It was one of only a few in the world, passed down through three generations of Osman men. The violin's thick varnish glowed magnificently, but one could still make out tiny nicks, marks of a previous owner's obsession.

Selim would open the case occasionally, just to have a look. It hadn't been touched in over a decade, and he was content to know that the instrument was unblemished by his own fingerprints. He kept its existence a well-guarded secret, locked away in its case on a high shelf at the back of his closet. The instrument would endure.

Selim was not used to the sound of another person breathing in his room. He wanted to reach out and touch her, to whisper, "Wake up," but he did no such thing. He just sat in his chair, separated from her by a dense space that seemed to pulsate as the chair rocked toward, then away from her.

Perhaps sensing his eyes upon her, she awoke a half hour later and turned to him, her face suddenly seeming younger, fuller. With her eyes half closed, she smiled drowsily, then pulled the sheet back over her.

They'd yet to share a single daylight hour, yet Selim was already convinced. Ayda Turkman was nothing like the bevy of young, eager opportunists and spent socialites who'd come prancing through his home and life. They'd come with their agendas, some to feel young again, others to feel important, but all seeking a kind of validation they'd not found within themselves. But they'd all come to understand that they had no place in Selim's future, so they'd slink out of his bed in the middle of the night, with makeup smeared and high heels dangling in their hands.

But not Ayda. It seemed to Selim that Ayda was not a woman who doubted herself. She was a woman who knew exactly who she was and why she'd come. Most of all, she knew her worth.

He watched her as she slept. It occurred to Selim that while she had little in common with those other women, there she was in his bed, lying in the very same spot where only a few days prior, a well-heeled jezebel had lain.

Looking at her now, he felt suddenly ashamed that he'd brought her to his place. He wanted her out of his life and back on her pedestal. She was a rising phoenix. He was a fading star. Though their paths might have briefly crossed, they were heading in opposite directions. He'd no desire to see her dragged down with him.

"You should leave." His husky voice startled her from sleep.

He stood up and made his way over to the night table, pouring himself a glass of water from the pitcher on the dresser. He took a long sip, then placed it back down, branding a dark wet ring on the mahogany.

"Leave? But it's so early?" she answered.

Selim scanned the room. Her clothes were strewn about the place. He gathered her purse, stilettos, and pink lacy bra, and found her satin dress in the warm, rumpled bedsheets. "I've got to get to work." He handed everything to her in a messy pile.

As he searched in his closet, she rose and left the room, returning several minutes later with a cup of steaming black coffee. "I hope you don't mind," she challenged him in a sassy, irreverent tone, then tucked herself back under his Egyptian cotton sheets, her coarse black hair splayed against the propped-up pillow. She held the porcelain mug with two hands and sipped cautiously as a small plume of steam rose between her dark eyes.

He took note of a narrow gap between her two front teeth as she pursed her lips and blew air across the steaming liquid surface. No one else would have noticed, but his brother Ali had had that same tiny gap between his teeth.

"Why are you looking at me like that?"

"What?" He was jolted to attention.

"You're staring."

His eyes darted to a framed portrait of Ali by the nightstand. Forever fourteen, the lanky boy with the cheerful grin held a checkered ball between the cleats of his shoe and the bright green grass. Hidden beyond that grainy image, that tiny gap would remain forever.

"It's just that you remind me of someone." He draped his jacket over his shoulder before heading for the door.

"Is that why you brought me here?" she called back after him.

He halted his step and turned back to face her.

"Or perhaps it's why you want me to leave?"

He could feel the muscles in his face stiffen as he studied her. Her brash observation had caught him off guard. He felt exposed, even under attack. "*Excuse* me?"

"What?" She sat up and smiled. "I thought you liked my big mouth." She reached for her coffee and took a deep sip, tilting the cup up against her face.

He shook his head and scoffed, then took a few steps toward her. "You'll burn yourself like that." He reached over and took the cup away from her, returning it to the coaster by the bedside. "I've gotta get to work. Make sure to close the door all the way when you leave."

Plopping back against the pillow, she sighed theatrically. When she did, Selim couldn't help but smile. "I'll call you," he shouted back, though he knew he wouldn't. Then he grabbed his briefcase and headed out.

From his office in Maslak, Selim managed a dozen shopping centers throughout the city and several hotels near the airport. They were not the prestigious properties his family had once owned—luxury resorts along the Turkish Riviera, hotels in the Galata region—but he was proud of his work. Selim Osman had established himself as a formidable player in the world of Turkish real estate, despite the fact that the old family money had been confiscated along with the throne of the sultanate.

In the aftermath of World War I the region was in a state of chaos as the victorious allied powers sought to disband the empire, leaving only a fraction of land under Turkish control. It was then, in the fall of 1922, that the Osman imperial family, Selim's family, received word that the Turkish armed guard, led by a zealous young nationalist, was preparing to overthrow the sultanate. Just four years after he'd ascended the throne, Selim's great-grandfather was forced to abdicate.

The Ottoman era drew to a close as the secular Republic of Turkey was born.

Life in Istanbul changed drastically under the command of the country's reformer and national hero, Mustafa Kemal Atatürk. The lattices and opaque curtains that had once separated men and women on the trams and ferries, even in the university classrooms, were removed. Turks shed their traditional garb and donned a more "civilized," European style of dress. Women stopped wearing the veil. Men gave up the fez and caftan in lieu of Panama hats and British-cut suits. A new Turkish alphabet was implemented and women were brought into the workforce.

President Kemal Atatürk had ushered in a kind of rational Islam, where religion and science might coexist. And though he insisted that the government remain secular, he had no intention of banishing faith from the Turkish home. On the contrary, he proclaimed that Islam was a faith to be worshiped voluntarily by individuals, rather than forced upon all by the state. As to be expected, many among the religious clergy opposed his reforms, and yet the people rallied behind their blue-eyed, fair-haired national hero.

And though the creation of the Turkish Republic had been years in the making, it had taken just one day for the Osman royal family to be rendered obsolete. It was years before they were issued passports and granted Turkish citizenship, but once they were, the family was relegated to the ranks of ordinary, albeit esteemed, citizens of the new republic. For the first time in over six hundred years, the Osmans were forced to contend with the humdrum pace of ordinary life.

Selim Osman was no exception. He got to work at his desk, first paying his bills, then checking the monthly rent deposit slips before clicking through the news headlines and scouring his in-box. He deleted a bunch of junk mail until nothing remained but a single e-mail from his property site inspector. The subject heading read: SQUATTERS STILL INHABITING PROPERTY SIX. The cursor hovered over the message for a long moment, until finally he sent the unopened message to the trash. He rubbed his eyes and sighed deeply. For months, his inspector had been warning him that a man and a young child had taken up shelter in the otherwise uninhabited building. They'd have to be evicted, of that he was certain, but turning out the homeless was a thankless job he was none too pleased to do. And yet his inspector was under strict instructions not to take matters into his own hands. If it had to be done, Selim would see to it himself.

Just then Miro, the office manager, knocked on the door. He presented Selim with news of the day's pertinent events. A commercial tenant in the financial district was behind on his rent and could not be reached, and a water tank in one of the hotels was leaking and perhaps needed to be replaced altogether. Other than that, he was going down to pick up some lamb kebabs from the street vendor below, and would Selim like a skewer or two?

Selim spent the rest of the morning researching prospective new properties before enjoying his kebab and listening in on a long-winded conference call with some of his investment partners in Ankara. Later on, he took a taxi to property six, the small hotel near the airport where the squatters had taken up shelter. He'd been wary of turning anyone—much less a child—out onto the streets, but with a planned renovation scheduled to begin in just under a week, he now had no other choice. They'd have at least a few days' notice to locate a new shelter before the concrete-mixing trucks and jackhammers arrived.

Selim paid the driver and stepped out into the lot. He reached into his empty pocket, then scolded himself for having forgotten to bring along the building's keys. He circled the crumbling structure in search of an unlocked entry point, noticing a floor-to-ceiling frame half shielded by a loose wooden plank. Pushing the plank aside, he stepped through a space large enough to hold a door. "*Merhaba? Hello?*"

He headed down the hall, stopping before an open door, where a young boy slept on a thin mattress. A balding mutt lifted its snout and yapped loudly in his direction.

Startled awake, the boy leaped from his mattress and attempted an escape through the doorway. He stumbled over a pile of dirty clothes as he tried to maneuver his way past the stranger standing before him.

Selim took hold of the frantic boy and stooped down to address him. "It's all right," he tried to assure the boy before lifting his hands in the air. "You're not in any trouble."

"Please don't call the police," the boy pleaded while his dog carried on yapping. "We can leave."

Selim looked around and noticed a pair of men's slippers. A loaf of bread. A bottle of disinfectant spray and a roll of paper towels near a bathroom. "Who sleeps there?" Selim motioned in the direction of a second mattress across the room.

"I do." A quiet voice sounded from behind. "My name is Ozgur."

Selim turned to discover a rail-thin man with a bandaged leg standing in the doorway.

"We're leaving. Just give us a few minutes," the man said. "Emre, get your things. We have to go now."

Selim's resolve softened as he watched the man hobble across the room. "What happened to your leg?"

He picked up a duffel bag and placed a few folded shirts inside. "Work accident. Crushed under a falling steel beam."

Selim felt his insides contract as he imagined the excruciating pain the man must have endured.

"They don't employ cripples on construction sites," the man continued as he made his way toward the bathroom. He emerged a moment later carrying a bar of soap, a toothbrush, and a shaving kit.

"Well, you can't stay here for free," Selim muttered more to himself than to the man standing before him.

The man frowned, then motioned for his son to follow. He tried to push past Selim, but Selim held out his arm and blocked the doorway. "Hear me out. I said you couldn't stay for *free*. I didn't say you couldn't stay."

The man laughed bitterly. "Do we look like we have money? Emre sells gum and batteries on the side of the highway just to help us get some food to eat."

"You don't seem to understand. I have no problem employing someone with an injury."

He stared at Selim, his mouth hanging open. "No." He shook his head and dropped his hands to his side. "Are you kidding?"

"I'm trying to offer you a job. You can both stay here."

The man covered his mouth and looked on with wide, blinking eyes. "It can't be true," he mumbled under his breath.

"You'll be paid like everyone else," Selim continued. "Except for a small rent deduction for this space. Renovations start next week. What do you say?"

"What do I say?" The man dropped his bag, tipped his head up, and closed his eyes. "*Mashallah!*" he cried up to the roof.

"Yes!" The young boy jumped forward and wrapped his arms around Selim's long leg.

Ozgur then stepped forward, clasped Selim's hand, and shook it ecstatically. "Thank you, effendi. You won't regret this!"

Upon returning home late that evening, Selim discovered that Ayda had not left. In fact, she sat on his couch wrapped in his terry cloth robe, her hair wet and her feet bare. The television sounded, though she didn't seem to be paying any attention. Rather, she was crouched over with her feet on the edge of the coffee table, painting her toenails a bright shade of red.

Selim had fully expected to return home to an empty apartment. "You're still here?" He announced his arrival with both a statement and a question.

"Oh, hi!" She glanced up and smiled, but then went on painting her toenails.

He scratched his cheek and examined her oddly. "I don't understand," he said cautiously.

"What's that?"

"*Why* are you still here?"

She looked up and scrunched her brows as though *she* were the one confused. "You said you'd call me," she said matter-of-factly.

An awkward silence hummed between them.

"*And?*" He drew out the word.

"Well, you forgot to ask for my number." She smiled casually, then rose from her place and handed him a piece of paper. "There it is." She nodded toward the scrap while heading back to her seat.

His eyes widened as she slumped back onto the couch. He stared at the paper in his hand and shook his head in disbelief.

"You seem irritated. Is it the nail polish?" She held up the bottle and shrugged innocently enough.

Is this a joke? Selim wondered. He didn't know if he was more annoyed or amused.

"Found it in your medicine cabinet. Perhaps an old girlfriend's?"

When he didn't answer, she bit her lip and continued to tease. "Or is it yours?" She tapped her chin and tilted her head. "Though I really don't think this color suits you at all."

"You're a real trip, aren't you?"

"I've been called worse," she said, reaching for a pack of Marlboro Lights resting on the coffee table. His eyes moved to the glowing tip of her cigarette as she lit up and inhaled. "I'd prefer you didn't smoke in here." It was the very least of his concerns, yet the only one he could voice.

She seemed to contemplate this for a moment before standing up to look out the window by the couch. She took a few more puffs, then tossed the lean cigarette over the edge.

Selim mumbled something as he headed away from the sofa and toward the balcony doors. It was the anniversary of the accident and his battered heart was grieving. The last thing he needed was this girl in his way. "This really isn't a good time," he said before opening the doors and stepping out into the cool night. The sea beyond was dark, illuminated only by the reflection of light from homes along either side of the shore. From the suspension bridge to the north, the taillights of speeding vehicles shone in streaks of red. "Not a good time," Selim repeated under his breath.

The engine of a motorbike roared in the distance of his memory. *Slow down, Brother. Slow down!* His palms gripped the iron railing and he found himself leaning against it with all his weight.

"Well, I'm staying!" she called from behind, shaking him out of the memory.

He spun around to face her through the open balcony doors. *"Why?"*

Back on the couch, she leafed through the worn pages of a magazine before finally looking up. "You know why."

He was taken aback by her steadfast tone.

"Do I need to spell it out?" She placed the magazine beside her, then pointed a finger at the world beyond the side window. "You know as well as I do, *they* don't know what it's like." Her tone was stern, if not accusatory.

Understanding more than he cared to admit, he studied her seriously.

"I'm tired of walking alone," she admitted. "I know you are too."

As he stared back, he felt his resolve melt away, his back and limbs seeming lighter than before. He rubbed his eyes, exhaled deeply, and felt himself surrender. Walking straight back to the couch, he lowered himself onto the cushion by her side. He tilted his head back, closed his eyes, and tried to make sense of it all. The night they'd spent together had been surreal. For the briefest moment, she'd even helped him forget. The reality of his grim life, however, had returned that morning, reminding him of what he'd always known. That his was a hurt sure to last a lifetime. In his heart, he knew there could never be room for anything more than pain. In his heart, there could never be room for love.

Ayda Turkman deserved so much more.

He sat forward, then shook his head as if to say *This isn't a good idea.*

She brought her hand to his cheek and smiled. They sat beside each other for a few quiet minutes before he reached for her hand and wove his fingers through hers.

18

For the next few weeks, Ayda cooked dinner for him, looked after the hydrangeas on the small balcony garden, and kept the place tidy. Oftentimes he was welcomed home by the wonderful scent of börek, savory meats ground with onions and peppers stuffed away into fried pastry dough. She served him mint tea with a dash of pine nuts that gathered in a floating loop along the rim of his steamy glass. He'd come home from work and sip his tea quietly through a small cube of sugar held between his teeth and the tip of his tongue. Sometimes he'd read a book or play online poker with strangers who went by names like *Tommyboycruze* or *Jesusismyhomeboy*. Then he'd return to bed for something that might have looked like love, but hadn't yet been named.

Her loving satisfied him in a way that made his pain a little duller, a little less real. In his dreams, he spoke to Ali. "So much time has passed, and you're still so young," but it was not Ali who'd answer.

"Darling, I'm not young, I'm old. I always have been."

"Ayda, is that you?"

"It's me," she would whisper. "What's wrong?"

"You should leave," he'd say, though the squeeze of his hand begged her to stay.

But being a woman who knew what she wanted, Ayda paid him no heed. She stroked his hair and draped her arm over him before pushing in close and falling back to sleep.

And though initially Selim had not wanted her there, he'd succumbed to her charms and let down his guard without even knowing it. Still, he told himself that this was nothing more than a fling. Though he had a half-empty closet in his study, he made a point of offering her only a few dresser drawers. Rather than take offense, Ayda shook her head at him, as though she were dealing with a silly, stubborn child. "I'll make a man of you yet, Selim Osman," she teased. All the while he continued to convince himself that she'd never get hurt because he'd keep it casual, take it one day at a time.

And while she laughed off his hesitation to commitment, he knew such a thing was no laughing matter. Ayda Turkman deserved to be with a good man. He told himself that one day she'd come to see this on her own. On that day she'd pack up her things from the few drawers she'd been allotted, walk out the door, and find a man who could offer all the love his sad heart never had to give.

It was 7:30 a.m. Selim sat on the living room sofa, leafing through the morning paper and sipping on his espresso. He folded his paper and tossed it on the table, catching a glimpse of the weather forecast for the day.

It was set to be a cool February morning with scattered rain throughout the day. "February," Selim wondered aloud. Had it really been three full months since Ayda Turkman had settled into his home and into his life? The days had sped by.

Ayda strolled down the hallway wearing a dangerously chic white pantsuit and red-soled Louboutin pumps. Her dark hair fell in loose waves, styled with a curling iron.

"You're up early."

She made her way toward the couch, leaned over, and kissed him quickly. "I've got an early breakfast." She glanced at her watch, then made her way to the open dining room, placing what appeared to be a journal on the glass table.

Selim sat forward. "What's that?" He got to his feet and made his way over for a closer look. Its moss-green linen case was embellished with silver stitching, mirrored beads, and loose threads where some stitching had come undone. The notebook was fashioned with the same tawdry fabric that covered countless knickknacks sold throughout the Grand Bazaar.

Ayda's long fingers hovered over it. As Selim looked at her, she turned toward the sea. Her dark eyes met his in their reflection on the glass window, and she stood while the waves lapped over them.

"What is it?" Selim nodded in the direction of the notebook.

She stepped away from the window, vanquishing the phantom that had been floating over the glass. "It's my journal," she said, hugging her arms to her chest.

"What do you write about?"

"Everything. Nothing." She shrugged. "I've been writing since I was a kid. I didn't have anyone to talk to." Her hands fell to her sides and she stood a little taller. "That's why I began to write. It just made me feel better. It's hard to explain, but when I wrote in it and read through it, it reminded me that I was someone, even if no one else knew it."

Selim frowned, his discomfort obvious. "It makes sense."

She glanced down at her watch. "I have to go," she said while heading for the door. "I'll be back in a few hours." She brought her hand to her mouth and cleared her throat with an *ahem,* then took hold of her purse and key and stood absolutely still, staring back at the notebook.

It was only a moment before her motive became obvious.

Selim followed her to the door and pressed his palm against it, preventing her from passing. "This isn't a good idea."

When she didn't answer, he took hold of her arm. "Ayda."

Her expression stiffened.

"What you want"—he shook his head—"it's something I can't give. Not to you. Not to anyone."

She averted his gaze. "I don't have to believe that."

Adjusting a few loose strands of hair, she took a deep breath and left without another word.

When the door closed behind her, he pressed his fingers against his temples and headed toward the bedroom. The morning episode did little to help the spreading ache behind his eyes and in his head. He withdrew a nearly empty bottle from his bedside drawer, then popped a few pills before returning to the living room.

The journal baited him from the dining room table. Ayda wanted to be known, and yet to know and be known was the very thing Selim Osman feared most.

He eyed the journal suspiciously. For a moment, it seemed as though the faint sheen of its green jacket had glared right back at him from atop the dining room table. He got up to fix himself another of cup of coffee, circling the table as he made his way to the kitchen. The journal had become his home's new center of gravity, and everything now seemed to revolve around it. He glanced at it warily as he made his way back into the living room. Selim lowered himself onto the couch, then rose as quickly as he'd sat.

He paced the room anxiously, knowing all too well that their relationship had gone far enough. More than a few times, he'd warned her that he had no interest in forming deep ties—not with her, not with anyone—and here she was, practically insisting that he read her diary. What was it that she saw in him? That didn't matter. It was only a matter of time before she'd be convinced of everything he'd been telling her all along.

Ayda's journal continued to call out to him from the glass table. Another moment passed before he found himself drawing nearer, until finally he took hold of it—or it of him?

He glanced at his watch. He'd be late for work if he started reading now.

Work be damned.

He opened the journal of Ayda Turkman and this is what he learned.

Ayda was born in a tenement in Tarlabaşi, a crumbling shantytown just a few miles from some of Istanbul's most elegant and renowned hotels. Since the age of four, she had studied and lived at an underfunded all-girls orphanage at the fringes of the city.

Her mother lived in a bunker with a dozen other women at the toy factory outside Istanbul, where she worked twelve-hour shifts. She'd take the bus into the city on Saturdays to visit her daughter. As gifts, she'd bring trinkets that she swiped from factory assembly lines, key chains and stuffed dolls intended for tourists frequenting the souvenir shops in and around the Grand Bazaar.

On her sixth birthday, Ayda's mother arrived with a big box tied with a white satin bow. "Every girl needs at least one good dress," she said before handing over the package.

Ayda tore away the wrapping and opened the box. Inside, she discovered a cherry-red eyelet sundress with a cinched waist and a full skirt. She slipped the dress on and twirled until she was sick. It was the most beautiful thing she'd ever seen.

When the girls weren't studying or doing chores, they'd watch old

Shirley Temple videos donated by a wealthy foreign couple years back. Not minding that they understood little of what was being said, the girls would sit on the tattered sofa of the "family room," clapping and wriggling as the little lady with the corkscrew curls sang and tap-danced to the tune of "On the Good Ship Lollipop" and "Animal Crackers in My Soup."

Ayda would sway her arms and commit to memory the words to songs she didn't comprehend. She'd run up and down the hallway stairs in her bright red dress, riding on banisters and curtsying, insisting that one day she too would be on the big screen, singing and dancing like an American movie star.

Taking note of the frivolous behavior little Ms. Shirley Temple had inspired, the headmistress denounced the tapes as foreign filth, then threw the entire box of VHS tapes into the trash. Though she and her friends spent a full day sulking, Ayda soon found new ways to amuse them and herself. She fashioned mancala games for her and her friends, using egg cartons for boards and jelly beans for chips. Other times she'd cut out paper dolls, build castles out of cards, or play leapfrog in the yard.

For as long as she knew her mother would return, she kept finding reasons to smile.

And yet for Ayda Turkman a happy childhood was not meant to be.

The orphanage would become her permanent home the day of the big earthquake a year later, when the shoddy roof of the factory collapsed, trapping hundreds of assembly-line workers inside. Every Saturday for months, she would put on her good dress and spend the afternoons looking out the window, waiting for her mother's visit. But as the months dragged on, Ayda grew fearful that her mother might never return.

Her friends and classmates tried to reassure her. It was suggested that perhaps her mother had met a wealthy oil tycoon, a shipping magnate, or a royal Saudi who had whisked her away to Europe, where the two were perhaps honeymooning. It had happened to one of the girl's half sister's third cousin, and it was agreed upon by all that if such a thing could happen once, surely it could happen again. It was only a matter of time, they assured her, before her mother and new father would come to collect her, and when they did, they'd arrive in a brand-spanking-new chauffeur-driven Mercedes-Benz.

But not all of their theories regarding her mother's continued absence were as benign. Aysegul, the oldest girl of the bunch and the only one to have her ears pierced, suggested that perhaps her mother had been taken as a domestic slave and was locked in a basement somewhere in the rural countryside. Still, she made a point to tell Ayda that there was no need to worry. Surely it would just be a matter of time before her mother attempted an escape and returned to claim her daughter.

After nearly four months, the emergency relief workers who had been on the ground that day discovered that a few of the victims' family members had slipped through the cracks and never been made aware that their loved ones had perished.

When the headmistress called Ayda into her office to share the news, she hugged Ayda for the first and only time, then gently tried to explain that her mother would not be returning. But it was Ayda who was soon trying to comfort the headmistress. She assured her that—like the cartoon she'd watched that morning—her mother had simply bumped her head and could not recall the address of the building. She'd come as soon as she remembered. It wouldn't be long at all.

Ayda grew up in that orphanage with dozens of other girls, sharing tears and beds and memories of parents once known or only ever imagined. Not truly accepting that her own mother could be gone, she began instigating all kinds of trouble and acting out.

During dinnertime one evening that same year, she sneaked into the headmistress's chamber, a cramped space just down the hall from where the girls slept. She unrolled a dozen reams of toilet paper all throughout the room, then tossed a stack of magazines out the window. Sweaters and socks and shoes were flung about the place. She smiled while looking around at the mess she'd made, concluding that perhaps a few finishing touches were in order. With a blunt crafts scissor, she cut the bedsheet to strips, then filled a cassette player deck with a tube-full of toothpaste.

She took credit for her actions, feeling little guilt or remorse, and demanded to be sent home. The headmistress—herself a poorly developed product of the orphanage—whipped Ayda as she'd been whipped by her own headmistress back in the day. Then she turned Ayda around, looked straight into her eyes, and informed her bluntly, *Your mother is dead.*

And so it was that Ayda came to the understanding that her mother would never come back. The meaning of that ugly word was now crystal clear. She cried all through the night. "Dead means *dead*!" she shouted into her pillow. Though her friends sought to console her, she pushed them away.

She could not be comforted.

Her mother was *dead*.

Accepting that reality did not bring Ayda even the smallest measure of closure or lessen the pain of her mother's absence. Over the course of the next decade, she grew increasingly defiant. She'd be caught shoplifting, sneaking boys into the house, and cheating on exams. By the time she was fifteen, she was flunking every class.

On the eve of her birthday, Ayda's derelict behavior would finally catch up with her. It began ordinarily enough, with a bottle of stolen vodka and some cigarettes from the tobacco shop down the road. After unveiling the contraband to a close group of her most mischievous allies, they all agreed to hold off partying until midnight, when everyone else was sleeping. At the stroke of twelve Ayda would officially turn seventeen.

Minutes before midnight, five teenage girls descended the stairs and entered the deserted common area known as the family room. They giggled and whispered while taking swigs of vodka, then spent a few clumsy moments lighting cigarettes in the dark. Soon they were laughing fiendishly, choking on smoke and spilling their secrets. A carelessly handled match fell to the couch, causing a slipcover to catch fire. Quick to snuff it out with the frenzied blows of a nearby chair cushion, they burst into laughter before discovering the headmistress standing at the base of the stairs. She was gripping the banister, eyes narrowed and an angry expression on her face.

Ayda was quick to take responsibility for the fiasco. She didn't want to see her friends punished for a scheme she herself had concocted. The sleeping girls were woken up and informed of Ayda's latest misconduct. Called out from their beds and made to stand by, Ayda was instructed to lie down on her bed, buttocks up, before she was whipped with a man's belt reserved for just such occasions. Alcohol was haram—forbidden according to the Koran.

She was prohibited from attending classes and assigned to kitchen and cleaning duties for the next few weeks. One day, while she was scrubbing the communal toilet bowl, the door swung open and one of the staff members popped her head in. "You're done here. Go pack up your things." Without waiting for a reply, she disappeared as quickly as she'd appeared.

In the afternoon, Ayda was called into the main office and told that her time in the orphanage was over. She was a corrupting influence on the other girls, a cancer that needed to be cut out before it spread. Hard as they'd tried, they'd failed to shape her into a respectable young woman. The headmistress went on to explain that although it was beyond the scope of her mandate to arrange marriages for the girls in her care, she'd made a special exception in Ayda's case. She'd identified a suitable match, someone she believed would be capable of disciplining her where she had clearly failed.

Ayda was given a Koran as a parting gift, along with an empty orange crate in which to store her belongings. They weren't much anyhow, an oversize pair of two-toned shoes, three or four gray uniforms, a few lipsticks she'd kept hidden through the years. And the red eyelet dress from what seemed to Ayda a lifetime ago. Though she'd long ago outgrown it, she'd never considered leaving it behind.

A little over an hour later, at the base of the stairs in the family room, Ayda was introduced to her future husband, a man three inches shorter than she, with an oily head and a big round belly. She knew right then and there that she could never marry him.

As he looked her over, he flashed a creepy grin exposing a gold-capped front tooth. "Her hair always this wild?" he asked. His leering eyes took stock of her every inch, though his words were directed at the headmistress.

"I'm afraid so, and I should warn you, Mr. Dogmaci, she refuses to cover it."

With his wrinkled sleeve, he wiped the sweat from his forehead, grunted, then licked his lips. "I'll take care of that." He reached for the ends of her tangled ringlets before taking her crate from her. "Meet me at the car," he instructed before turning around and heading toward the lot.

She was bid farewell by her friends, who hugged her one last time. They stood in their uniforms, huddled in the doorway of the building's entrance, waving good-bye as the rusty hatchback pulled away from the only home she'd ever known.

All throughout the car ride, Mr. Dogmaci chatted on his cell phone while Ayda watched the world slip away like a river running in the wrong direction. They passed palaces and old crumbling mosques. Streetcars bustled by and deliverymen on bikes went about their business. Gypsy children begging for change threw themselves at the windshield at each traffic light, and Mr. Dogmaci barked out the window and threatened them with his fat fists.

Stuck in the afternoon traffic, the car stopped beside an old lady with an ancient face and silver hair cascading about big black eyes. While Mr. Dogmaci was busy laughing on his cell phone, Ayda rolled down the window.

The old lady approached and extended her hand. In it, she held a single red rose. Ayda accepted this gift without a word, the only true gift she'd received in the decade since her mother's passing.

A half hour passed before the car stopped outside a half-built structure at an abandoned construction site. Exposed steel columns protruded up from the top few levels, and a broken-down tractor lay in a nearby ditch.

He got out of the vehicle and led her up the dusty path to a ground-floor studio. Ayda looked around the place. There was a bare mattress on the ground and a toilet but no sink, separated from the rest of the room by a curtain stapled to the ceiling.

"Let's eat!" Mr. Dogmaci announced. He prepared a single piece of broiled chicken. "You'll be the one cooking the meals from now on," he explained. When he was done eating, he offered up the remnants of his meal to Ayda. "There's nutrition in the marrow," he said as he passed her a plate of bones.

After clearing away the dishes, she retreated to the mattress. Exhausted and hungry, she dozed off into a fitful sleep while Mr. Dogmaci watched foreign videos on the outdated television set.

She wasn't sure how long she'd been asleep before she woke to find him unzipping her jeans. She struggled to get to her feet, but quickly realized she didn't stand a chance against his two-hundred-plus pounds. "Stop fidgeting! You know I didn't get a penny for you."

She pleaded for him to stop, but he went on rationalizing.

"No one would have taken you in," he said as he yanked the jeans from around her ankles. "I'm a charitable man, you understand?"

Ayda thought to scream, but when she turned toward the window and saw nothing but an abandoned lot, she blotted away her tears, gritted her teeth, and forced herself to yield to his touch. When he was done, he pushed her from the mattress and told her to sleep on the floor.

Ayda waited until she could hear him wheezing in his sleep. Then she gathered her things and headed to the door, snatching Mr. Dogmaci's long overcoat on her way out. She slipped away from that drab apartment and on to her unknown fate, running alongside a beaten sidewalk for a quarter of a mile before stopping to catch her breath and dress herself properly.

With nowhere to go, she joined the invisible class of Istanbul's underworld, taking shelter at first in the cavelike nooks in the city's ancient crumbling walls, and later along the embankment of the river, beneath a more recently built bridge. It seemed to Ayda somehow safer, as the police could often be spotted patrolling the area at night. There she lived alongside squatters and river rats, sleeping on a bed of gravel and grass in the shadows of two enormous concrete columns. To put off the advances of vagrants and lurking predators, she'd behave like a feral child, ranting and screeching incomprehensibly at any strange man who dared to approach.

At night she'd wash herself in the fountains of public parks. And when she was hungry, she'd scavenge scraps from the Dumpster of a nearby café. This went on for a few weeks until she was discovered sifting through the trash with a half-eaten pizza crust crammed between her mouth and fingers.

Expecting to find no more than a few stray cats clawing through her bins, the restaurant owner approached with a bright flashlight and a tall broom in hand. What she found instead was a disheveled teenage girl in an oversize man's coat, crouched behind her plastic garbage bins. The kind woman invited Ayda into her kitchen, where she served her up a bowl of hot lamb stew. Later that night, she offered Ayda a basement to sleep in as well as a job working in her restaurant.

Ayda spent the next two years waiting tables, sweeping floors, and scrubbing pots until her skin began to flake. It seemed as though she were destined for a lifetime of servitude when one day the restaurant manager told all the staff to take the week off, as the restaurant had been rented out to a production crew who thought it a charming location to film the opening scenes of a sitcom pilot.

For the first time in two years, she was granted paid time off from work. She could hardly believe her good fortune. Sensing that somehow her luck was about to change, she headed over to the bazaar and spent a fifth of her savings on a cheap red dress. *Every girl needs at least one good dress*, she remembered her mother's words.

Ayda headed away with her recent purchase, swinging her shopping bag and hoping for the break she so desperately needed. She hadn't thought it through and she didn't have a plan, but of one thing she was certain: she'd not be scrubbing pots forever. Ayda sat on the film set in her polyester frock, waiting to be noticed, for three days straight. She paid close attention as the actors delivered their lines, take after take, scene after scene, envisioning herself as one of the actors strutting about on set.

On the fourth day, something rather serendipitous occurred.

A sudden shriek rang through the air as one of the supporting cast members tripped and fell while walking in high heels on the old cobblestone street. Her gasps and groans were soon met with the sound of sirens, and an ambulance with flashing lights arrived to cart the actress away.

Ayda watched the director shake his head frantically as the ambulance pulled away. "What are we going to do now?" he shouted at his crew. "We need to finish the opening scene *today*! We're not working on an unlimited budget, people!"

Ayda smoothed down her dress and made her way over to the director. She tapped gently on his shoulder, causing him to turn abruptly.

"What!" he barked at her.

"I know all the lines. You can finish shooting today."

The muscles in his face began to droop. He stared at her blankly before his eyes narrowed and his face reddened. "Who the hell is this!"

"I know the lines," she repeated calmly.

"Anyone know who this is!" He spun around, shouting to no one in particular.

She swallowed a knot rising in her throat.

He blinked a few times, then shook his head. "Listen, sweets, this is a professional production company. Experienced actors only. Go home."

He turned and walked away, and as he did, a strange thought dawned on her.

If it was experience that he wanted, she had more than her fair share. Enough, in fact, to last a lifetime. She'd not give up now. Not now, not ever.

"I have experience!" She hurried after him and planted herself directly in his path. She thought back to the lonely years of her childhood. She thought back to the rape, her escape, and the cold nights she'd spent sleeping beneath a bridge.

"Believe me"—she looked up at him with all the determination she could muster—"I have experience."

He frowned and cursed under his breath before spitting on the dry dirt and tossing the script in her direction. "You have one shot," he said, eying her sternly. "You better not be wasting my time!" And to his crew he yelled, "Let's retake the last scene where the character's introduced!" He marched off and left Ayda standing in her cheap red dress, clutching the script in her arms and whispering thanks to Allah.

Later that day, after landing the part, she resolved to never again wait for anyone or anything to give her the life she dreamed of.

She would take control of her destiny and seize that which she wanted most in life. She'd pay no heed to the rules of propriety, to her lowly status, or to those who had urged her to remember her place. Never mind that she was an uneducated orphan with no money or good name to speak of. She'd live by her wits and follow her instincts. They'd not yet led her astray.

As Selim read on, he discovered that the next several years would bring Ayda fortune and fame. She'd rise to become one of the nation's better-known television stars, all the while learning how to navigate her way through a web of hangers-on and admirers who—had they come across her years prior when she was homeless and living on the street—wouldn't have bothered to drop even a five-kurush coin into her cup.

He'd managed to read just over three quarters of the journal when he heard footsteps from down the hall. The turn of the knob and the click of the latch announced Ayda's arrival. She stepped in, her hair soaked and her mascara running down her cheeks. At some point in the past hour, it had begun to pour. Selim hadn't even noticed.

Her eyes moved to the journal that lay open on his lap.

He studied her for a long moment. Setting the journal aside, he stood and made his way to her. He now knew more than he ever wished to know, more than he ever hoped to understand.

There was something about that realization that frightened him to the core.

And yet Selim forced his fears aside, took her face in his palms, and wiped away the streaks of mascara running down her cheeks. Beneath his blackened thumbs, her skin was warm with shame. The hems of her pants were muddied, and her hair—just hours before perfectly coiffed—was pulled back and soaked in a tangled bun.

The sight of her brought tears to his eyes.

He took her in his arms, not sure if he was crying with her, crying for her, or perhaps crying for himself.

19

Since the day Ayda had left her journal out, they'd not spoken of it again. The days slipped by, and as they did, Selim found himself trusting more easily. He listened to her jokes, laughing even at the terrible ones. And when she burned his eggs, he ate them and assured her they weren't all that bad. She woke by his side and slept when he slept. In the mornings, they'd head off toward Maslak, Istanbul's business district. He'd drop her off at the production studio where she worked before traveling a few blocks farther to the basement parking garage of his office building. While they drove, he'd be entertained by the silly questions that always arose during her playful morning moods.

"If I were mute? Would you like me anyway?"

"Even more than I do now."

"What if I could remember every song ever played on the radio. Would you think that was strange?"

"That doesn't count. You *do* know the words to every song on the radio."

"What if I told you that I was a jujitsu world champion?"

"I'd look forward to being taken down."

"What if you came home one day to find I'd seared off my eyebrows in a cookstove accident. You opened the door and there I was. All done up, minus my eyebrows."

He turned to her and eyed her seriously. "Don't joke about that. You know how I feel about your eyebrows."

He gave up his jazz tunes and acquiesced to her pop music tastes, saying nothing when she rested her bare feet on the leather dashboard and belted out cheery Tarkan tunes.

Before he knew it, six months had passed. Ayda Turkman had taken a chance on him, and when she did, cracked open a door that had long been sealed. For the first time since the accident, Selim was experiencing a small measure of peace, no longer coming undone at the sound of every engine roaring along the freeway.

But while the pain in his heart had taken a backseat, the pain in his head had not. Week after week, the ache wore on, until one day it seemed to explode. On that morning, Selim drank black tea infused with jasmine, nearly overdosed on ibuprofen tablets, and stayed in bed all day. Ayda begged him to see a doctor, suggested he not work too hard and take more time to rest.

He didn't disclose to her what he suspected to be true. That the raging pain in his head was the physical manifestation of his guilt, a guilt that he'd naively thought he could do away with. The past half year with Ayda by his side, he'd challenged its power over him. And with her there, he *had* managed to suppress it. But as he'd always suspected, as he'd always *known*, his was a hurt that would never release him.

It was his second visit to the doctor that month. Selim filled out the necessary forms and returned the clipboard to Denize, the pretty nurse who took his blood pressure each time he visited. "We're glad you could make it. Your wife was quite insistent that we make some time for you this week."

"My *wife?*" He was intrigued and amused all at once. "She called here?"

"Oh several times. Mrs. Osman said that if we didn't hound you after your first appointment, you'd never come in for a follow-up. She said to keep trying until we reached you. That we should never expect a call back."

"Wow." Selim sat back. "She said all that?"

"Your wife really cares about you." She smiled as if to say, *You're one lucky man.*

He didn't correct her, didn't explain that Ayda was not his wife, only looked up and nodded.

"Make yourself comfortable," she continued. "We'll call you in when the doctor is ready to see you."

Selim took a seat in the brightly lit waiting area. He reached for a stack of newspapers, then leafed through the national daily. The entire front page was taken up by just one article. He skimmed the story and learned that the nation's most prominent writer would stand trial for the crime of "damaging national unity" under Turkish law 3713. The novelist, a world-renowned Nobel laureate, was being punished for broaching the topic of the Armenian genocide in his most recent book. He faced up to three years in jail.

His crime? Daring a nation to come to terms with its sins and its shame.

Upon reading the article, something stirred within Selim. He didn't stop to consider why this particular injustice so moved him; rather, he spent the next few minutes making a mental list of powerful family friends and acquaintances, individuals who might be called upon to aid in the man's release.

"Selim Osman, the doctor is ready for you," the receptionist interrupted his thoughts. "Straight ahead, fourth door on the left."

He put down his paper and headed along a narrow corridor tiled with yellow-and-white-checkered squares. He was instructed to remove his shirt and change into a blue gown. A few minutes later Denize came in and took his blood pressure. She asked a series of questions, nodding sympathetically as Selim went over his symptoms with her for the second time in weeks. "Headaches, night sweats, blurry vision."

"Now, as the doctor stated during your last visit, it's most likely nothing serious, but we'd still like to go ahead with a few tests. Better safe than sorry."

Selim smiled blandly, then nodded. He was happy to get this over with, if only to appease Ayda.

"The procedure will be relatively simple," Denize explained. "You'll be sedated. A thin tube will be placed through your nose and up toward your sinuses so we can collect the sample we need for testing." She went on to caution, "There may be some discomfort. Some soreness for the next few days."

Selim leaned back and kicked his legs up onto the exam chair. Rather than on the procedure ahead, his thoughts rested squarely on the fate of the novelist.

* * *

A week later, Selim received a phone call from Denize. "The doctor wants you to come in."

Selim opened his leather planner and flipped to the calendar at the back. "How's this Wednesday?"

"Can you make it in this afternoon?"

"I've got a meeting later today." His eyes scanned the pages of the calendar. The week was completely booked. It hadn't been easy, but he'd finally gotten an appointment with Abdul Gurat, an influential member of Turkey's government. He was one of the few men in parliament with enough clout to gain amnesty for the imprisoned writer. Selim had discovered that Gurat actually rented apartment space in one of the buildings he owned in Etiler. They were to meet later in the day at Gurat's home, where Selim would propose to cut the minister's rent down to almost nothing. He was hopeful that this gesture might help "convince" him of how unjust imprisoning the man would be.

"Selim, the doctor needs to see you."

A moment of static sounded between them.

"Selim?"

"Um, yes." He cleared his throat.

"It's about your test results. Can you come in today?"

"Wow, you guys must really like having me around," he joked, though the crack in his voice exposed his worst fears.

"When's the earliest you can get here?"

Silence.

"Selim? Are you there?" she asked through the crunching sound of static.

He glanced at his watch, then took a deep breath. "Still here, Denize," he said in a singsong tone.

"So when should we expect you?"

He dropped his chin and covered his eyes with his free hand. "I'll be there in an hour." He put down the phone and called his receptionist on the intercom.

"Call the minister, cancel my appointment."

"Effendi, it was not easy to get that appointment. I doubt he'll want to reschedule. He's a very proud man."

"Tell the minister an emergency has come up."

"But, Effendi—"

"Just do it."

It was only a ten-minute drive to the doctor's office, but somehow, it seemed the less time he had to speculate as to his diagnosis, the better. At the clinic, Selim was shown into the doctor's office, a space just big enough for a desk and two chairs. He made his way calmly, ready to accept whatever fate held in store.

A car alarm sounded outside. The doctor rose and made his way to the window overlooking the concrete parking lot below. He peered out for a moment, then shut the window, effectively muting the shrill sound. Dr. Ehrlich shook Selim's hand and gestured for him to sit down in a maroon upholstered chair. It was considerably lower than the swivel chair Dr. Ehrlich occupied, and Selim felt uncomfortable as he tried to straighten his posture.

"The results of your biopsy came back this morning," the doctor said, his spectacles bobbing up and down with each frown. "It's a rare form of cancer."

Selim's body slumped into the cushion as the doctor continued speaking.

"Sinus cancer typically strikes men over the age of sixty, and almost exclusively people of Asian descent. You really don't fit the profile at all." The doctor told him these things gently, trying to assuage the shock he likely expected from Selim, a shock that never came, because Selim had been expecting it all along.

"No one could have foreseen this," he continued. "If you opt for the surgery, there's a chance to increase your life expectancy by a few more years." Precisely how many? He could not say. He went on to clarify that without the surgery, he could not expect to live much longer than a few months.

It was not long before the bitterness gave way to a strange sense of relief. It occurred to him now that it was only fair—perhaps even *just*— that he too should die young. Cancer lived in the empty spaces behind his cheek and nose and jaw. Imaging had determined that it had most likely spread and infected the bone structure throughout the left side of his face.

And yet it was still less painful than the guilt. The guilt had spread through every bone in his body. For fifteen years, he had held himself responsible for Ali's death. Selim was the elder brother. Wasn't it his job to keep Ali safe?

Selim was experiencing a profound relief. It was as though he'd been held underwater for all these years, and now—having burst through to the surface—he was freely gulping lungfuls of air into his chest. For the first time since his brother's accident, he sensed order in his universe, that everything was finally as it should be. A life for a life. This realization filled him with calm.

"You must be feeling so many different things," said the doctor. "Do you have anyone you can talk to?"

He thought back to the video games he and Ali had played as children. *Baba* had brought the games back from business trips in America, and all the neighborhood boys would come to the Osman villa in Ortaköy to watch Selim and his brother battle with green aliens that took away lives just by zapping their neon bug eyes. In English, the words *Game Over* would come across the screen. "You're dead," Ali would scream. "My turn!" Selim's thumbs would ache and his eyes would sting from long hours in front of the television screen. In the end, he was usually relieved when the aliens would come with their spinning saucers, shine a light over his bleeding human remains, and zap him into a galaxy far away from home.

Game Over.

"Talk to me. What's going through your head?" the doctor pressed on. "Selim, say something." Dr. Ehrlich's lips were moving but Selim caught only scraps of what he was saying. "Treatment in New York . . . experimental surgery . . . buy yourself some time." Soon the room was quiet except for the whir of the ceiling fan overhead. Dr. Ehrlich handed Selim a glossy white folder that read "Coping with Cancer."

He stood up and the two men shook hands. "There's a lot to think about, but the New York surgery, if you turn that down, there's nothing left but half a year at best."

It was well deserved, poetic justice at last. He'd go to New York, where he would likely die on the operating table. If he survived, it wouldn't be for too long. He'd be looked after by strangers. He'd be mourned by none.

It's as it should be, Selim thought to himself.

"Book the surgery," Selim said matter-of-factly. "Book it for the end of the month. I need two weeks to get my affairs in order."

"Yes, Selim. I'll call New York and have it arranged. Might I also suggest, there is a wonderful counselor who can help you digest this information. She can help you prepare to break the news to your loved ones too."

Selim's thoughts went to Ayda. She'd shattered his defenses with her bright eyes and silly jokes, but it was her smile that had disarmed him completely. And when she'd offered up her heart, against his better instincts, he hadn't turned away. He cursed himself now for believing that the happiness of the past six months was something that could have lasted, something he deserved. While he could forgive himself for playing the fool, he could never forgive himself for hurting Ayda Turkman.

There could be no safer place for her than estranged from his touch.

The doctor cleared his throat, interrupting his thoughts. "So I'll have Denize get you the number?"

"That won't be necessary," he said quietly before nodding politely and heading away.

Game Over.

20

Selim returned to his office, not dropping so much as a hint to those around that anything was amiss. There was no need to pretend or temper his behavior in any way. Things felt perfectly natural. For once he felt comfortable in his own skin. And why shouldn't he? He was dying. Things were as they should be.

He went about his business, sitting in on an investor conference call, drafting a few e-mails to send later in the day. After work, he met up with Ayda and some of her actor friends for dinner and drinks at Sunset Lounge, a hip restaurant and bar. He laughed when they laughed and smiled when they smiled, though their jokes and lighthearted observations fell on deaf ears. On the car ride home, he kept his eyes on the road ahead, only half listening to Ayda as she prattled on about her day. There was a fight with her producer, and an angry coworker had thrown a punch. She rubbed her bare heels as she spoke, then lamented a choice in shoes that had left her feet covered in blisters.

It all sounded as though from a distance. He caught mere snippets of what she was saying, the rambling anecdotes of the living. Selim felt himself a mere spirit, floating farther and farther away.

Later in the evening, he was already in bed when she called back to him from her dressing table. "So you haven't mentioned anything."

He rolled onto his side. "What about?"

"I assume it's all fine. I know you would have said something otherwise."

"I'm not sure what you're talking about."

"Your appointment today." Her eyes were wide as she shook her head. "Were you going to tell me how it went?"

"What would you like to know?"

"What'd the doctor have to say?"

He examined her reflection in the vanity mirror. "He said it was nothing." Fifteen years of lying and he still could never get used to the sting of it. "Just a sinus infection gone untreated too long. He prescribed some antibiotics. The symptoms should be gone in a few days."

"See." She turned around and smiled. "It doesn't hurt to go to the doctor every once in a while. You could have been rid of those headaches months ago."

He frowned, then pulled the covers up over him.

"I was worried there for a moment. I mean, you've been complaining of headaches since I've known you. I'm happy it's all taken care of now."

"Yes," he said while adjusting the pillows behind him. "It's all taken care of."

"Good." She sounded cheerful as she picked up her brush and began combing her hair. "Did I mention that my agent says there's a leading role for me in a feature film?" She put down the brush when he didn't respond. "Did you hear me, Selim? A real movie. I've wanted to get out of television for so long." With her back to him, she again addressed him through her reflection in the vanity mirror. "Most of the filming will be done in Germany." She opened a drawer and withdrew a few hair pins. "I told him I wouldn't do it. I wouldn't want to be away for six months. There's so much I would miss here." She stood from her place and let her robe slip to the floor in a small heap.

Selim studied her.

The thought that she might forsake her dreams for him had always been frightening, but never more so than on that day. He knew now that giving up *anything* for him should never have been an option—not for Ayda.

Reaching for his phone, he feigned a lack of interest. "Like what?" He turned away from her as she tucked herself under the sheets. "Istanbul is an awful place," he continued. "You said yourself you wanted to get out of television. This is your chance." He unlocked the screen and began setting the alarm. As he did, it occurred to him that the real countdown had begun. Time was running out, for both him and for the imprisoned novelist. If he couldn't secure the pardon before the trial date, the man would most likely rot in prison for the next three years. This was the work of ultranationalist conservatives whose stranglehold on free speech was being used to quash all voices of reason. "Everything's going to shit," Selim grumbled as he turned back to face her.

"What's going on with you?"

What's going on? he thought. *I'm toxic, that's what's going on.* "I'm just saying, you should get out while you can. You see what they're doing to that writer Taguc?"

"I see that it's eating you up. Why do you care so much?"

"Taguc is willing to risk everything—his career, his family, his very life. All to expose the truth."

"What is the truth?" Ayda challenged him.

He turned to her and took a breath. "Our nation has a glorious history, but a very dark past too." He waited for his words to sink in.

After a moment, she waved her hand ceremoniously. "You may continue."

"How can we truly embrace the glory of our nation when we refuse to come to terms with the sins of the past?"

She looked at him briefly, then threw her hands in the air. "Why didn't anyone tell me I was dating a philosopher?"

"Is that what we're doing?"

"I was making a joke, and yes, we *are* dating. Let me take this opportunity to make an introduction. Selim, this is Reality. Your acquaintance is long overdue."

"There's nothing funny about what I'm telling you." He shook his head. "Embracing only one part of your truth. How can a person live like that?"

"A *person*?" Ayda examined him quizzically. "I thought we were talking about a nation."

"We are talking about a nation."

"You said person."

"I certainly did not."

Selim tossed off the covers and sat up. His eyes went to the framed portrait of Ali at the bedside. *Slow down, Brother. Slow down!*

"Selim?"

"I'm all right."

"What is it?" she asked tenderly as she came to his side.

He shook his head and covered his ears as the sound of shouting pedestrians and screeching tires ricocheted through his mind. He fumbled for the remote and quickly turned on the television set. Flipping through the channels, he settled on a late-night stand-up routine. He sat unmoved as the canned laugh track drowned out the hideous racket in his head.

"Selim," she said gently. Her fingers made their way to his shoulder. "You can tell me. You know I love you."

He wanted so badly to reply in turn, but instead just cleared his throat and shrank away. Somehow, she'd managed to position herself in the very center of his life. Selim was sure she could be in no more dangerous a place. "I'm no good for you." His voice sounded gruffly.

"What are you afraid of?"

He was quiet as he contemplated the question. "I just don't want to hurt you."

Her hand caressed his face before she leaned back against the headboard. "Don't you see, Selim? I'm not the one you're hurting."

In the two weeks leading up to his departure, Selim distanced himself from Ayda. When she'd urge him to tell her what was bothering him, he'd accuse her of meddling. "I don't need another mother," he'd snap. "One was plenty."

"This isn't about me," she'd challenge him.

"This is *only* about you." He'd recoil from her touch. But fooling an actress was no easy feat. Not in the least when all he really wanted was to take her in his arms and hold her there forever. He was certain that his cruelty was a kindness. He did everything he could to drive her away. Ayda Turkman was not a woman who would put up with being poorly treated, he reasoned. Strong-willed and independent, she would walk out on him any day now, write off the entire relationship, and think him a jerk.

The idea of her loving him, losing him, mourning him—it was a punishment Ayda didn't deserve and a sacrifice he could never hope to merit.

Two nights before he was to leave, Selim entered his walk-in closet, stepped up onto a folding stool, and withdrew the Stradivarius case from the high shelf at the back of the closet. He lowered himself onto the carpet and sat with the case laid out in front of him. After a time, he opened it and let his fingers hover over the instrument.

"It's beautiful." Ayda's voice sounded from behind.

He looked over his shoulder and found her standing there. Her smile was so kind, he felt himself flinch.

"Do you play?"

He shut the case and fastened the latches. "I wouldn't play this violin even if I could." He rose to his feet, mounted the stool, and returned the case to its rightful place. "It's far too precious for that." As he tried to brush by her, she took hold of his arm.

"Selim."

"What is it?" His voice bristled.

"I don't know what's going on," she said quietly, "but it's gonna be okay."

Gazing at her for a long moment, he nodded, then brushed past without another word.

Selim Osman treated Ayda Turkman with the same misguided adoration with which he had quarantined the Stradivarius in his closet. He was afraid to touch either one. He was determined to ensure that nothing would ever again be damaged on his account. The instrument was silenced, but it was also safe.

In the morning, Selim headed to his office for the last time and wrote checks for the electricity, cable, and phone bills. "I'm taking a few months off," he told Miro, his office manager and longtime protégé.

Miro just stood there, wide-eyed and not fully comprehending.

"So you'll be in charge of identifying new investment opportunities and strategies. All final decisions will go through you," Selim continued.

"Effendi," Miro spoke cautiously. "This really isn't the time for gallivanting around Europe. We're about to close the deal with Gulhemet for the new shopping plaza. The whole thing might fall through if he finds out you've skipped town."

"Don't worry about it."

Sitting upright in the chair across the desk, Miro eyed him nervously. "Are you going to tell me what's going on here?"

"Just taking some time off. I was over at Gulhemet's office after I left here yesterday. I had him sign off on the documents right then and there. The shopping plaza's a done deal. You've got nothing to worry about."

Despite Selim's reassurances, Miro looked worried.

"I have no doubt you can manage things here on your own, and to prove it, I've upped your salary. I think you'll be pleased when you get your new paycheck."

"Effendi, I don't know what to say."

"You'll also find I've allotted you six percent equity share in the properties I own." He handed a manila envelope over to Miro. "It might not sound like a lot, but when you account for all the properties we've acquired over the years, it adds up quite nicely.

"It's all there in the documents." Selim nodded toward the folder on the desk. "All you need to do is sign the papers and the lawyers will do the rest." He stood up, rounded the desk, and patted Miro on the shoulder. "You just keep doing what you're doing. You've got big things ahead."

Selim worked until early evening, taking great care to ensure that all his affairs would be in order for Miro. As the sun was setting, he headed to the hotel to say good-bye to little Emre and his father Ozgur. Over the past few months, he'd grown fond of them both. He'd drop in on them occasionally, and they'd share some dried fruits and drink some tea. Emre liked to talk about sports, which would always lead to a spirited debate. He was fiercely loyal to Istanbul's Asian soccer team, Fenerbahçe, though Selim insisted it would be Galatasaray on the Europe side to take the Turkish Cup that year. And though he usually came with gifts, on this day he came with more than the usual.

"I'm going on a trip," Selim explained to Emre once he'd arrived. "I brought you some things." He handed over a set of American DVDs, some chocolates, a soccer ball, and a Fenerbahçe jersey. "Lucky number ten." Selim turned the jersey over and held it up. "Şanlı's number, I know he's your favorite."

Emre's eyes lit up. "Thank you! Thank you!"

"Why don't you sit with us while we have our dinner?" Ozgur invited Selim as he boiled peas and carrots over an electric stove.

A small table was set with paper napkins, plastic plates, forks, and knives. Selim thought back to the years of his childhood, when they'd all have dinner at six o'clock sharp, he, Ali, *Baba*, and Mother. *Baba* would stroll in from work in his Italian suit and place his briefcase by the door. Mother, always in a pretty dress with her hair piled high, would beam with pride when her husband entered through the front door. She'd offer him her beautiful white smile and a kiss on each cheek before beckoning him to the dining room, where a steaming buffet awaited.

A wave of sadness passed over Selim as he took a seat by Emre's side. The boy sat in an oversize purple T-shirt that came to his knees. His skinny arms poked out like sticks and his dark eyes were wide. "You remind me of my brother." The words were quick to escape Selim's lips.

"You have a brother?"

He scolded himself silently, then looked away. "I actually forgot." He glanced down at the watch on his wrist and pretended he had somewhere to be. "I have an appointment in fifteen minutes!" He shrugged as if to apologize, then got to his feet and headed for the door.

"Please stay with us, please!" the boy called out as he followed Selim down the hall, trying to catch up. "I'll be your brother!"

Selim picked up his pace.

"Slow down, Selim, will you?" Emre called out.

The memory of an engine roaring cut through him. "Leave me alone!" Selim snapped as he rounded the corner at the far end of the hall. When he reached the lobby, he stopped and turned back slowly. His heart was beating fast. He made his way back up the dark hallway toward Emre, who stood under a fluorescent light, tears in his eyes. Selim crouched down and put his hand on Emre's shoulder. "I'm sorry," he whispered. Selim spotted Ozgur peeking out into the hallway. He swallowed hard, then took a deep breath. Selim kissed Emre's forehead and left without another word.

Selim got in his car and drove north along the highway known as Ataturk Boulevard, but after fifteen minutes on the road, instead of turning east onto the exit leading home, Selim just pressed the pedal down and sped on. Where he was heading, he hadn't a clue. All he knew was that he wanted to be somewhere else, to escape his home, his past, his self. He cruised beyond the urban sprawl past the forests until he was driving off-road along a bumpy path leading to a ledge overlooking the Black Sea. Through a crack in the window, he could hear the muted chatter of diners stationed all along the balcony of what he presumed to be a local fish restaurant just beyond the brush. He took note of a few cars scattered around before realizing that he had driven into the restaurant's parking lot.

It seemed that Selim had driven as far north as he could, and yet it had taken him no longer than an hour to get there. That was the problem with Istanbul, he mused bitterly. Running away, you could go only so far before you ran out of road. Instead of turning back and heading home, he turned off the ignition, rolled down the windows all the way, and focused only on the sea. The crashing of waves soothed his nerves while the taste of salt in the air cleared his mind and his senses. He closed his eyes and soon after fell asleep.

A knock on the roof startled him awake. "Having some car trouble?" a man said.

Selim squinted and sat up.

A young man in a waiter's uniform was crouching over. "Need me to grab some jumper cables from my trunk?"

"That won't be necessary." Selim grabbed the keys from the center console. "Thanks."

The man headed toward an old broken-down Fiat as Selim started the engine. He was about to pull away when he decided to check his blinking phone instead.

It was 11:37 p.m. He had six missed calls and ten frantic text messages from Ayda.

He rubbed his eyes with the palm of his hand, then drew out a long breath before typing out: *Just saw your messages. Sorry . . . Fell asleep at the office . . . Phone was on silent.*

Her response was almost instant. *Glad you're ok. Was worried.*

Be home soon, he tapped back.

K. Exhausted, going to sleep now. See you in the morning. xx

When he arrived home, Selim made his way through the hall into their bedroom. He stripped off his jeans and top, lowered himself onto the bed, and pulled the covers over him.

That night, more than any other, seemed especially dark. Beside him, he could hear Ayda breathing soundly in her sleep. He turned to her and drew his arm over hers, then kissed her one last time.

He went to sleep that night painfully aware of the small duffel bag packed and hidden beneath the bed. He'd had it prepared for some time. He was now as ready as he'd ever be.

21

Early the next morning, Selim awoke and said farewell to the world he knew. He'd already said his good-byes to his office manager, to Emre and Ozgur too, and even to his precious Stradivarius. And yet, he couldn't bring himself to say good-bye to the woman he loved.

On the bedside table, he spotted an envelope addressed to him in Ayda's handwriting. Perhaps it had been there all night, but it had been a dark, moonless night and he'd not seen it until now. He tore it open gently, removed the pink stationary, but stopped short of unfolding the note. The sweet smell of rose potpourri was more than he could bear. If he read her words, he might not be able to leave, and to leave was the kindest thing he could do. She would hate him, she would curse him, and then she would move on with her life. She would not mourn his death like his mother and father had mourned Ali. She was a survivor. He placed her note back on the night table.

As she slept, he dressed quietly before retrieving the bag beneath the bed and heading out of the room.

And though he could not bring himself to read her note, he found himself writing two of his own. He placed one in the kitchen and one in the safe.

It was time to go.

Ayda awoke to find Selim gone from bed. The night before, she had returned from the doctor's office the happiest she'd been in years. Her suspicions were confirmed—a life was growing inside her. She was two months' pregnant. Selim had grown more reticent with each passing day, so she had decided that a note would be the most suitable way to tell him. She'd gone to the calligrapher on her way back from the doctor, purchased an entire box of overpriced rose-scented stationary, and used six sheets of paper before she was content with her note. Now that note sat by the bedside, no longer in the envelope that she'd sealed the night before.

"Selim?" she called out to the apartment. When there was no response, she made her way into the kitchen, half asleep and still puffy-faced. "Selim?" she called out once more before deducing that he'd gone out to pick up some muffins and coffee. *A celebratory breakfast,* she thought to herself. She ran her hand over her belly and smiled. Selim Osman would make a wonderful father. And though he'd been unable to bring himself to say the words, she'd never once felt unloved. They'd not planned for a child, but perhaps a new life would give new hope. Perhaps it was all he ever needed.

A mustard-yellow morning light came streaking through the window and settled on a Post-it note stuck upon the refrigerator door.

Ayda—
Check the safe.

She tore the pale yellow square from the door and examined it closely. Turning it about, she found nothing else written. Looking around the apartment, she found nothing out of place. And yet she had a sense something was terribly wrong. She hurried to the bedroom, found her cell, and selected Selim from her favorites list with shaky fingers.

"The number you have reached has been disconnected," a mechanical voice informed her. A creeping panic began to take hold of her. Reading over the note once more, she heeded its directive and made her way to the living room and over to the safe that she'd never before had access to. The iron handle was cool to the touch and gave way easily beneath her trembling grip. Inside the safe, she found dozens of velvet pouches containing the jewelry his mother had left behind. She emptied the contents on the glossy wooden floors. Strands of pearls lay in a small tangled heap. She lifted a heavy necklace before her, shocked by the abundance of red rubies dangling like cherry clusters. There was an emerald, at least eight carats, surrounded by radiant diamonds and cast in a platinum setting. There were dozens of solid gold coins in every size and from every corner of the globe, and a beautiful pear-shaped diamond.

She quickly returned the valuables to their pouches, then shook her hands once as though ridding herself of something dreadful. There was something eerie about those treasures, though she couldn't say just what.

She tore away a letter she noticed on the inside door of the vault. Selim had written with impeccable penmanship:

Ayda,
I've left Turkey. You deserve to be loved. You deserve so much,
but I have nothing to give you, just the contents of this safe.
They're not much, but anyway, now they're yours. Please don't
wait. I don't want you to look for me. I don't want to be found.

Before heading to the airport, his driver cast a curious glance at Selim as he lifted the bag to load it into the trunk of the old Bimmer. "Traveling light, effendi?"

"I suppose I am." The duffel contained just a few T-shirts, several pairs of sweats, socks, a stack of underwear, and some bag filled with toiletries. It also contained a book of celebrated Middle Eastern and Islamic poetry his grandfather had given him years back.

"You must have big shopping plans. Fill up this suitcase." The driver patted the loose fabric, which nearly flattened under his palm. When Selim didn't answer, he shrugged, placed the duffel on the empty backseat, and ferried his boss toward Ataturk International Airport.

They headed through the narrow winding streets along the edges of cliffs leading through the hills and overlooking the flat tin roofs of Istanbul's shantytowns. On the side of the dusty road, Gypsy women and child panhandlers waved down passing vehicles, selling sympathy, roses, bottled water, and squares of honey-glazed baklava. Selim moved the duffel from the seat beside him and placed it on his lap. He'd originally planned to bring no luggage at all, but he figured with his Middle Eastern skin tone, the TSA might give him a hard time. It was well known that American security guards were suspicious of passengers arriving from the region, especially those who did not possess a return ticket. Though his bag was small enough to carry on, he thought it best to check it instead.

On this day especially, he wanted no more trouble.

At the airport, he made his way through security with ease, then approached a magazine stand in a souvenir shop.

He picked up a glossy tabloid known for its coverage of Turkish celebrities.

Flipping through it hurriedly, he tossed it back on the rack before sifting through another.

"I need to find it," he whispered to himself.

"Can I help you, effendi?" A store employee approached.

Ignoring the teenager before him, he flipped through magazine after magazine. "Sir, I'm sure if you just told me what you were looking for, I could help you find it."

But Selim went on like a madman, skimming page after page of half a dozen magazines before his eyes finally settled on the image before him.

"This one." He breathed a sigh of relief. "I'll take this one."

"She's hot." The teenage boy was still hovering over his shoulder. "I take it you're a fan?"

Selim rummaged through his pockets, withdrew a few lira, and handed them over without a word.

After boarding the plane and settling down in his seat, Selim popped a sleeping pill. He removed the complimentary headphones from the sealed plastic bag, tried all twelve channels on the plane's entertainment system, but heard only static. A mother stood in the aisle rocking a wailing baby. The other passengers glared with frustration as flight attendants shook their heads and shrugged with an air of understanding self-righteousness.

A half hour later, just moments after take-off, Selim's ears began to pop as the pounding in his head worsened. Once the seat-belt sign was turned off, he waved down a flight attendant with a short blond bob. "I'll have a Johnnie Walker," he said as she stood smiling over him.

"There's a charge for alcohol." Her voice sounded as though they were both submerged in water.

He swallowed a few times, trying to clear the bloating sensation in his sinuses. After rummaging through his pockets, he handed over some cash and soon was fast asleep.

Eleven hours later, Selim's plane landed in New York City.

After checking himself into the hospital, he was prepped for a half day of surgery scheduled for the following morning. The doctors informed him that the tumor was close to his brain. Experimental in nature, the procedure really had no precedent, and there was a chance he might not survive, a fact he was fully aware of. Still, to die quickly and painlessly on the operating table was preferable to the alternative. Months of painful disintegration, with Ayda trapped by his side. At the very least, he'd spared her that misery.

22

Selim Osman tried to open his eyes, only to discover that an oozy yellow film had enveloped the world. Sensing a pressure along the left side of his face, he gently peeled away the bandages, unwrapping the large one diagonally from around his forehead, cheek, and head.

He spent a few hazy moments wondering who and where he was. They were oddly peaceful moments, free of the guilt and angst that had come to encompass all that it meant to be Selim Osman. But the tranquility soon wore off along with the pain medication, and Selim could again recall not only his identity but also the circumstances that had brought him to this place.

The experience wasn't anything like the movies or books, where shell-shocked accident victims awoke from some near-death collision, mistaking the whitewashed walls of a hospital room for heaven, a sweet-faced nurse for an angel. No, Selim understood that against the odds, he had survived the removal of a cancerous tumor that had spread from his left sinus cavity up to his brain. He felt a mounting pressure in his head and a racking pain in his stomach. He looked up at the fluorescent bulbs overhead and knew immediately that this was not heaven.

Three days after his surgery, he finally mustered the courage to examine himself in a small hand mirror. Left unscathed, the right side of his face was still even and smooth. The right brow was still dark and thickly forested, a reminder that he had once been a handsome man.

The left brow, having been shaved for surgery, was growing back in patches of dark fuzz. Just as the doctors had explained before the surgery, the left side of his face had been opened and the tumor, along with all the infected bone and muscle, extracted. His abdomen was sliced open and tissue was removed to try to fill the void where half his face had been. Pieces of his femur were used to create something resembling a cheekbone, a jaw—anything that might help restore the impression of a face. But despite these efforts, the left side of his face swelled and sank like the hideous jowls of Munch's screaming ghosts.

He tilted the mirror and discovered that in the very spot that he had most loved to be kissed, the doctors had carved out a clean, round hole. It was through this hole in the base of his throat that Selim now breathed. He could see the edges of the hole wiggle as he sucked in air from the outside world.

Several days went by before he found the strength to walk. The operations—one to remove the cancer and the other to remove tissue and bone to reconstruct his face—had left him weakened, and as a result, he trudged warily down the glossy halls with one hand always on the corridor handrail. He was six feet tall and moved stiffly, dragging each leg cautiously as though at any moment he might crack.

As he walked, the right side of his face was the flag of Ottoman pride and a testament to a centuries-old heritage of glory. The right side commanded respect and took it without asking. Selim Osman had sealed business deals and mergers. He had melted powerful business moguls into the seats of their chairs. The right side bore the glory of the Osman royal dynasty.

It was the left side that bore the shame.

Ten days had passed since Selim had awoken from his surgery. The usual background noise of bleeping instruments filled his room. A fly struggled overhead, caught in the light panels. Outside, a boy on a gurney in the hall giggled. The laughter receded, but Selim's ears still rang with the memory of youth and a nostalgia for days gone by.

It was the second Friday of the month, a lovely spring day in May. Sunlight poured through the windowpanes, barring the room in shadow and light. Selim Osman curled his frame into a fetal position as a plump middle-aged nurse wiped him down.

She held a wet sponge with the very tips of her short, stubby fingers, bathing him with the same repulsion one might bathe a flea-bitten stray.

Selim looked away, ashamed that at thirty-two he was being washed by a stranger. Every so often she would say, "Very good, Mr. Osman." When she was done sponging his back, she came around to face him. She peered into his eyes with such intensity that he was forced to look back at her as she smiled sweetly, her fat cheeks gathering into two pink rolls.

"Are we done?" he said, shivering.

She nodded, then patted him down with a rough towel.

"Anything you need?"

"I'm fine."

"And you?" She poked her head over the partition and addressed the stranger on the other side.

"I'm all right," someone said in a gruff voice.

Selim had not thought to request a private room. In fact, he'd not planned for anything at all. He'd not envisioned a future for himself beyond the surgery.

At three o'clock that afternoon, a young woman in a yellow summer dress entered his hospital room. As her low heels clicked against the floor, Selim looked up.

"Excuse me," she whispered. "Just visiting my father." She passed the foot of his bed, disappearing behind the pale blue curtain that divided the room. The legs of a chair screeched against the tiles as she made herself comfortable.

"Hi, Papa," Selim heard her say.

"*Chérie*, I've missed you." The man's voice was hoarse, his breathing louder than his words.

"Let me help you."

"That's all right, I can do it on my own."

Selim could hear the man fidgeting with the manual controls to adjust his bed.

"How am I feeling? I'm fine. It's you that I'm worried about. Tell me, how's the portrait coming along?"

"Not too bad, still working on it, but haven't been able to get the eyes right."

The legs of the chair screeched once more against the tiles. Selim could hear the woman shuffling her things.

"I found this box in the attic," she said after a few minutes. "There's a bunch of old stuff inside. Some photos, I thought you might want to see them." When he didn't answer, she continued: "I looked through them."

"Did you?" The man sounded concerned.

"I didn't recognize a single person in those pictures, Papa. Not a *single* one besides you."

"No. You wouldn't."

"And what about this picture here?"

"Which one?"

"This black-and-white one, where you're standing in front of a large steamship. You were so young and skinny. That's you, isn't it? And who is that beside you? Is that your mother? What about the boy with the zigzag scar above his eye? Was he a friend? You always said you didn't have any photos from France."

A thick silence blanketed the room, and Selim was convinced he could hear the old man breathing.

"Papa?"

"Put the box away."

"I'm sorry," she said. "I'll put it back where it was."

"No. Just leave it, now that it's here." A quiet moment passed. "What is it?" he asked.

"This ring was in the box." He could hear her going through her bag for a moment. "It's beautiful, Papa. Is that a ruby?"

"I honestly don't know. Go ahead. Try it on."

"Really?"

"Just take it. No point leaving it in an old box for another forty years."

"It's a little tight."

"Good. It won't slip off."

"There's an inscription."

"Where?"

"Right here, beneath the band."

"Ah, yes. I remember seeing it before."

"Any idea what it means?"

"I've always wondered."

They sat for some time, not speaking, with only the sound of ambulances coming and going in the parking lot below.

When she finally emerged from the other side of the curtain, Selim had the vague sense they'd met before. She had a long, lean face framed by free-flowing pale hair that fell in messy waves to her elbows. Her nose was distinctive yet appealing, punctuated by high cheekbones, softly rounded brows, and a small red mouth.

She kept her eyes to the ground and a large canvas tote slung over her shoulder as she moved across the room. Folding her fingers around the strap, she exposed a crimson gem, bold and luminous against the backdrop. As she passed Selim's bed, she glanced up and smiled, offering a glimpse of luminescent eyes from behind her long blond wisps.

Moments after she'd left the room, the strange aroma of sand and sea lingered behind.

It was the very first scent he had been able to pick up since the surgery. Selim felt as though he'd somehow been reborn.

23

As his only child left the room, Mr. Herzikova lay in his hospital bed contemplating the many secrets he'd held throughout his lifetime. The discovery of the box had aroused his daughter's curiosity. She wanted to know about the parts of his life that he longed to erase from memory. Death was imminent. Death would finally lay to rest the secret burdens of the past.

He examined the tin box she'd left behind. Plastered on the lid was an old French poster he'd stuck on years back—a pinup girl in a polka-dot dress with a bright red flower in her chestnut-colored hair. The old latch was rusted and jammed tight, and in his weakened state he struggled to open it. Inside were scores of old photos, postcards, and tickets from the annual Marais street fair. Though she'd gone through the box, there was no way his daughter could have understood just what these items had meant to him. He was relieved that his pain remained only his own. Just as he was about to close the lid, he spotted a gold chain peeking out from beneath a stack of postcards. He withdrew the chain and opened the locket that hung from it, bringing it to his lips for several moments before returning it to the box.

He called the nurse's aide and asked her to place the box under his bed. When she left, she neglected to pull the curtain back behind her. Mr. Herzikova looked over at the man in the bed beside his own. A young foreigner—the latest in a rapid succession of critically ill patients to be housed alongside him—moaned groggily.

Unlike his roommate, Mr. Herzikova had no bandages to show or surgical wounds to care for. Aside from his baldness, there was no outward indication that he was dying. Like the secrets he would take to his grave, Mr. Herzikova's cancer was invisible to all, but not very far from the heart.

And though he could never have known it, he had been guided by an invisible hand. Every step he'd taken and each decision he'd made had moved him to the exact place he now occupied, to the bed in room 301, beside a man whose name he didn't even know.

But of course the old man could know nothing of this. These were the movements of a universe in motion, a universe in search of balance.

24

David Rumie was raised in the same Marais district that had once been flooded with Paris's Jews. He was brought up alongside his twin brother, Edward, in a two-bedroom apartment just above their family's bakery. The boys celebrated their birthdays each year on Bastille Day. And though they'd been born on a day marking freedom, they'd entered the world in the third year of the Second World War.

The war dragged on two more years before the Nazi army was forced to retreat back across the Seine and Paris was liberated. Hundreds of church bells sounded throughout the city in celebration and crowds gathered to cheer and dance as General Charles de Gaulle headed a victory march through the streets. From every open window in Paris, people sang "La Marseillaise," France's national anthem.

It would be eight more months before Adolf Hitler would shoot himself in the head and end the war completely.

But of course the boys had been too young to remember any of this.

Theirs was a happy childhood spent traversing the sidewalks of busy boulevards and the courtyards of vast green gardens. After church on Sundays, they'd zigzag their way through a maze of rickshaw carriages and grocery trucks, sampling goods from wagons full of fruit and nuts and dropping their leftovers into the hats of curbside beggars.

And while the boys grew together, their dreams for the future did not. David was content with the notion of taking over his father's shop one day. So for as long back as anyone could remember, he'd been working on weekends alongside his parents, Marie and Carle, in the cozy bakery.

He'd stand outside the door with a tray of snacks, drawing in new customers as he doled out samples of honey cake and custard croissants.

His twin brother, Edward, preferred to spend the afternoons on the building's roof, fashioning paper planes from advertising flyers and the glossy pages of magazines. From the rooftop of the crumbling building, planted between the chimney stacks and the steady rumble of the rusty radiator, Edward launched all sorts of airborne origami. From that rooftop, he launched his dreams of someday serving his country as a pilot in the French Air Force.

By thirteen, not only had the twins' dreams diverged, but they looked wildly different as well. And yet it was never expected that they should resemble each other; they were fraternal twins, after all. David was tall and lean with pensive, wide-set eyes, a shy smile, and a handsome cleft in his chin. Edward was five inches shorter, broad-shouldered, and huskily built, with suntanned skin, clear eyes, and an open air about him.

As the boys grew, so did the gossip. Even the closest of neighbors began to question whether David was the couple's natural child, for David resembled neither of his parents. Where had he gotten that fair skin and those almond-colored eyes? And wasn't it odd that at the age of thirteen, he'd already grown a head taller than his father? It seemed that everyone in the neighborhood wondered about David Rumie—everyone, that is, except for the Rumies themselves.

It was the end of the last day of school when David and Edward descended three flights of stairs to the busy boulevard below. The sixteen-year-old twins had just finished their second to last year of studies at the lycée. All around, classmates and friends cheered and slapped one another's backs, eagerly anticipating the fun and freedom that summer would bring.

After saying their good-byes, the boys headed home, strolling past coffeehouses, stray cats, and flower merchants. They turned into the narrow alleyway leading up to their second-story apartment, leaving behind the hustle of the boulevard. The alley grew quieter as they ascended the shallow hill. Suddenly David felt something sharp strike his shoulder.

"Swine!" a voice shouted from behind. A small pile of stones in one hand, Jean-Pierre Prideux stood with three of his cronies. He was almost seventeen, a year older and half a foot taller than most of the other boys in their class. In his other hand he held a glass bottle of soda. "Thirsty?" He stepped forward as though he were going to offer David a sip.

Edward stepped up instinctively. "Hey! Knock it off!" He dropped his book bag and moved toward Jean-Pierre.

"I heard a rumor that your brother is a pig. What do you have to say about that?"

Edward froze. The expression of astonishment was apparent to all. He looked over at David and the two boys exchanged confused glances.

"So you didn't know? It's impossible to have brown eyes if both your parents have blue." Jean-Pierre laughed harshly. "I thought the Krauts had slaughtered all the swine in Paris."

"Edward, you can go. This doesn't concern you," Sebastian, the smallest of the three boys, stepped in. It was clear Edward would not budge.

"So you're a Jew lover?" Jean-Pierre squinted as he stared down Edward.

"I don't understand."

"Just get out of here!" He picked up Edward's bag and shoved it hard against his chest. "Now!" he demanded. Edward stumbled back and fell to the ground while Jean-Pierre shifted his attention to David. "But not you. You're not going anywhere." He smashed his bottle against the crumbling bricks as his three accomplices wrestled David against the wall. The shrill sound of the impact echoed through the alley and a stream of fizzy soda descended downhill toward the boulevard.

Jean-Pierre held up the broken bottle and examined it while Edward scrambled to his feet and looked on in horror. "If you're a pig like they say you are, you should be circumcised." He raised the jagged glass up to a single ray of light that streaked diagonally across the alley.

David struggled as the three boys kept him pinned against the brick wall. His head twisted from side to side as he tried to bite the forearms of his aggressors.

Jean-Pierre took the bottle and held the sharp edges up to David's face. "You want to be a good piggy, don't you?" He offered a toothy grin. "We can help you."

"No!" Edward shouted as he came barreling from behind, then leaped upon Jean-Pierre's back and dug his fingers into the sockets of his eyes.

Within seconds, Edward was pinned to the ground with Jean-Pierre kneeling over him. He took the soda bottle and struck it across Edward's face, eliciting a bright stream of blood from a deep gash above his eye. "I don't know what I find more disgusting, a Jew or a Jew lover." He spat in Edward's face, stood up, and began kicking him in the gut.

Edward, doubled over and twisting in pain, cried out as he was being pummeled.

"Next time I'm gonna take out your eye," Jean-Pierre snarled, then stopped to catch his breath.

The three others gave David one final shove against the wall before they released him and sauntered off the way they'd come.

Blood trickled down Edward's face, leaving bright red spots all along the length of his shirt. He took a few wobbly steps and almost collapsed before David pulled him against his chest and nearly dragged him up the narrow cobbled street to their home.

When they arrived, David could see Marie rolling dough behind the counter through the window. A few customers were hunched over the pastry case having their pick of chocolate croissants and marmalade biscuits.

As soon as she caught a glimpse of him waving frantically through the window, Marie dashed out of the store and set her sights upon Edward. "What happened?" she shouted as she hurried to their side. "Edward!" She lifted his limp head in her hands, though his neck gave way and his body slackened against his brother's chest.

"Grab hold of his legs!" David shouted as he ascended the stairs backward.

"Who did this?" Marie pressed as she lifted Edward's heels off the ground.

"Just follow my lead, slow and steady. That's it. Just a few more steps."

"Tell me what happened!" Marie cried out as Edward's ankle slid from her grasp and banged against the last few steps. "Open the door!" David said, still hugging his brother's back up against him as his mother hurried around to follow his directive. "Let's lay him on the couch."

"Who did this?" Marie begged him for an answer.

"I'll tell you all about it later, but for now, you need to call for the doctor, *Maman*. That cut won't heal on its own."

Thirty minutes later Dr. Renaut appeared with his black doctoring kit. Edward moaned groggily as the gash above his eye was sewn up.

When he was done, the doctor gave Marie instructions on how to clean and care for the wound. She in turn paid him with what few francs she had, promising to get the rest of the money to him by the end of the week.

Once Edward was sleeping soundly in his bed, David lowered himself onto an armchair beside the couch. "*Maman,*" he called to Marie gently.

"What is it, son?" She sat with her eyes closed and her head resting against the sofa back.

"Son? Is that what I am to you?"

She opened her eyes and sat up. "David?"

"It's suddenly so obvious," he continued calmly.

"What's this about?"

"I often wondered about my brown eyes. It seemed so unusual. You, Papa, and Edward, all with your blue eyes."

"David, what's happened?"

He leaned forward and took her hands in his own. "Just tell me."

"Tell you?" Her voice was almost a whisper.

"The truth."

Marie looked into David's eyes.

"It will be all right," he assured her. She opened her mouth but could not get a word out.

"I know it now. I just need to hear you say it."

"I prayed this day would never come." She gazed at him lovingly. "We tried our best to shield you both from the rumors." She lowered her head and continued quietly: "But I suppose the truth always finds a way of surfacing, doesn't it?"

"*Maman,*" David pleaded.

Her words, so soft, fell upon him like a gossamer. "You were born to the family Herzikova," she told the wide-eyed youth.

Her-zi-kova. The name settled in his mind and heart like a beautiful song he could not shake.

She reached for a heap of yarn, her fingers quickly going to work on the scarf she'd been knitting throughout the week. "She was lovely," Marie began after a long, lingering silence.

He fought to catch his breath. "My mother?"

Marie winced. "Your birth mother."

Now David struggled to speak. "How—how did you know her?"

Marie placed her knitting to the side, then drew a deep breath. "She came into the bakery one day."

The Herzikovas had visited the bakery often. In fact it was their special spot, a place they'd frequented on their first date, a place that had brought back memories of laughter, sweetness, and love every time they'd visit.

It was on the Jewish holiday of Passover, in the spring of 1941, that David's father, Jacob Herzikova, first laid eyes on his future bride. He caught a glimpse of her soft, round face through the lace partition that separated men and women in the tiny synagogue of the Marais district in Paris. After services, he inquired about her and discovered that her name was Haya and she was only sixteen, ten years his junior. She was the daughter of a widowed doctor who could barely make ends meet. David was from a prominent family of bankers and was a well-respected member of France's burgeoning Jewish community.

With her father's permission, Haya and Jacob spent the following Sunday together. He invited her to view art at a charming gallery he knew over on rue Soufflot before they strolled over to the Luxembourg Gardens, where they enjoyed a cup of tea and the nostalgic tunes of an accordion sounding from somewhere on the far end of the vast green lawn. In the afternoon, they hailed a taxi and headed back toward the old Jewish quarter. There he took her to a bakery he patronized often, one he claimed served up the very best chocolate éclairs and bread pudding in all the city. When the two arrived, the flush-faced, pretty *pâtissière*, Madame Rumie, kindly handed them two pastries for the price of one.

"*Merci beaucoup, madame,*" Haya thanked her with a bright smile.

"Call me Marie." She wiped her powdery fingers against her apron. "And do come again!"

"*Bien sûr, Madame Marie!*" Jacob called back as they headed for the door. "We'll surely be back soon!"

Outside the shop, they devoured their éclairs as children might do, stopping only to marvel at the pastry's doughy shell and creamy fill. When they were done, Jacob reached out and with his thumb wiped a smudge of chocolate icing from her lips. Blushing, Haya turned away, and when she did, Jacob felt his insides melt.

The following Friday, they boarded the Métro early in the morning and headed toward his family's château just east of Cherbourg. Jacob's mother came to collect them at the station. A few scattered clouds shone with yellow streaks of sun and the scent of honeysuckle filled the air. They spent a few hours in the orchard, getting to know each other better and picking apples his mother would bake into a pie later that day. They traipsed through the garden between a fortress of sweet-smelling roses and a wall of ivy that cloaked the south side of the house like a lush, green blanket.

After dinner, he escorted her to the outskirts of the estate, where they sat with legs dangling over the edge of a crumbling stone wall. As he looked at her, he felt his whole self beaming. "It's hard to look at you without smiling."

She turned her cheek and kicked her heels against the wall, a smile creeping on her face.

He mustered all his courage. "Can I kiss you?"

She turned to him, and when she did, he knew he need not wait for her response. Three months later, the two were engaged.

The Nazis had occupied France for nearly a year and life was becoming more difficult for the Jews of Paris. Jacob imagined that he would wait a year to marry his fiancée so she could at least reach her seventeenth birthday, but when the Nazis began rounding up thousands of foreign-born Jews, Jacob decided they should push up the wedding. No one knew if they might also be taken away or where they might be taken to.

Jacob Herzikova was determined to move forward with the wedding as if there were no war. The Jewish community was abuzz, as the guest list was rumored to contain no less than two hundred names. Talk of the wedding served as a dreamy respite, a fairy tale for the Jews of the Marais. They could talk of the impending dangers, of the anti-Semitic laws that were being advanced day by day, but it was much more pleasant to discuss the upcoming wedding. Those invited gripped the invitation with anticipation and desperation. The swirling calligraphy seemed to promise a secure future; *ne vous inquiétez pas*, it seemed to say. The world was not coming to an end. On the contrary, the future held merriment and celebration. This was a dangerous delusion that the community could ill afford to indulge in.

The ceremony would take place in the same synagogue Jacob's parents had been married in some thirty years earlier, and the reception to follow would be in a large banquet hall adjacent to the sanctuary. As a surprise, Jacob arranged for all the sweets to be provided by Haya's favorite pastry chef, Madame Marie of the Marais district bakery. In the three months they'd been engaged, the cafés and restaurants of the City of Light had shut their doors to Jewish customers, but not Madame Marie. Time and time again, she would welcome them into her cinnamon-scented nook with her congenial smile and chubby, open arms.

The night before the wedding was a crisp October night. The city streets were bleak and desolate, as the Germans had imposed a strict 9:00 p.m. curfew throughout Paris. The only signs of life seemed to be billowing forth from the rooftop chimneys lit up beneath the yellow glow of the moon.

In the still of night, the banquet hall dripped with freshly picked flowers and crystal candelabras. The tables were set with satin linens and fine porcelain china. Silver cutlery gleamed expectantly as the chefs busily prepared the feast that would be served for the occasion. It was to be a Friday morning celebration, early enough that the guests would still have all afternoon to prepare their Sabbath dinner meals. For just one lovely day in October, the war would cease to exist. Hundreds of the district's Jews would not have to wait on ration lines like paupers, but would dine leisurely as the carefree bourgeoisie they had been not long ago. The bride, groom, guests, flowers, china, and chuppah all waited anxiously for the sun to rise.

But such a celebration was not meant to be. That night the Nazis set fire to six synagogues in Paris. The porcelain china shattered. Perfectly polished cutlery shot through the night like shrapnel. Scorched Torah scrolls and rose petals curled hideously in the inferno. A number of the would-be guests were rounded up by the Nazis, never to be heard from again.

In the morning, Jacob wed his bride in the cold, damp basement of the chief rabbi's home. There were no guests. There were no flowers. The bride did not wear white.

That night they consummated their marriage quickly and quietly. Both of them wept silently. David Herzikova was born nine months later.

"You should be resting," Jacob said when he found Haya standing in the doorway with a basket in her arms. She had given birth only a week earlier, and he found it odd that she should be out of bed and walking about.

A little hiccup sounded from the basket.

"I can go out and fetch whatever you need," he continued. "Why not go back to bed?"

"You've heard the reports," she said quietly.

"Reports?"

"Of death camps."

"Haya, you're wearing a coat and hat. *Where* are you going?"

The look in her light eyes said everything he needed to know.

Jacob turned away and gritted his teeth.

"In the east," she went on.

"Rumors, all rumors!" he said defiantly.

"Ovens, Jacob. They say they are sending Jews into ovens!"

"*They* say a lot, don't they?"

"We have a son to protect."

"It's just panic in the streets."

"They're barbarians, Jacob."

"They're Europeans! As are we!"

"Don't you see what is happening around us?" she said. "Your parents, my father, where have they been taken?"

"You know very well. They're rounding up laborers street by street."

"It's not like Papa not to get in touch. He'd send word if he could."

"You're worried. It's understandable. But the able-bodied are sent to labor camps. Work! That's what they want us for. It's a fact of war."

"And what of those who cannot work? The sick, the elderly, and the children? Where have they gone to, Jacob? Tell me, where have they been sent?"

"I've got friends at the municipality and they've assured me—"

"We haven't any friends, Jacob. Open your eyes."

"A few more weeks. We've at least a few more weeks. And who knows, the war could be over by then," he said lamely.

"They're rounding people up, block by—"

"This will all be over soon."

"Days, Jacob. They're coming for us. One, maybe two. He's not safe here with us."

"For God's sake! He's seven days old!"

"We have to find somewhere else for him."

"He should remain with his parents, with his people!"

"It's too dangerous now, Jacob! You know that as well as I do. When this is all over, we'll come back for him. A few months? A year? The war can't drag on beyond another year, can it?"

"I think I hear the kettle," Jacob said numbly.

"I haven't put the water on to boil."

He looked up toward the kitchen door. "I swore I heard the kettle whistle."

Haya swallowed hard. "Perhaps you should go in and check."

"A good idea," he said wearily. He rose slowly, carefully, the weight of his decision bearing down on his shoulders. He stood there looming over the basket for a long moment without daring to touch it. Then he disappeared into the kitchen to check on the imaginary whistle of an imaginary kettle.

When she walked out the door, Jacob was not there to stop her. Several hours later she came back empty-handed.

Two weeks after giving up their son, Haya and Jacob were caught hiding beneath the loose floorboards in the kitchen of their home. Nazi officers arrived with dogs, which were unleashed on Haya while Jacob was held back and made to watch. They were beaten and dragged away, leaving only a trail of blood along the dusty road up to the house.

On the sixteenth of July, in a brutal roundup the French authorities referred to as Operation Spring Breeze, the Herzikovas, along with thirteen thousand other French Jews, were sent to the Vélodrome d'Hiver, a racing stadium in Paris that Jacob had frequented as a child. He had fond memories of the place, of cheering crowds and sticky peanut chews. Toward the end of a tight race, his father would start huffing, then leap out of his chair, red-faced, as the cycling contenders rode across the finish line. He loved that stadium and each year had anticipated the start of the spring racing season.

Now, in the midsummer heat of 1942, they were left in that racing stadium without food or water. The stench of feces and sweat hovered in the air, while flies and ticks plagued those imprisoned. On the fifth day of their confinement, they were transferred to Drancy, an internment camp on the outskirts of Paris. After a few months of forced labor and slow starvation they were swept up like ants and loaded onto a train bound for Auschwitz. Jacob was twenty-seven and Haya was seventeen. The young couple was torn apart, separated between cattle car four and cattle car five. For several days the train wound its way east. Maggots nested in Haya's pus-filled wounds, while Jacob fought for air through the small slivers and holes in the planks of the train. Once the train crossed over into Poland and pulled up to the camp's entrance, some would be pointed to the smokestacks. Others selected for "labor" would pass beneath a sign that read WORK WILL SET YOU FREE. But Jacob and Haya never did pass beneath that sign. In fact, they never got off the train. Somewhere along the tracks between Drancy and Auschwitz, David Herzikova had become an orphan.

25

"We shared an unspoken bond, your mother and I," Marie explained to David. "You see, we were both due to give birth at the very same time. Toward the end of our ninth month, she came into the bakery, and the bulge in her belly was gone. Before I could congratulate her, she said something strange to me. 'I hear you are expecting twins, *n'est-ce pas?*'"

"But you were not expecting twins?" David's voice was sober.

"Just the one. But I understood what she was asking of me. The round-ups, the lootings, rumors of death camps in the east. Your mother slid a basket over the counter and told me she'd return for you as soon as it was safe. We hid you until Edward was born two weeks later. Everyone just assumed I'd given birth to twins."

David swallowed hard. "She never came back."

Marie frowned.

He nodded.

"They left something." She shuffled to a closet at the end of the hall, returning with a small tweed sack. "For you," she said, then handed over the sack.

Dust flared out as David struggled to loosen a knot in the drawstring. Inside, he found several gold coins, the deed to a property in Cherbourg, and a locket on a long gold chain. Within the locket, he discovered a photo of his late mother, the expression on her face peaceful, the thick curls in her hair apparent despite being pulled back into a low chignon. He traced the edge of the locket's frame with the tip of his finger and gazed at the photograph.

Then very slowly he kneeled as mourners do. After a moment of absolute stillness, he wrapped his arms around Marie's legs and wept in the lap of the only mother he'd ever known.

After that day, David refused to return to the Catholic boy's school and officially adopted the *nom de famille* given to him at birth, Herzikova. With Edward by his side, he visited his family's impressive château northwest of Paris, on the jutting seaport of Cherbourg.

It was a devastating sight. The grand chalet looked more like a mausoleum than a vacation spot. When the Nazis invaded Paris, they had scoured the coast for grand structures they could confiscate and convert into army bases. Bullet shells littered the grass, peeking out from overgrown weeds and tall, swaying wildflowers. Disjointed cannon artillery loomed over the edge of the low, rocky cliffs, boasting empty threats to the passing sailors of the English Channel.

From the public records he'd gathered at the land registry office, he'd discovered that the château had been in his family for the last three generations. He imagined that it had once been a place of weekend and summer getaways, where his father, along with his siblings, had retreated in their youth, away from the hustle and smog of the Marais.

Blossoming trees flourished in the property's apple orchard, which had not succumbed to years of neglect. He tried to imagine his parents and grandparents sipping on fresh cider, breathing in the ocean air. *What were their names?* he wondered. *What did they look like? Did they play the piano like he did? Were they lonely like he was? No, they were a real family. They had each other. But then the Germans came one cool night in June, their bombs overhead, and their U-boats just off the shores of this rocky retreat. They took them away . . . And the big house was empty.*

"I don't know who I am," David said to Edward as they gazed up at the crumbling beauty of the majestic château. They sat in the tall grass, uprooting daffodils and listening to the sound of the waves. "I only know who I'm not."

Edward put his arm around David but said nothing. Then he fashioned a paper plane from pages of an old newspaper scattered about the abandoned property, and jettisoned it over the edge of the cliff toward the glowing horizon.

* * *

A year later, in July of 1959, David took the few gold coins his birth parents had left him, bid farewell to his adopted parents, and immigrated to a region that had, just over a decade earlier, been known as Palestine.

The Rumies had risen early that morning to take the long train ride to the southern port of Marseille. Before boarding the ship and waving good-bye to the people he had known as mother and father, David turned to Marie and looked into her kind eyes for the last time.

"*Mon petit.*" She pulled David against her. "Don't forget, you are always *my* boy."

"*Maman,*" he tried to reassure her. "We *will* see each other again soon."

She stepped back, took a deep breath, and straightened her shoulders. "Of course we will," she said matter-of-factly. At that moment she did what he knew she would; she pursed her lips and contorted her face into something resembling a smile.

"Go," she shooed him. "Get on your boat . . . The world awaits you."

He looked up at her and smiled. He would always be *her* boy.

"Hurry," she whispered. "You don't want to miss it."

In that moment he almost dropped his suitcase. He almost turned back because the person on that dock was *almost* who he was, *almost* who he needed to be, but in his heart, he knew that when you were searching for your soul, *almost* didn't count.

His father stood by her side, beads of sweat pinning his shirt to his big round belly. He hugged David one last time, then shook the boy's hand. "I will pray you find what you are looking for." He kissed David. "Write often." Then, with the Polaroid camera he'd purchased for the occasion, the baker took a photograph of his family, two boys who had once upon a time been twins, and standing between them, the brave woman who had risked her life in loving a child marked for death.

Marie took the photo from her husband, then shook it impatiently to speed the image to the surface. She handed it to David. "Keep it in a safe place."

Edward dragged his fingers through his hair and shook his head. "This is your home," he said in a hush so their parents wouldn't hear.

"I need to go," David whispered, "just like you need to fly."

He shook his head once more before putting his arms around David for a long moment. "I almost forgot," he said, pulling away hurriedly. "I've got something for you." Rummaging through his jacket pocket, he yanked out what appeared to be a palm-size scroll.

"What's this?" David asked.

Edward handed it over. "Open it."

David unrolled the parchment and laughed heartily at what he discovered. Within the scholarly-looking scroll was the saucy image of a French pinup girl in a red and white polka-dot dress. She wore a bright red flower in her chestnut-colored hair and smiled coquettishly while pulling back the hem of her dress, exposing just the tiniest hint of the white knickers beneath it.

Edward's eyes popped with excitement. "Doesn't it look just like Justine?" He hovered over the poster with the enthusiasm that teenage boys possess. "She even has the same polka-dot dress!" he said while tapping the glossy print. "It looks like her, doesn't it? I got it for you. Do you like it?"

"Justine?" David feigned ignorance.

"Ah, come on! I see you looking at her whenever we go into her father's shop."

"Right." David smiled sheepishly.

"Of course she never looks back." Edward's voice trailed off into a hearty chuckle before his tone turned serious. "It's just a reminder," he said quietly.

"A reminder?"

Edward dug his fists into his pockets and looked out toward the sea. "Of everything you'll be missing over here."

David rolled up the parchment and lowered his gaze. "I don't need to be reminded."

They embraced each other one last time. Edward stepped away and took hold of David's shoulder.

Each offered up an apologetic glance before Edward turned without a word and headed back to the train station.

It was nearly midnight by the time Edward arrived back in Paris. Having encouraged his parents to lodge overnight in Marseille and relish the fresh ocean air, Edward returned to the city on his own with plans to oversee the bakery the following day. He was glad that his parents would have some time to rest. He knew how badly they needed it. The previous night, he'd lain awake in bed, listening to his mother weep in anticipation of his brother's departure.

As he ascended the dark alley leading to the bakery, Edward encountered Jean-Pierre Prideux, along with his three cronies. They staggered through the street, the stench of cigarette smoke and booze on their breaths. This time they had brass knuckles and blades with them. At the first flash of the blade Edward knew he didn't stand a chance. It was one against four.

Instinctively, he turned to the empty space where David should have been. Though he tried his best to fend off his attackers, Edward received a beating that shattered his leg and ruptured his spleen, but of all the blows he had suffered, there was just one that would leave him pain to last a lifetime. A fist to the face, brass knuckles to the eye.

Slowly the curtain would fall.

Blinded in one eye, he could never hope to fly.

26

Standing on the upper deck of the steamship, long after the dock had disappeared into the horizon, David withdrew the photograph that Marie had given him from the inside pocket of his jacket. Poised before the enormous steamship beneath a bleach-white sun, there he, his brother, and his mother stood. Marie appeared between her sons, short and shapely in a paisley dress and matching pillbox hat. To her left, David stood tall and lean in a light-colored summer suit. Edward was positioned to her right—splendidly attired in his Sunday best—with one hand in his pocket and the other draped around her waist.

As he stared at the photo, he couldn't help but focus on the jagged gray scar above his brother's eye. That mark was the last physical remnant of the beating Edward had endured on his behalf a year earlier.

A sudden chill passed through him. Not wanting to relive the traumatic events of that day, David returned the photograph to his pocket. Then he headed to his cabin below deck and collapsed on his paper-thin mattress. While he slept, the metal springs poked him as they recoiled and bounced to the undulations of the rough seas. After a short nap, he made his way to the ship's kitchen for a cup of tea that he hoped would soothe his stomach and calm his nerves.

There he befriended the head chef, a jolly bewhiskered drunk with a heart of gold. At his invitation, David spent the afternoons baking with the kitchen crew, teaching them the secrets of nutmeg and cocoa, as well as his mother's most coveted recipes. In the evenings, he lay up on the deck, mapping the constellations and counting shooting stars. By the end of the journey, he'd been offered a job working with the kitchen crew.

Not without some reluctance, he'd declined. He hadn't gone this far to turn around and go back the way he'd come.

The ship had journeyed east along the Mediterranean, landing nine days later at the bustling port of Haifa in northern Israel. From there David hitchhiked east, less than an hour later finding himself in the fishing village of Tiberias, situated on the Sea of Galilee. He wandered through the marketplace, peopled by a raucous mix of Arab and Jewish merchants, each boasting the superiority of his own fish, dates, or olives, and spent the rest of the morning drifting through the streets like a ghost. Scouring the faces of stubble-jawed sabras and bearded Arabs, he probed the eyes of passing pedestrians. He needed a place to stay. He was hoping to find someone, anyone, really. And maybe, along the way, himself.

Exhausted and thirsty, he wandered beyond the market, reaching a fishing harbor along the western shore of the sea. The tops of tall palms swayed in the warm summer winds, and when David turned from the sea, he discovered a town surrounded by low rolling hills and the crumbling remains of an ancient wall the Byzantine emperor Justinian had built centuries back.

Just a few yards away, a burly fisherman with sand-colored hair and a pink nose stood knee-deep in the fresh waters, struggling under the weight of a loaded fishnet. The man's boat bobbed gently against smooth boulders, nestled deep in sand and peeping out from the shoreline's burgundy reeds. The veins in his forehead bulged as he strained to lift his net from the boat and retrieve his catch.

A good omen, David thought to himself as he marveled at the fisherman's tremendous bounty.

With nowhere to go and nothing else to do, David decided to make himself useful. He dropped his suitcase and rolled up his sleeves, then approached the red-faced fisherman. They exchanged quiet nods, and David grabbed hold of the net. Together they heaved it out of the water and dropped it onto the elevated wooden dock. The trapped fish wriggled feverishly, their bluish scales scintillating in the sunlight. His suit was drenched, but he felt alive.

"*Toda,*" said the big man. His face was soft and thick. Perspiration gleamed on his fat, sweet face as he leaned over, trying to catch his breath.

"Do you speak French?" David asked in his native tongue.

"A bit," the man replied. "Thanks to the endless hours I spend haggling with new immigrants. As I always say, if it was cast out from Babel, you'll hear it in the market," the fisherman mused.

"I just came from Paris," David explained. "I am looking for a place to stay and for work too."

The man thought for a second. "Well, I could use an extra hand here on the dock. I can't pay a lot of money, but we have an empty room in our house. It's just over there, on that hill. You can stay with us if you work." The man's tone was warm and welcoming.

David looked out to where the man was pointing and smiled for the first time since his arrival in Tiberias that morning.

He had a good feeling about the fisherman. He appeared to be in his midforties, with big white teeth in a wide-open smile. His tea-green eyes glistened as he wiped the sweat from his brow with the inside of his arm.

"I'm Judah," said the fisherman. The two exchanged a handshake, David's hand sinking deeply into the sweaty warmth of the fisherman's massive palm.

"David. David Herzikova."

After distributing the day's catch to a string of merchants in the market, Judah and David headed up to the fisherman's home, a one-story cottage at the top of the hill overlooking the Sea of Galilee. The dirt path leading uphill was patchy, winding, and steep. The engine of the pickup roared as Judah pressed the gas. Anxious that the worn tires of the pickup would skid and send the old Ford careening downhill, David shut his eyes and pressed his long frame back up against the tattered canvas seat cushion, grasping the dashboard with one hand and the door handle with the other.

Judah laughed gaily. At the top of the hill, he brought the vehicle to a halt beneath the shade of a low olive tree, then stepped out of the truck, leaving the keys inside and the door ajar behind him. "Hose down the back of the truck!" Judah instructed as he walked away. "The pump's over that way." He dropped his fishing gear on the dry grass and left his boots at the door before entering his house.

David obliged, uncoiling the thick rubber hose from its harness and jacking the pump until a steady stream of cool water spouted out. He hosed down the back of the pickup, washing away the smell of the day's catch. When he'd finished, he returned the hose to the harness and let the rusty truck bake dry under the steady sunshine.

Removing his shoes, David left them at the foot of the oak door beside the fisherman's. His slim-fitted loafers looked dainty next to Judah's thick lace-up boots.

The house was small, the walls decorated with antique maps and bookshelves crammed from end to end. The blue-and-white flag of the newly established Jewish state was tacked up over a fireplace, in which Judah stored what appeared to be unused netting traps and tightly bound reams of fishing string.

His wife, a slender woman with naturally rouged cheeks and a lean, angular face, led David to his room, a cozy nook just off the kitchen. The wrought-iron bed frame was fitted with a stripped twin mattress. There was no closet, just a low dresser with three stubborn shelves. David didn't mind. He hadn't brought much with him anyway. Beside the bed, a large window looked out onto the overgrown property.

"Judah removed them," she explained when David's eyes wandered to the bare curtain rod. "He says real men rise with the sun." She shrugged with raised open palms as if to say, *Men will be men.*

David gazed out into the garden through the open window. There was an orange tree, tall and blooming, surrounded by uncut grass and flowering shrubs.

"There are fresh linens in the closet, some soap under the sink. The laundry line is out back," she said to David as he continued to stare out the window and take in his new surroundings.

"*Merci.*"

"Supper at half past six."

He thought she might be an austere woman, but just before she turned to leave, she smiled kindly, her teeth hidden but her eyes gentle.

That evening David had dinner with Judah the fisherman and his family. He had one daughter, a slight girl with tanned skin, dirty blond hair, and a heart-shaped mouth. Her eyes cast down, she said little throughout the meal. But every so often she'd look up and smile shyly. David admired her delicate wrists and soft, youthful hands as she handled her cutlery.

Just beyond Judah's seat at the head of the table hung a portrait of a

woman wearing a black and gold brocade gown in the tradition of centuries past. Her hair was covered in a netted cap of opal, and upon her
neck rested an impressive strand of black sea pearls. Perhaps most striking were the deep blue eyes with which she seemed to survey the room.

"My family has resided in Tiberias since the the second half of the
sixteenth century," Judah explained to David, noticing his interest in the
portrait. He took a long sip of his Kiddush wine. "We are descended
from an Ottoman Jew. She arrived in Tiberias from Istanbul quite suddenly without a friend or family member here to greet her. It's believed
that she brought this painting too." He twisted around and glanced up
at the portrait behind him. "Is this an image of her likeness, or perhaps
that of another? Who can be sure? It was so very long ago." He turned
back to David. "They say she came from aristocracy." Judah laughed,
then rested his elbow on the table, causing it to wobble momentarily.
"We, descended from high society. Can you believe it?" He lifted his
hand toward the ceiling, pointed out the peeling paint over head, and
shook his head as if to say, *We've come a long way.*

His wife reached over with her bangle-clad wrist, took her husband's
hand, and pressed gently.

"Now why she left Istanbul in the first place, that part of the story is
lost," the fisherman continued. "She settled here along the sea, with a
mysterious fortune and a loyal entourage. They were all practicing Jews
who went about their business with quiet dignity, babbling among themselves in their native tongue, only the girl refused to speak. They say she
roamed about Tiberias like a ghost, speaking to no one, just whispering
to this ring here." He pointed to the ruby ring his wife was wearing.
"There is a small inscription in the band. They say it's old Ottoman, but
me, I don't know what it means." He shrugged as his wife slipped the
ring off her finger, then handed it to David for closer inspection.

"*C'est magnifique,*" David said as he turned it about beneath the flickering candlelight.

The stone was flawless, its color, intoxicating. The ruby was a deep,
sumptuous crimson. The same color of the aged red wine from Bordeaux
David had only been allowed to sip on Easter and at birthday celebrations.
Looking over its gleaming facets, David couldn't help but wonder
where it came from. It was a question he'd asked a thousand times before, but until that moment, he'd only ever asked himself.

That night, for the first time in his life, David celebrated the Sabbath. The candles, the challah, the sweet red wine. Judah, the red-faced man with the easygoing smile, his soft-spoken wife with her silk headscarf and gold bangles—it all felt like something that had been lost.

And so it was that Judah brought David Herzikova into his home.

Though he hired the boy as a fisherman, he took him in as son.

The fisherman understood all too well that contrary to appearances, David Herzikova had not traveled lightly. Though he'd arrived with just a single bag in tow, any caring eye could glean that his spirit was straddled by the weight of something more.

The fisherman never did ask David about his family. He sensed that—like so many others who had traveled alone from Europe to the Holy Land—the boy had likely come to this place to lay a haunted past to rest. To bury his sorrow, as most likely he'd never had a chance to bury his dead. And maybe here, in this historic homeland of his people, he'd come to witness the dawn of a new day. Perhaps here, in the land of milk and honey, he'd set off on his future.

27

Work as a fisherman was not a tidy affair. David soon learned that his pleated slacks and cotton vests were useless at sea. His new attire consisted of synthetic trousers cut off above the knee and waterproof moccasins he wore when stepping along the rocky shoreline on the occasion the boat needed towing.

At dawn, David and Judah would board the weathered boat and set out to cast their fishing nets with the hopes of catching a fat school of tilapia, flounder, or mullet. After hours, they'd return and unload the day's catch onto the flatbed of Judah's pickup and circle around to deliver orders to a handful of shopkeepers in the bustling marketplace. The first delivery went to Adon Haddad, a sabra in a straw hat who carried a foul-mouthed parrot on his shoulder. Farther down the market, they'd deliver flounder and tilapia to the Russian, Sasha Chekov, a hulk of a man with a keloid scar across his neck. On sweltering days, he'd take off his shirt, revealing rock-solid abs and the words *God is my judge* tattooed in Hebrew across his chest. But their best customer by far was Miss Hula, a middle-aged spinster who liked to pinch David's cheeks and compliment him on his rosy hue and fine broad shoulders. She was especially impressed with his Parisian accent and cackled when he said something she liked the sound of. She accosted him with slobbery kisses on the cheek, speaking in a singsong whine as she recited the petty gossip she herself invented and spread throughout the village. Later they'd head down the road to the Arab market to deliver catfish, because, as David learned, catfish did not have scales and therefore were not kosher.

The work was arduous, but David enjoyed the warm summer sun on his bare back and shoulders and the cool breeze that sometimes rushed south from the Golan Heights. His arms grew muscled from working the sails and drawing up the day's catch. His lean face bronzed and his almond eyes brightened whenever he looked out upon the rippling waters of the Sea of Galilee.

At his Catholic school, he'd been taught that these were the same waters Jesus had walked upon. He'd never believed that story until now. Even if Jesus was just a man, the lake held magic, of that he was sure.

Saturday was the only day David did not work. While everyone was gathered in the synagogue, David, ashamed that he could barely read Hebrew or recite prayers, would wander the ancient streets of Tiberias. He'd wonder how his brother and parents were faring; he'd written once or twice, though he'd yet to hear back. Still, he didn't harbor any resentment or remorse. His brother would be finishing up his first month of aviation training right about now. He was glad Edward was carving out a path for himself—they'd agreed all along that was something they each needed to do. As for his parents, they were now short two sets of hands behind the counter. He imagined they were particularly busy in the shop.

Nearly three months had passed since his arrival in Israel, and though summer had ended and the rainy season was now upon them, the temperatures were still pleasant enough to stroll through the streets in a light overcoat. In the quiet calm of the Sabbath, while the fisherman's family gathered with friends and neighbors at the synagogue, David wandered the streets before coming across an elderly Arab man, Sheikh Mohammad.

Sheikh Mohammad was a Sufi mystic, a spiritual adviser who would interpret dreams for shekels. He was a short, round man with white hair and snow-sloped brows. Bowlegged to a crippling degree, he required two canes when he walked, resembling more a gnarled tree trunk than a man as he moved. Bearded youths in skullcaps snickered as he shuffled past. In return he would look up at them and smile, his eyes so soft and sweet that the boys would suddenly become ashamed. His were eyes that could melt lies on the tongues of their bearers and turn the hearts of bragging criminals.

David found Sheikh Mohammad in the metalworkers' bazaar, sitting atop a wooden crate under a tin roof dangling with pots and pans. He dropped a few coins in the old man's can.

The sheikh looked up and smiled. "You're a stranger here?" he asked in simple Hebrew.

David felt his face flush, embarrassed it was so obvious.

"You are searching for something?"

He contemplated this for a moment, not sure if he'd properly understood the sheikh. *"Ani lo yodea."* He explained that he did not quite understand.

"Boey." Without waiting for a reply, the man rose to his feet, grasping the handles of both of his canes. "Come," he urged.

David made no effort to move.

"Yalla!" He wobbled clumsily as David followed two steps behind. He kept his arms ready, half expecting the old man to collapse like an accordion with each step. Down a quiet alley and across the empty square, Sheikh Mohammad led David toward an unassuming building, then followed the hedges around back, stopping at the entrance to its cellar. The rusty iron doors stuck out from the ground as if open arms ushering for them to enter. Fast-paced chanting and the rhythmic beat of darabukka drums echoed up the narrow stairwell. The two descended slowly and steadily, their arms linked as their heads bowed beneath the low ceiling.

Inside, a dozen men stood in long white robes, banging drums and stamping their bare feet, bells jingling about their ankles with each step. Several men in tall burgundy hats took to the center of the room with arms stretched out before them. They began to twirl in an ecstatic dance like the spinning tops David played with as a boy.

"What is this dance?" David whispered in the basic Hebrew he had acquired since his arrival.

Sheikh Mohammad stared up at the boy. "This is no dance." He turned away and let his eyes fall upon the whirling dervishes, their majestic robes floating out from their waists in a perfect circumference of symmetry and grace. "This is a prayer with all the body, heart, and soul."

As the beat intensified, the dervishes tilted their chins and stretched up their arms toward the heavens. The walls of the cellar grew tipsy with the drunkenness of men's spirits, and David felt a rush of excitement. He leaned in close to the sheikh. "Why do they do this?"

"Kol haolam mistovev," the sheikh explained slowly so David might understand. "All the universe is whirling," he said while drawing a ring

in the sky with his finger. "The moon is whirling around the earth. Our earth is whirling on its axis, forever around the sun. Other worlds, the constellations. The clouds in the sky and the stars in the farthest galaxies. We are not careening aimlessly through the universe. All the heavens and all the earth whirl eternally in perfect accord." He took David's hand in his thick leathery palm. "These men whirl because they are at one with the universe."

There were words the sheikh had spoken that David had perhaps misunderstood in translation or failed to grasp at all, but somehow the message the kind sheikh sought to impart still came through. David looked into the sheikh's eyes, stepped forward into an empty space, and with outstretched arms began to whirl.

28

When Marie and Edward filed an official complaint at the old police station, they were politely informed that without a cooperating witness or tangible evidence, there was no way they could charge Jean-Pierre Prideux with assault or any other crime, for that matter. "But they've torn his retina," Marie charged. "He's blind in one eye!"

"Madame, not to worry. We'll head over to Monsieur Prideux's flat and check into his alibi."

Later that evening, Marie received a phone call from an officer down at the station. "Monsieur Prideux claims he was fast asleep in his bed on the night in question. His father confirms this. Well, why would the man lie? Madame, with all due respect, Monsieur Prideux is a very well-respected member of our community. If he says his son was with him at church . . . *Oui, oui!* Of course we are serious about bringing the perpetrators to justice, but perhaps your son is confused about who the aggressors were. He did sustain head injuries, as you yourself have claimed . . . Madame, I do not appreciate your tone . . . Yes, of course we are doing our very best . . . We are certainly not going to drop the case. We'll continue our investigation until we bring the criminals to justice."

And so it was that Jean-Pierre Prideux, son of a decorated war hero and grandson of the retired chief of the Marais district police, escaped punishment for his crime, and Edward's dream of becoming a pilot in the French air force was snuffed out forever.

The letter came eight weeks after the beating:

In light of recent events, it is with much regret that we are forced to rescind your acceptance to the National Aviation Academy. As you are well aware, the safety of our students and pilots has and always will be our number one priority. While your visual impairment restricts you from our aviation training program, we welcome and encourage your application to an administrative position within the academy.

Edward folded each corner of the letter until it took on the winged shape of his dreams. He examined his creation before crushing it in the palm of his hand.

"I will never forgive you," he whispered that evening to the bed where David had once slept. The old floral sheets were drawn taut over the thin mattress where a brother should have been. *I was never a twin*, he thought to himself. Not even a brother.

That same week Edward received a letter addressed to him with a foreign stamp sealed with the mark of the newly established Jewish state. He placed it in the pocket of his oversize blazer and went about his day in no particular hurry. Since his graduation, he'd been working in the downstairs bakery. Business had slowed to a crawl, as two more pâtisseries had opened up just down the street. Marie and Carl had begun circling the neighborhood by bike, loading up their baskets to seek out new customers. But no matter how delicious the bread pudding or chocolate-glazed éclairs, these days they were barely able to make ends meet.

Edward greeted the customers slowly. When they asked for the usual chocolate crêpe or custard croissant, he moved sluggishly, eliciting irate glances. He made no attempt to mitigate his limp, but exaggerated it as an expression of disgust with everyone and everything. When the sun began to set, he closed up shop for the evening, then wiped down the counters and slowly swept up the powdered sugar and crumbs from the floor before heading around the corner and mounting the stairs to the family flat. In his pocket, he still held the letter.

It was a cool night in September, but with the furnace lit in the parlor, the Rumie household was warm and quiet. Edward held the envelope in his hands for several minutes. Then he tossed it into the furnace without bothering to open it. The next week he found yet another letter in the post, this time addressed to his parents. This time he tore open the envelope. David was working as a fisherman and had settled in a lush region of Israel called Tiberias. He was saving up his earnings to come back for a visit, perhaps around Easter if he could. How was his brother's aviation training, he wanted to know, and could they please write back as soon as possible?

Week after week Edward fueled the furnace with David's letters. Some were about his newfound Jewish identity, others about living under the constant threat of war. The more lighthearted letters were about the girl who'd caught his eye, the daughter of the fisherman for whom he worked. Her name was Nastasia, and with her help, he was making great strides learning the language, *Ivrit*.

Soon the letters began to show concern: *Has Papa thrown out his back again? What's going on there? Is someone ill?* And always they ended, *Why haven't you written?* And by early November they had turned bitter. *I know you raised me as a Catholic, but please respect my decision.*

While Marie worried constantly about David's fate, Edward busied himself sifting through the mail each day. "Don't worry, *Maman*. I'm sure he's just busy. We'll hear from him any day . . . any day . . . *No, Maman*, there was nothing in the post. I'll check first thing again tomorrow . . . He's bound to write one of these days."

Four months after his brother's departure, Edward finally wrote back. He did not mention the beating he endured and the weeks of painful rehabilitation. He did not mention that he'd been blinded in one eye, that the aviation academy had rescinded his acceptance, or that his leg had been shattered along with the only dream he'd ever had. Nowhere in the letter did he say what he often whispered between clenched teeth at night: "You should have been there for me, as I was there for you."

In neat block letters, he informed David that his abandonment of Christ had devastated their parents. His decision to live as a Jew and settle in Israel was tantamount to abandoning the family who had saved him from certain death. The letter concluded: "Please do not write again."

And so the months dragged on and the Rumie household was quiet. Marie and her husband became more reclusive and melancholy, fearing the worst had happened to their son. Perhaps he had gotten swept up in a skirmish with the Palestinians; maybe he was lying dead in a ditch somewhere.

As his father and mother grew more depressed with each passing day, Edward's conscience had begun to gnaw at him. He began neglecting the bakery. Crumbs and food bits were scattered all over the unswept floor tiles, and customers spotted mice scurrying about. Even the most loyal customers would no longer visit the bakery. Marie and her husband had become listless from worry.

And as time passed, Edward began to appreciate the severity of his actions. He waited every day for David to write again, for the opportunity to be able to storm his parents' chamber waving a tall white envelope in his hand. "It's David! He's all right!" He dreamed of the day. He just needed to wait, just wait for one more letter. They'd be able to check the return address and contact him, and in time, his offense would be forgiven. They would be a family once again.

And then it came. When Edward spotted the envelope in the mail, his heart leaped as he grasped it with frantic desperation. He tore at the seal in breathless gratitude and unfolded the letter inside. Just ten tiny words. Nothing more, nothing less.

> *You have broken my heart.*
> *I will not write again.*

Edward felt panic rising in his chest. He turned the envelope about several times over. Nowhere had David written his exact whereabouts. The envelope did not bear a return address. Out of scores of letters David had sent, it was the only one to survive the furnace. "I'll find you," he promised that night to his brother's empty bed. "I'll find you."

In the morning, Edward made his way to church and confessed his sins to Father Jean-Mari from behind the stenciled partition of a booth that smelled of dust and sweat and ladies' perfume. He returned home certain that absolution was not his to be had and told his parents the very same words he had told the priest. He would find David, he swore. He had a lead, Tiberias! He knew that David had settled there.

A week later, Edward found himself on a steamer bound for Haifa. Once there, he paid an Arab youth a small fortune to escort him to Tiberias, and upon arrival, began asking around about a young French boy. "His name is David," he said in a frantic huff. "David Herzikova." He held up an old photo to anyone who would stop to look.

And then a break. A fisherman with an Algerian accent pointed Edward to a small cottage nestled on a hill in the distance. "But the boy you look for, he left last week," explained the man as he went about skinning his latest catch. "He went with the father of his fiancée to fight."

"*Fiancée?*" Edward wondered aloud.

"They became engaged just before he left. Anyway, he's with the army now. I don't know anything more, but I'm sure you can get more information at army headquarters in Tel Aviv." The man wiped the sweat from his brow, then continued skinning the fish atop his wooden chopping board. "The girl, she is studying somewhere in Jerusalem, living there with her mother," he continued, but Edward was already pushing past overeager shopkeepers to find his way to the closest bus stop.

Several hours later at the administrative offices of the Israeli Defense Forces, Edward faced one brick wall after another. "We don't give out information about our soldiers," a Moroccan hulk of a man told him. "It's for security," he said as Edward, exhausted and dejected, leaned over on the counter that separated one man from the other. "Someone else in charge? I am in charge!" the man barked. "What do you think this is . . . We don't run a telegraph service . . . Stop crying! What do I look like? I'm not your mother. Pull yourself together, there's a war going on, man!" And after another fifteen minutes of pleading, "*Beseder, beseder*, okay, I'll pass the message, but don't get your hopes up. There are at least a few dozen David Herzikovas in the army. It will take some time to locate the right one."

Edward returned to France and waited for word of his brother.

He'd find himself waiting twelve months more.

The following year on Christmas Day, an administrator from the offices of the IDF phoned to say that David Herzikova had been discharged from service. He and his wife had left the country. And what of the message Edward had been trying to send to him? Had David at least gotten the message?

"What message was that?" the man inquired. "No, I didn't know there was any message to be delivered, but the good news is he's alive and well! Where is he? Oh, I'm sorry, sir, we don't keep such detailed information."

Edward released the receiver and looked up. His mother and father stood in the shallow doorway, eager-eyed and awaiting news. He dropped his head to his lap. "He's alive."

29

There was a sudden knock at the door.

Then another, but Hannah Herzikova just went on painting, paying no attention to the unexpected visitor. Instead, she looked about her makeshift studio. Sunbeams reached through the window, creating a dazzling plume of sun-sprinkled dust that settled gently on the wooden floor, whose uneven planks had already weathered two floods that year.

The studio was converted from an old barn that once upon a time housed horses. It was just a stone's throw from her home, a Norman Rockwell creation with giant windows and a splintered front porch. The house was at the bottom of a bowl-shaped plot of land, so several times in the month of May, it flooded. Unlike the studio, it had been elevated onto stilts to halt the floodwaters from rushing in and sweeping it away.

In her studio, Hannah left her equipment and works hanging on protruding nails that had once been used to hang horseshoes and saddles and old leather reins. Countless portraits of neighbors covered every inch of the walls. Some were proud, like Mr. Gottlieb from across the way. He moved like an old ugly bulldog, wobbling in all his magnificence, growling deliciously when he mumbled. She painted Mrs. Rhodes, her ancient face as wrinkled and enchanting as the etchings on a treasure map, her white hair in a glorious pouf. There was the portrait of one-eyed Mrs. Ethers, who wasn't one-eyed at all, but simply could not see out of the cracked lens in her spectacles. Their eyes, dark and gleaming, surveyed visitors like a thousand brooding Mona Lisas, hanging high above the floodwaters that seeped up through the floorboards, leaving an inch or so of water.

While many of Hannah's friends lived in the city, renting out small rooms in the Village or Williamsburg, she was happy to be back home in Connecticut. The city was just a twenty-minute ride away, with trains heading out every other hour.

She'd graduated from college four years earlier, in a springtime outdoor ceremony overlooking Washington Square Park and a colorful string of nineteenth-century rowhouses. And though she'd never forget the ceremony or the celebratory brunch they'd shared afterward, it saddened her to think that her mother never would or could recall that milestone, or any other for that matter. Alzheimer's had long since claimed her mother's mind. The memory of that day, as with so many others, was one she shared only with her father.

She'd originally rented a pocket-size studio space in the city with two other girls, taking a part-time job teaching art appreciation to elementary school students. In the afternoons, she'd return to the cramped quarters to focus on her *real* work, the portraits.

When she'd learned about her father's illness two months earlier, she quit her job and moved home right away. Where time had once been an inconsequential factor in the life of Hannah Herzikova, it was now something very real. Whereas her mother's dementia had slowly crept upon them, her father's cancer had come barreling into their lives with no prior warning.

She'd begun painting his portrait six weeks earlier, but for the past few days had found herself at a standstill. There was something missing, something not quite right. She'd never faced this problem before with the other portraits. They'd all seemed to just spring to life beneath her carefree brushstrokes, but now she simply could no longer proceed.

"Hello? Anyone there?" Hannah was startled to attention. She'd completely forgotten about whoever was at the door and was in no mood for visitors. The conversation with her father earlier in the day had left her disturbed. A lifetime spent under the same roof, and she still couldn't shake the feeling that the person she loved most in this world was the person she knew least of all. Leaning in toward his portrait, she studied it up close. She was no more than a few inches away, and yet when it came to understanding David Herzikova, she was light-years from where she needed to be.

The next knock sounded more boldly, this time on the windowpane. "Hello there!" A blurred figure had his forehead pressed up against the glass. "Hello!" The sight of arms waving in her direction forced her to her feet.

"What is it?" She made her way to the door, but stopped short of opening it.

"I'm looking for David Herzikova," a raspy male voice sounded. The man had a thick French accent, like so many of her father's friends and acquaintances; only this was a voice she did not recognize. "I knocked over at the main house," the unfamiliar voice continued. "No one seems to be home."

Hannah glimpsed back through the window. Outside, an assortment of chipped terra-cotta pots dotted the walkway up to the main house. Her eyes followed the gray stone path up to the kitchen window, where she met her mother's eyes from behind the green window dressings.

"That's right, no one's home," Hannah lied.

"Would you open the door?" the man asked politely enough.

She reached for the knob, then let her hand fall away. "I'm sorry," she said decidedly. "But I've really got to get back to work."

"Can you at least tell me when he'll be home?"

"I don't know when he'll be back," she called back as she headed away from the door and back toward the portrait.

Sitting before her canvas on a low folding stool, Hannah quickly forgot about the stranger who had come calling. Looking over the portrait, she realized that to the untrained eye, the painting of her father might very well seem complete. His image showed on canvas just as the man himself appeared in life—handsome, austere, and utterly elusive. The long, straight nose, the dimple in his chin, and the stubble along his strong jawline—it was all perfectly precise.

And yet there was something about the eyes that didn't seem quite right. The elongated distance between them was correct, but it was the expression that was incomplete, inexplicable at best. What was David Herzikova concealing behind that blank stare? Was it pride or shame? Joy or sorrow? She'd used all the colors of her palette, but no matter what combination she tried, she could not produce the image of a secret.

She knew she had to get it right, even if it meant having to start the portrait again from scratch. Hannah reached for her keys and slung her sack over her shoulder. What she needed, now more than ever, was to look into his eyes and discover the truth. There was no telling how much time he had left.

30

As the week wore on, Selim watched as each day his roommate's lids drooped a little further. The girl worked feverishly to finish her father's portrait, his whole life captured in eyes that would see long after his would close forever. She sat while she worked, her canvas propped on a wooden easel by her father's side. She seemed to paint in a trance, pressing her tubes frantically to get out the last drops.

It was a Thursday morning, six days since she'd first begun painting the man. Selim had started to anticipate her arrival.

As she had the previous days, the girl arrived just around the time the breakfast cart was making its rounds. She made her way across the room and offered up a courteous, tight-lipped smile before quietly kissing her father's forehead. Then she got right to work.

As the hours passed, her tired gaze flickered between the canvas and the man in the bed beside it. Visiting hours drew to a close, but the girl remained by her father's side, painting, always painting. Time slowed to a crawl, and all that seemed to change was the shifting light of day. All the while the girl still worked on the portrait.

Booming voices softened as the corridor lights were dimmed for the night. And still she stayed, stopping occasionally to whisper sweet words to her father as he faded in and out of a fitful sleep. Eventually, one of the nurses stopped by to inquire about an after-hours visiting pass. The girl just straightened up and sighed, then pulled from her sweater a laminated badge clipped to a string around her neck.

It was well past midnight by the time she'd laid down her brushes, packed up her paints, and for the first time in a week, collapsed her folding stool. It occurred to Selim that perhaps she'd finally finished working on her painting, or perhaps she'd just given up.

As she carried her stool over, resting it up beside the door, she glanced up at Selim. "Have I been keeping you up?"

His eyes had been on her all through the night. "No," he lied.

Making her way over to his side, she introduced herself. "I'm Hannah." Her low voice rustled with the sound of her breath, while the name itself somehow boasted of life.

Life. It was something that was not his to have, not for much longer anyhow. As he reflected upon his wretched state, warm tears made their way down the side of his bandaged face, and for the first time that night, Selim turned away from her.

"Good night, Hannah." He closed his eyes and pulled the sheet up to his chin. Though they'd only just met, he was soothed by the sound of her name on his lips.

"Good night."

She awoke early the next day to the sound of trucks hauling trash in the cul-de-sac below. She stood up from the hard wooden chair by her father's bed and turned to examine the canvas in the daylight. The paint, wet and dreamy the night before, was now bone dry and coarse to the touch.

She awoke, and her father had died.

Jewish law dictates that the dead be buried as soon as possible, and so the next day, over a hundred people gathered under wild oaks and cedars to say good-bye to David Herzikova. In the Jewish cemetery, dozens of friends and family members stood quietly as the rabbi recited the mourner's prayer, the kaddish. Every so often, the crowd would chant "Amen" in unison.

Twenty yards away, a black Town Car was parked on the side of the glistening tar road that wound through the cemetery. Two of the four tires were up on the grass. No one but Hannah seemed to notice the car or the silhouette of what appeared to be a man in a fedora seated beyond the tinted windowpane. She saw the shadowy figure lift a square cloth to his face, and after a moment lean back and disappear from view. As they lowered the wooden casket into the ground, the black Town Car slipped away, and Hannah said good-bye to her father for the last time.

Back at the old house on stilts, she and her mother sat shivah. Hannah watched as her mother, Nastasia, took a sip of her black coffee and looked out the living room window. It was unusually humid weather, and the room dripped with moisture. Hannah moved to the window as Nastasia pressed her fingers against the windowpane. Her concentration seemed spread over the outside lawn. "Where have the banana trees gone?" A small measure of panic rose in her voice. "Who would cut down my trees?" She turned around and looked at all the people gathered in her living room. "What are they all doing here?" she whispered to Hannah.

Hannah knew that her mother was somewhere else entirely right then, back in a small cottage in Tiberias, overlooking the Sea of Galilee.

As more visitors arrived, Hannah led her mother to cushions and pillows piled on the floor. Jewish law forbids mourners from sitting on couches or chairs, relegating them to mats on the floor as means to express one's grief.

Visitors offered their condolences as they munched on cashews and dried dates. All throughout the room, neighbors and friends exchanged memories of David Herzikova. While he was loved throughout his community and had many good friends in America, David's past was shrouded in mystery. Large blocks of his life had been kept private, shared only with his wife Nastasia, who could not recall much of the past now anyway. David Herzikova was a man of secrets—secrets that were now buried six feet underground.

3 1

In the seven days since her father's death, Hannah Herzikova had not come to the hospital once. He'd no reason to think she would, except perhaps to collect the portrait she'd left behind. By the time the breakfast cart rolled around each morning, Selim knew he'd spend another day alone.

It was Thursday, three weeks and a day since he'd arrived in New York. From the drawer in the bedside table, he withdrew the glossy magazine he'd purchased at the airport. He flipped through it several times before he found what he'd been searching for.

He tore the page away, then carefully folded it and tucked it within the yellowed pages of his grandfather's poetry collection.

It was then that the smell of the sea filled the room.

Selim turned and let his black eyes fall on the sliver of body exposed through the crack in the door. The door yielded, revealing her in full. Dark shadows ran the length of her cheekbones and high slinking neck as her bright eyes shone against her ghostly complexion.

Hannah Herzikova made her way through the dark room and toward the window shades.

"Don't," he called out, but she'd already opened the blinds, allowing the sunlight to pour in. He'd just removed his bandages, as he did every couple of days, to allow his wounds some air. Self-consciously, he lifted his hands to shield his face from the light.

Her eyes slid to the hole in his throat, his sealed lid, and the swollen mass of his left side before breaking away. That the right side was unaffected in any way only made the left side that much more difficult to look upon. Selim knew that. And by the sidelong look in her eyes, he suspected she felt it too.

"I'm sorry, I can put them back down if you want me to."

When he didn't answer, she came around and approached the chair by his side, the pleats in her dress rustling over her narrow hips. Her broad, bare shoulder sloped casually as she slid her oversize tote down the length of her arm, letting it fall to the ground with reckless ease.

The bed that her father had once occupied was empty. The portrait of David Herzikova was now resting against the wall beyond the foot of the bed, aligned with the retracted room divider.

"I'm sorry for your loss," he managed to say.

Her eyes welled up and it looked as though she were going to walk out. Instead, she turned and forced a sad smile. She glanced at the painting, then sighed disappointedly. "I never did get it quite right."

"I like it," he said matter-of-factly.

"What do you like about it?"

He took a moment to think it through. "A lot of things."

"Like what? Specifically?"

"Maybe the eyes."

"The eyes?"

"I feel like I know him just by looking at the eyes."

She took a moment before quietly asking, "Really?"

"You seem surprised."

"It's just . . . I was having a hard time . . ." Her voice trailed off as she dropped her chin and dragged shaky fingers through her sand-colored hair.

"They say the eyes are the windows to the soul. I imagine a soul is a difficult thing to paint."

She lifted her head as her hands fell to her sides.

"You did good," he said quietly.

She shook her head. "There were so many things I didn't know about him."

"You knew him." A moment passed before he was overtaken by a coughing fit.

She reached for the cup by his bed and bent to hold it to his lips. His eyes met hers. Covered in tubes and tape, his hand touched her hand as he grappled for the cup. He took a few shallow sips before his cough subsided.

Hand to hand, skin to skin, they were suspended in the current of air between them.

Hannah's hand slipped away as she stepped back clumsily. He studied her for a long moment, and she tore her gaze away, letting it escape to the clock on the wall.

"You have somewhere to be?" He stared on unflinchingly.

They heard footsteps in the hall, and the soft jingling of keys and loose change grew nearer. In the doorframe, a tall man with sharp, angular cheekbones stood studying an open manila folder. A stethoscope hung around his neck.

Dr. Rosen, a senior member of the hospital's oncology unit, leaned against the door panel as he continued shuffling through the papers in the manila folder.

"Selim, how're you today? The nurses say you barely touched your morphine drip this weekend. That's great to hear. So the pain is going away?"

"I'm okay." He attempted a smile.

Dr. Rosen loosened the stethoscope from around his neck and plugged his ears with the instrument.

"Deep breaths," he instructed as he slid the metal tip beneath the opening of Selim's gown. "I want to wait a few more days before we begin the treatments." He removed the stethoscope earpieces and backed away. After writing something in his notes, he capped his pen and returned it to his pocket. "We should talk about what's going to happen as we move forward."

Hannah reached for her bag and headed for the door. "Excuse me, I shouldn't have barged in like this. It's obviously a bad time. I'm sorry."

"Hannah," Selim called after her.

She stopped and turned in the doorway.

"Same time tomorrow?"

She swallowed hard, nodded, and disappeared from view.

32

The next day at noon, she was back as promised.

Her hair was pulled back into a messily braided bun, loose strands forming a delicate frame for her face. In her white linen dress, she appeared to Selim strikingly bare. She wore no bracelets, no watch, no polish on her nails. Her only adornment was the ruby ring, bright against her fair complexion.

She smelled familiar. Fresh and cool, but damp and rich. She smelled of the sea, and for a moment, he was transported seven thousand miles away, back to his home on the shores of the Bosphorus. Selim looked up at her, astounded. The scent filled his memory.

"You smell like the sea."

"Is that supposed to be a compliment?" She pulled her hair back, then sank into the chair by his bed. "The sea here has cigarette butts and garbage floating in it, probably a few dead bodies too."

A stocky attendant in an ice-blue uniform showed up, offering Selim a selection of snacks laid out on a purple plastic tray. He frowned and waved the tray and the nurse away with his bony hand. He turned to face Hannah, serious and alert.

"I'm glad you're here."

The rough strap of her leather bag whipped against the glossy floor as she let her purse slip from her lap. She sat unmoved as the contents spilled onto the floor.

She swallowed the knot in her throat, then looked around at the mess she had made. Her lean fingers reached for a lipstick, a few scattered coins, and a vintage-style compact mirror, cracked open on the floor.

When she'd gathered her belongings, she rose and stood in her place as though waiting for instruction.

"Are you okay?"

She frowned and swept the tip of her shoe against the floor, dodging the question. "I'm not going to bother you. Brought something to read with me." She held up a book as she spoke.

"Bother me? I asked you to come."

She nodded, then sank back into the seat of the chair and buried herself behind the thick book.

He examined her curiously as the minutes passed.

Her uncertain gaze crept over the edge of her book.

"Hannah?"

She placed the book down in her lap.

"You're not reading?"

She looked over at the portrait of her father, then turned her attention to the steady drip of IV fluid in the bag by Selim's side. Leaning forward, she slid the book under her seat. "I don't feel like reading anything right now."

"We could talk?"

She dropped her chin and looked away. "I don't want to talk." Her emerald eyes sought refuge in the shadowy crevices of the dark room. "I don't want to talk," she said a little more loudly this time.

He raised his hands. "Fair enough."

So they sat quietly for the next few minutes, listening to the sound of pigeons flapping their wings on the window ledge, and to the whir of small aircraft flying low over the dark river. At some point during that stretch of silence, he tore away the monitoring device clipped to his finger.

"Give me your hand."

Observing him oddly, she considered his request before pulling her chair in closer and extending her arm.

He took her hand in his own, then turned it so that her palm was exposed. Cautiously, he dragged his finger across her skin, drawing an *H* over her palm.

Hannah flinched. "It tickles," she explained, though Selim didn't loosen his grip.

A. Her wide eyes trailed his precise movements as he carried on.

N. Her body shivered to his touch.

N. His finger continued to glide across her pale skin.

A. The muscles in her hand loosened until her palm melted into his.

H. She looked up at him.

Hannah. Everything else seemed to have fallen away.

Outside, clouds were roiling in the hot gray sky. A wet wind poured through a narrow crack in the window as he loosened his grip and let her hand slip away.

Her eyes sparkled while her lips came to a part. "Selim?" she whispered.

He brought his finger to his mouth and hushed her with his eyes. Their bodies were still and their breathing slowed to a stop. Only the universe breathed for them.

33

Something strange was happening to Hannah. Her father was gone and her mother merely a shell of the woman she'd once been. Hannah was grieving for her losses, yet a new energy had taken her by force, a stranger from room 301.

More than ever before, Hannah began spending long hours in the studio, late into the night. She'd bring her paintings to his hospital room in the mornings and cover his wall with every scene the eye could capture. There were college kids in backpacks listening to iPods on the subway, hipsters in fedoras wearing lace-up combat boots. There were street musicians strumming acoustic guitars beside open cases filled with jumbled bills, as well as fiery sunsets, lovers kissing, children laughing. However she could, Hannah would take bits and pieces of the outside world and give them to Selim. Through her paintings, she hoped he might escape beyond the walls of room 301.

In the afternoons he'd sleep, dreaming of sweet halvah and sugar-coated pineapples sliced into yellow half-moons. His dreams took place in days gone by, when his mother still smelled of lemon and cinnamon spice, when she'd bring home bundles of licorice strips from the sweet-shop and take him to grassy fields along the shore, where they'd fly kites shaped like goldfish, dragons, and butterflies.

He'd tell Hannah of these dreams, the landscapes of different colors, iridescent hues of violet, blue, and pink. Of his hometown: Istanbul, the streets winding and a bit crooked but lovely and really very charming, much like her smile.

And while he dreamed, she'd sometimes wander into nearby museums.

She'd pass through white halls filled with Greek sculptures. Faces that looked like gods, bodies that were indestructible. Drawing inspiration at every turn, she'd pass through the Impressionist hall and let herself be absorbed in the paintings, moments that perhaps had lasted for only a second, but were immortalized by the artists who'd dared to capture them.

Oftentimes they'd take walks down the hall, passing room 307, where during lunchtime, dozens of visitors could be heard chatting gaily and doting over the eighty-something-year-old matriarch staying there. Her family would feast on home-cooked meals they'd brought over in stacks of metal baking tins. They'd wave Hannah and Selim in, inviting them to a taste of their delicious rice pilaf, flatbreads, and chutney.

When he was sick from his chemotherapy treatments and could barely get out of bed, she'd read to him from the works of Kahlil Gibran, the Lebanese artist, poet, and writer who believed happiness could not be contained without the carvings of sorrow deep within one's soul. She'd stay by his side until late into the evening, until he insisted that she leave, go home and work on whatever piece she was currently painting.

When he was feeling well enough, he'd read to her from his grand-father's poetry collection. Musings of the wise ones: the enlightened Hafez, the Afghan Rumi, the eleventh-century mystic Al-Ghazali.

He even shared with her a poem said to be centuries old, written by an illustrious ancestor of his named Suleiman. Though it had been passed down through the generations, his grandfather had scribbled it down on the very last blank page of the book. It was his hope that such a precious family heirloom should never be lost, that it should always remain close to his grandson's heart.

He kept his eyes on the page as he read and translated each verse for Hannah. All the while, she sensed that he knew every word by heart, as though the poem had originally been born of his pen, as though the poem had somehow been his own.

> "Throne of my lonely niche, my wealth, my love, my moon-
> light.
> My most sincere friend, my confidante, my very existence,
> my Sultan
> The most beautiful among the beautiful . . .

My springtime, my merry-faced love, my daytime, my
    sweetheart, laughing leaf . . .
My plans, my sweet, my rose
I'll sing your praises always."

34

Beneath the chair opposite Selim's bed, David Herzikova's tin box lay untouched. Week after week, it stayed in that space, concealed, then revealed, by a warping shadow that came and went each day.

The box had been left in the room alongside the portrait of her father. Why Hannah had refused to take it home, Selim couldn't comprehend. Perhaps it meant little to her, or perhaps it meant everything. Whatever the case, she'd come and go often, stepping past the thing as though it were yesterday's paper, or maybe tomorrow's.

Harking back to the conversation he'd overhead months earlier, Selim recalled her father sounding anxious when asked about the tin. His breathing had been harsh and his voice uneasy when instructing Hannah to put the box away. There was something inside that box that had set the man on edge. What was he hiding?

Secrets.

Selim knew all about secrets. He could sense the existence of one trapped in the box.

Reaching for the poetry book stored in the dresser by his side, he pulled out the glossy clipping planted between two nearly translucent pages.

Like Hannah's father, Selim had withheld the truth from someone who genuinely cared for him. He questioned himself now as to why he'd done it. It wasn't that he didn't love her. Looking at Ayda's image, he wondered if perhaps it was because he'd loved her too much.

With that one realization, it was as though he'd pulled a string, and with it, his twisted logic began to unravel. "I'm sorry," he whispered to no one and himself.

The sound of Crocs slapping against the floor tiles startled Selim. He looked up to find a nurse with a clipboard, taking notes a few feet beyond the edge of his bed. There she stood, mere inches from the box.

Secrets.

How was it that they were meant to protect when all they seemed to do was upset lives?

"Hey." He looked up at the nurse across the bed, then nodded to the chair behind her. "Would you do me a favor and hand me the box under there?"

She pulled her thin lips back into two pink threads. "This one here?" She let out a little squeal while squatting to retrieve it.

"That's it."

Selim examined the container, a storage tin that might have once served as a schoolboy's lunchbox. Plastered on the lid was a poster featuring a pinup girl in a polka-dot dress with a bloodred rose tucked up in chestnut hair. Selim drew his fingers across the curled-up edges of the parchment, trying to smooth them down as best he could. He wondered about the poster. He wondered why the man had kept it.

His chewed fingernails struggled to unfasten the tight latch as Selim considered the fate of his own memories. Would they die with him or would they, by an act of celestial kindness or, better yet, by courage on his part, be passed on to live in the consciousness of another? Perhaps they might only ever reside in a box such as this.

And who would inherit the Osman Secret Chronicles? They had been passed from generation to generation, from one man to the next. Centuries of wisdom and recollection had been preserved and passed down throughout the ages. Those memories deserved to be salvaged. But what of a man who never had any children? What of a man who had taken away the life of a boy and all the memories he would never live to have?

Slow down, Brother, slow down! The memory came tearing through his mind like the motorbike that had torn through his life.

Pop! The latch suddenly unfastened and the lid burst up. Startled, Selim shook his head, then turned his attention to the contents of the box. Sifting through dozens of photos, he discovered a gray-scale world framed by white perforated edges. He picked up a picture of a matronly woman in a pillbox hat, flanked by two young men—all three standing before a massive steamship.

There was no mistaking David Herzikova, with his prominent chin and curious eyes, was the youth on the left. On the other side of the woman was a husky-looking fellow with a scar above his eye. Selim flipped the photo over. *1959.*

He went through the others. The same boy featured in nearly all the pictures. He studied that boy, and as he did, he had the strange sensation that the boy was studying him back. He felt his shoulders tense up as a cramp spread up along the back of his neck, settling behind his ears and along his jaw. *It's just a picture,* he assured himself. He slowly lifted his chin up from the photo and discovered an elderly man in the doorway, leaning against a cane. There was no telling how long he'd been there.

Selim dropped the photos back into the box and secured the lid hurriedly.

"Edward Rumie," said the man. He poked his head farther into the room and looked around.

His wrinkled face, the lines around his mouth, reminded Selim of the worn pages of his grandfather's poetry collections. His eyes were a mystery, shielded from view by the oversize opaque lenses of black wraparound glasses. The man took a few steps toward Selim's bedside.

"Do I know you?" Selim asked, shifting uncomfortably. He was sure he didn't.

Edward Rumie made his way to the wall opposite the bed and set his sights on one particular abstract mural. "I'd be surprised if you did," he said. "Mind if I sit for a minute?" The joints in his knees cracked as he lowered himself onto the upholstered chair beyond the foot of his bed. "I've been trying to find someone." The elderly man suddenly seemed distracted. Though he couldn't see his eyes, Selim was sure the man's gaze was on the box, inspecting the girl in the polka-dot dress. "Whose is that?" The man seemed startled.

"The box?"

"Yes, the box."

Selim reached over and placed it in his bedside drawer. "It's mine."

"Yours?"

"Mine." He was surprised by the firmness in his voice.

"Right." The man scoffed. "That's a French pinup from 1959. I've seen only one in my lifetime. Well, two, counting that one."

Selim shrugged his shoulders. He'd spent half his life guarding secrets. One could say that it had become second nature. Now he found himself guarding one that didn't even belong to him.

"It's from the Marais. I should know."

"Then it's from the Marais," Selim acquiesced before turning away.

"So that's your box." The man leaned forward and smacked his lips together. "Maybe you're from Le Marais. Maybe you speak French too?"

"I do."

"Like a Spanish cow, I bet you do," the man mumbled under his breath in his native tongue.

"There are as many as five official languages spoken in Spain," Selim replied in near-perfect French. "Another three that enjoy recognition status and two others that are used unofficially."

The old man's pout flattened out into a wry grin.

"And I wouldn't underestimate cows," Selim went on blithely. "They're highly intelligent creatures."

Beaten at his own game, the old man shrugged, then glanced over the artworks hanging on the walls on Selim's side of the room. He gestured at the paintings before turning back to Selim. "Not bad." Floor to ceiling, together the paintings looked like the mosaic tiles of a sanctuary.

"Not bad at all," Selim replied.

"Who did all this?" His voice took on a tender tone.

"A friend."

The man quietly contemplated this. "Good friend."

Selim nodded. "She may be the best."

"You're very lucky."

Selim hadn't thought of himself as lucky. He said nothing.

"I'd have done anything to be loved like this." The old man seemed to be talking only to himself.

After a few moments, he headed to the door. When he reached it, he turned to Selim and with his cane drew an imaginary circle in the air. "*This*," he said, pointing with an air of instruction, "this is a labor of *love*." His cane came down quietly. He smiled, tipped his hat, and left the room.

35

It was a cool, bright morning when Edward Rumie came around again. Without a knock or salutation, he burst in for the second time that week, making himself comfortable once more in the chair beyond the bed. "I want to meet the artist."

"Nice to see you too."

"Where is she?" the old man huffed.

"I see you've been brushing up on your manners."

"Do you expect her to be in soon?"

"It's not even nine." Selim set his sights on the clock across the room. "You *do* know there are set visiting hours."

"I guess she's busy. Yes, she must be very busy."

"Do you wander around the hallways harassing every foreigner you come across?"

"I don't discriminate," the man said pointedly.

Selim sighed and turned back to his newspaper. "I don't know when she'll be back."

"Mind if I wait?"

"I guess not."

They sat in silence for a few minutes while Selim flipped through the newspaper. He discovered a half-page article detailing the latest turmoil surrounding the Turkish novelist's imprisonment on the charges of "damaging national unity" through his writings. A peaceful protest in defense of the novelist had turned violent and tear gas had been un-leashed on a crowd of marching university students. A large photo de-picted a man with multiple piercings and a young girl in a head scarf holding up a sign that read: "Free Taguc! Free Speech! Free Turkey!" Selim read on and learned that the trial had been postponed yet again, and that the author faced up to three years in prison for depicting an Armenian character as a victim of genocide. He was among scores of writers and journalists charged with violating article 8 of law 3713 for his supposed "attack" on the nation's unity.

Selim thought of Gurat and of the canceled appointment that might have freed the man. Still, even then it would not have been enough. There were more writers and journalists being prosecuted for speaking their minds.

The old man cleared his throat loudly, interrupting Selim's thoughts and bringing him back to reality. He looked up.

In his rumpled linen suit, Rumie stared shamelessly from his place opposite the bed.

"Mind taking off those glasses? I feel like I'm sitting across from the Terminator."

The old man seemed pleased. "I'll take that as a compliment."

"*Why?*" Selim shook his head limply. "Look, do you plan on sitting here all day?"

"I have no other plans. Nowhere to be."

Selim closed his eyes as though the act of not seeing might make the man disappear.

"What time did you say she'd be back?" Rumie looked at his watch, then glanced up at the door.

"I didn't say." Selim turned from the man and settled his attention on the heart-monitoring device beside his bed. His eyes lingered on the machine, its electric waves and black backdrop reminding him of days past when as a boy, he would play with the glowing pegs of his Lite-Brite set.

Once, long ago, he was just a boy.

Once he was a child.

A wave of sadness passed over him as he realized the Osman dynasty might end here, perhaps in this very bed, beneath a coarse white sheet between two metal rail guards. He had no children, and as Dr. Rosen had delicately informed him, even if he managed to make it out of here and live a few more years, the treatment would most likely leave him sterile.

"Well, where is she when she's not here?" the old man asked suddenly.

"I'm not sure."

"You don't know?"

"You'll have to ask Hannah."

"Ask me what?"

The two men turned to find her leaning in the doorway, sunglasses riding low on the bridge of her nose and a blank canvas tucked under the arm of her cropped denim jacket. "What's going on?"

She stripped away her glasses and let her bag fall to the ground as she made her way to Selim's side.

"You're here."

"I'm here," she echoed. She wove her fingers through a wavy halo of hair before making herself comfortable at the edge of his bed.

Edward Rumie stood and made his way toward her. "Hannah?"

"Hi?" she said curiously.

Rumie reached out and shook her hand. "I'm a big fan of your work."

"Thanks." She kicked off her ankle boots and tucked her legs under her. "I'm sorry, have we met before?"

"Edward Rumie." He smiled warmly, revealing a row of handsome ivory teeth, slightly misaligned like vintage piano keys.

"I have a gallery in Paris, and well, I'm sorry to barge in like this. It's just that I was looking for an old friend yesterday when I passed by this room and stumbled across your work. I must say, it's really quite astonishing."

Hannah glanced back at Selim, then smiled timidly. "Um. Thank you."

"I'll tell you what," Edward said while rummaging through his pockets. "I plan to be in New York a while longer. I may even move here for good." He withdrew a card from his wallet and handed it to her. "You see, I've found this great little space in Chelsea. A pop-up gallery, if you will. I've always dreamed of expanding and opening a place in New York. In any event, I was planning a kickoff exhibition, maybe next month or September, a sort of emerging artists showcase." He stopped and eyed her expectantly for a long moment.

"That all sounds really great," she said quietly. "What does that have to do with me?"

"Well, I want to exhibit your work, that's what."

"Oh, wow." Her eyes widened. "It's just that, I'm not an artist."

He turned his attention to Selim. "What is she talking about?" he sounded rather confused. "Not an artist?" His eyes scanned the dozens of paintings throughout the room. "No, no, no." He shook his head, then led her toward the door. "We're going to take you straight down the hall to have your eyes checked, and if there's nothing wrong with your eyes, and I suspect there isn't, we'll take the elevator down to two and have your head checked."

She turned her gaze to Selim. "It's not a good time. I'm not ready." She spoke low enough that perhaps Rumie might not hear.

"That one," Rumie pointed in the direction of David's portrait leaning up against the wall. "That *must* be the centerpiece."

"No . . . *no*," she stammered and moved to turn the canvas around so that only its blank side could be seen. "That one's no good."

"*Mais, c'est magnifique!*" He brushed past her, then carried the canvas over to the window to examine it under natural light. "This is it."

"I'm sorry." Her voice began to crack. "You don't want that one."

"But *why?*"

Her glistening eyes settled on her father's image. "He was a very special man. This portrait doesn't do him justice."

"You may be an artist, a great one at that, but you are no art critic."

She shrugged her shoulders and looked away. "What can I say."

"You can say yes." His eyes turned serious. "Say yes, and believe me when I tell you, this portrait *is* special. Every brushstroke and every shade is a testament to the respect and admiration you held for this man."

"You see all that?" Her voice was doubtful.

"I see you must have loved him very much."

She turned her chin to the ground and felt the tears begin to fall.

"It's all right there on the canvas," he continued. "This is something special."

And though she had no reason to trust him, as she looked up, Selim could tell she wanted so badly to believe him. She needed so badly to feel that this one portrait, above all the others, *was* special.

"All right." Her words were barely a whisper.

He brought his hands together, then kissed her cheeks.

"May I?" He reached for the newspaper on Selim's tray, then tore away the front page. He began folding its corners as Hannah and Selim looked on. After a minute he handed her a rose fashioned from the paper Selim had been reading earlier in the day. "I need at least twenty-five, maybe thirty pieces!" he said before heading away down the hall.

36

Four months after he first arrived, Selim underwent yet another second cycle of chemotherapy. Refusing to leave his side that first night, Hannah sat in the dark watching him sleep and listening to him mumble. He shot up suddenly, his body choking, desperate to rid himself of the contents of his stomach and the poison in his blood.

She reached out to him.

"I'm sorry."

"I'm here. You're going to be fine."

"I'm so sorry."

"Everything's okay."

"Forgive me."

"Do you need anything? How about some water?"

"You have to forgive me." It seemed he was still very much asleep. "Ayda." He took hold of her hand and squeezed. "Is it you?"

"Shhh. Try to rest now. I don't know an Ayda."

"Ayda?" His voice was frantic.

"I'm here, Selim. It's Hannah."

His breathing slowed.

"It's really you?" A quiet moment passed between them. "Ayda?"

She swallowed a knot rising in her throat. "Yes," she lied.

"Ayda." His voice was a whisper.

She took his hand and brought it to her lips.

"I'm so sorry. You forgive me?"

"I forgive you."

"Ayda?"

"Yes, Selim?"

"You love me?"

"I love you."

The next morning she helped him to sit upright and coaxed him from the bed. She thought nothing of the words he'd spoken in his sleep. He'd surely have no memory of them now. He'd been delirious, she reasoned, then pushed the odd exchange from her mind.

Selim dragged his legs over the edge of the mattress and stood slowly, seeming not to notice when his grandfather's poetry collection tumbled from the rumpled sheets down to the floor.

Hannah moved to retrieve it while he shuffled past to the bathroom. As she bent to pick it up, she noticed the frayed edge of a glossy scrap sticking out amongst the pages. She pulled the paper loose and discovered a torn-out magazine page folded down the center. Running water sounded from the tap as Hannah flattened the page out in front of her.

Half the space was taken up by the image of a stunning brunette with wide-set smoky eyes, full red lips, and a half-filled martini glass raised up to her chin. Though she could not decipher a single word of the accompanying article, the name he'd uttered in his dreams leaped out from scattered spots all across the page.

AYDA: The headline called to her loud and clear.

AYDA.

The sound of running water stopped suddenly, and she hastily folded the sheet, returned it to the pages of the book, and backed away hurriedly into the chair.

When Selim emerged, he glanced around as though sensing that something was not quite right. "What'd I miss?"

She shrugged her shoulders and feigned ignorance. "Let's go for a walk," she suggested.

Selim pushed the metal pole supporting his IV drip as they made their way through the hallway toward the ground-level courtyard. There she led him to a cool stone bench in the shade, where earlier that morning she'd set up her easel and canvas.

"I guess that's yours?" he asked suspiciously of the easel positioned beside them.

She crossed her legs and leaned back against the bench. "Set it up this morning."

"What's it doing out here?"

She shrugged and sank deeper into the seat of the bench.

"You're not going to paint my portrait."

She kept her emerald eyes on the fountain ahead but said nothing.

"Hannah, I need to hear that you understand what I'm saying. You're *not* going to paint my portrait."

She stood abruptly and turned to face him. "Selim, that's exactly what I plan on doing."

"No."

"No?"

"I won't let you."

"It doesn't matter if you let me or you don't let me. I've already begun it."

"The canvas is blank!" His hands shot up wildly as he spoke.

"In my mind. I've begun it in my mind."

"I won't sit for you."

"You don't have to."

"You're going to paint it from memory? You think you know my face?"

When she didn't answer, he continued on. "Damn it, Hannah. I didn't ask for this."

"No, and I doubt you ever would."

"I'm telling you now, I don't want to see it. All these people"—he dropped his voice to a whisper—"I know what they see."

"You don't know what I see."

"I don't want to know."

"If you could only see yourself the way I do." She made her way to the canvas. "I'm sorry, Selim, but I've made up my mind."

"Go to hell."

"I'm not going anywhere."

"And what if you do?" he asked.

"I said I'm not going anywhere."

"Promise me, Hannah? Can you promise me that?"

"I don't need to. I said it and I meant it."

He shook his head and dropped his chin.

"What is it?" Her tone softened.

He hesitated. "I'm scared."

"You're brave."

"I'm so scared."

"No one's ever been brave without first being scared."

"Do you even know me? *Really* know me?"

She thought about the things he'd uttered in his sleep the night before. Words he would never recall and she would never understand. She looked up. "I don't know a *thing* about you. Is that what you want to hear?"

"That's not what I asked."

She put down her brush and took a seat on the bench next to him. "All right, Selim."

"All right?"

"Yes, all right. I *do* know you. I can't explain it and I don't understand it, but I'm sure of it. I know you."

"Hannah?" he said quietly.

"What is it?" she asked, her voice strained by exhaustion.

He studied her emerald eyes for a long, lingering moment. "I know you too. I think I always have."

She began sketching out her vision for the painting, at first succeeding only with drawings of the right side of his face. Perched on her stool those first few hours, she tore through her sketchbook, discarding etching after etching as the hours passed. By midday, they were surrounded by a landscape of crumpled paper balls.

Perhaps there was something missing. Something she hadn't quite understood? It seemed Hannah could no more capture the left side of his face than she could the dark side of the moon.

And still she labored on.

They sat quietly. She, not wanting to be disturbed while she worked. He, slowly surrendering to the weight of the past.

Sitting across from Hannah, he felt safe. It seemed to him that they were now living in a world where he no longer needed to hide, not from her, not from himself. And so when visions of Ayda came to his mind, as they often did, he no longer found himself trying to push them away; rather, he allowed his guilt to speak its piece.

It had taken him only an instant to close the door and walk away—an instant to hurt another human being. He knew now it could take a lifetime to make it right. That was something he didn't have.

And what had become of little Emre? Was he still living in the hotel by the airport? Was it even still operating? Was he back to selling gum and batteries on the side of the highway? He should have been looking out for the boy. Emre needed a big brother. Not too many people got second chances, but if Selim ever got back to Istanbul, he would make things right.

After three days of sitting for his portrait, Selim underwent another dose of treatment. He endured forty-eight hours of nausea and vomiting. His insides felt as though they'd caught fire, his mouth and tongue and lips like hot coals he wished he could eject. By the third morning, the havoc in his body subsided. He changed into fresh clothes and tried eating something other than buttered toast. He and Hannah drank tea and played backgammon. Midway through the game, she tossed in her chips and admitted defeat.

"I give up." She threw her hands in the air.

"So you don't have a future as a backgammon world champion." His voice was raspy. "I'll have to find another way to support us," he went on teasing.

Her cheeks flushed at the mention of a future together, even if it was just in jest.

Mustering all his courage, he wove his fingers through hers, then settled his focus on the ring she wore.

"What is it?" she asked after a moment.

"Oh, it's nothing." He shrugged as his fingers fiddled with the stone. "Just reminds me of an old tale I once heard. Mind if I have a closer look?"

"Go ahead." She slid the ruby ring from her finger and handed it over to him.

He turned it around, his eyes widening upon noticing the inscription inside the band.

He looked up and for a minute was transfixed by her gaze.

"Well, what does it mean?" she asked.

A sudden déjà vu flashed through him: a fleeting vision, green and fresh and smelling of the sea. Leaning forward, he scoured the depths of her emerald eyes.

When he finally pulled away, the air between them felt saturated with wonder. Slowly and steadily, a strange thought crept through him. It made its way into his consciousness and rooted its seed firmly in his mind. There it was.

The Sultan's Curse.

It was something he'd always dismissed as an old wives' tale, marveling at the irony of that Osman family fable, that it should so closely align with his own cruel fate. But an actual *curse?* As far as he'd always known, the whole matter was just a heap of superstitious mumbo jumbo.

He was a man of reason.

Only now the reasonable Selim Osman could no longer be certain of the things he once thought he knew. Staring at this ruby ring with the old Ottoman writing clearly etched on the inner band, he was no longer quite sure.

"So what does it mean?" Hannah pressed him.

"Oh my god." He dropped his face into his palms and began to laugh.

"Selim?"

But he could not answer. He just laughed until he was gasping for air.

"What's so funny?"

"Nothing."

"Why are you laughing?"

He could barely catch his breath.

"*Why?*"

He wiped the tears from his eyes and shook his head, astonished. "Even if I told you, you'd never believe me." He leaned in once more and slid the ring back over her finger, then kissed her with every ounce of strength he had left. When he pulled away, he looked at her, astonished.

"I just remembered . . ." he mused aloud.

"What is it?" She lifted his hand to her lips. "Selim?" She looked at him strangely.

"Is it the twenty-ninth?"

"I don't know. Why?"

"Do me a favor, check your phone."

She dug through her purse, withdrew her cell, and flipped it open. "August twenty-ninth," she said, still looking at the screen. "Why do you ask?"

He took a deep breath and flexed his arms behind his back before collapsing against his pillow.

"Selim?" she pressed.

"Whether it's the first or last of many," he said, "I'm grateful I get to spend it here, with you."

"What are you talking about?" She shoved him playfully.

He lowered his voice but kept his eyes on the ceiling. "You see, I've only just realized that I've lived to see thirty-three." He blinked a few times before sitting upright once more and holding her stare. "Today is my birthday."

37

The next few weeks passed, intermittent periods of illness followed by periods of recuperation. As the summer sun waned and cooler days were ushered in, they'd sit under the terrace on the grassy lawn, Hannah still working on his portrait. He sat on the bench and she on her painter's stool. There were times they quipped and joked. There were times when they were silent too.

It was that time that came around just twice each year. A point when the sun reigned in perfect accord with the moon, a time when the hours of day were perfectly balanced with the hours of night. It was September 23—the autumnal equinox. It would not be long now before the cold air began wilting the flowers and laying the trees and bushes bare. Winter would come, and after that, life would sprout anew.

Slipping off his shoes, Selim moved barefoot from his place in the shade to a bench in the sunshine, savoring the feel of the earth against his skin, the burn of the sun on his chest and face and neck. September 23. Feeling the tranquility of that day, he knew that what he'd been missing was an equinox of spirit. To reach it, he'd have to first summon the strength within himself; he'd have to unburden his heart.

He fixed his eyes on some obscure point in the distance as Hannah continued painting. As a breeze came wafting in, lifting fallen leaves from the grass, Selim finally broke his silence. "It was I who was driving the motorbike" was all he managed for a time. Measured, dry of emotion, but mostly, just tired words.

The cool air licked his ears and stroked his hair, just as it had in the memory of that tragic day. "It was me." He nodded matter-of-factly and then dropped his chin and eyes to the ground. "Ali was begging me to slow down, but I didn't listen."

Hannah studied him for a moment, then picked up her brush.

He sighed and rubbed his eyes.

"Don't stop now."

He looked up at her.

She was still, her arm raised and her brush hanging in the air.

"So I confess while you paint? That's how it works?"

She looked away and began mixing colors. "That's how it works." She dabbed the paints together carefully and rinsed her brush clean.

So he spoke, and as he spoke, she went on painting.

There was a stroke for each word. A hue for every shade of shame. The panic in his voice was matched only by the urgency of her brush-strokes.

Ali sat perched on the backseat of his motorbike, his thin arms linked tightly around Selim. Selim had just turned seventeen, old enough to apply for a motorbike license, and Ali was just fourteen. *Baba* had warned Selim not to take Ali on the motorbike until he learned how to handle the thing, but flush with the brashness of teenage boys, Selim had ignored his father's directive.

They cruised through the narrow, crooked streets of the fashionable Nişantaşı neighborhood, marveling innocently at the beauty of Izmirian blonds, who sipped on cappuccinos and pecked at their food under the colorful canopies that stretched outward from the low-slung stucco rooftops of outdoor cafés.

The wind whipped through their hair as the engine sounded in the streets, disturbing the quiet.

"Slow down, Brother!" Ali shouted over the wind. "Slow down!"

"What?" Selim pretended not to hear, a rush of excitement coming over him.

"Slow down!"

Selim, intoxicated by the engine's power, pressed the gas pedal further. He swerved the handlebars from left to right, a cruel joke intended to frighten his little brother. Selim's long dark hair whipped against his cheeks and lids, so that he squinted to shield his watery gaze from the glaring light and ash of the wind. As the bike swerved, he pressed the pedal harder, laughing as drivers from oncoming vehicles sounded their horns angrily, some shaking their heads and others cursing.

"Slow down, Brother!" Ali's frantic voice rose again above the roaring engine and his grip tightened around Selim's waist.

Empowered by recklessness, Selim teased, "What's that? Can't hear you, little brother!" He snaked along the winding roads at speeds that frightened the curbside grocers and sent veiled women running in the opposite direction.

The sweet-charred scent of roasting shawarma made Selim turn his head. He caught a glimpse of three girls sitting at a sidewalk café. They seemed to be looking deep into the bottoms of their cups, at the dark swirling patterns produced by the gooey residue of Turkish coffee. Many believed those patterns held the secrets of the future. They smiled and laughed as a young lady with a bright green head scarf tried to predict what was yet to come. She did not foresee what the next few seconds had in store.

While his eyes were on the girls, he lost sight of oncoming traffic ahead. The bike clipped the edge of a gray Honda before swerving and colliding with a tall utility pole. When Selim opened his eyes, the woman with the green head scarf was leaning over him, her face contorted and eyes narrowed. It looked as though she was screaming, but Selim heard nothing. There was only silence.

Ali landed thirty feet away, beneath the tire of a truck that had been transporting crates of fruits and vegetables. People stopped and stared and rushed around, unsure of what to do. Watermelon bits, strewn about the street in wet fleshy clumps, rolled down the slanted alleys, and all else seemed to stand still.

His parents were still sitting vigil three days later when Selim returned home to collect some fresh garments and toiletries for them. He'd rushed up the stairs, hurried to their room to gather what was needed, then stuffed it all in a medium-sized duffel bag. Just as soon as he'd zipped it shut, the phone ring and he ran to retrieve it.

"He is gone" was all his father said.

Selim lowered the phone and looked out his parents' bedroom window. Below, the workmen moved about the property, business as usual, their long-poled nets skimming the pool's surface, their brooms sweeping the tennis court clear of footprints, Ali's footprints. At the side of the house, gardeners tended the bushes as though they still believed it was possible for life to grow.

In his heart, he held the secret that no one else could touch. He could convince others, his parents, the doctors, the authorities—they were all so sympathetic. No one doubted what he presented as fact. Only, no matter how many times he had lied to those around him, he could not lie to himself.

He had been driving the motorcycle.

He had killed his brother.

It was mid afternoon by the time Selim had finished his confession.

Hannah examined the empty half of his face, the blank space on the canvas that until now she'd been unable to imagine. In him, she was now able to detect all the elements of a Picasso painting, like *Les Demoiselles d'Avignon*, where a face was not a face, but a collection of exquisitely assembled broken shards. The effect was explosive.

Exhausted, Selim sat limp as she rinsed her brushes and wiped her forehead with her sleeve. "Go inside." She placed her hand on his shoulder.

He stood slowly and made his way to the automatic doors.

Hours passed with Hannah crouched before her easel, entranced by the revelations that commanded her brush. By seven o'clock, she was utterly drained. She'd somehow accomplished in just four hours what she'd previously been unable to envision in the span of a few weeks. Dusk had now arrived. The portrait was complete.

38

The news had not been good. The latest round of chemotherapy had been unsuccessful. CT scans indicated that the cancer had come back despite the surgery and treatments. The tumor had metastasized. Dr. Rosen had not needed to explain to Selim what that meant. He'd suggested a more aggressive treatment plan, to extend whatever "good months" Selim had left.

Though his body was failing him and there was no hope left, he was still able to look up at Hannah and smile. He had experienced an awakening within, like a slow, steady sun rising through him. It started in his core and spread throughout the dark shell of his body. It coated the lining of his being and seeped into each and every cancer-ridden cell. Selim finally understood what his guilt had never let him see—while the days he had left were swiftly falling away, so too were they becoming ever more precious.

After they received the news, Hannah and Selim sat beside each other for some time. Words could not capture the things that became clear in the eloquence of silent understanding. Soon it was Selim who had to console Hannah and assure her that she'd be all right and please don't cry because it breaks my heart, and wasn't that the only good part of me left?

It was a month since Hannah had met with Mr. Rumie in his downtown gallery. She'd selected over two dozen of her best works to be shown in an exhibition he'd arranged to showcase emerging young artists. In less than twenty-four hours, Hannah's paintings were to be exhibited.

"It's almost five," Selim said. "Go home and unwind. You have a big day ahead of you tomorrow." He collapsed back against his pillow and forced a smile. It was to be *her* big day. He'd not spoil Hannah's excitement by letting on just how badly he wished he could be there with her. He'd inquired earlier in the week, but Dr. Rosen had warned that in light of his weakened state, leaving hospital grounds for any reason whatsoever was completely *out of the question.*

"Forget it. It's not important." Hannah leaned forward, a thief stealing a kiss that should have been shared between them, but that she hoarded to herself since he had lost all sensation on his left side. And yet, when Selim closed his eyes, he could sense her kisses passing through him like puffs of air in the lungs of a drowning man. He thought to himself, *How odd is life that only through such pain should I discover such joy.*

She kissed him once, twice, three times, then pulled back and looked into his black eyes.

"You should go," she whispered in a tone so low, he was unsure if he'd even heard it. "Go now."

He sat up, not fully comprehending.

"You've lived your life with regrets. That's no way to die."

"I don't understand—"

"All the things you said as I was painting your portrait . . ."

"I was talking about another time, another life."

"But it's not another life. It's the one you have now."

"I have you."

"*Go.*" She cut him off and locked her eyes with his. "*Go back to her.*" Her words startled both of them, lingering like spilt wine that continued to drip off the edge of their thoughts because neither dared to wipe it away.

"Hannah," he finally whispered, his tone somewhat astounded.

"I know you've never stopped loving her." She lowered her chin. "I think you just stopped loving yourself."

He felt tears come to his eyes.

"It's not too late . . ." Her voice trailed off. He nodded slowly and looked around at the countless landscapes and portraits that lined the walls of his hospital room. Floor to ceiling, wall to wall, a collage of distant places and familiar strangers.

They held each other throughout the night, savoring the long goodbye. Beyond the shivering curtains, a silhouette of flapping wings shone briefly against the red harvest moon. And though neither could ever have known it, for just the tiniest fraction of a second—a unit of time so infinitesimally small, it could never hope to be observed—the universe came to a fleeting stop, shifting their paths ever so slightly before setting off once more.

In the morning, Hannah gathered her paints and her canvas under her arm. Walking out of the room, she stopped at the door. She drew her fingers across the raised numbers, her ruby gleaming brightly as she turned around to give him one last look. "I love you," she whispered, standing a moment longer. Just before heading away she added under her breath, "Love me next lifetime."

When Selim woke up, he saw the canvas she'd left by the door. At least four feet high and three feet wide, it was his portrait. She had painted him standing on the Bosphorus Bridge in Istanbul, the one that connects Asia and Europe. In the background, the sea rippled out and seemed to spill over the top of the canvas, as it did sometimes in his dreams. He studied his own face, a face no longer divided by pain and beauty, but a unified vision of the man he had once been. Looking at the painting, he saw the man he *still* could be.

Selim reached for the telephone by his bed and slowly dialed the number to Ayda's cell. It rang a half-dozen times before the voice mail picked up. "I'm not around, leave a message," Ayda's voice sounded cheery on the recording.

"Ayda, it's me."

On the other end, he was greeted by the cold space of nothingness.

For a few long seconds, he lay with the warm receiver against his cheek, breathing heavily into the mouthpiece. "Forgive me." They were the only words he could muster. In that moment, it seemed there was nothing else to say. "*Forgive me.*"

39

"You got some kind of party?" asked the driver, his face nothing more than eyes caught in the trappings of the rearview mirror.

"Something like that," she said after a long moment.

Outside, the clamor of evening sped past in a colorful array of dog walkers and urban business elites in gray suits. Chunks of Seventh Avenue tumbled by while the Town Car weaved through traffic and past the threat of changing streetlights.

"What's the celebration?" the driver pressed.

She looked down at her champagne-colored dress. "No celebration." She leaned back and closed her eyes.

A few minutes later she felt the car slow to a stop. When she opened her eyes she could see Mr. Rumie standing curbside with his arms latched behind his back. He peered into the window, then reached for the handle. She heard a click before the door swung open and the cool air rushed in. Arm outstretched, he reached for her hand and helped her from the seat as lovingly as one might have plucked the gardenias for his lapel.

She stepped out, her feet landing gently on the pavement. A wind grazed her cheeks, with a dash of crispness that seemed to confirm the arrival of fall. He held her hand as though inviting her to curtsy and guided her past a small horde of guests, humming a tune under his breath. When he reached the narrow stairs leading up to the gallery's entrance, he stopped. Then he turned to Hannah. "You've overwhelmed me with beauty this evening."

"I'm not beautiful. You should see my mother," she managed in an attempt to steer the focus away from her. Hannah had never been comfortable being the center of attention, and tonight was no exception.

"I'm sure she is," he continued, planting his cane into the ground as he spoke. "But your father was also a nice-looking man."

"Excuse me?" she wondered aloud.

"It's apparent from your work, of course," he added hastily. "Hurry, they're all waiting for you."

When she stood unmoved, he again gestured in a shooing motion.

"Aren't you coming?" she asked.

"I'm too old and ugly to spoil your debut." He winked. "I'll be right behind you."

Hannah made her way up the staircase and through the entrance of the Edward Rumie Art Gallery, stopping face-to-face with the life-size portrait of David Herzikova. Though it was the centerpiece of the exhibit, she still couldn't help but feel, even here, even now, that there was something missing, something not quite right. She turned away from his almond eyes because she could not bear to face him at this moment.

She spent the next hour mingling with art collectors and critics inside. Edward had made all the arrangements necessary to promote Hannah's exhibition.

"Ashish Rakesh." A young man with dark, sunken eyes approached her. "I wanted to congratulate you. I'm very impressed with your work." She smiled and shifted away, only to be assaulted by a man whose name came down on her like a stamp. "Jonathan Templeton, *New York* magazine." He flashed an immaculately capped smile. "When you've got a minute, I'd love to interview you for this piece I'm doing for the arts section of the upcoming issue." She heard her name roll off the tongues of East Side art dealers and French critics.

Just when she thought she'd found a moment to sit down and rest, she was accosted by a group of swanky lean-limbed ladies. Their hair and bangs were cut to the same disturbingly accurate, angular perfection as their black cocktail dresses and stiletto heels. They toasted their champagne and flashed double-edged smiles before quickly turning away and disappearing into the crowd.

Hannah shifted her attention to her portraits lining the walls of the gallery. Mrs. Ethers, the rabbi's son, the town's seamstress, all of the countless portraits—an expression of relief emerged for the first time upon the canvases. Relief that the power of their secrets, their ordinary joys and pains, were finally recognized for what they were: *extraordinary*.

Crystal chimed while the New York glitterati raised their champagne glasses and sauntered through the room dropping names and exchanging business cards. Critics seemed fascinated by her subjects, the "suburban bourgeoisie," one critic claiming that her portraits "speak louder than her muses would ever dare." After everyone who was anyone had arrived and introduced themselves to Hannah, the room grew quiet to the sound of a spoon clinking against crystal.

"Can I have your attention for just a minute," exclaimed Mr. Rumie as he made his way to her side. "I'm glad to see this great turnout tonight. Hopefully by now you've all had a chance to view the artwork on display, have a few drinks, and perhaps get something to eat as well." He lifted his handkerchief and patted the moisture on his forehead before continuing: "I'd like to take this opportunity to thank you all for coming. I hope you'll stay and enjoy a few hours more, but I would be remiss in my duties if I did not take a moment to formally present New York's riveting new talent." Turning to Hannah, he gestured in grand style. "Allow me to introduce to you all, Ms. Hannah Herzikova." A clapping sensation filled her ears as the flash of cameras filled the room. She got her bearings and smiled, then turned to Rumie, who held a glass of champagne for her. As the din returned to the room, he pulled away and searched her eyes. "Is something wrong?" His voice was crisp and clear against the murmurs and laughter that surrounded them.

"It's perfect." She took her glass and clinked her champagne to Edward's, downing more than she could handle. "Everything is perfect," she said, her eyes tearing a little.

He stood still, his mouth stiff and the corners of his steeped brows rising up over the edge of his black frames. He studied the champagne in his glass before his expression softened once more. Then he leaned in to whisper, "You did everything you possibly could for him."

"How does it feel?" a gray-haired waif interrupted. "Oh, by the way, the caterer did a hell of a job, Rumie. Send me his number, will you?" She smiled thoughtlessly, then popped an olive tartine into her mouth. "Brilliant!" she marveled and wandered off into the crowd.

Hannah reached out with both hands and touched his glasses. Cautiously, she slid the thick frames away from his face. He didn't try to stop her or pull away, just stood quietly as she examined his face unmasked for the first time. Above his eye, a prominent scar zigzagged horizontally. A gray-scale photo flashed before her eyes. A stout lady in a pillbox hat, standing between a lanky teenage David Herzikova and a shorter boy with a scar above his eye, all three poised before an enormous steamship.

"Who *are* you?" she asked.

He took his glasses from her. "Let's just say I knew your father when I was a boy."

She studied him for a moment. She was sure that somewhere in his gaze lay the key to a mystery locked away in a box.

Who was he? She wasn't sure. She wasn't sure of anything, least of all herself. Looking around, she felt desperately out of place. There was only one place she needed to be, only one person she needed to be beside.

"I'm so sorry," she stammered, "but I have to go."

"Now?"

"Right now."

"Okay." He squeezed her hand. "Get out of here. I'll cover for you." She smiled as she felt something like hope fill her.

"The Town Car's waiting outside. Consider it yours for the night."

"You're not angry?"

"Angry?" He shrugged his shoulders and chuckled. "At the risk of sounding condescending, I couldn't be prouder."

She turned to leave.

"One more thing before you go," he said as he retrieved an envelope from a pocket inside his jacket and handed it to Hannah.

"What's this?"

"It's something I received in the mail a while back . . . I've been meaning to share it with you for some time. It meant so much to me, and well, my dear, I know it will mean something to you too. Open it later. When you have some time."

She studied the blank envelope and placed it into her bag. "Thank you for everything." She hugged him and headed out with a longing she'd not known existed until that moment.

Edward rounded the room, sampling hors d'oeuvres and entertaining guests. A small knot had formed in the dark spaces of his throat, but still, he managed to charm buyers and critics whose stellar reviews he was counting on for his late brother's child.

As he made his way through the room, he stopped before the portrait of David Herzikova and stood up straighter than his brittle bones should have permitted. Looking up into the rapid brushstrokes making up David's almond eyes, he said aloud, "Forgive me, Brother, I know I'm too late. Forgive me." Then he straightened his bow tie and smoothed back his hair.

Though he had missed his brother, he would honor his dying wish. He would care for Hannah as though she were his own.

40

Hannah surveyed the empty room from the hall. A set of fresh, perfectly pressed bedsheets were tucked neatly around the edges of the bed. "Where is he?" Hannah asked aloud.

"Left a few hours ago," Dina, the on-call attendant, replied from her chair behind the nurse's station. "It was time for that boy to go," she said while rifling through her files.

Hannah's eyes looked back through the doorway to the chair beside the bed where she'd so often sat. While she'd spent the past few hours hobnobbing with strangers at her exhibition opening, she'd now give anything to get those few precious hours back. To have shared that time with him instead. She looked around the room. The portrait of Selim that she'd left by the door was nowhere to be found. Hannah breathed a grief-stricken sigh, but where she found pain, she also drew comfort.

Selim *had* taken the painting with him. It was now gone, a piece of her heart gone with it. A piece of her would always remain by his side. Hannah made her way over to Dina and leaned over the desk. "Where is he?"

"Went home," she said coolly. "Wherever that is."

"Who would know?"

"Try someone over at the desk in the discharge lounge."

Downstairs, she tried coaxing the clerical staff members into giving her some information. Their lips moved, but all she seemed to hear were the words "patient confidentiality."

As the Town Car drove away, it followed the familiar route north along the highway and over the bridge, beyond the towering shadow of

Manhattan's skyscrapers toward the small, sleepy town she called home. The windshield wipers were set to full speed but could do nothing to stop the rain that had begun pounding down. As they turned off the highway and drove through the streets to her house, the headlights stretched into the black night, illuminating just a few yards of the glistening road ahead. *He's gone.* The simple meaning of those words was finally sinking in, and with it, a sense of panic.

Desperate for fresh air, Hannah opened the window a crack, taking in the cool wind as raindrops splattered on her face. She breathed in the scent of bark and pine and leaves from the woods lining the road. This thick, wholesome scent of the earth had a sweetness that she wished could last forever. Everyone and everything was escaping her now.

She was no more than five minutes from her house when she noticed her cell phone light up in her bag. Having remembered that she'd silenced it at the start of the evening, Hannah now retrieved the phone from her purse, discovering a voice mail. Anxiously, she tapped the play button.

"Hannah, it's Edward." Edward's voice sounded low and clear. "I'm calling to tell you that the show sold out in the first few hours. Your paintings went to business moguls and enthusiastic young collectors. Quite a few more went to an anonymous buyer who phoned in during the show. My dear, you are a success in your own right." The old man cleared his throat, then continued: "In any event, as you may have suspected by now, there is another matter that I'm compelled to share with you tonight. As I mentioned earlier, I did know your father in his youth. In fact, I more than knew him. We were brothers. Just a few weeks before he died, I received a letter from him. Well, I suppose you haven't read it yet or I'd have heard from you by now. In any case, I think it's best you see it for yourself. It's right there in your purse where you placed it earlier tonight. When you are ready, Hannah, I will tell you the story."

Hannah stared down at her phone incredulously. She fumbled hastily through her purse before withdrawing the envelope she'd forgotten about. Only now did she stop to notice that the return address scribbled on the back was her own. Within seconds, she opened it and unfolded the letter. She recognized her father's handwriting immediately, as well as the stationery with the *D.H.* monogram at the top. With some measure of trepidation, she began reading the French words.

March 15, 2002
Dear Edward,

So much time has passed, but I've not forgotten you, nor the life we shared. Perhaps I'm nothing but an old fool, but it seems I can no longer recall what it was that tore us apart. Or perhaps it's that I simply no longer care to remember. All these years, I did what I could to hide my whereabouts from you. Did you search for me? I think deep down I always hoped you would.

I'll not mince words with you now. I'm dying, Edward. And nothing of the past seems to matter now. I have a daughter. Her name is Hannah. It may sound silly, but I do not exaggerate when I tell you that she is the most precious thing I have in this world.

All the hurt is gone. The bitterness has faded, and for the first time in my life, I can see clearly. She is all that matters to me. And it is my greatest fear that when I die, she'll be left alone in this world.

Selfishly, I write to you now, Brother, to ask that you grant me my dying wish. Reach out to my Hannah.

I warn you that she knows nothing of you or of our past. You see, from the time my Hannah was a little girl, all I ever wanted was to protect her. To give her a world filled with beauty and kindness and goodness. When she was little, I would tell her stories and fairy tales with happy endings, like our maman *used to do.*

But our story was not a fairy tale, was it? Ours was a tale I could not bear to tell, especially not to my Hannah.

I've mailed this letter to the old post office by the bakery. Perhaps, by some miracle, Mme. Lamberthe's daughter is still sorting mail behind the counter. Perhaps you still live nearby? I pray you come to America and find her. I pray you care for her, take her under your wing as though she were your own.

Do me this kindness, dear brother. Turn our tragedy into a fairy tale. When you do, tell my Hannah the story of us.

Your brother, now and forever,
David

41

The air was crisp, beckoning the city's inhabitants to take an evening stroll. Along the horizon, a few birds could be seen, their black wings flapping across a sun that hung like a glowing medallion in the plum-colored sky. Crickets chimed in the distance as the clouds of smoke from passing steamships filled the sky above the Bosphorus.

Hannah and Edward approached the building. It was a modest honey-colored villa with large windows and faded red shingles. By the entry, an orange tree blossomed, surrounded by a thin ring of fallen leaves.

"What if this is a mistake?" Hannah turned to Edward.

"It's not a mistake," he said matter-of-factly.

"I'm not sure I can do it. Go up there . . ."

"Of course you can."

She swallowed hard. "Come with me?"

"I will if that's what you want. But I don't think it's what you want, not really."

She drew a deep breath, then exhaled. "Maybe we should go back—"

"*Really?* To where? Where is back now, Hannah?"

"Back to the hotel. Back to New York. Back to before. Just back!" she nearly shouted.

"No, *chérie.*" He sighed, then leaned the weight of his body against his cane. "There's no going back. This world, it pushes you forward." He placed his hand on her shoulder. "*Go.*" He kissed her cheek and then turned away.

Reluctantly she stepped forward and pressed the buzzer lightly, eliciting

281

a low hum from the monitor. After a minute she tried again and waited anxiously before turning to Edward. "No one's home."

"Give it a minute."

She craned her neck upward and took a few steps back to see if she could observe anything through the second-story window of the seaside condominium. The shades were drawn in a long row of windows.

The melodious voices of muezzins began to sound the call to the Maghrib prayer. One after another they chanted from the countless minarets dotting Istanbul's skyline.

Hannah noticed a silhouette pass behind the drawn window dressings. Then the buzzer sounded back.

"I'll be here." Edward held the door open for her.

Beyond the entry hall a steep flight of stairs rose with no end in sight. She gathered the edges of her skirt as she ascended the stairs to the second floor. At the top of the staircase she rounded the corner and noticed a door slightly ajar. That was it. Apartment 2C. A sliver of light from inside settled across the green-tiled hallway floor.

The door eased open, revealing a small boy with big black eyes. His face and fingertips peeked out from behind the door until the voice within whispered something quickly, sending the boy scurrying out of sight. "Come in," a woman's voice, thick and full, beckoned.

Inside, a slender woman in an ivory suit looked up from the edge of a plush sofa. "You must be Hannah." She stood and made her way over. "I'm sorry it's taken so long." Ayda's dark eyes radiated warmth. "You should understand, Selim didn't *want* to be found."

Hannah lowered her chin and wondered if perhaps it had been a mistake to come after all. "I see."

"It's not what you think," Ayda quickly replied. "He cared for you deeply."

Hannah felt the lump in her throat begin to swell.

"I guess he just thought that seeing you again, it would just be too difficult for him." She offered up a sad smile. "He had his reasons."

"Of course," Hannah said meekly.

"Please, have a seat." Ayda closed the door and led her to the sofa. "You must be hungry?" she said as she gestured to a tray of assorted delicacies.

"That's all right. I have dinner plans at eight."

"That's two hours from now," she said while reaching for a plate. "The caviar is good. Have some."

Hannah looked about the low table. There was a large flat book on the dancing horses of Vienna, one of the collected works of Gibran, and another book on the history of the Osman imperial dynasty. Beside the coffee-table books, a few smaller books were stacked. Hannah reached for a novel by someone named Ahmet Taguc.

"Have you heard of Taguc?" Ayda asked as Hannah flipped through the book.

"The name rings a bell."

"He's the author who was imprisoned for discussing the Armenian genocide. When Selim came back, he made it his mission to free Taguc."

"Did he succeed?"

"I believe so," Ayda said as she withdrew a long cigarette from a carton by the table. "But he never did admit to me exactly what happened. All I know is that one day the funds in our bank account were drastically lower. That was the same day several ministers publicly came out to oppose prosecutions on the basis of 'Crimes Against Turkishness.' I always suspected that Selim was involved, but he never admitted as much."

"But why would he care so much about Taguc?"

"I don't think it had all that much to do with Taguc actually."

"Then what was it about?"

Ayda lifted her chin. "Selim was haunted by the past."

"His own past, though."

"Yes, but it was more than that." With her unlit cigarette dangling between her fingers, Ayda's hand moved as if casting a spell. "It was as though the history of the Ottoman Empire lived inside him. He carried all the glory with him, but also, he carried so much shame. I think he was looking for a way to lay it all to rest."

"He must have loved you a lot," Hannah whispered.

"He loved me," Ayda said quietly. "He loved us both." She frowned, then lifted the cigarette to her lips.

"Are you going to light that?" Hannah asked.

"No."

"Then—"

"I don't smoke," Ayda interrupted. "Haven't in years." She nodded toward a broken tower of children's blocks and an assortment of over-turned miniature race cars. "I have a son," Ayda finished the thought.

Hannah examined the cigarette quizzically, but said nothing.

"It's just something I like to hold in my hand." Ayda's voice fell to a whisper. "Something from the past, you see." She turned her attention back to her son. The boy popped his head up and smiled before moving toward the two of them. He was a skinny little thing, all knees and elbows. His thick dark hair was tousled, his purple lips smooth and narrow. The boy blinked listlessly, then rested his head in his mother's lap.

"This is Ali," Ayda said as the boy's lids drooped wearily.

"I didn't know—" Hannah shook her head.

"Neither did Selim," Ayda explained. "When he finally returned to Istanbul, I was still at our old place. It was late when I heard a buzzing at the door. I wasn't expecting anyone at that hour. I'd received a message from him the night before, but when I checked the security camera to see who was calling up so late, I didn't recognize the old man I saw. He was skinny and pale, with hunched shoulders and an oversize cap pulled low over his face. I thought the man had pushed the wrong button, so I said into the monitor, 'Sir, which apartment are you trying to go to?' He said, 'I'm trying to go home.' I said, 'You're confused, old man. You don't live here!' Then he turned and stared directly up at the lens with his big dark eyes. That was when I knew.

"When I opened the door, I just stood there, barely able to say hello. He took one look at my bloated belly and I could see the look of astonishment on his face. There was no way he could have known. He spread his hands across my stomach as though trying to feel the life inside me. I invited him in and we talked for a while. He asked me to stay with him. To be with him till the end. He said there wasn't much time. It was not something I needed to think over.

"A few months later, Ali was born and Selim was given a fresh breath of life. He lived another *four* years. Those four years were the most painful but also the most beautiful of my life." She played with Ali's long wavy hair as he rested in her lap.

"He's beautiful," Hannah said.

"Like his father."

Hannah reached for a silver frame resting atop a side table. She examined the photo of a skinny adolescent holding a soccer ball. "And this boy?"

"That's Emre. Selim was kind of a big brother to him. Arranged for him to attend a good school. Made sure he and his father were taken care of. He even left one of his properties to them in his will, a small hotel. They still come by often and visit."

"I knew so little about him," Hannah wondered aloud.

"I guess that's why he felt you knew him more than anyone else ever could . . ."

"I beg your pardon?"

"You knew him," Ayda explained. "I mean, *really* knew him, without all the noise and clutter and misunderstanding that comes with knowing too many details of a person's family history. It's one of the reasons he loved you so." Ayda's voice trailed off.

Hannah said nothing, just lowered her gaze to the ruby ring she wore.

"You never knew Selim the Osman," Ayda continued.

"I didn't," Hannah admitted.

"But you knew Selim the man. And that's all he was at the end of the day, really. People forget that."

"It's all I ever knew of him."

Ayda scooted forward and lowered her voice. "He once said it was as though he'd always known you."

"That's how it felt for me too."

"He said that in meeting you, it was like his heart had finally opened. He said that in meeting you, a curse had been broken."

Hannah thought back to the phone call she'd received two months prior from Ayda. Upon hearing the name, Hannah had understood the purpose of the call. Her heart dropped now as it did that day.

"I didn't break any curses," Hannah replied.

"Selim would disagree. You know, he once told me of an old family legend concerning a centuries-old debt." Ayda stared ahead thoughtfully. "I'd never thought much of it, but I must admit, after hearing about you, I couldn't shake it from my mind. After his death, I dug a bit deeper into the Osman Secret Chronicles." She leaned forward and crossed her legs. "It seems that the old family legend was recorded in meticulous detail after all. Who knew?" Ayda shrugged.

"I'm not sure I follow," Hannah asked. "What does this have to do with me?"

Ayda breathed deeply, then clasped her hands together. "The story is that when one of the Osman ancestors rescued the family of the green-eyed girl, it also salvaged her family's future descendants. For that action, a debt was cast into the fabric of the universe and hovered over her family. According to the legend, the debt could be repaid only when the green-eyed girl returned to grant a chain of life in return, when the saved became the savior, and the savior became the saved."

"Why are you telling me this?" Hannah's voice was nearly a whisper.

"I know it must sound crazy." Ayda squared her shoulder and sat up straight. "But I believe that you did that, Hannah. Selim believed it too. You paid the debt. You broke the curse."

Hannah just shook her head and rubbed her eyes. "That can't be."

"Can't it?" Ayda set her sights on the bright red stone and nodded in its direction. "That piece is an old family heirloom, isn't it?"

"Well, yes." Hannah flexed her fingers before flipping the ruby over, hiding it from view.

"And the inscription on the band, Selim mentioned it was old Ottoman writing."

Could this be real? Hannah questioned herself. She could not quite believe the tale she was being told.

"The girl in the story had a ruby ring, so wouldn't it follow to reason . . ." Ayda paused. Her eyes were moist beneath her steeped brows. Perhaps it pained her to do so, but it seemed she could not bring herself to finish the thought.

Shrinking back, Hannah managed to finish the sentence that Ayda could not. "That I am the green-eyed girl." Her eyes were wide as she whispered the words. For a long moment she just sat there, contemplating the magnitude of what she'd just uttered. Then she glanced up suddenly and shook her head. "But Selim *died*. If I had the power to break curses . . ." She pressed her lips together and closed her eyes.

"It doesn't matter that he died." Ayda interrupted. "We all die at some point. The only thing that matters is that in the end, he lived. *Really* lived. With joy. With love. Without regret." She took a breath, shook her head, and continued. "And I want you to know, I'll always be grateful for the bond that you shared. You brought him back to life. You brought him back to me."

Hannah studied Ayda for a long, lingering moment.

"And though our son had been conceived before you ever knew him, there was a very real chance that Selim would never have returned. That our son would have suffered the pain of feeling he was abandoned by his father, that *he too* would have gone through life without ever really living. As far as I'm concerned, that's as good as being dead. You see, it's not just about a family name or bloodline physically living on." She waited for the meaning of her words to sink in. "When Selim came back, he brought love back with him. I believe that was a gift you gave him." She leaned forward and placed her hand over Hannah's. "Selim understood it. So must you. It's love that grants life. It's what we pass on to our children. It's what they pass on to theirs. Don't you understand, Hannah? It's love that keeps a bloodline *alive*."

As Hannah took on the weight of Ayda's words, she felt a lightness spread throughout her limbs.

"Come, I want to show you something." Ayda stood, then motioned for Hannah to follow as she made her way down a corridor flanked with rows of framed portraits. "These are the Ottoman sultans. Selim's ancestors." They passed a framed portrait of a shriveled man with a hooked nose who wore an oversize turban. "Suleiman the Magnificent, our most celebrated sultan," Ayda explained before moving on to another portrait, this one of a young man with delicate features and a tinge of grief in his expression. Ayda turned back to her. "Murad the III. Selim liked this portrait very much." She continued down the hallway past the watchful guard of dozens of ancient sultans before coming upon the portrait Hannah had painted of Selim in New York. There he was, the man she'd known and loved. Looking at the painting now, she felt as though she was looking upon a piece of herself.

"Of course he wasn't a sultan," Ayda explained. Then, "I think by the end, he'd made peace with his past."

Hannah swallowed her grief as well as her joy as she made her way through the corridor. Looking back upon the portraits, Hannah had the vague sense she was passing through the rolling waves of time.

"This, this is what I wanted you to see." Ayda stopped at a door and opened it. Hannah stepped into a small room with deep crimson walls and a large mahogany desk.

She felt her world turn over as her anonymous buyer revealed himself. She looked up at a wall covered with fifteen works belonging to her first exhibition, paintings that'd once hung in Selim's hospital room in New

York. Set in silver frames, the portraits looked back at her with a deep, soulful sigh. She closed her eyes and let the dim light flicker on her sealed eyelids as she tumbled through a kaleidoscope of fire raging in a sea of sand and stars, waves of lavender fields yielding to misty lagoons. Willow tree branches enveloped Bosphorus blossoms, enlivened by brushstrokes of emerald and bright crimson . . .

When she opened her eyes, the air tasted of the sea, fresh, as though it had just been born.

"He said it's what had kept him going," Ayda explained, her soft voice settling over Hannah like a long soothing hush.

"He said it was a *labor of love*."

Hannah turned her gaze toward the window. Over the sea, a massive bird soared through the evening sky. It flapped its spotted wings once, twice, three times, before gliding off toward the horizon and disappearing.

Author's Note

Some time in my twenties I realized I did not know as much about my Sephardic, or Iberian Jewish/Middle Eastern, heritage as I would have liked. As the granddaughter of Syrian American immigrants who had emigrated from the formerly Ottoman-controlled city of Aleppo to the United States in the 1930s, I knew that my identity was in some way tied to my family's past. I felt that in understanding that past, I would come to better appreciate the person I was striving to become, so I began spending long hours in the library researching the history of Sephardic Jewry. As a young woman living, studying, and working in New York City in the twenty-first century, I felt compelled to understand that history through the eyes of another woman.

While searching for strong female heroines within the Sephardic historical narrative, I stumbled across the epic life story of the sixteenth-century philanthropist and activist Dona Gracia Nasi. Here was a powerful, independent woman who shared my very own cultural heritage. She was a woman who risked her life to save scores of Jews during the Inquisition, and who was instrumental in the underground movement to smuggle refugees out of Spain and Portugal and into more hospitable lands. When I thought about my own family history, I couldn't help but wonder if she was involved in rescuing my own ancestors more than four hundred years ago. The more I learned about Dona Gracia, the more captivated I became. It was not long before I decided to write a novel inspired by her legacy, a novel that would imagine the connections, both physical and spiritual, between our modern world and our past.

The Debt of Tamar is loosely inspired by real historical events, and while my goal was to stay true to the essence of the eras I have depicted, this novel is in many ways a fairy tale. To that end, I have taken liberties with names, dates, and events, altering them at will to imagine the book's narrative. Wanting to give tribute to Dona Gracia Nasi, but not wanting to do a disservice to her legacy or those unfamiliar with her real life story, I chose to use the name Dona Antonia Nissim. At the same time, I retained the actual given names of Dona Gracia's daughter and nephew as a kind of ode to the family that piqued my imagination and writing. The character of Tamar, as well as all subsequent characters portrayed as descendants of the House of Nissim, are completely invented and are not based on any historical persons.

Life for non-Muslims under Ottoman rule was not perfect, but for Jews fleeing Inquisition-era Iberia, like Dona Antonia, José, and Reyna, the empire served as a blessed refuge. While Jews were generally well treated in their new home, it would be false to assume that anti-Jewish sentiment did not exist throughout pockets of the general population, though it was in no way as vehement as the state-sanctioned anti-Semitism found throughout parts of Europe at the time. Still, Jewish life in the Ottoman Empire flourished during the reign of Suleiman the Magnificent, when many Jews rose to prominence in politics, diplomacy, medicine, and many other fields. While Suleiman has been remembered as a friend to the Jewish people and a great leader dedicated to justice, he was, like all human beings, a complex character. The Suleiman portrayed in this narrative is that of Suleiman the Legend, and as such, I depicted his persona in a way that best served the story line. The characters in this book portrayed as descendants of the last Ottoman sultan are imagined.

In general, accounts of sixteenth-century harem life are hard to come by, as life inside the sultan's harem was very much a private affair, with few outsiders allowed access. As such, details pertaining to the backgrounds of the legendary women who were sequestered behind those walls are murky. For example, Nurbanu Sultan, also known throughout history as Cecilia Venier-Baffo, may very well have been Greek, rather than Venetian, as many historians have claimed. Like many other women who lived behind harem walls, her origins remain a mystery to us today.

Though many secrets have been locked away in the unwritten pages of history, there is one historical truth that cannot be disputed. It is something that historical figures like Dona Gracia and Suleiman reveal in humankind, that we reveal in one another each day: While we, as human beings, are capable of inflicting tremendous suffering upon one another, so too are we capable of bestowing unbridled goodness on the world. It is my sincerest wish that *The Debt of Tamar* has helped illuminate that truth.

—Nicole Dweck

Acknowledgments

Getting a book published is no easy feat. Oftentimes, when people ask me how I did it, I am reminded of the many people who inspired me, supported me, worked behind the scenes and fought to see this book come to market. I couldn't have done it without the help of all those who believed in me and in *The Debt of Tamar*. Though my name is the only one credited on the cover, I would be remiss not to thank the many people who devoted hundreds if not thousands of hours to seeing this project come to fruition. So when people ask me how I did it, I think it's fair to say, I didn't do it. *We* did it.

At the very top of that long list of *We* is my editor, Melanie Fried of Thomas Dunne Books, as well as my agent, Stefanie Lieberman of Janklow & Nesbit Associates. Both powerhouses in their own rights, these two women worked tirelessly to see this project through, and though they were part of a great team, they each deserve special recognition for their dedication and drive, as well as the unique sets of talents and expertise they brought to this literary endeavor.

I'll start with Melanie. Every once in a while, you come across someone who has the potential to completely alter the course of your professional destiny. Melanie is that person. After getting a hold of the manuscript and reading it in the course of a day, Melanie championed the book to her colleagues and is ultimately responsible for bringing this book to market. None of this would have happened without her passion, her editorial vision, and her commitment.

Melanie, thank you for taking a chance on a debut novel, for turning a writer into an author, and turning my dreams into realities.

Thank you to my publisher, Thomas Dunne Books, for taking on this project, to Laura Clark, Staci Burt, and Janet Chow, for their efforts in expanding the scope and reach of this debut novel, as well as to all the wonderful people in the marketing, art, and sales departments for all the behind-the-scenes magic they made happen.

To my agent Stefanie—

With my head in the clouds and my creative spirit unleashed, thank goodness I had you by my side to keep me anchored in reality. While you helped me cultivate my artistic vision, you also stayed grounded and focused while guiding me through the complex publication process, always with my best interest in mind. A heartfelt thanks to you, Stefanie.

I would also like to acknowledge my early readers, fellow authors John Campbell and Ross Clark, for having worked with me on my earliest drafts and supported me throughout the writing process, as well as my first writing teacher, Mr. Thomas Sheridan, who fostered in me a love of writing and creative expression. A special thanks to Laura Klynstra— who created the beautiful cover you see on this book—as well as to my family and friends, who were forced to read through dozens of pre-publication drafts and never once complained. To my father, who cheered me on when I began to lose steam and never wavered in his support, thank you from the bottom of my heart. To Lora, for giving me the spark I needed to finish what I started. There is also the very talented writer, Kelly Massry, for whom I have the utmost respect and appreciation. She has given me her professional and personal guidance during the later stages of this project and for that I am grateful.

To my mother, the words "thank you" seem entirely insufficient, but somehow, those words are all I have to express the overwhelming appreciation I feel for the support you've shown me throughout this process. Thank you for the hundreds of hours you spent pouring over thousands of manuscript pages and countless drafts, for being my greatest advocate, friend, mentor, and fan. Thank you for believing in me before I believed in myself. None of this could have happened without you.

To my husband—You are my rock, my muse, my friend, my love. All that we built and all that we share is a story more moving than any tale I could ever conjure or dare put in writing. Our son is the light in my day and the smile on my lips. I am so happy he looks like you. Thank you for giving me the gift of family—for bringing true magic and wonder to my world.

Finally, I'd like to acknowledge my late grandparents, as well as the friends I have known that are no longer with me in this world. You've inspired me in ways that only you and I will ever know.

I am forever in your debt.